THE JUSTICE FACTORY

*The Seventh Detective Inspector
Christy Kennedy Mystery*

Paul Charles

D0996144

Other books by Paul Charles published by
The Do-Not Press:

The Christy Kennedy Mysteries
I Love The Sound of Breaking Glass
Last Boat to Camden Town
Fountain of Sorrow
The Ballad of Sean & Wilko
The Hissing of The Silent Lonely Room
I've Heard The Banshee Sing

A novel concerning The Beatles.
The First of the True Believers

Thanks a million to Jim Driver, a man solid, true and undaunted by the dark forest; to Andrew and Cora for showing the light; to the music of Jackson Browne, Nick Lowe and George Harrison for helping while away the hours in the Rovers Return; to Ed Lake for editing; to Peter Bergman and David Torrans two outstanding booksellers, vocal, not to mention effective, in spreading the word. BIG, BIG thanks to Catherine for the red pen and taking hold of my hand.

Chapter One

FUNERALS ARE FOR dead people. So why do so many of the living show up? Maybe they hope, if they turn out for funerals regularly enough, they'll get a good showing at their own. But then again, what does it matter? They're never going to know who goes or doesn't go, because... funerals are for dead people.

One Thursday morning Detective Inspector Christy Kennedy of Camden Town CID was standing in a rain-soaked graveyard distracting himself with such thoughts, and waiting for the recently deceased Daniel Elliot to be laid to rest. Although it was the middle of July, London had endured seventy-two straight hours of sheet rain. Every time Kennedy found a solid piece of ground to stand on, in a matter of seconds it would start to give way under his feet.

No doubt the delay of the arrival of the funeral procession was due to the slowness of London traffic in the rain, Kennedy thought. He headed off to stand under the largest tree in the graveyard, not for shelter so much as for the firmness of ground he thought he'd find close to the trunk. Kennedy disliked funerals. They were for dead people. But now and again, as on this particular morning, he was professionally obliged to attend. There was a social reason as well: Daniel Elliot was a friend of Kennedy's ex-girlfriend, ann rea. Kennedy had met Elliot a few times while working on a case concerning Elliot's daughter. It hadn't altogether been a pleasant experience but Kennedy had been impressed with the way Elliot had dealt with the situation and had continued to be supportive of his daughter, Bella Forsythe.

Miss Forsythe, currently detained at Her Majesty's pleasure, was here on a morning's compassionate leave. She was handcuffed to two guards. At the far end of the graveyard Kennedy could just about pick out the silhouette of Forsythe, her guards, and the lonely figure of ann rea, separated from the trio by about two yards of mucky earth and quite a few gallons of water.

Kennedy saw the hearse draw up at the gates of the graveyard and watched about a dozen old soldiers stiffly hobble around to the rear of the hearse. Kennedy made his way over to the freshly dug grave. Bella Forsythe was standing at its foot between her guards; all three were soaked to the skin. ann rea had come better equipped, in a body-length, see-through mac and a pair of Wellington boots. She walked over to Kennedy as he arrived and kissed him politely on the cheek. She nodded to him, saying nothing. Kennedy walked over to Miss Forsythe to offer his respects. She ignored him completely, looking straight through him as though he didn't exist. Maybe in her life he didn't exist. She just continued to stand, hands restrained by her side, and directed her stare down into her father's grave.

The coffin bearers – eight instead of the usual six – made their precarious way along the path towards the mourners, slipping and sliding all over the place. Kennedy half-turned towards them and made to offer assistance. The undertaker, positioned at the front of the coffin, gave a discreet shake of his head that no one but Kennedy would have noticed.

Kennedy turned back to the grave and followed Forsythe's gaze down. In the split second that he thought he saw two marbles in the mud, Forsythe let out a scream so loud and sinister it would have frightened a banshee. ann rea ran over. The security guard on Forsythe's right raised the palm of his free hand towards her, as his partner turned towards their captive. He seemed to think she was being overcome with emotion and wanted to offer her some comfort.

Forsythe was having none of it and pushed him away. He stumbled in the mud and fell to his knees, barely managing to keep himself from falling into the chasm. Forsythe kept staring and screaming at the top of her lungs. She was trying to raise one of her hands to point.

Kennedy moved closer to the edge of the grave and looked down into the mud. For a second he nearly offered a scream of his own. The marbles he thought he had spotted were not, in fact, marbles after all. They were a pair of open eyes and, as the rain washed away the soil around them, it became increasingly clear that they were still attached to a body, albeit a dead one.

Chapter Two

'SO IF IT hadn't been for the rain they would have gotten away with it?'

So spoke Detective Sergeant James Irvine, Kennedy's favourite bagman.

'Yes,' Kennedy replied, 'and that's the closest we're getting to seeing the perfect way to dispose of a body.'

'Are we to assume that it's a regular method, or a one-off?'

Kennedy looked at Irvine, unable to stop his shoulders drooping in disappointment.

'Sorry, sorry,' said Irvine quickly, before Kennedy had a chance to reply. 'Of course we can't assume anything at this stage in the investigation.'

On this answer, Kennedy's shoulders returned to their original position.

A good forty-five minutes had passed since the cuckoo body had been found. The graveyard had been cleared of mourners, who had been moved to the sanctuary of the church to give statements. The several dozen solemn brethren were replaced by an even larger group of Camden Town CID Scene of Crime Officers (SOCO). The mourners and the police resembled one another inasmuch as they all dressed predominantly in black. Bella Forsythe had been transferred to North Bridge House, the oldest building in Camden Town and workplace of Kennedy and his colleagues. The remains of Daniel Elliot had been returned to the undertakers in nearby King's Cross where his coffin was opened and checked for further irregularities. None were found.

Irvine left Kennedy by himself, staring into the open grave. The corpse had been joined in the pit by a forensic team, who were carefully excavating the body. The more earth they removed, the more the smell of rotting meat threatened to overpower them. The rain might have stopped, but it was still a miserable job.

The corpse was male. Once black-skinned, he was now reddish-green, having met his maker wearing a shiny emerald-green suit. His T-shirt, originally white, was now an inconsistent chocolate colour and his hair was matted with soil and mud. His facial features had been made indistinguishable by the inevitable processes of death.

As the SOCO photographer snapped away, an additional two officers eased themselves cautiously into the grave and gingerly started trying to lift the body out.

After a few minutes it became clear that manpower alone was unequal to the task. Irvine called a halt to their efforts and went scurrying off in the direction of the church, returning a couple of minutes later with a plank and a length of rope. He passed the plank down into the grave, and the four police officers – two at the head and two at the feet – struggled to roll the body on top of it. This done, they fed the rope underneath and passed the ends up to their colleagues to begin hauling. As it tightened, the white rope darkened, and the body rose unsteadily from the grave, limbs jutting horizontally, supported only by rigor mortis.

Pathologist Dr Leonard Taylor, kitted out in Barbour jacket, Barbour hat and green wellies and looking every inch the country doctor, completed a graveside examination of the corpse in about four minutes.

'No marks, no wounds, no sign of injury of any kind as far as I can see,' he began. 'I'd say by the state of the body and the presence of spiders our friend here has been dead for at least forty-eight hours.'

Taylor, unlike the majority of his profession, was not shy about guesstimating the time of death. He loved to offer his opinion, and consistently proved that his gut instinct was equal to the exact science.

'If you don't mind old chap, I'd like to take the body back to civilization,' Taylor continued, once the SOCO had searched the body, finding nothing.

'Fine,' Kennedy said. 'Please do.'

'I'll give you my provisional report by last watch today.'

Kennedy looked at his Simon Carter wristwatch. It was three twenty-nine. He guessed that the end of this particular day was going to encroach on tomorrow by at least a few hours. He also accepted the fact that another day was going to pass without him finding out, at his superior's request, who exactly had been letting the once-elegant building opposite North Bridge House fall into ruin. He watched the SOCO zip the corpse into a body bag, and just as they were loading it into an unmarked police van the heavens opened again, destroying what, if any, evidence remained in the graveyard.

The Detective Inspector braved the rain and watched his men at work. A group to his right were kneeling in the soil searching for footprints, and even when they found what looked like traces, they couldn't be sure if they were the prints of the mourners, the genuine gravediggers, the churchmen or the workers. They did, however, know for certain that they wouldn't be the footprints of the ever-efficient SOCO team, led by DS James Irvine. Another group were gathered around the trunk of a tree using white arc lights and a UV light to search for evidence. A third group were diligently examining the sides of the recently vacated grave.

'Look, sir,' Irvine said about an hour later, 'we're getting absolutely zero here. I'm not sure it's even worth hanging around. We've already bagged everything that's moveable but it's my bet that this graveyard is not going to offer up anything worthwhile.'

'I wouldn't be so sure, James,' Kennedy replied, the fingers of his right hand twitching furiously. 'Whoever left our friend in the grave was convinced that the body would never be found. He's not going to have been too worried about covering up his tracks…'

'Aye,' Irvine cut in, 'but the rain has certainly made amends for any carelessness.' He hadn't really meant to interrupt or contradict his superior but had committed both sins simultaneously.

Kennedy didn't react to either faux pas, and went on: 'Let's just walk through this for a while, James. Let's not pack up just yet.'

'Sorry sir, yes, of course, no problem.'

Both detectives headed over to the main entrance of St Pancras Old Church, located in the bend on the left-hand side of Pancras Road as you headed towards Kings Cross. The origins of the church were in the 13th century but it probably hadn't seen so many men in uniform since it had been used as a barracks for Cromwell's men in the Civil War.

'Now let's see what we have,' Kennedy began and then, when he appeared to be drawing a blank, he continued, 'what exactly do we have here, James?'

'Well, we have a freshly dug grave. The sexton of the church, a Mr...' Irvine paused as he consulted his notes, 'Mr Davy Stewart, told us that the grave was dug yesterday afternoon between showers. The work was completed by four o'clock. So, someone spots a freshly dug grave, something clicks in the weird and wonderful workings of the criminal mind, and he, or she, sees the perfect way to dispose of a body.'

'Let's back up a wee bit. How did they know there was a freshly dug grave here, James?' Kennedy began nodding back towards the graveyard. 'You can't see it from the street.'

'Good point, good point, sir,' Irvine said, getting into the swing. 'Insider knowledge, perhaps?'

'Nagh,' Kennedy replied, deadpan. 'Too obvious, too traceable.'

'But you've already said, sir, that our suspect didn't expect the victim to be found.'

'True, but at the same time he, or she, is not going to want to raise unnecessary suspicions by inquiring about freshly dug graves. It's hardly an official anorak hobby.'

They stopped talking and listened to the sound of the rain driving relentlessly into the ever-expanding puddles.

'Of course,' Kennedy continued, appearing to remember something. 'There was a piece in the *Camden News Journal* two days ago about the father of mass-murderer Bella Forsythe dying. I believe the story also carried details of the funeral arrangements and the fact that Miss Forsythe would probably be granted compassionate leave to attend. Come to think of it, that's probably why there were so many mourners here today. Even the atrocious weather couldn't keep them away.'

'Okay. Good. That all works for me, sir. So our murderer has a body he wants to dispose of and now he's found the perfect hiding place.'

'Right, but let's forget for now about whether or not the victim is already dead at this point and concentrate on how the murderer gets the victim to the grave side.'

'Car?'

They were standing by the churchyard gate. Kennedy made a 360-degree turn. To the right of the church and the surprisingly well-manicured grounds was a high wall, running down to the Fleet River. To the left, the graveyard was bordered by the Hospital for Tropical Diseases. Which brought him back to the gate. Kennedy looked back up the eleven steps to the church. His stare continued across the busy road to once-elegant Goldington Crescent with its forty-four windows overlooking the churchyard.

'Perhaps not, perhaps a little too public,' Kennedy murmured, as much for his own benefit as Irvine's. 'The best way to blend into the surroundings is to appear to be part of the furniture. So we have to think of the least obvious way of moving a body around a graveyard.'

'Gravediggers?

'Nagh, we're already covered for two of those.'

'How about people who would look after the graveyard; maintenance and whatever?'

'You're not thinking of landscape gardeners, are you? Would churches employ such professionals to look after their property? I have to admit, the grounds are in first-class condition around here.'

'Yep,' Irvine agreed, 'so someone has been taking great care of it, even as the rain is trying desperately to undo all their work.'

'Okay, good point, so we'd have to say that if someone, say across the road there, saw a man walking around the graveyard in overalls and with a wheelbarrow he wouldn't draw any unnecessary and unwanted attention.'

'Yep. So, for the sake of the argument, our murderer removes the victim,' Irvine offered, picking up Kennedy's thread, 'out of the back of a van, say wrapped in a tarpaulin, places it in a wheelbarrow and just wheels it into the heart of the graveyard.'

'He'd have a bit of difficulty getting a wheelbarrow up these steps,' Kennedy chipped in, walking down the steps.

'Yes, but not impossible.' Irvine countered, clicking his fingers to spur himself on. 'Maybe he places the empty wheelbarrow at the top of the steps and then throws the body in its tarpaulin over his shoulder, carries it up the steps and dumps it in the wheelbarrow. He then wheels the body across to the grave. Perhaps he digs the grave an extra foot or so deeper, dumps the body in the bottom and covers it with a layer of soil. He then simply wheels the wheelbarrow out of the graveyard just like you imagine he would have done every day of his life, and no one pays a blind bit of notice to him. Next he drives off in his wee van, confident that the gravediggers and the burial of Daniel Elliot are going to do the rest of his work for him.'

'That could work,' Kennedy said, rushing back up the steps and heading off in the direction of the grave, 'so what we need to check is if there was any extra soil visible.'

'Well that's easy, sir,' Irvine called after him. 'Both the gravediggers are still here. They were ready to do their work after the memorial service and we've kept them hanging around just in case.'

The gravediggers, with a little checking and a lot of moaning, confirmed that the grave had been dug an extra fifteen inches. 'At least,' they remarked in unison. However, no extra soil had been added to their original mound of extracted earth. Which meant of course that at least the equivalent of a body's volume of soil was missing.

Chapter Three

BACK AT NORTH Bridge House an hour later, Irvine and Kennedy were waiting for Dr Taylor to come up with something and hoping that the victim's fingerprints would show up in the New Scotland Yard file.

Kennedy hated running corpse photos in the press with the headline, 'Do you know this man?' There was something terribly undignified about that whole approach and he would only use it as a last resort.

The two detectives decided that they should use the opportunity to question Dr Bella Forsythe.

Kennedy thought it highly unlikely that she was involved in the death of the victim. She had successfully set her sights on the four men who had raped her early in life, and now she was paying society back for her crimes. She didn't seem too unhappy to have to do so.

Kennedy was aware that Irvine had had a soft spot for the beautiful doctor, so he offered to have someone else conduct the interview with him. Irvine insisted that he should be involved.

Considering the fact that, a few hours ago, Forsythe had totally blanked Kennedy, she received the two policemen warmly. Especially, it has to be said, Irvine.

'Goodness, that was weird, wasn't it?' she began before Kennedy had time to switch the tape recorder on.

Forsythe seemed different to him. She was like an athlete whose years of discipline and single-mindedness were over now that she had achieved her goal – a goal nowhere near as honourable as that of Linford Christie say, but which had nevertheless ruled her life as rigidly as those sub-ten-second dashes had dominated the sprinter's waking hours. She seemed more relaxed and more comfortable with herself. This was not to suggest, however, that she had gone to seed. Far from it: Miss Bella Forsythe was a strikingly attractive woman, a fact richly appreciated by DI Irvine, who spoke with mixed emotions when he exclaimed: 'It must have been terrible for you, all that carry on out there.'

Kennedy added: 'I was sorry to hear about your father.'

How weird was that? he thought. Here he was, offering his condolences to a woman who had murdered four men.

The important thing to remember, he reflected, was that, just because one person had murdered another, it didn't necessarily make her immoral or a ten-foot tall monster or anything like that. Or did it? Just because she had taken lives didn't mean that she didn't have to go to the toilet, that she couldn't cry, that she didn't need food. It didn't mean that she didn't want to look good, that she didn't have a conscience any more, and didn't mean that she wasn't human any more. That was a big thing, wasn't it? We'd like to think that our murderers are not human because of their inhuman deeds. We'd like them to die and disappear from the face of the earth just so that we don't have to be reminded of what our fellow humans are capable of. Perhaps criminals aren't really locked away for long periods to punish them so much as to give people on the outside a chance to forget them and their crimes.

But Dr Bella Forsythe's murders were murders of vengeance. She had sought out and killed the four men who had raped her up on Primrose Hill all those years ago, and she had received a certain amount of public support for her single-minded act.

And now, in front of Kennedy and Irvine, she seemed quite… well, normal. She certainly seemed to be at peace with herself and content with her station.

'I think it's for the best,' she replied, referring to her father. 'In reality he lost his life when my mother died. I think his main way of dealing with what I did was to blame himself.'

'Had you seen him recently?' Kennedy asked, as Irvine continued to stare.

'When I was first sentenced twenty-four months ago, he came to see me a few times. Later, when he moved back to London, he had difficulty travelling. But he'd write to me. I think we made our peace. I think he came to see that what I did was what a father should have done. Anyway, the last time I saw him in the flesh was maybe as far back as February of this year.'

'Did you recognize the body in the grave?' Kennedy asked.

Forsythe's mouth and eyes opened simultaneously to their widest extremes.

'Heavens, no! You don't actually think that I was in any way responsible for this death? No!'

Irvine and Kennedy remained silent as the second hand of the wall clock counted eleven seconds.

'No! Come on,' Forsythe said, breaking into a smile. 'You both worked on my case. You know my motive. I've settled all of my scores.'

'So you've no idea who it was, then?' Irvine asked.

'No, James, I positively do not!'

'Okay,' Kennedy announced, hitting the stop button on the tape recorder. 'I think we can leave it there for now.'

'What's going to happen to me now?' asked Forsythe as he rose.

'I believe our chaps are nearly finished in the graveyard and the funeral has been rescheduled for seven o'clock this evening,' he said. 'I imagine you'll stay here until then and, following the funeral, you'll be driven back to prison.'

'Would you like some tea or something?' Irvine asked as an afterthought, as he followed Kennedy out of the interview room.

'Yes, that would be delightful, James. I'm a bit peckish too. Any chance of something more substantial?'

'I'll see what I can rustle up for you.'

'I'm afraid this is the best I could come up with,' Irvine announced as he returned precariously balancing a makeshift tray with two teas, a couple of sandwiches, a bag of crisps and a muffin that was dangerously close to its sell-by date.

Dr Bella Forsythe jumped up to help him, only to be restrained by attendant PC Allaway.

'Away. Off with ye, man, we're fine here by ourselves,' Irvine said as he inadvertently used his left elbow to come between the conscientious constable and the convicted murderer.

'I'm afraid, sir...' Allaway began doubtfully.

'Okay, okay, fine,' said Irvine. 'Look, Constable Allaway, we're in the basement, right? So she's not going to go scurrying off through any window. Why don't you just stand yourself outside the door, and if the good doctor here tries to escape, you'll be perfectly positioned.'

'Well, it's as much to protect the prisoner...' Allaway opined, either recalling some rule or, more likely, being downright nosy.

'Yeah, yeah,' Irvine sighed, clearly losing his patience and taking the young constable by the arm. 'I'll tell you what: the doctor here will promise to shout out loud and clear if I start to molest her. Okay?'

Allaway looked to Forsythe, who was suppressing a fit of the giggles. She nodded her agreement eagerly and the constable made his way into the corridor.

'I'd forgotten just how much you really do sound like Sean Connery. It was just when you said: "Shout out loud and clear if I start to molest her." It's incredible, really.'

'Do you really think so?' Irvine asked, hamming up the Connery inflections a bit more than was usual.

'Oh, this tea is ghastly,' Forsythe said, nearly spitting out the brew. 'I remember the last drink we enjoyed together was somewhat stronger than this.'

'Yes,' Irvine replied after a pause. He refused to return her direct stare.

'Look, this is awkward, James. We don't have much time for niceties,' Forsythe began confidently. 'But there are a few things I need to say to you. I did like you. I liked you lot. We just met at the wrong time. I couldn't believe we met when we did. You'll be happy to know that you distracted me...'

'Obviously not enough,' Irvine said dryly, remembering her crimes.

'It's difficult enough, James...'

'Difficult? Annabella! You murder four men and then say that I nearly distracted you? Please!'

His obvious venom silenced both of them for a couple of minutes.

'I'm sorry,' he said.

'I'm sorry,' she said.

Then after another couple of minutes of silence, the sound of Allaway scuffing impatiently from foot to foot outside the door reminded them of the limited time they had.

'Look, James, I'm not going to apologise for what I did but surely you realise I had...'

'Please don't say that you had to kill them...'

'Of course I had to kill them.'

'There were other ways,' the lawman said.

'There was no other way, James.'

'Ah...'

'No, James, just shut up and listen to me, then you can say whatever you want to say,' Forsythe began rising to her feet.

Irvine made to protest, then thought better of it.

'Okay, I had to do what neither the law of the land nor my father was prepared to do.'

'But you've ruined your life...'

'No, James, I did not ruin my life, my life was already ruined. They ruined my life. You have to accept that fact. I have accepted that fact. Yes, I know I should have dealt with it and moved on and I certainly would have been able to deal with it if they'd been dealt with properly. Don't you see what's happening out there? Thanks to the liberals amongst us the country has lost its collective conscience. This scum think they can just roam the streets doing as they please. And why wouldn't they? When was the last time a criminal paid for his deed? I mean really paid? You, more than most, should realize where all this is heading, but no one seems either willing or able to do anything about it.'

Irvine sat quietly looking at her.

'Yes, but I, more than most, realise that we can't solve it by returning to the ways of the Wild Wild West.'

'Really, James? Are you really aware what's happening out

there? The Wild Wild West is like Disneyland compared to what's happening out there at the minute.' Forsythe broke into a sarcastic snigger. 'You know what? I'm probably in the safest place there is right now.'

'But Kennedy says that we can't afford to look beyond the crime otherwise we'll never be able to solve it.'

'James, Kennedy is naive and that's why he's able to solve his crimes, he loves the puzzles, that's why he was able to catch me. But there's a big, bad world out there and Kennedy ignores it entirely. He solves his cases, he catches the criminals, and then the justice system lets him down and lets them out to commit more crimes as quickly as they can be processed. Maybe the second time around, society has reached the stage where their evil is no longer considered criminal. You think it was wrong of me to end the lives of those boys, don't you? And you agree that I should have been punished for what I did to them. But what about some punishment for what they did to me?'

'Yes, yes, I know, but we can't exist in a vigilante state.'

'But we can exist in a state where four boys can rape a young girl and destroy her life, and then walk the streets as pillars of society? Hell, one of them even had political ambitions.'

'But we have to live within the laws of the land.'

'I was living within the laws of the land. I was working for the law and I, as an officer of the law, sought out the four boys and…'

'Annabella, they were hardly boys…'

'Yeah, you're right,' said Forsythe, relaxing a little. 'But I always saw them as the boys they were up on Primrose Hill. And I know you're angry because there was something between us. We were both aware of it. Even in that brief time we spent together something happened between us, and you think that if I hadn't done this, then maybe we'd be together. And I sometimes think too that, if I'd met you earlier, maybe my life would have taken a different direction. But James, you should never forget that, by the time I'd met you, one of them was already dead.'

She looked at him sympathetically before continuing. 'Do you ever think of me, James?'

'Yes I do,' Irvine replied simply and honestly.

'How come you never got in touch?'

Irvine couldn't contain a brief laugh.

'What,' Forsythe countered, 'you mean because I'm a convicted killer and you're a law-abiding policeman?'

'Something like that.'

'But I'm paying for my crimes, James. Don't you see that's the main difference between those four boys and me? They assaulted and wronged me indiscriminately; they broke the laws of the land on a macho whim. Then, to compound their crime, they lied to get away with it. Although I knew I was ridding the world of scum, I accepted my punishment and am content to do my time.'

'And that makes it all right?'

'No. Do you realise just how infuriating you are when you sit there and smugly say that to me? Of course it doesn't make it all right, but I would remind you I was not the one who committed the original crime. I was just doing what I had to do to get back at least part of my life.'

After another few seconds of quiet, she continued. 'Can I tell you something? I've had so many letters over the last few years from people who've been raped. From mothers whose daughters have been raped and in some instances murdered. From fathers and from brothers. And they all, each and every one of them, says thank you: thanks for getting a little of our own back. They find satisfaction, or peace, or some kind of resolve in what I did. One woman, a vicar's wife who had been raped by a friend of her father's when she was young, said that she couldn't condone what I had done. But she could see why I did it, and she said she thought it sent out a message to other would-be offenders.'

'It would only have sent out an effective message if you'd gotten away with it.'

'That's a bit of a change of tack, isn't it? The police line softening up a bit is it, James?'

'No,' Irvine started with a sigh. 'What I meant was that your vigilante approach would only succeed as a deterrent if you had gotten away with it. In the vicar's wife's theory, the rapist thinks:

"Oh, I won't rape anyone because they may come and murder me." In fact, taken to its logical conclusion, the rapist's logic would be: "If I rape her, then she's not going to murder me because she'll have to do time if she does."'

'Which equally means that if you, the police, locked up the bastards in the first place and threw away the key, you'd have all the deterrent you needed to keep at least some of the crime off the streets,' Forsythe said.

She changed tack. 'So you were thinking about me?'

'Yes.'

'I thought about you too.'

'Which one? Larry, Adam, Bono or The Edge?'

'Right, good. I must remember that one for the inside. It'll have them rolling in the aisles and keep me out of trouble.'

'Do you experience much grief on the inside?'

'Who, me? A lifer, a mass murderer?' Forsythe laughed. 'I'm queen of the castle. I'm left well alone, I can tell you. I've even had a few of the girls tell me they wish they'd done the same. You know what, James? You'd be surprised how many of the girls start off their life of crime following a rape. But I don't encourage the awe factor any more than is necessary to give me my space.'

'Do you have any visitors?'

'I got out to bury my only visitor today,' she said. 'I… I feel that my father's dying has completed the cycle. It's drawn a line under all of this for me.'

'So you've no other friends?'

'No, not really. Not at all, in fact. The few I had I lost when I went inside. Leonard's been kind. Dr Taylor, that is. He sent me a lovely note when I was sentenced to say that if I needed anything, anything at all, just to get in touch with him. I enjoyed working with him, I have to admit. Those were the two good things about my work: meeting him and meeting you. And at least he contacted me…'

'I often thought about contacting you or coming in to see you…' Irvine replied hesitantly.

'But you didn't?'

'No, I didn't. I wasn't sure of the reception I'd get. I didn't know how I fitted into everything.'

'You didn't remember the night we kissed?' Forsythe asked, her voice dropping to a barely audible level.

The door creaked. Irvine imagined Allaway had his ear so close to the wood that he'd penetrated the first coat of paint.

Irvine did remember their solitary kiss but his memory of it was of a truly soulless kiss. This, however, was not something he should bring up at this point so he went for the more gracious reply.

'Now there's a memory to warm the heart on a cold night. You know we probably only remember that kiss because nothing else happened. If we'd gone any further…' Irvine paused as though to consider what 'any further' could have been. 'Well, quite simply, the kiss might have been forgotten by now.'

'Perhaps,' she whispered, 'but I don't think so. Then again, I'm sure I've not got quite the same experience as you.'

She moved towards Irvine and caressed his cheek in an absent-minded kind of way. It looked like it was something she was bursting to do but wanted to make it appear casual.

'James,' she continued still in a whisper, 'I've thought about our kiss a lot. I've had a lot of time to spare to consider it and…' she hesitated. 'Blast! I don't have a lot of time for us to work our way around to this so I'll just come right out and say it. Would you mind if we kissed again? You know, give me something else to consider in my lonely nights. Blast! There I go, being flippant about it again and that's not what I want to be. The truth is, James, I just want to see if kissing you is as special as I remember or if the memory is merely an oasis in my desert.'

Irvine didn't say a word. He rose from his chair, took her hand and gently pulled her towards him.

They met in their second, but this time singularly spectacular, kiss.

Allaway knocked loudly on the door to the interview room and discreetly waited quite a few seconds before entering the room, by which time both Irvine and Forsythe had rearranged themselves.

'Detective Inspector Kennedy would like to see you, sir,' the constable said quickly. He was accompanied by a WPC.

'Right, yes, thank you,' Irvine replied. He got up from his chair and placed it carefully and considerately under the table, directly across from where Bella Forsythe was now sitting. 'Look... am...'

'Yes, it's fine, DS Irvine,' Forsythe cut in, deflating Irvine's awkwardness. 'Thank you very much for the... ah... for the nourishment. I'm quite sure that's enough to get me through the night.'

Irvine took Constable Allaway out of the room as soon as possible, hoping that he hadn't had time to note that none of the food from the makeshift tray had been touched.

Chapter Four

'WELL, AN EARLY break for us,' Kennedy announced as Irvine and Allaway joined him and WDC Anne Coles in his office. 'Our victim from the grave. His prints were on the computer. He's a Mr Christopher Lloyd, last known address 78b Kelly Street. And he's got form: a list as long as your eyebrows.'

'You don't seem all that heartened though, sir,' said Irvine, taking the last available seat and still awaiting the return of his land legs.

'Well, there is no such thing as a golden rule but usually when you get a break early in a case, you pay for it twice over with hard work later on,' Kennedy replied as he studied Lloyd's file.

'He's got convictions for handling stolen tyres, assault, indecent assault, attempted robbery – apparently he tried to empty the parking-ticket meter in Parkway – and handling stolen credit cards. It's all petty stuff apart from his last one, which was indecently assaulting an underage girl. He went to trial for that in March this year. He said the girl consented and apparently he got off.'

'But surely if she was underage,' Irvine began, 'even if she consented – and I'm assuming that when he said she consented he was admitting something happened between them – he should have been done for that?' He twitched nervously in his seat.

'Apparently not, James. The jury found him not guilty,' Kennedy replied closing the file.

'But someone else obviously not only found him guilty but they carried out their own death sentence as well,' Coles said, adding her tuppence worth.

'Right,' Kennedy began, straightening up in his chair. 'We need to find out a lot more about Mr Christopher Lloyd and what went on at the trial. At this stage, we can't assume that his death is connected to it.'

'Have we had the autopsy report yet, sir?' Irvine asked.

'No, not yet, we just got the report straight through from the fingerprint department. Taylor expects to have something for us by the end of the day. Let's check Lloyd's credit card details for the last week of his life. Let's also check his phone records for the last week and see who he was in touch with. Hell, if it helps us, let's even rummage through his dustbin.'

Something was troubling Kennedy. It was all just a bit too pat. The body of a petty criminal is found and already they have a motive and perhaps even a healthy suspect list. Kennedy was convinced that whenever they got into the details of the family of the underage victim, it wouldn't take long for a few suspects' heads to pop up on the horizon. This worried him. Experience had taught him that things were rarely as simple as that.

But in this case, where Christopher Lloyd was found by the skin of his teeth – more like by the skin of his eyeballs – spoiling an ingenious method of disposing of the body, well, then it all appeared to be wrapped up and delivered to him on a plate. He realised he was guilty of the biggest sin he lectured his team to avoid – making assumptions. He had a long way to go before he could start to draw any conclusions. A journey always starts with one step. It was time to take it.

'Okay. WDC Coles and myself will go and visit 78b Kelly Street. DS Irvine, you take Constable Allaway here with you to the courthouse and see what information you can gather about Mr Lloyd's trial in March.'

Chapter Five

ALLAWAY DROVE AND Irvine considered his encounter with Dr Bella Forsythe.

Snogging a convicted murderer while she was under his jurisdiction – what was that all about? He tried to examine his feelings for her. He returned to his earlier conclusion that, if they'd had time to play out their relationship in a normal manner, he'd have gone after her and lost interest the minute she'd said yes. He knew it was a major character flaw on his part. He frequently wished it were otherwise.

But Forsythe hadn't said yes. They'd had two dates. One drunken and one where they'd had dinner and he'd kissed her at the end of the date. He'd remembered the kiss as being indifferent at the time, but it had obviously made a big impression on her. She still seemed to be preoccupied with it. Mind you, at the time of the original kiss she'd been preoccupied with murder so perhaps her memory wasn't all it ought to be.

He couldn't believe he was even considering this. *She'd taken four people's lives, for heaven's sake.* Yes, but those four people had taken her life just as surely as if they had ended it that night on Primrose Hill. *She'd lied to get away with her crimes.* Yes, but they'd lied to get away with their crimes. *She'd used her professional position to help her carry out her crime.* Yes, but at least one of them had used his professional position to help hide and deny his original crime. *She'd broken a commandment: Thou shalt not kill.* Yes, but they'd also broken at least one of the commandments, if not several. *She should have left it to the law of the land and the justice system to ensure the four of them paid for their crime.* Yes, but the justice system had failed her when it had allowed the lies of the four boys to stand. And the Bible did say:

An eye for an eye and a tooth for a tooth. Wasn't that all she had done? Obeyed the Bible?

Irvine thought it was funny – no, not funny, funny was the wrong word. He couldn't believe that he, a policeman, was justifying people taking the law into their own hands. That was bad enough, but if he was interpreting his own feelings properly he was also suggesting that they should get away with it.

Well, one of them, at least.

But surely it was his job to uphold the law, not to kiss a mass-murderer in the basement of his very own place of work? It was a great kiss though, he had to admit. Maybe it was because she was no longer preoccupied with planning murder, or because she had just recently lost her father, her last remaining contact with the outside world. Maybe it was out of a desperate need to make tender contact with at least one other human on this planet that she kissed him. For his part, Irvine thought that second kiss was all that Forsythe claimed the first one was.

Maybe its power was in its finality.

Neither of them had spoken a word at the end of the encounter. They had remained in each other's arms until Allaway had given the discreet knock on the door. They had disentangled from each other and a few seconds later, Irvine and Allaway had left Forsythe and a WPC in the room and headed off to see DI Kennedy. Chances were that Irvine and Forsythe both knew they would never, ever see each other again.

Irvine pushed all thoughts of Dr Forsythe out of his head as he arrived at the Camden Courthouse up on the right-hand side of Plender Street. Walking through its imposing doors, he couldn't help wondering if courts of law were built so majestically to make everyone, particularly the guilty, feel humble.

Irvine suddenly had another thought: would the officers of the court hand over files just because the local police asked for them? Surely there were proper channels to go through, miles of red tape and triplicate paperwork to be filled out and signed.

The simple answer was yes and yes. Yes, they were able to collect a transcript of the trial and yes, they would have to go through the red tape for the rest should they need more. Irvine wasn't sure if this was the normal procedure or if they'd just been lucky enough to meet a helpful officer of the court.

On the drive back to North Bridge House he started to read the file. He wanted to make sure that he was familiar with all the contents before he saw Kennedy again.

Mr Christopher Lloyd was charged with unlawfully having sex with Miss Eve Adams, who was fifteen years and ten months old at the time of the alleged offence. It was a pretty sordid affair, as far as Irvine could ascertain from the file. Miss Adams, who was still at school at the time, did some casual labour for Mr Lloyd on his weekend stall up on Camden Market in the Stables, selling antique radios and second-hand CDs. Mr Lloyd went to great pains to claim that he did not in fact employ Miss Adams. Sometimes he would give her some money – usually a fiver or a tenner – when she covered for him. They had met ten months previously. Mr Lloyd was an acquaintance of a friend of Miss Adams' mother. Mr Lloyd was thirty-two years old at the time of the incident, married but separated, with two children. He claimed that Miss Adams had several boyfriends. He also claimed that he overheard her and her friend, Miss Madonna Duncan, discuss the fact that she was sleeping with her then-boyfriend.

On the night in question, a Monday, just after Coronation Street, which Miss Adams had watched on a small portable television at the back of Mr Lloyd's stall, Mr Lloyd and Miss Adams started messing around in the way Mr Lloyd claimed they'd done several times before. Miss Adams was sitting on Mr Lloyd's knee for several minutes. She got up to turn off the television. This much they agreed on (apart from the fact that they'd fooled around a lot before). Lloyd, who changed his evidence twice, first claimed, when he was picked up, that absolutely nothing had happened. When medical evidence clearly showed something had happened he said they had been messing around but that she had claimed he'd raped her only because she'd asked for a job and he wouldn't agree. Then he changed his story to say that they were boyfriend and girlfriend and she'd made up the story because she was annoyed that he wouldn't take her to Denmark for a weekend. He claimed that although both of them were undressed, only his finger was used. Miss Adams' consistent story was that after she turned the television off he grabbed her, knocked her legs out from underneath her, held both her hands above her head with one hand while he removed her trousers and his own with his other hand. He then, she claimed, proceeded to have unlawful sex with her.

Miss Adams went home and didn't say anything to her mother. Then, after several minutes, went around to Miss Duncan's house where she told Miss Duncan's mother that Mr Lloyd had raped her. Mrs Duncan took her straight to North Bridge House, where specially trained officers counselled, questioned, examined and cared for her. Mr Lloyd was arrested and charged the following morning.

Mr Lloyd was remanded in custody until March of this year when the case went to court. During the course of the trial Mr Lloyd changed his evidence.

Due to their tender age, Miss Eve Adams and her friend Miss Madonna Duncan had given their evidence by video link. The other witnesses were Mr Manfred Hodges, the adjoining stallholder and a friend of Mr Lloyd; Mrs Christine Duncan (Madonna's mother); Mrs Angelina Adams (Eve's mother); Dr Susanne Reiger (the doctor who physically examined Miss Adams); Miss Adele Scott and Mrs Margaret Hutchinson (the prosecution's expert witnesses); Mr Wesley Cane (the defence's expert witness); WPC Jenny Lowe; DS Victor Savage, the arresting officer; and Derek McClelland, a character witness for Lloyd.

There was the usual argy-bargy between defence and prosecution: a bit of point-scoring on both sides. There were a few boobs on the part of the police, including a failure to seal the scene of the crime immediately, and a few from the defence, who got their knickers in a twist with one of their own witnesses, Mr Manfred Hodges.

The judge had given a fair summing-up but, overall, even reading it several months later, it seemed a pretty open-and-shut case to Irvine, especially with Lloyd changing his story.

And still the jury was not able to find him guilty.

But someone had found him guilty though, as WDC Coles had claimed a few hours earlier. Or was his death totally unrelated to the Eve Adams incident?

Irvine knew that Kennedy wouldn't go down the road of the unlawful sex charge exclusively. No, he'd use it as one line of his investigation but still look elsewhere. Until, of course, he had a reason not to.

Again, Irvine's mind wandered to the Dr Forsythe case. She, too, had been raped. What would Kennedy's line have been on that one? Would he have assumed those charged by Forsythe to be the guilty parties just because she'd accused them?

There were similarities between the cases. But when Irvine was reading the notes on the case, was he putting his spin on it just because he knew what had happened to Dr Bella Forsythe? Could the truth really be that, yes, Miss Eve Adams was indeed promiscuous? Could they have been fooling around and then one thing have lead to another? Yes, maybe they'd crossed a barrier they'd never crossed before, but had they done so with each other's consent? Then, afterwards, because he wouldn't take her for a weekend in Denmark or because she regretted it – had she falsely accused him?

Clichés are clichés because they are frequently truths and none more true than the one about there being two sides to every story. Obviously only one side could be truly truthful. And all of it, at the end of the day, was about the truth. Could both sides passionately believe that what they were saying was the truth? Could Miss Eve Adams be lying? But even if she was lying about the sequence of events, surely it was still a case of statutory rape? Why had Christopher Lloyd not been charged with statutory rape?

Chapter Six

'HOW ARE YOUR exams going, then?' Kennedy asked Coles once they'd started on their short journey from North Bridge House.

'To be perfectly honest, I'm really enjoying them. I know you're not meant to but I do.'

'Hey, that's fine, much better enjoying it than it being a slog. And I'll tell you what, unlike in my day, you're not going to make any progress in the police force these days without the exam results.'

As she swung a left out of the gates of North Bridge House into Gloucester Avenue, Kennedy grinned. 'Would you listen to me. "Unlike in my day…". I sound like I'm from the ark.'

'Oh, I'd say there's a few miles left in you yet,' Coles replied as she turned right into Oval Road, adding a belated 'Sir' as she took another quick right into Gloucester Crescent.

Kennedy sat wondering why he'd made that last remark. He wasn't trying to impress the extremely attractive and even more efficient WDC Anne Coles, was he? And her response, was that meant to be encouraging or patronising? It was so difficult to know these days. There he was again, marking the passing of time on his own clock.

Now he felt that even though it was only a short journey, it was going to take longer than he wanted. Coles turned right into Inverness Street and then left into Arlington Road. When he was being driven by Irvine, neither of them minded the silences, but with Coles, both of them seemed to be struggling to find something to say. Then he realised that it had nothing to do with her. Something deep down inside of him had accepted that he was going to the house of a person who had recently lost their life and there was a good chance that a mother, a father, a sister or a brother, a partner or a wife, a son or a daughter or some combination of these was going to greet him, not even suspecting how devastating his news was going to be. Now his original fear over how long the journey was going to take had changed and he wanted the journey to take longer, to take forever in fact.

As Coles turned into Camden High Street, Kennedy offered: 'It's funny, you know. I'm in my mid-forties but I never thought I would be starting to feel old at this stage.'

'Do you feel old, sir?'

'No, and I think that might be part of the problem. I think maybe I should be feeling older. But there's another part of me that's thinking, "hang on a minute, it's only a short time since I was feeling young" so what's happened to all the time that's meant to be in-between?'

'Perhaps middle age really comes after old age?', Coles suggested as they moved from Camden High Street to Chalk Farm Road and the traffic started to ease up again.

'You know, you might have something there. That kind of makes sense. Old age is the end of your career and middle age is your retirement period when you're apparently rejuvenated and spend most of your life on the golf course.'

Coles broke into a hearty laugh. 'You know, if we market this new concept properly we could make our fortune, sir.'

'You mean you think we've discovered eternal youth?' Kennedy said, getting in the flow of it and very much enjoying this lighter moment.

'Well,' Coles continued carefully negotiating the traffic as she turned right into Hartland Road, 'in a way we have. We just need to make sure we keep it our secret so we can make a few pounds out of it when we need to. In the meantime we'll have a bit of fun with it ourselves.'

They both seemed to consider this for a few seconds and as they reached the junction of Clarence Way, where they took a right turn, Coles seemed compelled to qualify herself. 'I mean, of course, sir, having a bit of fun by the fact that we've discovered the secret of eternal youth but not sharing it with anyone else.'

'Of course,' Kennedy agreed without hesitation, sparing her embarrassment. They were now turning left into Castlehaven Road. Kennedy raised his right-hand index finger to the houses they were passing. 'You know, all the people who live in all of these houses are going to be pretty annoyed with us when we eventually market and sell them this fabulous secret of ours.'

'Yes,' Coles replied, clicking an 'ah well' with her teeth. 'The magic of secrets, sir, is that they are only secrets if hardly anyone knows about them.'

'Kelly Street is next right I think,' Kennedy said. 'So what you're saying is it's best to keep this exclusive club to only two members?'

'Absolutely, sir,' she replied as she eased the car to a perfect stop outside 11 Kelly Street.

'Okay, I can live with that,' Kennedy said and he continued under his breath: 'It's a bit like the Elusive Butterfly Club.'

They made their way up the steps to number eleven and pressed the doorbell marked 'Lloyd.'

About twenty seconds later, as Coles was about to give the bell another ring, they heard a high-pitched musical voice say: 'And the Lord's blessing to you. It's Mabel Lloyd here. What can I do for you on this fine day?'

Kennedy and Coles announced themselves and half a minute later the owner of the voice, all fifteen stone of her, was standing in front of them.

'Come on in, won't you,' she commanded in her singing voice. 'I can't abide doing the Lord's business on the doorstep. You're very welcome into our home.'

The Lloyd family had the top two floors of the house. They had obviously lived there a considerable time, so homely was their set-up.

'Is there anyone else with you?' Kennedy asked when he and Coles were sitting with Mrs Mabel Lloyd in the living room.

'Only the Lord,' came the joyous reply.

Kennedy noticed Coles look around the room, taking in the lack of dust, the honest no-name furniture, the family photos and religious images around the walls, and a painting of three roses just above the mantelpiece. The thick white carpet was now off-white and worn, but still very clean.

'Your husband?' Kennedy offered.

'Oh, God rest his soul, Jesus took him nine years since.'

'I'm sorry,' Kennedy said realising this was going to be painful.

'Oh no, don't be sorry for James. He enjoyed the spirit of our Lord each and every day of his life. No, it's just Christopher and myself now. Well now, Christopher hasn't been here for a few days to be honest. He's a good boy, Christopher, but he does get into trouble, he tries too hard. Yes, basically that's his problem: he tries too hard. He tries too hard in everything he does.'

Then something quite remarkable happened. Right before Coles' and Kennedy's eyes, Mrs Mabel Lloyd physically and mentally changed. She suddenly became businesslike.

'Okay, officer,' she began brushing down her light blue and red-rose floral dress. 'What's he been up to this time?'

Kennedy saw several ways to proceed but he preferred not to beat about the bush. The truth was a blow that could never be softened.

'I'm afraid I have some bad news for you, Mrs Lloyd. Your son Christopher was found dead earlier today.'

At first she smiled at them. It was a smile that said, 'Oh don't be silly, you must mean someone else.' But from the look in their eyes, she saw that they didn't. Then she started to bawl like a baby. Kennedy couldn't find another way to describe it. Babies always look so helpless and desperate when they cry. It's as though, if someone doesn't solve their problem, their world will end right there and then. And once they've been sorted out, the cry changes into a 'why didn't you do that for me sooner?' kind of cry. Mrs Lloyd's cry would take no such turn.

The sheer volume of her crying scared Coles. She went to comfort the older woman but her fear kept a barrier between them.

Kennedy stepped in, sat beside the woman and took her in his arms. Mrs Lloyd's arms dwarfed him, nearly hugging the life out of him. In times of death you cling to life.

Coles made her way through to the kitchen.

Kennedy didn't offer any of the 'there, there, it'll be alright' type of comfort. He knew that for Mrs Mabel Lloyd it wasn't going to be all right.

It was never going to be all right ever again.

He let her cry and she rocked gently in his arms.

Coles returned several minutes later; it could have been five, it could have been twenty, Kennedy didn't know. Mabel Lloyd used the interruption as an excuse to pull away from him and start to compose herself. Coles offered tea. Both Mabel and Kennedy accepted, and Mabel started ploughing her way through a box of Kleenex tissues. Tears still streamed down her face.

'What happened to my baby?' Mrs Lloyd eventually asked.

'We don't know exactly yet,' Kennedy began. 'He was found... a couple of hours ago.' Kennedy hoped WDC Coles would take his ever-so-slight pause for a sign that he wanted to spare the grieving woman the details.

'But was it an accident? Was he in his car? I don't understand.'

'He was found in mysterious circumstances. He is currently being examined...'

'Examined? Good Lord, but I thought you said he was dead.'

'He is dead, Mrs Lloyd. We have to examine him to ascertain what happened to him,' Kennedy said raising his arm to her back again. She turned around to him, a look of pure horror in her eyes.

'But you're not cutting my poor baby up are you, officer?'

'He's being examined by a Dr Taylor, a kind man,' were the only words Kennedy could find to say that would neither be a discomfort or a lie.

'Oh, he was a good boy, sir. Yes, he got into trouble sometimes but he really didn't mean any harm to anyone. That boy was just in too much of a hurry all his life, that was his only problem, you know?'

The problem with a shock, particularly the kind of shock that death brings, is that people are not properly equipped to deal with it. Mabel Lloyd's good nature took over. She looked like she thought she was behaving pathetically, sitting there and crying uncontrollably in front of strangers. She wiped the tears from her eyes as best she could and stopped her sobbing by gulping large breaths of air.

'Forgive my manners,' she said as she rose to her feet. 'Let me get you some digestives or something.'

'It's fine. We're quite okay, Mrs Lloyd,' Kennedy said, also rising.

She ignored him and walked towards the kitchen. Kennedy watched her go. And as if in slow-motion he saw, first her left leg, then her right, buckle beneath her, as Mrs Lloyd collapsed onto the carpet. The thud shook the entire room. Kennedy and Coles rushed over to her and awkwardly helped her back to the safety of the sofa.

She began bawling at the top of her lungs again. Kennedy sat beside her, while Coles rang for a doctor.

After a few minutes, Coles said: 'Is there anyone we can ring to come and be with you?'

Mrs Lloyd looked at Coles as if she was just seeing her for the first time. She started to say something several times but couldn't get her words to cut through her sobbing.

'It's okay. We'll stay with you for now,' Kennedy said and he gently patted her on her bulky shoulders. 'We've sent for a doctor who will give you something to help.'

'I'm alone apart from Christopher,' Mrs Lloyd eventually got out with great difficulty.

'What about your local clergy?' Kennedy offered.

Mrs Lloyd seemed to perk up a little at that. So, about thirty minutes later, the Reverend McGonigle, local GP Doctor Clive Bruce, WDC Anne Coles and DI Christy Kennedy found themselves sitting around the large circular table in her kitchen, drinking tea and talking about the recently deceased Christopher Lloyd.

Rather than tanking Mrs Lloyd up with sedatives and packing her off to bed, both Reverend McGonigle and Dr Bruce encouraged her to talk, to let her memories flow as freely and fast as her tears.

'He wasn't a bad boy was he, Reverend?' Mabel said a smile creeping across her face for the first time in the sorry episode.

'No worse than a lot.' said McGonigle diplomatically.

'Of course, you didn't know him as well as I did,' Mrs Lloyd replied. 'Christopher's main problem was that he was in too much of a hurry. Too much of a hurry to get out of short trousers, to start smoking, to get out of school, to join the army. To be going out with girls. To be getting married.'

'Now now, Mabel dear, the army did make a man out of him,' the Reverend cut in.

'You're right, it did. The army did the job that his father should have done if he'd lived long enough. But then, the army also punished him for being good. They promoted him too quickly. He wasn't ready for all that responsibility. He was a good soldier, yes, he took to it all like a duck to water, but he was still a child who needed to be able to have a bit of fun. But they made him an NCO too quickly. Yes, much too quickly.'

Kennedy stole a glance at Coles who was making notes in her notebook.

'But that's where the trouble started,' Mabel continued unperturbed. 'He just wanted to be one of the boys. He didn't want to be superior. And then one night, he was out for a drink with some of his mates, and a few of the juniors – who I'd have to say had had a tiny bit too much to drink at that stage – started to shout things at Christopher and his friend. A fight started and Christopher just defended himself. But as he was senior, they said he should have known better, and he was court-martialled. Thrown out of the army. Now how can you ever get over that, especially if you're as ambitious as Christopher? But we prayed for him didn't we, Reverend?'

'We sure did. We surely did, Mabel,' Reverend McGonigle said beaming from ear to ear.

'Yes, but the Lord didn't seem to listen,' Mabel replied, wiping the smile from Reverend McGonigle's face. 'Because then he met Valerie. A nice wee girl really, but neither of them were ready for marriage, let alone the two kiddies they had. And now I never even get to see the wee mites any more. They don't come to see their doting granny. The sins of the father really do fall on the children. And since then, he's never been out of trouble. It's all been petty stuff. But once the police have you in their system…'

Mabel stopped mid-track, looked at Coles and Kennedy and, obviously thinking better of her original tack, continued with only the slightest batting of the eye. 'Well, he was found not guilty on all those trumped-up charges, wasn't he?'

No one replied.

'I thought if you took the Lord into your heart and lived a decent life, He would look after you?' Mabel said, addressing the Reverend.

'Well, you know…' the Reverend prevaricated. 'The Lord sent His son to this earth and had Him die on a cross so that we all may be forgiven…'

Mabel made to protest but Reverend McGonigle lifted the palm of his right hand up to God to silence her, and silence her he did. 'So you see, He didn't spare His own child. There was something that He had to show – forgiveness – something He had to feel – compassion – something even that He had to endure – pain – so that His flock could be protected and continue. And when Jesus' time on this earth was completed, God took Him back to heaven to sit at His right hand and now He's taken our dear Christopher back to heaven.'

Kennedy prayed that Mabel wouldn't cut in with 'to sit at his left hand.' It was a silly thought and he felt guilty for having it, but it had just popped into his head. The Reverend's words seemed to offer Mabel some comfort because she stopped asking questions and appeared to start reminiscing.

She was rocking back and forth and gently singing to herself when Kennedy and Coles made their apologies and returned to North Bridge House.

Chapter Seven

'SO WHAT DOES a petty criminal do to get himself murdered?' Irvine asked himself aloud. The team was back in Kennedy's office, having brought each other up to date on their newly acquired information.

'Let's not be in such a hurry,' said Kennedy. 'If you push too hard, you'll find nothing there to meet your resistance. To push effectively, there has to be some sort of resistance,' he went on, mainly to have something to say. As he said it, he realized that it might have sounded just a tiny bit pompous. But it wasn't simply because he liked the sound of his voice that he said those words. Sometimes, with a case as with a puzzle, you just needed to make a start. You may wish to go back and rub out what you've done and begin all over again, but at the very least you'd made some sort of a start. And even if you did have to go back again, well then, wasn't that just because you'd learnt more and were then able to proceed with a bit more confidence?

Kennedy and his team learnt from Dr Taylor that Christopher Lloyd had died as a result of poisoning. High levels of aluminium phosphite had been detected in his bloodstream. The good doctor had advised Kennedy that Phostek tablets, which contained 57% aluminium phosphite, were generally available from agricultural suppliers for pest control – specifically rabbits and moles. Another clue that pointed them in the direction of a professional gardener of some sort, Kennedy thought, but he didn't mention to the team. He did, however, make a note to find out more about the poison from Taylor.

'The main problem with the case for me,' Kennedy began wandering over to his 'Guinness is Good For You' notice board and pinning a labelled photo of Christopher Lloyd on to it, 'is that, in reality, we do not have a crime scene to work with.'

'You mean no murder scene, no clues?' Coles offered.

'Well yes, I suppose so, but at this stage I'd settle for just the scene of crime. There's always something to be learnt from the scene of crime, even if it's only in the way that it's been cleaned up.' Kennedy sat down at his desk before continuing. 'And there are always some clues to be found around the body.'

'For instance?' Coles asked.

'Well, for instance, when you know the method of murder – in this case, poisoning – and you have the scene, you can reach a few important conclusions. For instance, was Lloyd restrained while the poison was administered? A lot of poisons are administered without the victim realising, you know, mixed in with their food or drink for example. The victim's totally unaware of what is happening until it's too late, if indeed they ever become aware at all.'

'If that were the case, would Christopher lead us directly to his mother?' Coles exclaimed in disbelief.

'If so, then she must have had an accomplice to carry out that whole sorry hoo-ha in the cemetery. That's doubtful, though…'

'At this stage it's too early to rule anything out,' Coles said, completing Kennedy's sentence with a guilty look.

'Did Dr Taylor find any sign of restraint on the wrists or ankles?' Irvine asked, raising an eyebrow at Coles.

'None whatsoever. The body, according to Dr Taylor, was very clean on the outside, if less so within,' Kennedy replied, making another note for himself. 'Yes, we need to find out exactly where Christopher Lloyd was murdered.'

'So we are adding "where" to our usual list of "who, why, how and by whom?"' Coles said, scribbling in her notebook.

'Yes, which should make it an easier case to solve,' Kennedy replied.

'Oh?' said Irvine, turning his raised eyebrow to his superior.

'Well,' Kennedy said breaking into a smile, 'the positive thing about all of this is that we are increasing our target size by at least 25%, so it should make it a much easier target for us to hit!'

*

Irvine returned to the graveyard at ten to seven that evening where he witnessed the eventual burial of Daniel Elliot. By the time he returned to North Bridge House just after ten o'clock, he reported to Kennedy that Bella Forsythe was present at the funeral and that she'd been escorted by two relief prison guards. He did not, however, mention to his superior that he had had another conversation with her and that she had asked him to promise to come and visit her in prison.

Irvine had said that he would see. He didn't want to say 'no' straight to her face. But say 'no' is what he thought he should have done. However, the more he thought about it, the more he realized that his feelings were not as black and white as that. So now he was happy that he'd delayed the final decision until a later date.

Meanwhile, Kennedy dismissed the entire team. His logic was slightly selfish. There wasn't really a lot more they could do that first night and he wanted his team fresh and keen the following morning.

He walked home to Primrose Hill alone. Irvine offered to drop him off, though it wasn't on his way. But Kennedy didn't want his day to be over quite so fast. He disliked days where he woke up, went to work, stayed there until late, came home and went straight to bed. Days like that were lost forever. At the same time, you couldn't stockpile your easy days; when they were gone, they were lost forever too. The quality of your day had to be of the utmost importance.

Kennedy could remember clearly the time he'd spent with Daniel Elliot and how the older man had viewed his impending death. Elliot said that if he had known that he was going to outlive his wife, he would have lived his life differently. He certainly wouldn't have been as health-conscious. He'd have enjoyed the odd extra glass of whiskey. He wouldn't have given up smoking. When middle-aged, he would have been less reluctant to tackle the big fry-ups he'd grown up on. He would have paced his life differently, and died closer to his wife. He believed that you owed it to yourself to enjoy your life as and when you were living it. He and his wife had always planned for his retirement. That was to have been when they were going to start to fully enjoy themselves together. All the sacrifices they made when they were younger were for this better time.

Then his wife had died.

Then he spent the rest of his life waiting to die.

Kennedy thought of Elliot's daughter, Bella, and how much of a trauma it must have been for her, and, equally, how gladly Daniel would probably have given up the remainder of his life in exchange for his daughter's redemption.

Kennedy had reached Magpie Corner on Primrose Hill and, instead of taking a right towards the Queens' corner exit, he headed straight up to the top of the hill. He started to think about Christopher Lloyd and what connection, if any, he had with Bella Forsythe or Daniel Elliot, whose grave someone had tried to hide him in. Was there anything to be learnt from that or was it purely a matter of coincidence?

On reaching the summit, Kennedy turned and looked over the zoo towards London. He was always inspired when he was on top of Primrose Hill. Why was that? Why, when you put a man atop a hill, does he feel good? Could it simply be that it made him feel bigger? He laughed out loud at that thought.

ann rea would have liked that. He missed having her around at times like these, missed having someone he could really talk to. For all her problems, ann rea always called things as she saw them. Kennedy found this refreshing. She was the one who felt their relationship should have been all or nothing, whereas he'd have been happy to compromise and remain friends. Now, sadly, after all they'd been through together, they'd never be able to return to the quieter pastures. Men could fall in and out of relationships with men, likewise women with women, but men and women rarely seemed able to do it.

Tonight though, he'd have given anything to go back to his house and find her there waiting for him. Waiting to talk to him. Actually, if he were being perfectly honest, he'd have liked ann rea to have been waiting in his house to do a little more than just talk to him. He laughed again, realising how quickly she'd have seen through such pretences.

He'd never been fully able to understand the subtleties of physical relationships. Mind you, it wasn't as though he'd enjoyed a lot of them, and of the ones he had, none had been as intense as that with ann rea. Kennedy tried to figure out if ending a relationship with someone was anything like giving up smoking or drinking, or cutting down eating. The obvious difference was that with the latter three addictions, one could, with a bit of self-determination, wean oneself off them. But when you stop loving your lover there are no in-between stages; one day you're in love and the next you're not. If you knew exactly when the relationship was going to end, you could stockpile several encounters for the long and lonely nights.

'Agh, it's been so long!' Kennedy called out into such a night.

He was hurting so much he could actually feel a pain in his chest and emptiness in the pit of his stomach. Why was that? His common sense told him that he and ann rea were better off apart.

He knew that, he accepted that. Yet he felt so intolerably lonely. This was an experience he had rarely suffered in his life, and mostly, when he did, he was okay with it. And it wasn't that he wanted or really needed to be physical with ann rea; he knew that he couldn't. He was just longing for that specialness he'd felt when they'd been together. That closeness was the only drug he'd ever missed and, for him, it was stronger than sugar, nicotine or alcohol; it was as intoxicating as all three put together.

What was it in his make-up, Kennedy wondered, that didn't make him turn to any of the other three drugs when he was suffering so? Why was he not compelled to seek comfort in someone else's arms? He recalled the line from Paul Simon's 'The Boxer':

I do declare there were times when I was so lonesome I took some comfort there.

Not seeking after such comfort did not make Kennedy feel any better a man. Mind you, he reckoned, looking out over the multi-coloured lights and gentle movements of London, where would he be able to find a pair of arms in this city to offer him such comfort?

Then he realized why he didn't really mind the life of bed to work and back to bed again. It ensured the simmering loneliness remained beneath the surface. He grew annoyed at not being able to deal with this stuff better. The annoyance gave way to the solace however when he considered that greater men than he – men like Bob Dylan, Ray Davies, George Harrison, Paul Simon, Nick Lowe and Paul Buchanan – seemed equally ill-equipped. At least they all had their songs and their music to help them along the way, the exact same songs that now acted as bright lights for the mere mortals who followed on the same sharp-stoned paths of desolation.

Kennedy resolved to return to the comfort and safety of his home at the foot of the hill and play Nick Lowe's classic album, *The Convincer*, at least once. The magical music wouldn't completely heal all, or indeed any, of his wounds, but it would at least cover them up so that he wouldn't have to look at them as he got on with his life. He wasn't sure Mr Lowe would be so pleased to discover his music being compared to Elastoplasts, but the thought of the healing going on all around him was nevertheless a great comfort.

He felt embarrassed, being a man in his mid-forties and still getting hurt this way. He felt even more embarrassed at having witnessed the circumstances of Christopher Lloyd and yet still being preoccupied with his own petty problems.

He thought of Mabel Lloyd and the pain she must currently be going through, and suddenly all thoughts of his own circumstances evaporated into the cold midnight air as quickly and as quietly as the white fluffy clouds passed across the path of the moon. He soon became distracted with the case. This ability to push all his personal anxieties beneath the surface by tuning into his current case made him wonder if he worked the way he did, so compulsively and so completely, as a way to fight back the pains of loneliness.

It hadn't been so bad before he met ann rea because he didn't know what he had been missing out on. He had his work to do and he just got on with it. Kennedy wondered whether, if he'd known then what he knew now, he would have given up on the chance to meet her. He knew there was only one answer to that question. He started to think about music again, and how brilliant it was to think of something on the way home that you desperately wanted to play and the thoughts filled your head about how much you were going to enjoy it, and its different tracks and string arrangements, and on and on. Then he thought of ann rea and her love for music, and he thought about how, when you met up with someone – boy or girl, man or woman – you are subjected to an entire new collection of CDs. He wondered what music his next girlfriend, should there ever be one, would turn him on to.

The detective let himself in though the front door of 16 Rothwell Street and, despite his previous resolve, went straight to bed.

Chapter Eight

KENNEDY'S FIRST VISIT the following morning was to see Camden Market stallholder, Mr Manfred Hodges. Accompanying him, WDC Anne Coles seemed totally bemused by all the colour and characters on display, even at ten o'clock on a Friday morning. Although the majority of the market people had a reputation for getting to work at the crack of lunchtime, both the police officers were surprised to find the Stables part of the market in full swing. Manfred Hodges was currently managing two stalls; his own, where he sold Corgi Classic Models, and Christopher Lloyd's radio and CD stand.

Kennedy, content that yesterday evening's darkness had given way to a cool, sunny morning, felt good about making Hodges their first call; he must have been a real friend of Lloyd's for he not only continued running his stall but he'd also been the only person to speak up on the dead man's behalf at the recent trial.

'Good morning,' Kennedy began, as he and Coles flashed their ID cards. 'I'm Detective Inspector Kennedy and this is Detective Constable Coles. We'd like to ask you a few questions about Mr Christopher Lloyd.'

'I heard the terrible news yesterday evening,' Hodges said, freezing in his tracks. 'Look… oh… yeah… this is Ivan, my son Ivan. Ivan, could you watch the stalls while I have a chat with these two people in the back?'

Hodges led the two police through a multicoloured bead curtain, which served as a partition between the shop part of the stall and the office-cum-storeroom in the back. One of its walls was packed from floor to curved ceiling with cardboard boxes, labelled on the ends in black felt-tip pen. Although the room was small and packed, it was clean and tidy. Hodges invited the police to take a seat on a wooden trunk, which made an 'L' shape with his desk. It wasn't really big enough for both of them so they had to sit quite close together. Neither seemed to be bothered by the arrangement and both accepted Hodges' offer of tea.

'Yes, a friend of Mabel's – Chris's mum – rang me late last night,' Manfred began as he started the brew up. 'His poor mother, as if she hasn't been through enough in her life.'

Manfred flopped out on his swivel chair, electric kettle still in his hand. He was in his mid-fifties, slim, clean-shaven, with strikingly thick black hair. He was casually dressed in newly-pressed denim jeans and German national football shirt. His semi-sporty look was completed by white socks and Dunlop Green Flash pumps. His accent didn't betray the roots of the flag his shirt flew. He spoke very precisely, in a way that the English seldom master.

'How long had you known him?' Coles asked, perched precariously on the trunk.

'Let's see… I've been here since 1984 and he came along about five years later. Yes, it was either 1989 or 1990 so that would make it about twelve years or so. He was quite young then and was convinced he was going to be a millionaire by the end of the Millennium. That was his main goal. I'd always try to explain to him that the best way to make money wasn't always to go off in search of it. The best and most effective way, I'd tell him, was to find something he really wanted to do, something he had an interest in and was good at. Once he'd managed that, then if he applied himself he had a chance of making some money. But he used to just laugh at me.'

Hodges swung around and plugged the kettle in on his desk. Then he picked up a maroon Corgi Jaguar Mark II.

'You see,' he began offering the model to Coles for examination, 'here's a case in point. I've been into Corgis since I was a kid. I've always been collecting them and I knew instinctively to keep all the boxes in mint condition. And I'm the perfect example of how you can make money, good money, out of your hobby.'

Hodges took the car from Coles and carefully passed it on to Kennedy. 'So how much do you reckon this one is worth?'

Coles and Kennedy looked at him with blank expressions on their faces.

'Oh, come on,' Hodges continued, feigning impatience, 'hazard a guess. You two should have the inside track on this particular model. It's Inspector Morse's Jaguar.'

'Oh,' Kennedy began, preparing to offer a figure if only to encourage a degree of civility between them. 'I'd say… maybe as much as twenty pounds?'

'And yourself, Miss Coles?'

'Oh, not as much as that… maybe a fiver?'

Manfred Hodges broke into an expansive smile as he took the Corgi back again. He laughed as he said: 'You're both way off. This little beauty came out in 1991; it was one of the first television tie-ins and it was priced around £5.00. Now you'd have very little change out of £200.'

'You're kidding?' Coles said.

'Absolutely not,' Hodges replied happily, returning the Corgi to its pride of place. 'I never kid about prices. They've done another two editions of it since then where they've corrected their original mistakes, like the colour of the seats on that one is cream, as you can see, whereas in the real Jag and the later model the seat colour is brown. And then in Corgi's final version they've included wing mirrors. But going back to my first point. I didn't start to collect Corgis to make money; I collected them because I thought they were beautiful models and now, almost as a by-product, I do make a very good living out of it.'

'So you're saying that Mr Lloyd never had similar passions?' Coles said.

'Well, music perhaps. I mean, it was the only thing that he consistently talked about and he was always playing some racket or other in the back, but he didn't seem to have any interest in either making it or being involved in it. I suppose the radios were another of his passions but he was quite lackadaisical about even that. I mean, he knew a bit about them but he never really seemed to apply himself to learning more. He discovered he could buy them cheaply. He had a couple of people who restored them for him and he could always move them on at a tidy profit. But he never did more than that. For instance, on our patch here, we get so many Americans coming through these Stables it's phenomenal. I tell you, there are probably as many Americans passing our stalls as all the other nationalities put together. Now, they love my Corgis and they pay top price for them, always do. They never haggle, they just seem happy to find some of the rarer models. Then they'll stop and look at Chris's radios and they'll think they are real cute, and then they'll find out that they're wired up for the UK – you know, square-pin plugs – so they'll walk on,' Manfred said and then hiked his shoulders as if to say 'Now isn't Chris a silly Willy?'

His smirk disappeared as he continued. 'So I say to Chris, "Why don't you put a converter or transformer or something on them and then our American visitors will be able to use them back home and they'll snap them up? You know, the dollar is doing well at the moment." And he says, "Nagh, it's disrespectful, it's not the way the radios were meant to be." So I say, "Good point, good point, then why don't you get a contact in the States to supply you with original American radios and then you'll be able to sell to both the Americans and the locals?" I even told him I would have some of my American Corgi dealers track down some radio dealers for him. And he says, "Nagh, I don't know anything about them." So I say, "Well, why don't you learn?" And he says, "Nagh, I couldn't be bothered." And on and on we'd go. But I tell you if only he'd applied himself, if only he hadn't been in such a hurry... Oh yes, that's another thing I tried to get him interested in, only because I felt there was a direct connection. Did you ever see one of those big original Wurlitzer jukeboxes? They go for twenty thousand pounds sterling upwards, and he even told me he saw the odd one or two when he was out on his trips to pick up the radios, but again it was, "Nagh, couldn't be bothered." I think that was his favourite saying. Apart from the radios, he was turning over a couple of hundred pounds sterling with the CDs but the good customers, they don't want to be buying grubby second hand CDs – these are people with money. Money that's burning a hole in their pocket if you ask me.'

'Tell me,' Kennedy asked, feeling that perhaps Manfred had run with that topic for long enough, 'did you know Miss Eve Adams?'

Manfred Hodges swivelled nervously back and forth, feet planted firmly on the seagrass flooring. He started to mouth a word but didn't speak it. He repeated this process several times before saying: 'Look, I thought all that was behind him. He was tried and found innocent, surely that's enough to ensure that even the police force let it rest?'

'I know he was your friend, sir,' Kennedy began.

'I didn't speak up for him just because he was my friend. I went to court because I believed he was innocent, and the court obviously agreed with me.'

'I wasn't suggesting that you testified for him because he was your friend,' Kennedy continued calmly and quietly. 'I respect the fact that Christopher Lloyd was a friend of yours, and I don't wish to upset you about the case with Miss Eve Adams. But I do need to find out as much as I can about Mr Lloyd's life. Now, obviously this was a serious incident, and only by digging into this sorry mess can we hope to find out what happened.'

'So you think that someone murdered Chris because they feel he got off with the rape charge?'

'Well, that obviously is one possibility,' Coles said, 'but there are several others. We have to eliminate as many as we can from our inquiries.'

'You think maybe Eve or one of her family killed Chris because of what happened?'

'We haven't even thought that far yet, sir, but it would be helpful for us if you could give us as much background information as possible,' Coles said, as Kennedy tried to find a comfortable spot on the trunk. He was so close to Coles he could smell her perfume. Kennedy hadn't a clue what it was, apart from the fact that it was very feminine and appealing. He was careful not to shift around on the trunk so much as to compromise Coles.

'Yes, okay, certainly I'm willing to help; what do you need to know?' Hodges said.

Kennedy repeated his earlier question. 'Did you know Miss Eve Adams?'

'Yes.'

Kennedy was surprised; he'd been expecting more.

'How did you know her?' Coles asked.

'She used to hang around Chris's stall,' Hodges replied. 'She was there all the time in fact. In the early days it was her and her mate, Madonna Duncan. Madonna's sister, Dionne – as in Warwick – used to date Ivan, my son and assistant, who you met on the way in.'

'Yes,' Coles replied, jotting the names in her notebook.

'Actually, Ivan told me after all this sorry mess that his then girlfriend, Dionne – their relationship was a casualty in all of this – brought Madonna to the stall once. A few days later, Madonna turns up at the stall with Eve. I know that the whole thing of going to the market in Camden Town is quite romantic and adventurous when you're a teenager. It's not as if Eve and Madonna lived in Wimbledon, which I personally find to be quite beautiful. I go down there every year for the tennis and I love it. I could easily live down there if I could afford it. But there you have it, the other man's grass is always greener, particularly if it's on the centre court.' Hodges chuckled at his own joke. His laugh was quite embarrassing. To Kennedy it seemed totally out of proportion.

'So, Mr Lloyd,' Coles said pausing to clear her throat, 'did you meet Miss Adams around that time?'

'Yes.'

'When would that have been?'

'Towards the end of the summer last year – the middle of August, I believe,' Hodges replied immediately.

'So, did she just start hanging out around the stall or something?' Kennedy asked doggedly.

'Oh, you know what it's like. They'd come here, Madonna and Eve, and try to ingratiate themselves with Ian by offering to go and fetch his tea or coffee from the stall down by the main gate, and then one day they arrive with two cups of coffee. And I thought, "Great, they've brought me a cup."' Hodges laughed abruptly. 'No such luck. It was for Chris of course. And then it seemed like they were here all the time, and then only at weekends when they went back to college, and then Madonna apparently found a boyfriend and Eve started coming around by herself. And whereas Ivan had always been civil to Madonna because she was his girlfriend's sister, he was never really warm towards Eve, so she started to hang out more with Chris on his stall. And after a while she'd be minding the stall when Chris would have to nip off somewhere to do a deal or something.

'By the end of September she was playing truant from college to be on the stall. And when they'd packed up at the end of the day they'd go in the back to watch television. I'd told him to be careful. I reminded him that, even if he was separated from his wife, he still had two children he was responsible for. He'd just say, "Nagh, no bother, she's only a kid." Then I'd point out to him that she might be a child, but she had the body of a woman, and he'd say, "Whatever." That's all either of them would say: "Whatever." You can't interfere too much in other people's lives, can you?'

Kennedy heard a beseeching note in Hodges' last question.

'Well, the problem then becomes something else,' he began, trying to show a little sympathy. 'You start to be accused of being a busybody.'

'Yes, you're correct,' said Hodges, brightening a little. Then he glanced at his shirt and he seemed to remember something. 'And I certainly can't afford to be considered a busybody.'

'And then what happened?' Coles asked.

'Well, then she became part of the furniture and that's it, really,' Hodges replied and, on seeing the quizzical look on Coles' pale face, he continued: 'Oh, you mean the incident? Yes, well, as I say, they'd always be disappearing in the back to watch television. On a couple of occasions Chris even asked Ivan to mind the stall for him as he and Eve went in the back. I forbade Ivan to do that. I didn't want to condone any of their carryings-on.'

'Carryings-on?' Coles probed.

'Well, you could hear them, couldn't you?'

'Hear them doing what?' Coles asked because Kennedy had chosen not to.

Hodges looked decidedly uncomfortable. He started swinging his seat back and forth again. He simply said: 'You know.'

'Well, we don't actually,' Coles pushed, a bit of a red flush creeping across her cheeks.

'You know?' Hodges repeated this time glaring at Kennedy.

'Are you suggesting, Manfred,' Kennedy began, trying, unsuccessfully, to create a little space between himself and Coles on the trunk top, 'that Mr Christopher Lloyd and Miss Eve Adams were enjoying sexual relations?'

'Yes, I believe so.'

'You believe so?' Coles spluttered in apparent disbelief. 'But she was underage and you still stood up in court and claimed he was not guilty of rape?'

'The charge was one of rape, not of statutory rape officer. You know better than I that age is an issue in the second case only.'

Coles started muttering so Kennedy asked: 'We don't need to get into that here, so can we move on to the incident in question?'

'Okay,' Hodges replied visibly relieved. 'Early in October last year I was here cleaning my stock – dust fades the paint on the Corgis, you know – and Chris and Eve were in the cramped back room next door. It was a Monday; they were watching Coronation Street apparently, and she was sitting on his knee. They both agreed on this point but that's where the stories start to differ. According to Chris she was sitting on his knee and they started messing around with each other; they disrobed each other and Chris claimed something may or may not have happened. She claimed she was sitting on his knee watching the television.' Hodges appeared to see the question in Coles' eyes so he answered it: 'Because there was nowhere else for her to sit. She said he started messing around with her, she asked him to stop and he wouldn't. She claims she shouted for help to try and scare him into stopping. She claimed he got "animal with her," – her words – held her hands behind her back, pulled down her trousers and raped her.'

'She didn't know that you were next door?' Kennedy felt compelled to ask.

'No,' Hodges sighed remorsefully, 'and that was her mistake. If she had known that, she wouldn't have claimed that she shouted out.'

Coles looked at Hodges.

'What?' Hodges said. 'Look, I'm innocent. I didn't do anything.'

'That's perhaps part of the problem, sir,' Coles replied a little too sweetly, Kennedy thought.

'If Chris had been charged with statutory rape, believe me I would never have acted as a witness at his trial, please believe me; but that wasn't his charge and quite frankly I could never work out why.'

'Tell me, sir,' said Kennedy, trying to dig the questioning out of its dead-end. 'When was the last time you saw Christopher Lloyd?'

'That would have been Sunday lunchtime,' Hodges replied, grateful for the lifeline.

'And how did he seem?' Kennedy asked.

'You know, since the trial he seemed to be a little more blithe. We talked about it and he felt his luck had changed. He thought it had taken a long time to get on the correct track but now that he was, he was determined to make the most of it. He promised me that now that the courts had redeemed him he was going to ensure that he'd never get on the wrong side of the law again.' Hodges paused for another loud, sudden laugh. 'I think you refer to it as "keeping your nose clean". Now, to me, that means making sure that you don't catch a cold or flu.'

'Um,' Kennedy continued, choosing to ignore Hodges' last remark, 'did anyone ever show up here threatening Mr Lloyd?'

'No, certainly not, the market would never have stood for it. They run a pretty tight ship around here you know. I'm impressed by how legit they keep it.'

'Okay, did Mr Lloyd ever discuss with you any trouble he might have been in?' Coles asked.

'No. As I say, he was generally a happier man since the out-come of the trial. He didn't seem to be experiencing any prob-lems, or at least not as far as I could tell.'

'And on Sunday, the last time you saw him, was there anything out of the ordinary in his manner or behaviour?' Kennedy asked as he rose from the trunk for the first time, leaving behind Coles' warmth.

'Nope. He was here working away in the morning,' Hodges replied, also rising to his feet. 'He had a very good morning. He gave Ivan a few bob for the work he'd done for him during the past week – I make sure that Ivan declares all the money he earns, by the way – said he was off to lunch with his mum and asked us to lock up his stall. Sunday trade is a bit iffy; you just never know. I think our best take has been a Sunday but I wouldn't be surprised if our lowest take was also a Sunday. So there was nothing unusual there. Then we both took Monday off and he didn't show on Tuesday or Wednesday, didn't show yesterday, and then last night I received the telephone call.'

'Had that ever happened before, him not showing up?' Coles asked.

'Well, the last time he didn't show up was when he was remanded in custody on the rape charge, but apart from that he usually kept us posted of his movements. I mean, he'd be off chas-ing old radios sometimes for as long as a week or so and his stocks would grow quite low, but I didn't think that that was the case in this instance.'

'Did you try to contact him?' Kennedy asked.

'I rang Mabel on Tuesday in the early afternoon and she said she hadn't seen him since lunchtime on Friday last. But she thought he might have had a new girlfriend and that was why nei-ther of us was seeing a lot of him.'

'Had he been absent from the stall a lot before Sunday?' Coles asked, sliding to the middle of the trunk.

'No, he was around most of the time.'

'Did his friends come around the stall?' Coles asked looking at her notebook.

'There were a few old boys who came around the stall but they weren't really friends, they were sourcing radios for him and they'd check in with him regularly,' Hodges replied, and then walked across to the bead curtain, which he parted widely with his right hand. 'Ivan, what was the name of Chris' friend? You know, the one who sometimes picked him up on a Friday or a Saturday to go off clubbing. You know the guy I mean, the one who was always saying "Whatever"?'

'Oh yeah,' Ivan replied. Neither Kennedy nor Coles could see Ivan but they could hear his shaky voice. 'Greg. I think his second name is something like Whitehead.'

'Yes, that's it,' Hodges confirmed. 'Gregory Whitehead. I should be able to remember that because his hair is white. Well, more like blond, but you know what I mean. Greg was probably Chris's best mate. At least he was the most regular. They went way back, I think.'

'Do you know where we could reach him?' Kennedy asked, happy for a new bit of information.

'As it happens I do,' Manfred Hodges replied as he returned to his desk chair, which he spun around to face the desk. He took a large blue book out of a drawer. 'Chris has stayed around at Greg's on more than one occasion so he gave me the telephone number for there. It's quite close to here, I believe.'

Coles wrote the name and telephone number down in her notebook and Kennedy thanked the stall owner for his time.

'I imagine we'll need to talk to you further,' were Kennedy's parting words.

'Why do you think Lloyd wasn't charged with statutory rape?' were Coles' first words when they were out of earshot of Manfred and Ivan Hodges.

'Well, I'd say we must have been pretty convinced that we'd get him on the main charge,' Kennedy replied as they walked towards the market gate. 'You know what it's like on the statutory charge. All the defence counsel needed to do was to say that Eve had told him she was eighteen and then produce a photograph where she was all dolled up to the nines, and he'd probably have walked. Here, let's have a proper cup of tea from George's stall. That'll give us a bit of a kick for the rest of the day.'

'Okay,' Coles replied, trying to work up a bit of enthusiasm. 'This must have something to do with the rape charge though, don't you think?'

Kennedy turned back from the stall and offered her the briefest of smiles.

'Sorry, sorry, sorry,' Coles gushed. 'I know, never put the cart before the horse.'

Chapter Nine

ON RETURNING TO North Bridge House later that Friday morning, WDC Anne Coles overheard two junior police officers speaking in the reception.

'What's happening between Kennedy and ann rea?

'Oh, I hear they've split up.'

'Is their break-up serious?'

'Yes.'

'Will they get over it?'

'Not this time.'

'Why?'

'Apparently she loves the new Radiohead album and he can't stand it.'

Chapter Ten

AS DS JAMES Irvine ploughed through the court files, Desk Sgt Tim Flynn tracked the credit card company and Constable Allaway chased the telephone records. Meanwhile, Kennedy and Coles were back on the streets of Camden Town. Coles had rung the number for Greg Whitehead, three times in fact. The first two times there was no reply, but the third time a cheeky-chappie type of voice answered, 'Hi, what's up?'

Twenty-nine minutes later, Coles and Kennedy were standing in the living room of Whitehead's plush pad in a recently converted block on Jamestown Street. Whitehead slid open the wall-to-ceiling windows of his living room to reveal a balcony that overlooked the Regents Canal and, if you'd a giraffe's neck, afforded a view of Camden Lock. He invited the members of Camden Town CID to join him on the balcony and offered them a glass of, he assured them, freshly squeezed orange juice.

Kennedy noted that Greg Whitehead took to Coles immediately, and with every move he made he seemed to go out of his way to impress her. Kennedy thought Whitehead was too laddish, too much part of the 'FU' generation for Coles. He looked like he'd come straight from the set of TFI Friday. In another way, Kennedy found himself envying Whitehead and his approach. Whitehead and his mates lived their lives totally for partying, drinking – maybe even a little cocaine – and pulling girls for no reason but to pleasure themselves. Relationships were a drag and uncool. Mind you, the new 'lad' society had been responsible for spawning the 'ladettes,' who were nothing less than an in-your-face, female version of their male counterparts. So if one pulled the other then neither lost out. But male or female, they all seemed compelled by a desire to live their lives to the fullest and right on the edge.

And what was wrong with that?

Nothing really, Kennedy thought, it might even have been preferable to the alternative, excepting of course that the morning after always seemed and felt like the morning after and not the brilliant first day of the rest of your life. So all of Whitehead's aluminium furniture and black, white and silver Prêt A Manger décor seemed like nothing more than the stage-set to a shallow lifestyle. A bit harsh perhaps, Kennedy thought. Whitehead seemed to be enjoying himself, putting on his show and strutting his stuff for Coles in his loose black slacks, baggy grey T-shirt and bare feet.

'You're obviously here about Chrissie,' Whitehead started the proceedings following a rather large gulp of OJ.

'Yes,' Coles replied. 'We understand you were a good friend of his.'

'Friend? Yes. Good friend? I'm not sure. He wasn't really hip to my scene any more. Cash is not to stash, it's to blow, you know, and Chrissie... well, I kept asking him if he was sure that he wasn't related to the other Lloyds, you know the high-street banking company. But, we went way back and so we occasionally hung out together, no big deal you know. He was good fun once he'd loosened up and had a few bevvies inside him.'

'How did you meet?' Coles continued.

'We went to school together, darling.'

'So, you had known him a long time?.

'Well, not that long,' Whitehead said running his fingers through his dishevelled, natural-blond hair. 'I may not be looking my best this morning – it was a rough night – but I do assure you that I'm not that old.'

'Oh, I'm sorry. It's just that, you know, using the word "darling" is quite old fashioned isn't it?' Coles replied without batting an eyelid and then, before Whitehead had a chance to recover, she continued: 'So you were friends to some degree. Tell me, when did you see him last?

Greg Whitehead paused for another gulp of orange juice.

'Sunday last – just after lunchtime, in fact,' he said, at length.

'So you joined him and his mum for lunch?' Kennedy asked somewhat bemused.

'No, no, he wasn't at his mum's place for Sunday lunch – he crashed here on Saturday night, you see. We were both out on the town on Saturday night.'

Whitehead paused and looked directly at Coles. 'Neither of us got lucky though.' And then to both police officers: 'We came back here extremely hammered though, and watched a sports channel until about four-thirty in the morning, then we slept through 'til lunchtime on Sunday. Then he headed off to the stall and that was the last time I saw him.'

'Where exactly did you go on Saturday night?' Coles asked.

'Oh, we had a couple of drinks at the Spread Eagle, followed by a quick pizza at Parkway Pizza. Then we headed down to the bar at Café Delancey and ended up at Camden Palace.'

Kennedy considered Whitehead and Lloyd's big night out. He still found it hard to believe that men and women and boys and girls went out hunting for each other. Of course he was well aware that it happened and he supposed, on reflection, it was all down to pot luck if you were: (a) going to find someone and (b) going to enjoy some kind of relationship with them, no matter how brief and (c) going to find a relationship that would last and blossom into something special. Yes, he did believe that it was probably better if you met someone naturally and for things to develop of their own accord. But either way, the whole situation was pretty preposterous, wasn't it? The whole thing of two people living together as one; each has a mind and thoughts of their own, and individual thoughts are the rust on a relationship. No matter how much you were in love, or how much you thought you were in love, there would always be a time – and it might only last for a split second – when one, or maybe even both members of the couple would think: 'Do I love them less than they love me?' or, 'Do they love me less than I love them?' or even, 'Did I really love them in the first place or am I just with them because I couldn't find anyone else and I didn't particularly want to be by myself?' And how much did you really know and understand your true feelings anyway? Kennedy wondered.

For instance, a man and a woman get together and share that special intimate moment – the same intimate moment that more and more people are starting to mess around with – but at that point of intimacy there is certainly no human, particularly no man, who is not physically and mentally moved. Something spiritual happens, no matter how brief, and you feel to some degree connected with the universe. It might just have something to do with the fact that you are aware at that precise moment you just might have created another human. Now that's a mighty big thing to do, maybe even the biggest thing that a human can do. So with all the mental, physical, spiritual and chemical reactions going on, some of us lesser mortals are going to feel that they are experiencing true love. Kennedy thought it was a bit like the song said: 'It can't be influenza, so it must be love.'

But then, Kennedy felt, the more you tried for these special moments and the greater the number of people you tried to experience them with, well, of course it was logical that you were going to start to doubt your feelings. It seemed to him that the truth was that there was no one special person who you could meet and fall passionately in love with and live happily ever after with. The reality was that there were several people. At the end of the day it was a lot like when you were younger and you were playing street football, or hockey if you were a female, and you were all standing around together in a group while the two captains pick their team, alternating between one man (or woman) at a time from the group. Obviously the best players are going to be chosen first, leaving the dregs at the end. So maybe that meant that Whitehead and Lloyd's approach was right after all: get out there in the market place, pick the best that's available before someone else does and forget all this crap about whether or not she's really the one for you or whether it's real love.

As far as ann rea was concerned, Kennedy was convinced that she was the one for him and that they were meant to be together for the rest of their lives. But because she had felt exactly the same way in her previous relationship, she doubted her real feelings for Kennedy and, if anything, she was scared by his total conviction that they were a match. Did this mean that in Kennedy's next relationship he would be the cynical one just because of his experience with ann rea? Hopefully not, he thought. If anything, he felt he was now preparing and disciplining himself to accept someone less than perfect.

He found himself sighing out loud and gradually tuning out his own thoughts to listen to Coles questioning Whitehead.

'And did you get to spend any time with anyone during the course of the evening?'

'Well, we chatted up a few dolls at the Palace but in the end we sussed that they were just after free drinks so we moved on.'

'Did you find out their names?' Coles persisted with this line; Kennedy wondered if she was still annoyed at being called 'darling.'

'Yes, as it happens, Chris was talking to a girl called Tamsin who had long, black hair all the way down to her bum. Mine was called Jeanie.'

'You didn't manage to get their telephone numbers, did you?' Coles said, pen at the ready in jest.

'No, um... we didn't manage to collect the digits,' Whitehead replied, choosing to look directly at Kennedy. Like all blond-haired people, he found it hard to hide his embarrassment.

'Did you bump into any mates of yours during the course of the evening?' Kennedy asked.

'No, you see that's why I was hanging with Chris. All my mates, the guys I normally hang out with, had flown over to Dublin for a blast and, well, you see I'm a bit stretched financially at the moment so I chose to stay in London. Normally I would be with my real mates on a Saturday night – I wouldn't be hanging with Chris – he's, well, as I said, he's not really hip to the scene any more. Well he wouldn't be, would he? He's got an old lady and a couple of rugrats, hasn't he?'

'Did he say anything to you about any trouble he might have been in? You know, about anyone giving him grief?' Kennedy asked, taking up Coles' slack.

'No – I had the feeling, though, that he was pretty determined to keep his nose clean after getting off on the rape charge. But of course you know he was found not guilty on that charge, don't you?'

'Yes,' Kennedy replied with a warm smile. 'That's such a strange thing to say.'

'No, no, I wasn't insinuating anything or anything like that,' Whitehead offered quickly. 'It's just that Chris was saying over the weekend that although he was found not guilty by the jury, he had been tarred with that brush and he felt most people thought he was guilty.'

'And there was nothing else troubling him?'

'Not that I was aware of, no.'

'Tell me, sir,' Kennedy said backtracking over Coles' question, 'did you go to his trial?'

'Good grief, no,' Whitehead began, rubbing both his hands on his upper thighs. 'I mean, to be perfectly honest with you, the problem I find is that when someone screams rape you never really know whether it's true or not. I didn't want to get caught up in it, so I kept my distance.'

'You mean to tell us that even though he was a friend of yours you didn't know whether or not he'd raped someone?' Coles jumped in.

Whitehead sighed; he looked at Coles and then at Kennedy with a 'shall I tell her or will you?' kind of look and then he looked back at Coles.

'Am I my brother's keeper?' Whitehead asked. 'No!' he said, answering his own question. 'Look, here's the thing – it's not meant to sound profound or pompous or anything but do we ever know what each other are capable of? If you'd asked me, say, a year ago if Chrissie Lloyd was capable of rape I'd have said an unequivocal no. I'd have said: "of course not." But after this incident occurred, you start to think, you know, maybe he was egged on. You know, the signals were mixed and it went just a bit too far to stop...'

'Even though she said an unequivocal no?' Coles said, looking at Kennedy.

'Darling, please climb down from your high horse before you fall off,' Whitehead snapped back. 'Look, you asked me a question and I was trying to give you an honest answer. I was trying to work out under what circumstances this could have happened, and what I was trying to say was that before all this, I would have told you that Chris wasn't capable of such a vile act. You know, I could tell you with my hand on my heart that Chris was not someone who would go out and prey on someone and pull them into an alley or a ditch and rape them. But then, when he was arrested, I will admit that even I, a friend, started to think: "There's no smoke without fire." So I was thinking that yes, maybe he did rape her and I wanted no part of that so I stayed well away.'

'What was Mr Lloyd like at school?' Kennedy asked.

'Oh, he was different, totally different. He had all these great ideas about what he was going to do and about how rich he was going to be. I don't mean he was flash or anything like that but he just dressed well and looked good and if you wanted to pick an example of someone who was cool, you'd pick Chris. Do you know what I mean? He's wasn't flash, he was just cool. And then it all started to go wrong for him. He got bogged down with the little things that went wrong, and instead of just getting on with life, he'd get preoccupied with these things.'

'Things like?' Kennedy asked.

'Oh, things like having a few pints too many when he was in the army. The army was his career fast-track, you know. He was going to put in a few solid years working his...' Whitehead paused and considered Coles, 'working his whatsits off and then come out into civvies a few steps ahead of the rest of us and go into management in whatever was current at that point. But then, as I say, he got drunk and got into a bit of a barney, got court-martialled and not only was that the end of that but he'd also ruled himself out of the next Olympics, if you know what I'm on about.

'After that he started this car-tyre thing up. That surprised me. It was a bit menial for Chris, but he worked hard at it. He had a little lockup over the other side of the market in Hawley Road, and it all seemed to be going quite well until it was discovered that his tyres were in fact stolen. Chris claimed he thought they were legit but he got done for that.

Then another time he'd a few bevvies in him and he was with this girl who was drunk and they were getting down to it and she started hitting him, just thumping him about the head. He pushed her away but she kept on coming back and hitting him and she was laughing all the time, and then he whacked her and knocked her into the middle of next week and he was up on a sexual assault charge – apparently just because they were both naked at the time it was a sexual assault. If they'd been dressed it would have been assault only.

Then the silly beggar got caught trying to break into the parking-ticket machine on Parkway. God, when I think back on it, his life's been a disaster. Then there was the credit card thing where he claimed he was just holding them for a mate of his who was meant to collect them; turns out this mate was detained at the pleasure of Her Majesty on the Isle of Wight. But you see, if you take his view on all of this, the innocent view, he was a victim of circumstances.'

Whitehead paused as if in thought, and a warm smile appeared on his face.

'When he met Valerie he really wanted to get married – I think he thought that marriage would solve everything for him but it didn't, and then I think he thought that if he started a family everything would work out and when that didn't, one wife and two kids later he started to get preoccupied with the mess. You know, in the early days he was a great chap to hang out with. He had all these great dreams and ideas and then he started carrying all this baggage and then it became a case of: "Oh, here comes Chris, let's cross to the other side of the road."'

Greg Whitehead stopped talking and took another large swig of OJ, emptying his glass. He rolled the remains around in his mouth before swallowing and continuing.

'You know what he reminded me of? He reminded me of an Olympic hopeful; someone who felt convinced they could win the gold medal in the 400 metres and was the favourite to do so.

And he trains and trains and just as he gets to the Games he realizes that he's peaked too soon and as a result he wins only the bronze medal. For him it's a disaster. He doesn't think: "Great, I was third!" He thinks: "Shit, I wasn't first."

And then instead of thinking: "I'll try again in a few years," he spends all his time preoccupied by the fact that he was robbed, you know, his rotten luck had robbed him. And so he tries to take shortcuts for the next Olympics and pretty soon it's his preoccupation with failure that gets in the way of his goal. Well, I suppose in a way Chris never really got over his initial failures. He was always running into the wind, and you know,' Whitehead continued, pausing for effect as he quoted the *Pocket Essential Book of Wisdom*, 'it's just as easy, not to mention far more prudent, to run with the wind.'

Coles raised her eyebrows but said nothing. Kennedy had a weird vision of Christopher Lloyd's corpse running in slow-motion into the wind.

At that moment they were all distracted by an incident down on the canal towpath. Someone had snatched a tourist's handbag. The victim, an elderly woman, screamed and shouted until someone gave chase. The thief was no match for them and was caught within ten yards. The sprinter manhandled the bag from the thief's grasp and was just about to return the bag to the old lady when the thief shouted something about the handbag. The sprinter gave the handbag to the old lady, calmly turned back to the thief, flung both his arms around him in a bear hug, carried him to the edge of the canal and dropped him in.

'Did you know any of Lloyd's colleagues?' Kennedy asked after the commotion had died down.

'No. I met Herr Hodges several times. He's a bit of a character but honest as the day is long, and that's about it. I knew Chris dealt in antique radios but not a lot more than that. He never really talked about his work when he was out. He didn't seem all that interested in it, to be honest.'

'I was thinking about some of his other colleagues,' Kennedy added.

'I thought you might have been,' Whitehead sniggered. 'No, not at all, I'd no time for any of that carry-on.'

Again Coles raised an eyebrow, just a hint, but enough for Whitehead to pick up on.

'Come on, officer,' Whitehead complained, looking back into his apartment. 'I've got too much to lose. You know what's more important, as I was always telling Chris. In this life it's much better if you put all your energies and creative resources into legit projects. It's like running with the wind, you'll get much further on the same amount of energy.'

'But you were aware of his activities?' Coles asked.

'It's public knowledge, isn't it?'

'Yes it is,' Kennedy replied, smiling at Coles. 'I think that's all we need for now. If there's anything else you can think of, please give us a ring. Bear in mind that we'll probably need to see you again.'

'No problem,' Whitehead said showing them to the door.

As they returned to the car, Coles asked, 'Do you think he was trying just a bit too hard to tell us that he was legit and that he'd never get involved in any of Lloyd's dodgy deals?'

'Perhaps,' replied Kennedy, but his mind was elsewhere, so Coles, following one of Irvine's tips, drove him back to North Bridge House in silence.

Chapter Eleven

'HAVE YOU MADE much progress?' Kennedy asked Sgt Flynn as he walked into the reception. Coles was parking the car to the rear of the House, which looked more like a Spanish villa than one of North London's oldest buildings.

'Yes sir,' Flynn replied proudly. 'London©Card have just faxed over Mr Lloyd's account for the past month.'

'Excellent,' Kennedy said, browsing through the paperwork as he walked back to his office.

The Detective Inspector placed the London©Card statement sheets on his desk and made a cup of tea. Then he sat down with a new pack of Walkers Chocolate Chip Shortbread and a clean, yellow foolscap notepad. He alternated between dunking biscuits with his left hand and running a pen down the statement line by line with his right, occasionally pausing to make a note on his pad or take a bite of perfectly moistened shortbread.

Kennedy wrote:

Greg Whitehead didn't mention visit to Johnny Fox's.

Country trip 17th June

Restaurant bill on 18th June off patch.

Either other (business) credit card or all cash!

That was that; not as much as he'd hoped for, but maybe more than he needed. He went to visit Irvine in his shared office. Irvine was absent; his colleagues didn't know where he had gone. Kennedy grew frustrated. He knew he shouldn't but he couldn't help it. They didn't have a lot to go on, so they were depending too heavily on the little that they did know. He went to PC Allaway to see how he was getting on with the telephone records. Allaway had a lot to go through; Lloyd had three phones – one at the Stables, another at home (separate from his mum's number) and a mobile. Kennedy left Allaway plodding away through the detailed phone bills, buzzed WDC Anne Coles and requested the car.

Five minutes later she picked him up at the front door.

'Where to this time, sir?' she asked as Kennedy clicked his seat-belt into place.

'Let's visit the Stables,' he said. 'It's going so slow in there I need to get out and try and find something else. What we need isn't going to come waltzing up Parkway and into our laps.'

'Any new developments?'

'Nothing much on his credit card statements except that Lloyd and Whitehead seemed to make one extra stop on the Saturday night out. They stopped off at Johnny Fox's on the High Street and had a bottle of wine.'

'Why would he not have told us about that?' Coles asked.

'Maybe they scored some drugs there and he thought that by not telling us about their stop off we wouldn't know he was into that. Or maybe even they were so drunk he forgot all about it. Then Chris took a little trip down Swindon way around June 17th. And he used his credit card at WH Smith in Swiss Cottage. There's nothing really unusual in that except that it's a wee bit outside his patch. And that was it.'

Kennedy paused thoughtfully, then went on. 'It looks like most of his business was done in cash. Either that or he's got a company credit card somewhere.'

'Maybe invoices and cheques?' Coles offered.

'Possibly. Possibly,' said Kennedy. They were passing over the Regents Canal and then under the railway bridge. 'Let's just turn into the Safeway up here on the left, there's an entrance to the Stables up there.'

'I know it,' said Coles.

The units in the Stables area, called stalls in deference to Camden Market, were of two types. The first, under the roof of the original Stables, were divided up by the stall-owners' wares, curtains or temporary walls made of wood and plasterboard. The Stables were originally built to house the ponies that transported goods, predominately whiskey for a long time, from the Roundhouse to the nearby Canal. For about half a mile a raised roadway had been constructed, and beneath this were the arches and catacombs which made up the second type of unit.

These were somewhat larger and more secure than those at the Stables end, with several of the owners having their own lockable doorway. Manfred Hodges and Christopher Lloyd shared one such arch, the third one on the right as you came in from the Safeway entrance to the market.

The German spied Kennedy first.

'Ivan,' Hodges declaimed, 'it's the Camden Town police force again. Quickly, you'd better hide all that stuff that fell off the back of the lorry.'

'What lorry?' Ivan replied dumbly.

'It was just a joke, Ivan.'

'Whatever,' said Ivan, tidying up the CDs on Lloyd's stall.

Manfred gave the police officers a 'kids – what can you do?' shrug and said: 'And how can we help you today?'

'Oh, we just wanted to have another look around Mr Lloyd's stall.'

'Perfectly fine with me. Mind you, I'm not sure that if it wasn't – fine with me that is – it would make much difference. Hey, would it, Ivan?'

Ivan mumbled another 'Whatever' as he continued his work.

Lloyd's stall was packed with traditional radios. The majority were placed about the shelves of the room but Kennedy was drawn to three that were locked away in an glass-fronted display cabinet. To Kennedy they looked absolutely wonderful. The central one was a rose-fronted Celestion Radiophone. Hodges had obviously done his homework and he was prepared to share this information with his potential customers by marking the radio as a 1926 model and valuing it at £2495. The one to the left was a Bush 1959, which was in perfect condition and was priced up at £1395, whereas the poor cousin to the right was Philips at a mere £895.

Hodges unlocked the padlocked door to allow Coles and Kennedy access to Lloyd's office.

There was something strange about walking in on someone's private space, particularly when that person had just died. Kennedy thought that you got to see first hand how ill-prepared any of us are for death. Lloyd, from the look of his office, had many uncompleted tasks; jobs and chores he had been certain he would get back to at a later date. He probably never doubted he'd ever have a chance to get back to them. Perhaps he would even have liked to have found a way to postpone them until a later date. Yes, he'd have liked to have found any way to avoid the work… though perhaps not the way he had.

The office housed a large desk, a single swivel chair, a Sony television on a matching white fridge, a vacuum cleaner, several videos but apparently no video player, a number of radios – all in various stages of refurbishment – and five plastic storage crates packed with CDs and stacked on top of one another. The crates were marked '70s', '80s', 'Punk', 'American' and finally – Brian Matthew's favourite, Kennedy thought – 'UK 60s Beat Groups.' The floor was covered with a threadbare red carpet very similar to those sold by one of the neighbouring stalls, and the walls were covered with posters proclaiming the delights of two-valve radios and such like.

Kennedy removed a couple of resealable plastic bags from the inside pocket of his deep-blue hooded windcheater. He took a newspaper from the top of the desk, checked there was no handwriting on it, and spread out a double-page in the middle of the carpet. Then he took the green rubbish bin from beside the desk and tipped its contents out onto the newspaper; he and Coles crouched on their knees on either side and started to work their way through the rubbish.

'Sometimes there's just nothing to beat the good old-fashioned police legwork,' Kennedy said, unconsciously stealing a glance at Coles' legs. Her Black Watch tartan pleated skirt had ridden up over her knees revealing an extremely shapely bit of thigh. 'No, goodness, I didn't mean that.'

'I know you didn't,' Coles replied as she gave Kennedy an 'It's okay, it was innocent' shrug of her shoulders. She then tried to straighten up on her haunches, perhaps trying to reclaim a bit more of her decency, lost her balance and fell over backwards. To Kennedy's eye it appeared she was disappearing in slow motion and he'd enough time to reach out his hand, which she caught immediately and regained her balance. She stood up straight, dusted some imaginary dust from her skirt and white shirt. 'Oh, let's forget ladylike for now shall we?' she said, and got down on her hands and knees over the rubbish.

They found several scraps of white paper rolled up into tight little balls, which they unravelled and set on top of each other to read later. They also found five discarded Galaxy Chocolate Whole Nut wrappers; an empty pack of Players cigarettes, though there were no ashtrays around so Kennedy assumed it must have belonged to a visitor; a Safeway supermarket bag, crumpled up; a Michael Bolton CD case; three white, polystyrene cups with the dregs of tea or coffee visible at the bottom; a black Pilot Hi-Tecpoint V5 pen; an Osram 'Classic Pearl' B22d bayonet cap 60-watt light bulb and box for same; a penny; several paperclips of varying colour; the polythene wrapping for a light tester; and a crumpled-up photograph of a woman and two children, Lloyd's estranged family, as it turned out.

Kennedy had Coles bag the contents while he took the scraps of white paper to the desk and sat down to examine them. The first one had the name 'Michelle' and a telephone number on it. The second one had no telephone number or name, just the letters 'Y&A' and the numbers 21.15. The next one contained a list: potatoes, tea, eggs, bacon, bread, beans and Lucozade. Then one in different handwriting saying: 'Greg rang – he'll ring you later.' The next one was back to the original handwriting: 'Ernest. Badminton. Three Philips 60s —£50 each ?? Thur morning 10.15.' And the final bit of paper – again in the original handwriting – had the name 'Dionne' and a telephone number on it. Kennedy sealed all the crumpled bits of paper in a plastic bag and turned his attention to the contents of the desk.

Right in the centre of the desk was a copy of The *Camden News Journal* with a story on the front page proclaiming Christopher Lloyd's innocence; to the right-hand side of the desk was a Ferrari mug containing several pencils and pens, while on the opposite side was an orange-coloured Roberts Radio. The remainder of the desktop was remarkably clear. A tray slid out just under the desktop to the right, directly above a stack of three drawers. The tray contained a plastic inlay that housed paperclips, numerous low-denomination coins and a card from the Trattoria Lucca Restaurant.

The top drawer contained catalogues from various auctions around the country. The second drawer contained a file full of invoices, all of which were marked 'Paid', and an envelope stuffed with correspondence from the courts and his solicitor. Also in this drawer was a copy of the Yellow Pages, growing bigger by the year but already capable of adding at least three inches to one's stature. The bottom drawer housed a two-thirds-full bottle of Bushmills Whiskey with two glasses, ten CDs and a portable CD player.

'Well, we didn't get very much here did we?' Kennedy said to himself.

'I've never seen such a tidy office,' said Coles. 'And I can't for the life of me remember the last time I was in one that didn't have a computer. Do you think it's possible that someone has already been in here and tidied up?'

'Herr Hodges would be the most likely candidate. He's the only one we know with keys,' Kennedy replied. 'But let's just leave it for now until we've amassed some more information – something tells me we'll come calling again at his door before very long. In the meantime, let's grab a bite of lunch on the way back to North Bridge House.'

'You'll get no arguments from me on that one, sir,' said Coles, noticeably perking up.

'Let's just go to Café Delancey for a quick snack, shall we?'

'Suits me,' Coles replied as she engaged the car's first gear and pulled out onto Chalk Farm Road from the rear of the petrol station, setting the dials for the centre of Camden Town.

Chapter Twelve

THE REASON KENNEDY hadn't been able to find Detective Sergeant James Irvine on his earlier trip around North Bridge House was because the resourceful detective had, for the time being, finished his work on the Christopher Lloyd trial file and was making his way to interview the first person on his list, Valerie Lloyd – Christopher Lloyd's estranged wife.

Irvine and DC Allaway were both visibly shocked as they were shown into the second-floor flat on Edis Street. Irvine assumed his own reaction stemmed from his prejudice. He chastised himself for assuming that the family home of a coloured petty criminal would be a bit of a hovel, which was much the same as assuming that all Scotsmen wore kilts and drank whisky by the pint pot. Yes, some certainly did and yes, a lot of criminal families didn't live in the most luxurious of places, but Valerie and Christopher Lloyd had gone to great trouble to ensure that their two children grew up in a nice, comfortable home.

On top of which, Mrs Valerie Lloyd was polite and courteous, and she had two of the best-mannered children Irvine had ever met. Whitney, the daughter, was nine years old, and Michael was four. Their mother showed Irvine and Allaway into the living room and excused herself to make coffee. Irvine had found living accommodation generally fell, not into the two categories that letting agents would have you believe, but three: unfurnished, furnished and homely. The Lloyds' flat in leafy Primrose Hill most definitely fell into the latter group. The living room was clean, tidy and toy-free. There were several vases with flowers and two bowls packed with fresh fruit. The walls were painted a warm terracotta. A few prints hung on the walls, and over the fireplace was a large framed photograph of the Lloyd family, all spruced up and smiling for the camera. On top of the fireplace, which didn't look to have been used in anger for the last forty years, were several smaller photographs, many of which included Christopher Lloyd. Irvine chose a very comfortable-looking seat by the fireplace while Allaway crossed the room to look down onto the street. The living room, surprisingly enough, did not have a television on display but there were two radios: one a 1953 Sky Queen, manufactured by Ever Ready, and the other a much grander affair, a 1946 Ambassador, complete with its own built-in bookcase. The Ambassador was the feature of one entire wall and if the CD rack beside it was anything to go by, Christopher Lloyd had done a bit of conversion work on the original model. Both were in pristine condition and the Ambassador was polished so you could see your face in it.

Irvine sank back into the plush chair. He thought of Valerie and Christopher Lloyd and he thought about himself and Bella. There wasn't really a lot of difference, he thought. Well of course, there was the obvious difference in that Christopher Lloyd had recently been murdered whereas Bella was a convicted murderess herself. Apart from that, both Lloyd and Forsythe were involved in crime, to varying degrees, and both had people who weren't involved in crime but who cared about them. Lloyd enjoyed the love of his wife, his two children and his mother, and Forsythe enjoyed the love of her father and Irvine. Irvine suddenly realised that Forsythe's father had recently died and that left only him to care for her. Did he really count? Why was he reluctant to go and visit her in prison? Why was he thinking about her so much? If she was on the outside and following her chosen profession as a pathologist would they, as was the case with the majority of Irvine's relationships, have passed liked ships in the night? Was he only preoccupied with her because she was incarcerated? Was she only attracted to him because he was the only man she'd permitted to enjoy any degree of intimacy with her? It was only a kiss, for heaven's sake – two if you counted their recent encounter – but it might just have been the most intimate moment she'd shared with anyone. I'm flattering myself, he thought. Of course she'd been married to a Mr Forsythe, her maiden name was Elliot; where was Mr Forsythe now, when she needed him? Was she in fact just forming an attachment to Irvine because he was the only person she knew?

'The children will be in shortly with some goodies,' Valerie announced in a voice that was but a few decibels above a whisper, but still loud enough to break into Irvine's thoughts. 'But in the meantime here's our liquid refreshment.'

Valerie lowered the tray carefully down onto the coffee table in front of Irvine and about five feet from the fireplace.

She looked over at Allaway and smiled at Irvine. 'You can tell your colleague to come away from the window. You won't lose the wheels of your car around here.'

Allaway did as he was bidden, mumbling about being amazed by how beautiful the tree-lined street was.

'Yes, one of the best things Christopher ever did,' Valerie said as she poured the coffee into three white bone-china cups. 'He bought this place with the money he got from the army when he left, plus a little we'd saved. It was right around the time Whitney was born and he said we needed to have a comfortable family home. He insisted the flat was to be in my name so that we'd always be protected. He really was a good husband,' she stopped, disturbed by the noise of the children just about to enter the room, and then added, 'and father' as an afterthought.

Whitney and Michael proudly bore two plates each; Whitney's contained scones with steam still rising from them and Michael's bore a variety of biscuits and pastries. Irvine and Allaway protested that they'd spoil their lunch, and were tut-tutted by Valerie who said: 'You realise, of course, that the scones were all baked by Whitney, so eat up now or...'

'Of course,' Irvine replied immediately. 'They look absolutely delicious.'

Both children started to laugh. It was a stifled giggle at first but then as Irvine said, 'Good heaven's, what's the matter?' they burst into full-scale guffaws.

'He sounds just like daddy when he was watching the videos,

doesn't he, Michael?' Whitney barely managed to get out the words through her laughter.

'Goodness me, I say,' Irvine said, sending the children into further convulsions.

'Christopher, their father, was a very good mimic. He could do most voices but the one he did best was James Bond and you sound just like him.'

'Aye, that's been said before,' Irvine replied, reassured to know what was behind the episode, and they all helped themselves to coffee and treats. The children were dismissed to their room with the promise that they could watch a video if they were well behaved.

'They're as good as gold really,' Valerie said as the children left the room, closing the door behind them.

'Aye, very well behaved, I'd say,' Irvine said and then waited to see if his accent caused any more ripples of laughter. When he saw it was safe to proceed he offered: 'So Christopher bought this place for you?'

'Well, he bought it for all of us really, for the family,' Valerie replied, returning her cup and saucer to the tray to free up her hands to jam one of her daughter's delicious scones. 'And you know what? No matter how bad times got for him, for Christopher – and I knew for a fact that they were pretty scary sometimes – but no matter how troubled he was, he never once even suggested selling this place or taking out a mortgage on it.'

Valerie polished off one of the scones and used a serviette to remove any traces of jam from her face, which benefited greatly from her extremely subtle hints of make-up. Valerie Lloyd was barely 28 years old, Irvine figured, but she looked like a mum; someone whose life would always take second place to her children. She looked like she would look like a mum for the rest of her life. She wore a long, shapeless black dress and black flip-flop shoes. Was she in mourning? She was just this side of overweight, about five-foot eight, and her jet-black wiry hair was pulled up into a bun at her crown.

Irvine wondered if this was really it. Was all of this, the dead husband, the clean home, the cute kids, was that the sum total of this woman's life to date? Was that really what life was all about? Was this really the end of all her plans and all her dreams?

Irvine couldn't imagine Valerie Lloyd's reality. She had her priorities; her existence had meaning and contented her in a way that Irvine, were he aware of it, would envy.

'Do you get to see Lloyd's mother much?'

'No, we don't. That's sad for the children though, because they should know their grandmother. But when we wanted to get married Mabel stood against us. We wanted to get married in a church and she said she would stand up and testify against it if we tried. In the end we just got married in a registry office. I was fine with it but it really hurt Christopher. He so badly wanted to do it right. I knew I wanted to be with him. It didn't matter what we had to do or not do to be together.'

'So did Christopher and his mum not get on?' Irvine asked.

'They got on fine; he was a good son, as well you know. It was just she was too religious for Whitney and Michael. Christopher said it would be fine later when they had minds of their own, but he wanted to keep them away from all her prejudices that had tried to keep us apart.'

'I'm not sure I understand,' Irvine said, hoping he wasn't probing too much.

'You see,' Valerie said in an even quieter voice than normal, 'a couple of years before I met Christopher I had a relationship with another man and... well, I got pregnant and it just wasn't right so I had a termination.'

'And Mabel got to hear about this?' Irvine said.

'Yes, she found out from one of her congregation, people who used to live next door to us. When Christopher first took me home and I met her, she was as nice as pie, and then, just as we were making our plans for our wedding, all of this came out.' Valerie sat up straighter in her chair as she continued. 'We hadn't spoken for ages before this morning when she phoned me. She rang up to make her peace. Now that we've both lost someone we love it's like at last we have a common bond.'

'How long had you and Mr Lloyd been separated?' Irvine asked as he finished his cup of coffee.

'About three years, I think,' she replied, offering Irvine a refill, which he refused.

'That's quite a long time, isn't it?' Irvine continued, not really sure where he was going with this.

'What, too long to be by myself?' Valerie said grimacing slightly.

'No… well, maybe yes,' Irvine conceded.

'Yes, with all this spare time I have, I suppose I should be getting myself tarted up and getting out there on the pull with my mates,' Valerie said and started to break into another chuckle.

Irvine thought it was funny that she laughed with a louder, more confident voice than the one she spoke with.

'Yes, I see what you mean,' he conceded.

'I suppose in a way we didn't really split up,' Valerie started, appearing to search for her next words. 'It was more that our relationship changed. I mean, he wasn't cheating on me or anything like that – not that I know of anyway – it's just that it wasn't working on that physical level. I think it was simply that he fell out of love, or maybe he realised that he'd never really loved me in the first place. We did run into things a bit fast, I know. So he moved back in with his mum; there were no great fights or anything like that. It was just that once we were that but now we're this. And he was still an attentive father to Whitney and Michael, and then I sat him down and told him that I didn't want him running off behind my back and going with any girls. I wanted to know about them. I didn't want any gossips sniggering about us behind our backs. I knew he'd be showing an interest in them so I wanted to know about them. But he was respectful towards me. He never brought anyone around here and when he took Whitney and Michael out he'd never have any girlfriends in tow. He never took any girlfriends around to his mum's house either.'

'Did he have any girlfriends that you knew of?' Irvine asked.

'I believe he had a fling now and again,' Valerie said, breaking into another throaty laugh. 'He wasn't shy and he was a man. No, no. I'm sorry, I didn't mean it like that. I didn't mean for you to think that he was a man and he'd want to have his way no matter what because then you'd think that he raped that little girl. He didn't rape her, you know. I went to the trial once – once was all I could bear – but he was found not guilty. Did you know that?'

'Yes, we knew that,' Irvine replied hoping that as he was doing all the talking, Allaway was doing all the note-taking.

'Good. But going back to what we were talking about, I'm sure he was dipping in the honey pot, but he was so desperate to get things in order I don't think he would have wanted to slow himself down by having a steady girlfriend. He would have wanted to sort everything out before he even thought about that.'

'When did you last see him?'

'About ten days ago, he came around to have tea with us.'

'What frame of mind was he in?'

'He was up. He was happy. He was being a good daddy, the way he always was. He fixed some of their toys, fixed the radio for me. I love listening to the radio. I could quite happily live without a television. It was Christopher who turned me on to radios. I used to think he was prehistoric with all his chit-chat and jive about old radios. But if you have something like that,' Valerie paused and turned and looked over at the radiogram in the far corner, 'well, you want to listen to it, don't you?'

'Yes, I suppose so.'

'Do you listen to the radio a lot?' Valerie asked.

'No, I don't actually. I always mean to listen to it more, more than just listening to the news, if only because my boss seems to get such enjoyment from it.'

'I live for my radio. Forgive me if you think that's a little strange, but for me the radio gets it exactly right. With the television everything is right there in front of you but on the radio, the fullness of the characters is a combination of the writer and your imagination. Those aren't exactly my words. I heard them on Woman's Hour.'

'You said you knew for a fact that things got pretty scary for Christopher recently. What exactly did you mean?'

'I know he sailed close to the wind. I'm not sure that he ever went into something knowing it was 100% illegal. I used to say to him: "Don't you ever ask yourself why they're selling something so cheaply to you?" But he'd always be looking for a quick pound and I'd send him up by saying things like: "God, even Del boy would have had the brains to see that one coming." But he always thought... he has this feeling that he was destined for greater things. I'm not kidding, he went through his life thinking that all of this was temporary and that someday it was all going to click into place for him and he'd be made, and he'd be able to look after us. I'd say: "Look Christopher, none of us are exactly going around in rags. We've got shoes on our feet and food in our stomach, so it's okay." But he'd just smile that smile of his that said "just you wait." It was sad really. I have to admit, his priorities were wrong. He was so hungry for tomorrow he forgot about today, and when you do that someone comes up and steals all of your todays on you, don't they?'

'Well, I have to admit, I've never looked at it that way, but I think you might have something there,' Irvine replied, then changed tack. 'I know this is hard for you, what with Mr Lloyd just being dead and everything...'

'No,' Valerie cut in, 'I've had three years to get used to losing Christopher. I was thinking about this last night – you know, about not feeling bad about his death – and I thought it must either be a delayed reaction or, more likely, I feel as bad as you would feel if you lost a friend. That's what I lost: a friend. And yes it hurts, but not as much as it would have done if he'd still been my husband. So it's okay really. I want to help you if I can.'

'Thank you,' Irvine said. 'I just wanted to know were there any of his associates who might want to do him some harm.'

'He never brought any of his troubles around here.'

'What about names? Did he ever mention anyone who he was working with? You know, a deal that had gone wrong or something like that?' Irvine asked shooting wildly in the dark.

'No, sorry, nothing. I mean, I know he shared a stall space with Manfred Hodges and his son Ivan, but I don't think there was a problem there. He had mentioned he was close to something. I know that everyone always says that but not Christopher. He didn't say much, but I got the feeling by little hints that he felt there was something around the corner.'

'Something on the radio front?'

'I'm not sure,' Valerie paused and appeared to be deep in thought for a few moments. 'Probably not, I imagine. I mean, I'm sure if it was a radio deal he would have been more candid about it. That's not to say he was being underhand about it. It was just a feeling, as I say. I'd hate, now he's dead, for you to think I was suggesting he was knowingly involved with anything underhand. It's just that, when you sail as close to the wind as Christopher did, it would be easy to cross the line accidentally. But I need you to know that Christopher was not like that. I don't know if it will help you with your investigations or anything but he was not a bad person. I think I ought to know that better than most, and there's no reason for me to give you a false impression now. That's what I believe.'

'What was he like around the time of the rape charge?'

'Very solemn. He hadn't been around here for ages, and then one day he rang and told me he was in custody. He said he was being held on a charge of raping the girl who hung around the stall. It's difficult for me to discuss this, but I thought about it a lot. I know girls nowadays are more mature and inquisitive for their age and I thought, knowing how frisky Christopher could get, that maybe things could have got out of hand. Then I felt sorry for her, you know, starting to flirt with this grown-up and then somehow it all got out of control and how scared she'd be, and I also wondered how she could put herself through all that if she wasn't being honest. And then I thought that the police wouldn't make such a serious charge and take him to trial if they weren't convinced that he were guilty. Then I started to wonder if it was that he was black and in the wrong place at the wrong time that things got out of hand, that someone had put two and two together and got five. Two people can have two very different takes on the same scene. But then I saw Christopher with our

Whitney when he was released and I knew there was just no way a father like Christopher could do this thing.'

Irvine was trying to think of what to ask next when Allaway asked his first question. 'Where were you on Monday night last between the hours of six pm and midnight?'

Damage done, Irvine decided to go with it and hear her answer for fear of Valerie Lloyd thinking they were playing a game of 'good cop, bad cop'.

'I had what I think could euphemistically be referred to as a sleep-over.'

Of the nine thousand, three hundred and twenty-five answers Irvine thought Valerie Lloyd could have given to that question, the one she gave was certainly not one of them.

Chapter Thirteen

'I JUST RECEIVED a call from DS Irvine, sir,' Coles said. Kennedy was already at his favourite table in the Café Delancey, in the corner of the back room. Coles had dropped him off at the front door and driven off to find a safe, which is to say legal, place to park the car. 'Yes, he's just finished interviewing Valerie Lloyd.'

'Did he find out much?' asked Kennedy, absentmindedly studying the menu.

'He told me he'd brief you on it fully when you get back. But he did say that the flat was beautiful, the kids were well-mannered, and that it didn't seem that Valerie and Christopher had been at loggerheads. Though Valerie and Lloyd's mother Mabel were. And Valerie apparently was out on a date the night Christopher was murdered.'

'Oh,' Kennedy said, setting the menu down. He didn't really know why he was reading it anyway. He knew what he wanted: the same thing he had every time he dined in the funky Café Delancey.

'It is incredible sir, when you really get down to it,' Coles began, after the waitress had taken their orders. 'Most of our work seems to involve relationships that have gone wrong.'

'Good point, good point. Perhaps instead of the government spending millions on crime prevention they should invest some of that money in helping people protect and nurture their relationships,' Kennedy half-joked.

'Maybe you've got something there. If everybody were happily in love, crime would drop drastically.'

'Yes, but it's the "another day in paradise" theory, isn't it?' Kennedy said, losing the smile on his face. 'Someone's going to be so in love he's going to want to steal something to keep his partner happy and that's how the circle starts.'

Coles stared deep into the table. It seemed to Kennedy that something serious lay behind her trancelike state. He didn't want to get involved, but he thought it would be rude and ungentlemanly not to try to draw this line out further.

'You're thinking of a lost relationship?' he said quietly.

Coles shook her head quite firmly as though trying to shake the thoughts from her mind. 'Ah, I was just thinking that maybe sometimes we try a bit too hard to keep something together that has already finished.'

She couldn't be referring to ann rea and himself, could she? Kennedy wondered. He decided to keep quiet and leave Coles to elaborate as she chose. She started to say something, but it was lost as the waitress arrived with their food; Kennedy's crispy bacon, fried eggs and rosti, Coles' healthier poached chicken and salad.

Coles persevered. 'They say people are too flippant these days. You know: "At the first sign of troubled waters one or other partner is off."'

'Yes,' Kennedy replied breaking into an expansive smile, 'and then they'll say something like: "In my day, you had to muck in together to get through your troubles. Once you were married that was it for life."'

'But don't you think there is a grain of truth in that? You know, that once you're married that should be it for life?'

Kennedy shrugged his shoulders as if to say 'How should I know?'

'All I know is, things aren't how they used to be in the good old days. Mind you, even then, people would complain, murder, steal, fight, commit adultery and divorce just as much as they do now,' Kennedy said, wanting to steer the conversation in a different direction to avoid ruining his meal.

'Yes, I dare say you're right. We're probably no better or worse at getting on with each other today.'

They ate in silence for a couple of minutes. If this had been a date it would have been awkward, but because they were colleagues it was excused by the extent to which both of them were immersed in their case.

'Have you ever lost a relationship you didn't want to lose, sir?' Coles asked with an 'in for a penny, in for a pound' sigh.

'I'm afraid so,' Kennedy said hoping that would be an end to the matter. Then, for a bit of insurance, he added 'And yourself?'

Coles sighed again, this time, it seemed, with exasperation. Kennedy wondered if that was because of his short answer or because of his even shorter question.

'Yes. But I think my main regret is that I might just have ruined it by trying a little too hard to keep it together,' Coles replied.

Okay, safe so far, thought Kennedy. She's left me the option of leaving it here or delving deeper.

He surprised himself by choosing option B.

'How can you try too hard to save something or someone that you want?' he asked.

Coles looked him straight in his green eyes. 'By staying and trying to save the relationship even though I knew the other person was sleeping with someone else.'

Now she had his attention. 'Really?' he said.

'Really,' she admitted. 'Tom was my first real boyfriend. Well, not exactly my first boyfriend but that's another story altogether. But we, Tom and I, did everything by the book: dated for a time before our first kiss, kissed for a time before our first night, and waited more time before moving in together. And we were, I thought, in love and started plan our lives together. It all went horribly pear-shaped when I discovered he was sleeping with someone else. I found a hotel bill in his pocket. Nothing unusual in that, I suppose, except that the hotel was about half a mile away from our flat. Maybe nothing odd there either, except that the check-out time was 9.38. That was pm, not am. So I followed him there one evening. It was comical really, looking back. I borrowed a long, black wig from a mate of mine and wore a long overcoat, even though it was the middle of June. It wasn't even slightly funny at the time though

'I eventually plucked up the courage to go into the hotel lobby. There he was, bold as brass, having a drink with the wife of a friend ours. She was very beautiful. And at that stage, we'd only been dating for about nine months. But, well... I thought I looked okay too. I was going to confront both of them there and then in the hotel lobby but at the last moment I changed my mind. I went back to our flat and decided to ignore the fact that he was cheating on me and to try and win him back so he would drop her. My logic was, that by not confronting him about it, our relationship would not suffer a terrible traumas that it couldn't recover from. It would be my secret, and because he would think I didn't know about it, we would get over it and just grow stronger and stronger together. I kept up the charade for seven more months. In that time he had affairs with four different women. It seems he could never say no to a woman. And because he didn't want anything other than sex from them, he must have presented something of a challenge.'

'What happened?' Kennedy asked, filling Coles' recent silence.

'By the time I did confront him our relationship was effectively over. He apologised and said that he just couldn't help himself. He said he was glad I'd found out. He told me he felt sorry for me, but that he could never change. He admitted he was chronically promiscuous. He just loved being with different women. That was his big hit, his drug: the thrill of being with a new woman. When we broke up, it tore me apart. I felt that I wanted him, no matter how thinly he was spreading himself. When I look back now I can see he was no big shake. But that's only with hindsight. At the time I was convinced that my life was over.'

'But you did get over him?' Kennedy asked, a little shell-shocked.

'Well, I suppose yes and no. Yes, in that I'm okay now. No, in that I haven't really had a serious relationship since Tom. Not that I think that all men are bastards, or that I think anyone I ever go out with is going to cheat on me. It hasn't been by design, it's just the way that it's worked out. But I'm beginning to wonder if we don't all have a flaw built into us, you know, so that we never enjoy true happiness for a long period of time. Is there some great danger in happiness that God is trying to save us from?'

'An unusual slant,' Kennedy remarked. 'I suppose if we subscribe to it, there is a bit of hope for us after all.'

He asked for the bill and paid it, despite protests from Coles, who was profusely grateful and only accepted his generosity on the condition that she could return the favour some other time. Once she had secured a firm promise, she went off to fetch the car.

Waiting alone, Kennedy pondered relationships and the inability of people to deal with them. He wondered if he and Coles and Irvine were unusual in seeming unable to hold down a serious one. Then he thought of Christopher and Valerie Lloyd and of the relationships at the centre of the majority of the cases he worked on. And as his change arrived, he reflected that perhaps everybody did have an inbuilt flaw that prevented them from taking too many steps down the road to happiness. He thought of all the good times he'd spent with ann rea and wondered how great it would have been really, if they'd lived in that state continuously. But a beautiful waitress with a degree in subtle flirting was passing him his change, and his ponderings were trailing off... He wondered, what did that say about him?

Chapter Fourteen

IT SEEMED LIKE a day for people to open up to Kennedy about their personal feelings.

Just after lunchtime, as promised, Irvine visited Kennedy in his office. Coles was already there and Kennedy was placing name cards on his notice board. Already on the board were the names:

Mr Christopher Lloyd

Miss Eve Adams – Brought rape charges against C. Lloyd. Worked for him on stall.

Mrs Angelina Adams – Mother of Eve.

Miss Madonna Duncan – Friend of Eve. Introduced her to Mr Hodges and in turn to Mr Lloyd.

Miss Dionne Duncan – Sister of Madonna's and ex-girlfriend of Ivan Hodges.

Mrs Christine Duncan – Mother of Madonna and Dionne and one who took Eve to police.

Manfred Hodges – Stall owner and friend of Lloyd. Testified on his behalf at trial.

Ivan Hodges – Son of Manfred and sometimes took care of Lloyd's stall.

Mrs Mabel Lloyd – Mother of C. Lloyd.

Mr Daniel Elliot – Father of Ms Forsythe. Lloyd was found in his grave.

Ms Bella Forsythe – Daughter of D. Elliot, convicted murderess. Present at graveside when Lloyd's body was found.

The poison.

Each card noted the name in large, neat handwriting at the top with a brief biography and a few relevant facts beneath.

'Ah good,' Kennedy announced when he spotted Irvine, 'we're just about to add Mrs Valerie Lloyd to our notice board. You can fill us in on some background.'

Fifteen minutes later everyone was up to date. Coles went off to see how things were progressing and to put names to all the telephone numbers listed on Lloyd's recent bills.

'Do you think Bella Forsythe and her dad have any connection with this?' Irvine asked as he looked at the card for Ms Bella Forsythe.

'It's too early to say, James,' Kennedy replied. 'Why do you ask?'

'Well, it's just that, you know…' Irvine said, uncharacteristically lost for words.

'Yes?'

'Well, it's just that she's done her crime and is doing her time and if she's not involved in this I'm not sure we should be pinning her name to a notice board as a "convicted murderer."'

'Yep,' Kennedy said, somewhat taken aback, 'that's true. Maybe it was a coincidence and maybe it wasn't. But until we know for sure we should keep her name on the board so that she stays in our mind.'

'She's rarely out of my mind, sir.' Irvine said half-apologetically.

'Sorry?' said Kennedy in disbelief.

'You know that, at the time of the last murder, I had feelings for Annabella?'

'Yes, I do remember, James,' Kennedy replied sitting up very straight in his chair.

'Well, at the time, I felt she was someone special.'

Kennedy resisted the temptation to say that Ms Forsythe was indeed someone very special; she was a fecking serial killer. Instead he contented himself with tidying his desk and giving his junior the opportunity to continue.

Irvine, his face flushed, went on. 'I have to admit that I'd pretty much gotten over her. It's just when I saw her yesterday, well… it brought all my old feelings back again. Now I don't know if it's because she's totally unobtainable that she seems to be my ideal woman, or if she really is.'

'Unobtainable? That's a fact,' Kennedy remarked.

Irvine had the good manners to laugh. 'But,' he continued carefully, 'I can't help feeling that she's human and as deserving of love as anyone is.'

'Yes, James, but you're a fecking po-liceman,' Kennedy said. Whenever he got frustrated, he had a habit of dropping back into Ulsterspeak.

'Yes I know that, but it's not like she's ever tried to escape her porridge. Isn't that meant to be the whole point of the legal system – once you've repaid society for your crime, you're allowed to take up your place in the world again?'

'Well James, forgive me. I'm trying to be honest here, but you do realize that by the time Ms Forsythe takes up her place in society again the only thing she'll be capable of taking up will be her bus pass. And what are you intending to do for the next twenty years? Save yourself?'

'It's just that, if things had been different…'

'Things are not different James. Ms. Bella Forsythe, née Elliot, murdered at least four men. She's a convicted murderer who's been incarcerated. She may or may not be involved with the murder of Christopher Lloyd.'

'Now come on, isn't that pushing her guilt a bit too far?'

'I don't know, James, and neither do you yet.'

Irvine paused to control his anger. 'But why would she want to murder Christopher Lloyd?' he demanded at length.

'We don't know, James. Perhaps she's turned into a vengeance-seeking white knight who thinks that Christopher Lloyd got off with rape just like the four chaps who raped her, and so she's taken it upon herself to act as judge, jury and executioner.'

'What? So she's used some of Harry Potter's magical powers to fly out of her cell at night, murder Lloyd and dump him in her father's grave?'

'That's possibly the most sensible thing you've said in the last few minutes,' Kennedy said, nearly staring through Irvine.

Irvine looked as though he was considering what Kennedy had just said and then they both broke into a fit of laughter.

'It's so unfair, though,' Irvine continued after they had both regained their composure. 'We let her down. She decided that the only thing she could do was take the law into her own hands, so that's what she did. I remember in all of it, in all of the time we were working on the Fountain of Sorrow case, that no one, not any of the families involved, ever suggested that the four were not guilty of rape.'

'I know, James, and I felt for her too. But we can't get involved in thoughts like that. You take a little child playing on the footpath with his bike and you take a drunk or a druggie in a car, out of their brains, and they come steaming around the corner, up onto the footpath where the child is playing, run him over and kill him. The driver will get off with, at most, probably a couple of years. When the father or mother of the poor kid who was run over then seeks out and murders our drunk or junkie, we can't for one second say: "Well, they got what was coming to them." That's not what we're paid to do, James. We're paid to solve the crimes and catch the criminals who commit them. At that point it's someone else's business, not ours. I don't for one moment believe that Bella Forsythe ever considered trying to get away with her crimes. I think the only reason they were so elaborate and deceptive was because she wanted to take her time getting her revenge. Once her task was complete, she didn't really give us much of a run for our money. There was that one ingenious little twist at the end, but the main thing is that she knew exactly what she was getting herself into, and she knew what the consequences of her actions would be.'

'But maybe if I'd met her earlier…' Irvine said quietly.

'What, you mean maybe if you'd met her earlier you'd have moved on, just like you've moved on from every girlfriend you've ever had? Take Rose Butler, for instance. Youse two were perfect for each other, absolutely perfect, but because she was there and because she was available you moved on. Who's to say exactly the same thing wouldn't have happened if you'd met Bella Forsythe years before? You're just wishing for something that you can't have, just like you always do, and once you can have it you don't want it. But now you've found the perfect solution: someone you can never have, or at least not for another 25 years or so. Wishing's not going to help you out of that one. It's like my Mum always says: "Wish in one hand and do a Jimmy Riddle in the other and see which one fills first."'

'Ah, Rose Butler,' Irvine sighed. 'I'd nearly forgotten about her.'

'I bet you haven't James, I bet you haven't.'

Kennedy wasn't convinced he had persuaded Irvine away from Forsythe, but he did know that if he continued with his warning he might actually drive him closer to her.

'Look, James, there's nothing wrong with going to see Ms Forsythe from time to time.'

'What, so that I can get her out of my system?' Irvine replied, raising his eyebrows.

'As I say, there's nothing wrong with going to see Ms Forsythe from time to time,' Kennedy continued. 'But next time you go, could you maybe find out if she has any strong connections left on the outside? In the meantime though, I need you and Coles to go and interview Madonna!'

Chapter Fifteen

KENNEDY DIDN'T KNOW whether or not he'd sent Irvine off with Coles just so he wouldn't have had to continue the Café Delancey conversation with her. He tended to think not. He liked to think it was more because he wanted to keep his people fresh and not have them slip into a routine. In retrospect though, he probably should have brought WDC Coles with him to his next interview, with Miss Eve Adams – the young lady who had charged Lloyd with rape – and her mother, Angelina.

Kennedy could feel the resentment in the Adams' household the minute he and WDC Jenny Lowe walked through the door. Eve's oldest sister saw a lot of her own nose before she saw the members of the police force. She refused to have anything to do with them and left the house immediately. Running away wasn't going to be the end of the matter, though.

Eve Adams took Kennedy and Lowe away from the domestic chaos created by a mother, two younger brothers and another slightly older sister.

'Be easy with my Ma, her nerves are shot,' was Eve's opening remark as she shooed the police into her small room at the back of the ground-floor flat in Talacre Road, just off Prince of Wales Road in Chalk Farm. 'She's on something or other. God, you'd need to be to be living in this madhouse with us lot. So, have you come to see me because someone did us all a favour and topped Chris? I've been expecting you.'

Eve had a habit of looking at Kennedy but with her head turned slightly away, as though she was continuously giving him a last chance. She chewed gum as if it were an Olympic sport.

'What have you heard so far?' Kennedy asked finding a chair in the small room.

'Just that someone had topped him and had been caught trying to bury him in a graveyard at midnight in a black magic ritual thing,' Eve said continuing her crooked stare and her noisy gnashing.

Kennedy smiled. 'It's interesting what's going around the streets then?'

'What, you mean he's not really dead?' Eve said impatiently.

'No, he's dead all right.'

'He lied, you know?' Eve said.

'Oh?' Kennedy replied, quietly surprised that she was prepared to get straight into it without any prompting.

'He said that I didn't work on his stall. He said I just hung around his stall because of Madonna and Dionne; I'm not going to do that for nuffink, am I? I worked on his stall because he paid me, didn't I? I'm not going to do anything for free, am I? Our lawyer didn't pick up on that, you know. If she'd just gotten into that and could have proved he was lying about that, which would have been simple – the German saw him give me money – then the rest would have been easy.'

'The German?' Kennedy felt obliged to ask.

'Hodges, the man in the next stall, Ivan's dad, you know? It was funny, the whole court thing. When you see it on the telly, you know with Ally McBeal, it's all so slick and funny, even the judges are funny, but in the real court there's all these court officers stuttering and stopping and starting and tripping over themselves. I thought it would be cut and dried, you know with the evidence and the fact that Chris lied. He lied at least four times. Once about me working for him and then he changed his statement three times. Kids tell lies for a bit of a lark, but grown-ups always lie for a reason, don't they?'

'Tell me, had you seen Mr Lloyd since the trial?' Kennedy asked.

'No,' Eve snapped. 'What, do you fink I'm stupid or somefink?'

'Did he ever try to contact you?' Kennedy asked.

'No. I already told you.'

'I know you hadn't contacted him but I just wondered...'

'No one contacted no one, right?'

'Have you finished college yet?' Kennedy asked, tempted to say 'school' but thinking Eve Adams might be insulted by the term.

'No, I was ill after the trial. The doctor put me on somefink and I couldn't concentrate on my work so I sat out my last six months – I'll never be able to catch that up, you know. My Mum can't afford to wait around until I get me education. She needs the money and she needs it now.'

'Can we talk a little more about the trial?'

'There's not a lot more to talk about, really. I gave all my evidence on the closed-circuit telly. I told our lawyer that I wasn't scared to go in and face him in the court but she said I wasn't allowed. I think that was a big mistake though, it could have put the jury off me; maybe they thought I was too scared to face them in the courtroom.'

'I imagine the jury would have been advised beforehand that you were too young to stand up in court and that you would be giving your evidence on camera,' Kennedy offered, before continuing: 'Was your father at the trial?'

'We don't have no father, he left us about two years ago. That's why my mother is at her wits' end, and Blair's no help either.'

'Was Blair your father?'

'No, Tony Blair innit; he's not big on one-parent families, is he?'

'Oh, right,' Kennedy said. He looked around the room as WDC Lowe asked Eve if she had a boyfriend.

Eve looked adoringly at a large poster of David Beckham with his Mohican cut, towering over the room.

'Nagh, not yet. I mean, you don't get to meet many decent geezers around here, and I know they're all after one thing,' Eve replied, choosing that point to return her partial stare at Kennedy. 'Nagh, I'm going to go out and make my money and get some independence before I start to think about any of that nonsense. Look at our poor Ma; she's in a hopeless situation and how's she ever going to get out of it, eh? How's my mother ever going to be able to get on top of things? Never, eh? We've got to all look out for her, that's what we have to do, and there's enough of us to do that properly for her. I'm never going to end up like that, never in a million years, I'll tell ya that for nothing.'

'Do you have an uncle or anything?' Kennedy asked.

'No!' Eve shouted. 'Oh I get it, you're trying to see if I've a boyfriend or a father or an uncle I could go to and get to top Chris.'

'I didn't realize I was that transparent,' Kennedy admitted.

'Yeah, well, you were. I'm afraid you're not going to wrap up your case that easy. Now, you tell me somefink.'

'I'll try,' Kennedy offered, hoping for a truce of sorts.

'Have you worked on lots of murder cases?'

'A few, yes,' Kennedy admitted.

'And did you solve all of them?'

'No,' Kennedy laughed, 'certainly not.'

'Good. You see, that was a little test I set for you. Most of the fuzz would have said yes, but I know that's not true,' Eve said and for the first time offered Kennedy a full-on look. She even stopped chewing her gum. 'No, actually my real question was, when someone is murdered like, is it true that they always die with their eyes open?'

'Not always.'

'You see, I was told that when someone is murdered they always die looking at the person who murdered them,' Eve said. Kennedy was going to offer his opinion again but, before he had a chance, she pushed on. 'And so I had this theory that if that was true, the person who was murdered would still have the image of the person who killed them – the murderer – in their eyes, you know, on the retina. So, all we would have to do to solve the crime would be to find a way of recovering the image. You know how in the computers, when you lose something that you're working on, there's a way to reclaim it? So I thought pretty soon, with all these computers your guys have, you'll be able to reclaim the image. Good, eh? I got the idea when one of the teachers showed us how to lose some of our work from the screen and then go back into the mainframe and pull it back up again. So why not go back into the retina and do the same thing?'

'Well, I suppose part of the problem would be,' Kennedy replied, trying hard not to patronize her, 'that the retina sends all its signals to the brain and when the body dies, the brain and all the functions that go with it die as well.'

'But isn't it the same as a computer?' Eve replied, growing enthusiastic for the first time during the interview. 'You know, when you turn it off it's not got any power but all the info is still in there, just waiting for you to turn the power on again?'

'Yes, but when someone is dead you can't turn their power – their life force – back on.'

'What about that geezer in America who was dead for nineteen minutes on the operating table and they brought him back to life? You see, what I thought was that they need to find some way of connecting the retina to a computer and then they could revive the body; you know, with those two paddles that they give you a shock with. They did that to my granddad once but it didn't do any good; that's how I got this idea. There was a tiny flicker on the screen when they gave him a shock and so my point would be, in that tiny flicker, he came back to life. Now if you already had the computer connected up to the retina then you could reclaim the image of the murderer.'

'What if the last person the victim saw was the person who tried to help them?' Kennedy asked.

'Good point, detective, very good point,' Eve laughed. Maybe she was happy to be treated seriously, Kennedy thought. 'I'll have to do some more work on my theory,' she went on. 'And when I do, the old bill'll pay me money for it, I know. That's why I'd like to've gone back to college – I'd like to've gotten into this computer shit more.'

'Perhaps you could go to night classes?' the WDC suggested.

'What, and end up like you with your white shirt, tight black skirt and your flat feet? No way! I want to do what he does,' Eve said pushing her finger very close to Kennedy's chest.

Kennedy could feel the plectrum pass slowly over the final chord; the interview had finished of its own accord. He hadn't learned much, but in any case, the more people you can tick off your list of suspects, the greater your progress.

Surprisingly, Eve Adams did bother to accompany the police back down to the lounge, where Angelina was waiting for them. As they came in, the two boys who'd been playing a Game Boy walked out. Their mother looked glazed and, Kennedy thought, defensive. She was knitting, and continued to do so throughout the entire interview, rarely looking up at either detective. Kennedy noticed that the flat was clean, if perhaps in need of redecorating. The living-room was cluttered, with a television and music centre in one of two alcoves by the chimney stack. In the other, shelves were packed with CDs, paperback books, music cassettes, magazines, and a crazy assortment of orna-ments. The other strange thing about the lounge was that there were no single-seater chairs in evidence. Instead, there was a mis-match of four sofas; one tartan, one dark blue, one light blue and one a well-worn orange corduroy. The sofas lined the perimeter of the room, while a large, low, stripped-pine coffee table occu-pied the centre of the floor, which was boards barely covered by a couple of coats of light blue paint.

The position of the sofas meant that Kennedy had to choose either to sit on the same one as Angelina or one that was a long way off. He elected not to crowd her valuable space, and sat across the room from her. The poised WDC Lowe sat on the same sofa as Kennedy but at the other end of it; it seemed to be a day for giving people space. Kennedy thought of Eve in her room and of the two brothers, wherever they'd gone. He thought of the sister whose closed door they'd passed; a sign on the door had very impolitely requested that everyone keep out. Another sign announced that 'All Goths are welcome.' He thought of the sister who'd left in a hurry when they'd arrived. He thought of a father who'd been unable or unwilling to cope, and where he might be now. He wondered, was this what family life was all about? It was never like this in The Waltons. Why that occurred to him at that particular moment he couldn't say, but it brought a flicker of a smile to his eyes. When Angelina and Eve's father had first started to date one another, had they been aware of what lay ahead? And if they had, would they have chosen a different life and a different partner? Would the one guarantee you the other? Eve had an idea of how to escape. Kennedy wondered whether this was where the seeds of ambition came from, when you tried so hard to succeed just to make sure that you avoided the devil you knew.

'Eve seems to be okay,' he said cautiously, trying to gauge how fragile the woman was.

'Aye, she's doing good, isn't she?' Angelina agreed, knitting-needles clicking away. She was chubby in a puffy, unattractive way. Her hair was wiry, white and thinning, and she wore a large pair of cut off ice blue denim dungarees with a multicoloured cardigan over them.

'Yeah, she was giving us a few very interesting suggestions,' said Coles, joining in the conversation as they all watched a bobbing purple ball of wool on the floor disappear into the large garment that was warming the mother's chubby knees.

'It's no thanks to Chris Lloyd that she's doing well,' Angelina said in a monotone. 'No thanks to the law either. You were all too busy to protect my little girl from perverts. Letting him back out on the street again. What was that all about? You never seem to do what you're paid to do, do you?'

'Well, we can only send them to trial, then it's out of our hands. But I'd have to say that if our colleagues chose to remand Mr Lloyd in custody, they would have thought they had enough evidence for a conviction. We can't be held responsible for the court's decision.'

'Aye, it's always someone else's fault, isn't it? And now it's all starting over again. Chris Lloyd is getting us into trouble again.'

'Well, I think it was more a case of getting himself into trouble,' Kennedy offered hopefully.

'Well, if he's not getting us into trouble again, what are you two doing calling on our doorstep, eh? Answer me that.'

'We have to try and find out what happened to him,' offered Coles helpfully.

'What happened to him was he got what he deserved. Right? And now you're back here troubling us again. I can't be doing with this, my nerves won't stand it. I can't go through all of that again. It'll be the death of me, you'll see,' said Angelina, her voice fixed in its depressing drone.

'Well, we'll try not to trouble you too much, Mrs. Adams, but there are a few questions that we must ask you,' Kennedy said.

Mrs Adams stopped knitting for the first time since they entered the room. She looked up at Kennedy and seemed to spend several minutes assessing him. 'What is it you think I can tell you that'll help you with this sorry mess?'

'Had you seen Mr Lloyd since the trial?' Kennedy asked, feeling she was now probably on a short fuse.

'No,' she said resuming her knitting.

'Do you know if Eve saw him since the trial?'

'What did she tell you?'

'She said she hadn't.'

'Well then, she hadn't. She never tells lies, does Eve.'

'What about your other daughter?'

'Which one?'

'The older one who left as we arrived.'

'Janice? You'd have to ask her for yourself but I don't see any reason why she would have seen him.'

'Was your husband aware of the incident?'

'It wasn't an incident, Inspector. It was a rape. Let's call a spade a spade, particularly in this case.'

'Okay, was your husband aware of the rape?'

'I wouldn't know. I haven't spoke to him for two years.'

Kennedy wondered if he was just imagining that Mrs. Adams' knitting rate had increased since they started this quick-fire part of the interview. He wasn't about to lose the momentum with any further such thoughts, so he pushed on.

'Would you know where we'd be able to get hold of him?'

'I have a number I can give you, though I'm not sure how much good it will do you.'

'Have you ever been to Mr Lloyd's stall on the market?'

'Once. Christine Duncan and myself went around there to see what all this fuss was that the girls were on about.'

'Was Mr Lloyd present?'

'Yes.'

'Did you speak to him?'

'Just a quick hello. He looked a bit sheepish to me.'

'Was Mr Hodges present?'

'Yes.'

'Did you speak to him?

'My father died in the war so I didn't have to speak to the likes of him.'

'Are you and Christine Duncan good friends?'

'Well, okay, you know. Mostly through our daughters.'

Kennedy adopted a friendlier tone. 'Are Eve and Madonna still best friends?'

'Yes, I suppose they are, but Eve doesn't go out like she used to, so they don't hang around together as much.'

'That's a nice new Game Boy the boys were playing with. Did their father buy that for them?'

'Yes,' Angelina replied, breaking into a loving smile. She stopped knitting for a split second, but as her eyes came up to meet Kennedy's, the smile disappeared.

Chapter Sixteen

MEANWHILE, ROUND THE corner in Athlone Street, DS James Irvine and WDC Anne Coles were interviewing Madonna Duncan and her mother, Christine.

Christine, unlike Angelina Adams, was less the walking wounded than a breath of fresh air. No coaxing or prodding or gentle handling necessary. 'Come in,' she said the minute they rang the door bell, 'come in. I've been expecting you.' Then she shouted upstairs: 'Madonna, come on down and make a pot of tea, we've got visitors.'

'Mum, I'm busy!' came a high-pitched whine from above.

'I'll busy you,' Christine screeched, totally uninhibited by the presence of the police. 'Get down these stairs before I come up for you.'

Mrs Duncan led Coles and Irvine into the lower of the two floors of the maisonette they occupied in a four-story Georgian house. Before long they heard what sounded like a baby elephant tumble down the stairs and then kick up an almighty racket in the kitchen.

'I don't know how many times I have to remind her that she's not the American Madonna,' Mrs. Duncan said, sliding into her favourite chair by the window. 'She can dance and sing just as well as the other one, but...' and she rose to her feet and began what Irvine imagined was her party piece, a little dance where she deliberately tripped over herself, before continuing, '...then again, so can I.'

At which point she collapsed into the chair in a heap of laughter.

Irvine thought it was funny, joining in the laughter. Coles obviously didn't and used the time to get her notebook out of her pocket.

'Okay,' Christine announced as the tea arrived, 'this is the wonderful Madonna. She's pretty in pink, isn't she?'

'Mum!' Madonna protested.

'Oh, shush,' Christine replied, playing mother and pouring everyone's tea. 'Now, do you want to chat to us together or separately?'

'Separately,' Coles said immediately, after a pause adding: 'please.'

'Okay, angel. You run along back upstairs to your bedroom and these police persons will call you when they need you.'

Mrs. Duncan wore a long, shapeless, lemon T-shirt, nearly long enough to be a dress. She was about five-feet four inches tall, and though she wasn't exactly overweight, she lacked contours. Underneath the T-shirt she wore a pair of navy-blue shiny slacks, and her blonde hair was partially hidden under a Clarice Cliff coloured headscarf. Although she was dressed in the traditional housewife indoor uniform, she had made no efforts to change when they arrived. She came across initially as a woman with a lot of front. Irvine imagined her thinking she had more front than Sainsbury's, but she didn't quite have the natural confidence to carry it off. For all that, there was something distinctly likeable about her.

'First things first, I'd just like to say right now that I think the bastard got exactly what he deserved,' Christine exclaimed before either Coles or Irvine had a chance to ask their first question. 'You can write down in your little book that I said that.'

'So, you're in no doubt about Mr Lloyd's guilt?' Irvine said, trying to get the interview started.

'None.'

'Why are you so sure?' Coles asked.

'I saw Eve the night it happened,' replied Christine.

'When she came around here to see Madonna after the incident?' Irvine said, again trying to wrest some control over proceedings.

'Well, she went home first and then yes, she did come around to see our Madonna.'

'Why didn't she tell her mother?'

'Have you met her mother? She's a nice person and all, I wouldn't hear a word said against her, but she's barely capable of getting out of bed, let alone running her family. So Eve came around here. And I swear to you, I knew something was wrong with her the minute she walked in through the door. She looked at me and didn't say a word. I didn't know what it was. It's impossible to read them sometimes, you know? She and Madonna are at the age where they don't have any small problems. So I didn't interfere. I said: "You want to go up and see Madonna?" and she nods "Yes" and so I send her on up. Then ten minutes later they come down together and Madonna says: "Mum, Eve's got something to tell you, haven't you Eve?" Our Madonna's sensible enough when she needs to be. So Eve comes in here with me, and Madonna goes off to make us some tea. Eve didn't say a word until Madonna came back in again. She wasn't really crying but you know that stage just before sobbing begins, when the nostrils are working overtime and you know the waterworks aren't far away?'

'Yes,' said Coles suddenly. Christine paused before continuing.

'Well, Madonna comes back in with the tea and Eve tells us all that happened to her. How they were watching Coronation Street and she was sitting on his knee because there was only one seat, and then she gets up after the programme and he follows her and grabs her from behind and pushes her to the floor. Oh, I could have swung for him, I really could. So then I tell Eve that she can do one of two things: she can either forget that it happened and get on with her life, or she can go to the police. I told her there were two main advantages in the "going to the police" approach. The first was that he'd be put away and she'd be saving some other poor girl from having to go through the same ordeal. The other was that she'd get counselling and be looked after proper, like. She made her own decision. I didn't push her. In fact, I even told her how humiliating it would be. But she went to the police. Madonna and me went with her, poor little mite, and we all went through months of hell. You know, there's that point before you go to trial where the people outside of your direct family don't know who to believe, and you know some people are looking at Eve and saying: "Right little slag, getting that poor married man with two children locked up", and then, just because everyone knows Madonna is best mates with Eve, she gets tarred with the same brush.'

'Surely...' Irvine began

'No, believe you me, that's what it's like out there. It's dog eat dog. But you know what was the most devastating thing for me in all of this, the thing that kept me awake at nights? It was that it could have been our Madonna that he'd raped. Just as easily. And I'll tell you now, if he had done, me and our Frankie would have gone up there and strangled the bastard right there and then. They don't deserve to live, these animals. They're inhuman. There's something basically wrong with their make-up and I'm afraid I have to admit I think they should be put down. But more often than not, if they have any money behind them they'll get a fancy lawyer to get them off the charge, and nine times out of ten they'll go out and do the same thing all over again.'

'Is Frankie your husband?' Irvine asked. He didn't want to break her flow but, to him, it was an important question.

'Good Lord, no,' Christine broke into a quiet little chuckle. 'We've never been married. But we've been together for seven years now, and I swear to you, we're more solid than most of the married couples I know.'

'So he'd be...?' Irvine prompted.

'Frankie Hammond, he'd be.'

'Thanks,' Irvine said. 'And where would we be able to contact Mr Frankie Hammond?'

'Well, this is his home,' Christine laughed. 'He finishes work at five-thirty most nights. He's usually back here for the six o'clock news. If it's more urgent than that, you can get him at Tyres R Us on Chalk Farm Road.'

'Oh, I know it,' Coles said.

'Let's go back to Mr Lloyd for a minute, if you will. Had you seen him since the trial?' Irvine asked.

'No, certainly not.'

'Do you know if Eve had seen him since the trial?'

'No! Definitely not!' Christine said, raising her voice.

'Had anyone you know seen Mr Lloyd since the trial?'

'No one I know told me they had seen Chris, no,' Christine replied, then qualified herself. 'To be quite honest I'm sure he wanted to keep a low profile. He knew he wouldn't be flavour of the month around here so he would have been looking after his own skin by keeping out of our hair, so to speak.'

'Could you tell me what you were doing on Tuesday last between 6 o'clock and midnight?' Coles asked.

'Yes, I can, as it happens. Me and our Frankie had the house to ourselves. We got an Indian takeaway, a couple of bottles of wine and a video and had some good old-fashioned recreation – a night in,' Christine said, trying to be coy but not quite pulling it off.

'Good,' Irvine said. 'Perhaps we should see Madonna now.'

'Yes, yes of course,' Christine answered, a little surprised. Perhaps, Irvine thought, because they were finished with her so quickly.

But Coles hadn't quite done with her. She had one more question and she delivered it in her best Columbo fashion, just as she and Irvine were about to disappear through the door en route to Madonna's bedroom.

'Oh sorry, I nearly forgot. Just one more thing. What was the name of the video you watched on Tuesday evening?'

'Ha, that old chestnut,' Christine smiled. 'It's Frankie's favourite, Emmanuel – I don't know how many times we've watched it but we always enjoy it.'

She winked at Irvine. Coles was already out of the door.

Unlike her mother, Madonna Duncan had not yet given up on the battle of the bulge. It appeared she had to put up an almighty fight though. When the detectives knocked on her bedroom door they could hear her grunting and groaning inside.

'Come on in,' Madonna said between large gasps for air.

She was on her back on the floor with legs up over her head

and her toes touching the floor. She was dressed in a pink leotard and a pink baseball cap, with a ponytail of her jet-black hair protruding from it. She rose to her feet, flopped back onto her bed and started to towel the sweat from her face.

'So, what can I do for you?' she started off all businesslike and obviously taking a page out of her mother's book on directness.

'We wanted to ask you about Christopher Lloyd,' Coles said starting off the proceedings.

'Who?'

'Mr…' Irvine started to offer an explanation.

'Oh, you mean Chris? We call him Chris. I've never heard him referred to as Christopher.'

'Oh, I see,' Coles said.

'Well, what could I possibly tell you about Chris that you don't already know?' Madonna said and then smiled, just like her mother had done. 'Unless, of course, I could give you the name of the person who murdered him.'

'Yes,' Coles replied, 'that would be handy.'

'Not to mention impossible. Is it true his body was cut into little pieces and spread over a graveyard?'

'No, it's not true.' Now it was Coles' turn to laugh. 'Whoever told you that?'

'Oh, that's the word going around. Me and my sister, Dionne, saw that disaster coming a mile off, you know.'

'What? Him being murdered?' Coles asked.

Irvine was happy to let her conduct the interview on the grounds that she might get more out of the teenager. He hoped he wasn't appearing to be the naive one.

'No, no,' Madonna said in a hurry, 'although if you move in his circles I suppose it's bound to happen to you sooner or later.'

'What circles would those have been?'

'Well, you know, my Mum's boyfriend said Chris was a petty criminal. He said it right from the beginning and that's why Dionne and me knew it would end up a disaster. I mean, apart from anything else, he was old; he was an old man. He had two kids, for heaven's sake! What did Eve want to hang out at the stall for?'

'Maybe it was just her first job, you know, earning her own money and having some bit of independence.'

'Yeah,' Madonna replied, sitting back up on the bed so she could throw her towel over the rail at the foot of the bed. It landed dangerously close to the wooden stool Irvine was perched on. Coles sat on a lower plastic stool closer to the head of the bed. 'But that didn't mean she needed to hang around with him afterwards and watch television and all that. My sister says that Chris claimed in court that he and Eve were boyfriend and girlfriend. But Eve said she wasn't. She's a bit... well she missed out a whole year at school because she was ill when she was younger and so she's a bit slow. I love her lots and she's my best mate but I do have to look out for her sometimes and I warned her that things could get out of hand. You know, he was an old man and old men...' and here she paused and looked at Irvine,' well, old men get a bit desperate, don't they?'

'Had you seen Chris since the trial?' Coles asked Madonna. Irvine knew by the look on his colleague's face that she was about to burst a gut.

'Well, no, not really,' Madonna replied as she absentmindedly took up a magazine that was resting on her pillow and started to flick through the pages, alternating her looks between Coles, the pages and Irvine.

'Not really?' Coles asked, apparently suspecting something more like 'Yes, really'.

'Well, Dionne made me swear I wouldn't tell anyone but I know what the police are like; if they find out you've told one lie, they think that everything you have told them is a pack of lies and I don't want to get into no trouble.'

'You're not going to get into trouble,' Coles offered gently, 'but you're right, you shouldn't tell us lies.'

'Well, it's innocent really; our Dionne wanted to accidentally see Ivan Hodges again, if you know what I mean. Yeah?'

Coles and Irvine both nodded that they knew exactly what she meant.

'So, we both go up the Camden Market and accidentally pass Ivan and his dad's stall and Chris was just leaving as we arrived.

I'm not sure that he even saw us but that one glimpse of him technically means that I have in fact seen him since the trial.'

'Okay, that's good, very good. Thank you for being honest,' Coles said and then looked at her notebook before asking: 'When would this have been? You know, your trip to Camden Market?'

'Saturday morning last,' Madonna replied, distracting herself. 'It's quite spooky really, isn't it? That was the last day of his life, wasn't it?'

'Yes, Madonna,' Coles said quietly and paused before continuing. 'Did Dionne manage to accidentally see Ivan on Saturday morning, after all?'

This question seemed to snap Madonna out of her dark mood.

'Yes,' she replied in a whisper, as if her mother was on the other side of the bedroom door. 'We hung around until his dad sent him for a couple of teas and we followed Ivan to the stall. I left them alone for a time and she came back skipping away. She wouldn't tell me anything but I think she arranged to see him that night because she was very happy for the rest of the day and got herself all dolled up that evening to go out.'

'You said earlier that your dad knew Chris was a petty thief. Had he told you this before or after the rape incident?'

'He's certainly not my Dad,' Madonna said coldly. 'He's my Mum's boyfriend. But he was warning us way before the rape. He mentioned it at the very beginning when our Dionne first mentioned his name as someone Ivan covered for occasionally on the stall. He actually said: "You'd better watch that one closely. He's been in trouble with the law."'

'Do you know how Mr Hammond knew of Chris, by any chance?', Coles continued. Irvine felt she was pushing it a bit with this one but he left her to it. Maybe she felt she had Madonna on her side.

'I think he said it was something to do with tyres, but I'm not altogether sure,' Madonna replied, getting stuck back into her magazine again.

'Well, I think that's all for now,' Coles said standing up. Irvine hopped off his chair.

'Oh good, that was painless, wasn't it?' Madonna said remaining on the bed. 'You're okay,' she said to Coles, 'but he's not much of a partner, is he? Does he always make you do all the work?'

Chapter Seventeen

'TWO MORE NAMES for our suspects list, I think,' Coles said as she negotiated the tricky corner of Athlone and Wilkin Street.

'Who? Madonna and her mum?'

'No,' Coles replied impatiently. 'Frankie Hammond and Dionne Duncan.'

'But Frankie was at home all night with Christine.'

'Exactly,' Coles replied, 'or so she claims.'

'Shall we pay Frankie a visit on the way back?' Irvine said, not really meaning it as a question.

Tyres R Us is diagonally across the road from The Roundhouse on the way towards Camden Lock, and not a million miles from Lloyd's stall in The Stables.'

Frankie Hammond was sizing up their vehicle on the forecourt as Coles and Irvine pulled up.

He automatically opened their boot and rummaged around for a few seconds.

'The spare needs a bit of work, but all the others look clean,' was the tyre man's greeting. He leaned against the passenger side of the car, wiping his hands on a rag.

Coles' and Irvine's collective response was to flash their warranty cards.

'Oh,' Hammond said, digging his hands deep back into his oily, navy-blue dungarees. Apart from the bib, his upper torso was naked and tanned, a combination of sunburn and a bit of weather-beating. His hair was cut to a 'number one', the skin clearly visibly through the white stubble. Irvine pegged the trim man as being in his mid-forties and well capable of looking after himself.

'We've just been up to see your wife and Madonna…' Irvine started.

'Madonna? What's she been saying? They're okay, aren't they?' Hammond said, quickly taking his hands out of his pockets and taking a step closer to the police.

'No. I mean yes, they're fine,' Irvine reassured him. 'We're looking into the death of Mr Christopher Lloyd.'

'Oh.'

'Yes,' Coles said. 'Is there somewhere we can go for a chat?'

'Oh, yes, sorry, we can use the tea room; it's always empty at this time.'

Irvine saw from the look on Coles' face that she wished she hadn't agreed to Hammond's suggestion. The tea room was small and all the walls were plastered with the pages from Playboy, Men Only and other such girlie magazines.

To his credit, Hammond apologised immediately, saying that he really was oblivious to it all now and offered to take them elsewhere. Coles assured Hammond and Irvine she was perfectly fine to stay in the tea room. Irvine found it more difficult; every now and then a shapely lady would catch his eye and he'd look at it in disbelief until another lady distracted him even more.

'Madonna was telling us that you knew Christopher Lloyd before the incident with Eve Adams,' Irvine said, seeking a mental distraction to all the pictorial ones.

'Incident?' Hammond replied. 'Incident? Surely you mean him raping Eve. Now, tell me this, how did he ever manage to get away with it? The inspector who was on the case was convinced that he was going to do time. He reckoned they had him good and proper on it and how long he'd go down only depended on the judge. And then, he walks away scott bloody free. You tell me how that works then?'

'We'd prefer to talk about how you knew Christopher Lloyd before the rape incident,' Coles answered.

'Do you mind if I light up in here?' Hammond said pulling out a grubby pack of Players and a green disposable lighter from his bib pocket and, before either Coles or Irvine had a chance to consent, he lit up, taking the first long, deep drag of a two-pack-a-day habit. 'Several years ago, one of the staff here was found nicking the odd tyre and the boss discovered that he was passing them on to one of our very regular customers, the very same Mr Christopher Lloyd.'

Hammond closed his mouth very tight and hiked his shoulders and eyebrows up, implying 'see what I mean?'

'Did you come into contact with him personally?' Coles asked, fanning some smoke in the badly ventilated room from her eyes.

'Well, I saw him around and that, but I had nothing to do with him then and I didn't want to have anything to do with him when I heard his name mentioned by the girls as someone who was working up at the market,' Hammond said. He paused as he used the free little finger and thumb of the hand holding the cigarette to remove a piece of tobacco from his pure white teeth. 'And what does a married man with kids want hanging around with a child like Eve? She may look grown up but she's mentally only a child.'

'So did you come into contact with him around the time of the case?' Irvine asked, feeling a bit nauseous now with the mixture of smoke and residue of body odours of hardworking men.

'I'd no need to, had I?' Hammond said. 'I mean, I saw him one day in court. I took a day off work and went to support Christine. It's been hard on her you know, because of the state of Eve's mum, Angelina. Our Christine, God bless her, has had to act as a surrogate mum for little Eve as well. But anyway, I saw him in court on that one day.'

'And that was it?' Coles asked.

'And that was it,' Hammond replied finishing his cigarette.

'Can you tell us what you were doing on Monday evening last between the hours of six and midnight?' Irvine asked quickly.

'Christine and myself had a quiet night in, an Indian takeaway and watched a video,' Hammond said, stubbing out the cigarette on the bare floorboards beneath his foot. He rubbed his chin and looked directly at Coles before continuing. 'I'm afraid it was a bit of indulgence on my part. The video was a personal favourite of mine, Emmanuel.'

'Each to their own,' Coles said feigning a smile. 'And could you please tell us what your were doing on Tuesday night between the hours of six o'clock and midnight?'

Hammond's face went the shade of red he should have turned when he mentioned Emmanuel, and with a few ums and ahs, and a stage laugh, he said: 'No, of course, the Indian and the video was on Tuesday night not Monday night, I was just confused.'

'He could have been genuinely confused,' Coles said to Irvine five minutes later as they were driving back to North Bridge House.

'Possibly,' Irvine agreed.

'It was a little bit cheeky,' Coles said opening the window of the car. Irvine imagined she wanted to clear the smell of the smoke and sweat from her nostrils.

'Perhaps, but at the very least it proved that Christine had phoned him to tip him off that we'd probably be visiting him,' Irvine said sinking into his seat and belting up. 'So, what was all that charade on the forecourt when we arrived?'

'Maybe they're just rallying around Eve,' Coles offered.

'Some people cling to this neighbourly thing a bit too much,' Irvine started, 'and some people just don't know when it's time to downright stop interfering.'

'Christine seemed genuine enough to me. I thought she seemed to care about Eve.'

'But it was the same with Annabella.'

'Who?' Coles asked, swerving to avoid a couple of Japanese tourists who darted out in the middle of the road in front of them. There was lots of bowing and smiling and nervous giggling as the teenage girls returned to the footpath with their lives.

'Dr Bella Forsythe, you know…'

'I know,' Coles replied.

'There were probably lots of people who cared for her after she'd been gang-raped but who was there for her beforehand? Who was there to protect her from the evil thugs in the first place? And then, when she rid the world of the scum, she's the one who's sent to prison.'

'James!' Coles literally shouted. 'Come on, you can't just murder four people and walk away scott-free.'

'Yes, and you can't gang-rape someone and walk away scott-free either, but all her attackers did. They'd got away with their crime, got away with it for ages to be honest,' Irvine replied passionately. He was angry with himself for raising his voice.

They both drove in silence for a few minutes.

'Sorry about that.'

'It's fine,' Coles replied.

'It's just that after meeting her again at the graveyard, I've been thinking a lot about her.'

'Oh?'

'Yes, I've been thinking how unfair it all is. We did our job, put her away, forgot all about her and got on with our lives,' Irvine said. 'And then I saw her again and I suddenly remembered that I had feelings for her, and I remembered how much I liked her and was attracted to her and wanted to get to know her. I was desperate to get to know her, Anne.'

'Oh!' was all Coles could reply, but Irvine noted that she didn't seem to mind the Christian name slipping into the conversation.

'I think I saw her about two or three times and then bang, she was in prison. And I have to admit that I forgot about her totally but equally I'd have to admit that I've not been the same since. I find I don't pay as much attention to women as I used to, it's all a bit half-hearted to be honest, and then I saw Bella in the graveyard and it all came flooding back again. Which was very weird, believe me, because I kept reminding myself that she is a murderer.'

'Yes,' Coles said.

Irvine wondered if Coles thought he was weird.

'I know you probably think I'm weird but…'

'I don't, I just wonder…' Coles stammered.

'You just wonder am I fooling myself that she's my perfect woman, you know, just because she's totally unavailable?'

'Well, now that you come to mention it…'

'You see, I knew it. DI Kennedy felt the same,' Irvine said dejectedly.

'You've told him about this? Coles hissed. 'You're not going to do anything about it, are you?'

'Yeah, and there's a lot that I can do about it, isn't there?'

'James?'

'You see, it's my own fault really. I have this reputation for loving them and leaving them.'

Coles blushed a little but said nothing.

'And after a couple of dates I'm not interested any more. But the truth is probably that I was just so desperate, and maybe a little impatient to meet the right person, so if it didn't work out I'd want to move on, and move on immediately.'

'But you can't really believe that Dr Forsythe is this person, this person that you've been waiting for, searching for?'

'I don't know, maybe not, but what I do know is that since I saw her again in the graveyard I've just not been able to get her out of my mind, and if I was a member of the cast of EastEnders, I'd say that "it was doing my bleedin' 'ead in." And then with this case, every time I think of Eve Adams and her accusing Christopher Lloyd of raping her, I start to think of Bella again. Do you think there can be any connection between the burial of Daniel Elliot and Lloyd's death?'

'And by extension,' Coles added, 'between Lloyd's death and Dr Forsythe?'

'Well, yes.'

'Too early to say, but it could just be purely coincidental, couldn't it?' Coles replied, offering her colleague a degree of support.

'You know they say that we make plans and then God laughs.'

'Oh, please don't go religious on me,' Coles said.

'No, no, I didn't mean that,' Irvine protested. 'I meant how weird it all was, you know. Someone plans this bizarre murder and this amazingly clever way of getting rid of a body and then God or someone or something sends the rain and uncovers the body of a man who turns out to be an accused rapist, waiting to share the grave of a man who was accused by his daughter of not protecting her against rapists. Come on, Anne, you have to admit, someone is having a big laugh at somebody.'

'Yes, put that way it is pretty bizarre, isn't it?' Coles said as she pulled into the car park at the rear of North Bridge House, where they saw DI Christy Kennedy and ann rea walking off down Parkway.

'I thought those two had split up,' Coles said aloud to herself, not caring to hide her disappointment from her colleague.

Chapter Seventeen

APPEARANCES CAN BE deceptive. Whereas WDC Coles *thought* she saw Kennedy and ann rea walk down Parkway *together*, what she actually saw was Kennedy and ann rea walk down Parkway *un*together. Local journalist ann rea had been passing North Bridge House just as the local detective was nipping down to Regents Bookshop to pick up something about antique radios. Both were equally taken aback to have met each other out of the blue and they made polite conversation until Kennedy could find a gap in the traffic to enable him to cross Parkway. He watched her from the opposite side of the road, strolling confidently away. He felt a distance between them that had never existed before, not even when he first spied her in the bookstore at Heathrow Airport and he didn't even know who she was. Kennedy felt a knot in his stomach and felt himself unconsciously swallow large gulps of air. She wasn't even offering him a quick backward glance; she was obviously moving forward with her life quicker than he was, but then he had been the one who'd been in love, hadn't he? He was wondering if they'd ever grow into being friends – not *just* friends but good friends – when he arrived at the friendly bookstore. He hoped they would become friends but if he felt as bad as he had from just a few words and a brief glimpse of her, it was going to take a considerable amount of time to reach that state. In the meantime, he had a case to throw himself into.

Twenty minutes later, panic attack over, Kennedy was back in the comfort of his office with his team and a mint copy of Jonathan Hill's illuminating *Radio! Radio!* Kennedy sent Coles out with Allaway to find and interview Janice Adams whose quasi-dramatic exit from her parents' home had made some kind of lasting impression on at least two members of Camden Town CID.

Thirty minutes after that, Irvine returned to say that he'd managed to track down the foreman of Christopher Lloyd's jury. The very same Mr Paul Wood was a computer operator and although he lived, and obviously voted, in London, he worked at the Jordan Factory up at Silverstone in Northants. So, working on the theory that there was no time like the present, Kennedy phoned Mr Wood to advise him they would be visiting him at the factory.

Irvine and Kennedy were back on the road again – at least that's what it felt like to Kennedy. He wasn't a great one for long car journeys, though. He was fine scooting around the streets of London but even then he felt it was more to his advantage – speed wise – to walk. Despite all Ken Livingstone's great promises of revolutionising traffic congestion in London, the situation was getting worse. Kennedy loved to let his mind skip off on various tangents and possible solutions for his cases while travelling. Being stuck in heavy traffic with highly visible road rage did little to encourage his daydreaming. Given a choice, he preferred either to walk or to travel by train. For some reason or other, the extra space one was afforded by train travel, and walking, seemed to encourage such flights of fancy.

But, for today, he was happy to scoot up by car to the picturesque Northamptonshire countryside to interview Mr Paul Wood, foreman of the jury at Christopher Lloyd's trial.

The Jordan Formula One Factory stood at the end of a narrow track directly opposite the famous Silverstone Racetrack gates. It seemed incredibly quiet for such an important organisation, assuming that at 3.30pm, lunch should have been long since completed. Irvine explained why.

'Paul Wood said it would be quiet today, sir. He said the majority of the team would be testing over at the racetrack.'

'Did he not need to be over there too?'

'No, he said it would be fine to stay behind and meet us. Apparently the only reason he occasionally goes is to hear Eddie

Jordan's wisecracks. One of the perks of the job, according to him.'

Walking into the reception area they were awed. The factory was state-of-the-art. It looked and smelt so clean that Kennedy thought it seemed more like a hospital than the glorified garage he'd been expecting. Perhaps mechanics and doctors had more in common than was generally thought. The receptionist buzzed through to Paul Wood who greeted the two Camden Town policemen less than a minute later.

Paul Wood betrayed his Brummie roots with his gentle drawl. He wore a droopy moustache and a Kevin Keegan hairstyle, which prompted Kennedy to whisper to Irvine as they were being led through to a reception room: 'I thought all of that style died off in the '70s.'

'Perhaps in Ireland, Scotland and London, sir,' Irvine ventured discreetly, 'but obviously not in the Midlands.'

Wood was dressed in black chinos and a yellow Jordan Honda Team shirt that displayed in various colours how heavily the team were sponsored. He did break with the party line on sponsorship with his footwear however, wearing a brand new pair of white Nike trainers.

Wood left the detectives in a room so clean looked liked it had just been redecorated. Its white walls were covered with various photos of cars and team owner, Eddie Jordan.

Both policemen made themselves comfortable at the table, which supported a large-scale model of the hi-tech Jordan Honda Team Formula One car, as Kennedy noted from the engraved silver legend underneath.

'Goodness!' Irvine said, following Kennedy's eyes to the engraving. 'It's next year's car and they're reverting to the Irish green from that horrible yellow they've been using for a few years now.'

Wood returned with a tray laden down with sandwiches, tea, coffee, milk, Jacob's Kimberley Biscuits and real white china. The three of them tucked in to their refreshments and the case of the Crown versus Lloyd.

Chapter Eighteen

WOOD MADE IT clear from the start that he'd really enjoyed his jury-service stint.

'For me, it was like being in a class where the teachers weren't, you know, speaking to you in a foreign language. I could understand and follow all the proceedings. I was surprised I was able to retain all the details. Some of the other jurors would sometimes ask me to recall various things, so, when the time came round, I wasn't surprised to be proposed as the foreman.'

Kennedy studied this 27-year-old man. He appeared very together, very articulate, comfortable with himself, eager for knowledge, well-spoken, ambitious; all the qualities, Kennedy imagined, that one really needed as the foreman of a jury.

Irvine was making short work of the freshly made egg sandwiches, which was fine by Kennedy as it left the delicious Jacob's Kimberley biscuits unchallenged. Wood sipped occasionally on Ballygowan Still Mineral Water as he started to talk.

'The judge always spoke in perfectly formed paragraphs. He came across as very kind, friendly and humble. He always had an open smile on his face for the jury. He would sit with various coloured pens fanned out in his left hand, while making notes in some predetermined colour-code of his. He looked like a judge, even when walking about disrobed and grey-suited, in the corridors of the County Court House.

'Christopher Lloyd received a fair trial; too fair perhaps. He was represented by one Mai Chada. If she'd been hoping to win her spurs on Lloyd's case she was always going to be disappointed. She was ill at ease and unprepared. She'd stumble around in her notes trying to find things to ask. Her questioning was mostly haphazard, as if she was searching wildly in the dark, hoping. On several occasions the judge actually had to ask Ms Chada's questions for her.

'I should probably point this out to you right at the start. To me this case was quite simple and very straightforward. Christopher Lloyd was guilty. I have absolutely no doubt whatsoever about that fact. I have to say that my opinion is based entirely on the evidence and had nothing whatsoever to do with the man's colour. The man changed his statement three times. Now, you don't change your evidence when you're innocent, do you? No, you adapt it because as the case unfolds, you and your brief become aware of the information the prosecution has. In the first instance – you know, when he was picked up right at the beginning of all of this?'

Irvine and Kennedy nodded that they knew when Wood was referring to.

'Well, when he was first picked up, Christopher Lloyd claimed that he hadn't touched Eve Adams. He claimed she had come up with the story that he raped her just because he wouldn't give her a job in his stall. Then, when the defence team and Lloyd discovered there was physical evidence confirming that he had, in fact, had sex with her, he admitted that they were boyfriend and girlfriend and that Miss Adams had claimed rape because he'd tried to drop her. When he found that that story wasn't holding much water, he claimed that Miss Adams had shouted rape out of spite because he wouldn't take her to Denmark, wouldn't buy her a mobile phone and wouldn't give her money.'

'But how come,' Kennedy started mid-bite, 'if you were the foreman of the jury and you were convinced he was guilty, Lloyd was found not guilty?'

'He was found innocent by the due process of the law that our country is famous for,' Wood replied, pausing for a sip of his water.

'A miscarriage of justice, you mean?' Irvine asked, wondering where this was going.

'No, not entirely,' said Wood, wiping some water that had spilt on his chin. 'We couldn't find him guilty. That doesn't mean he was innocent, it just means that on the day, we, as a jury, were not presented with a case that convinced us all of his guilt. When we first retired to the jury room to consider our verdict, I advised everyone that what we should do before voting was assess the evidence and to carry out a complete review of it, for everyone's benefit.'

'Sure, sure,' Irvine replied.

'No, I think you've got me wrong. I did that because I felt that some of the jury had already made up their minds during the trial – something we were very strongly warned against at the beginning and at the summing up.'

'How long did the trial last?' Kennedy asked.

'Four days in total,' Wood replied immediately. He paused as though waiting for the police to ask further questions. They didn't so he continued expansively: 'You know, it's a lot like this...' Wood gestured around the office and beyond.

'I mean the courthouse. It's so grand, so imposing, so humbling, but it could just as well have been a factory. You know, with all its different rooms, the canteen, signs everywhere, loud ticking clocks, notice boards and public-address systems for announcements. There was one largish room, which was the jury-selection room, and sometimes there'd be as many as two hundred people waiting in there to see which trial they were going to be jurors on. The administrative staff had their own space at one end of the room and the smokers were all closeted off in their own little area at the opposite end. It smelt stale; probably the combination of the heat of the radiators and the air that had already been used several times before it got to you. But everyone in that area – the admin. staff, the jurors, the clerks of the court and all the various briefs who travelled through the room on their way to the courts – all of us acted like we were on a normal day's work on the factory floor. The main difference was that that particular factory produced nothing but justice.'

'So, you had started to say you wanted everyone to review the evidence when your jury first retired to the jury room,' Kennedy said, taking advantage of a natural pause in the Brummie's narrative to try to get him back on track.

'Sorry,' Wood replied, snapping out of whatever it was that had distracted him and seeming pleased by Kennedy's prompt. 'Yes, yes of course. So, on the final day, we were all sitting around the table in the jury retirement room. Let's see now…' Here, Wood closed his eyes to help himself to recall the scene.

'Yes, let's get this correct now. Ah, there was the Irish lad, Sean O'Malley, to my immediate left. He'd been over working in the UK for about 8 years. He was a labourer currently doing some refitting work at Heathrow's Terminal 4. He had a lot of common sense, was about 30 years old and was one of the smokers – probably the leader of the smokers, in fact. Then to Sean's left there was Mary. Mary…' Wood seemed to struggle.

'Mary McGonigle,' Irvine prompted after checking his notes.

Wood opened his eyes, smiled for a split second then closed his eyes again and continued. 'Yes, Mary McGonigle. She was in her mid-twenties. I'd say she was cute but not beautiful. She was another of the smokers. She was a student; still at university, I think. She wanted to be a sculptress. She talked only to the jurors she'd been informally introduced to by Sean. But if she hadn't been introduced to you, then she'd listen to you when you spoke but never address you. She was Sean's mate; she hung out with him.

'Next at the table there was the reader, Miss Golding – Susie… no, Susan. Yes, that's it, Susan Golding. During any break in the proceedings she'd always keep herself to herself and have her nose stuck in her book. From what I could gather, she finished two books during the time she was on jury service and started on a third. She never wore even a hint of make-up but she was very striking nonetheless. I couldn't be exactly sure of her age – I'd say she could have been anywhere from 25 to 35 years old. Non-smoker.

'Then there was Michelle Roche. She had a very, very bad limp. I don't know why, but from the way she walked I'd say she'd had it most of her life. She was a smoker. From what I could gather she probably smoked more than most; you could always smell smoke on her clothes. She had long, very long, mousy-coloured straight hair and an even longer face. I'm not sure she was ever able to get a correct grasp of the evidence. She had a bit of a chip on her shoulder. I'd say she was in her early thirties.

Paul Wood stopped talking again. He closed his eyes even tighter, squeezing them shut until lines marked his white eyelids. His concentration was so intense that it prompted Irvine to plough through his notes again to see if he could find the name Wood was searching for. Kennedy raised a single finger to his lips, thinking that any outside interference would break Wood's flow and perhaps spoil his ability to recall the jury-room scene.

'Oh yes, I've got him. Maurice! Yes, to the left of Michelle Roche was Maurice Morrison. He was always smartly dressed and well groomed. He's a partner in a small advertising firm. He'd always be on his mobile during any of the breaks we had. He and I had a pub lunch a few times. He was a non-smoker and 34 years old. He was well capable of following the trial and picking up on all the subtleties of the evidence.

'Which brings us on to Andrew Sainsbury. He's easy to remember because he was a van packer for Marks and Spencer. Get it? A van packer for Marks and Sparks called Sainsbury?'

Kennedy and Irvine nodded that they had indeed got it.

'Maurice was nervous, very quiet and quite scruffy with a red complexion. He was in his mid-thirties and was happy for the trial to last as long as possible because it kept him off work.

'Next was Mrs Sheila Watson. She was 56. She said she was 56 years old and had been a Christian for 50 of those years. This was during our first conversation, you understand. She was our professional juror. She'd served on two previous juries. She was always talking about her other cases. She told us about one she'd been instrumental in solving, she claimed.

'In the trial in question, this chap was charged with GBH. He was accused of beating up some poor sod in the car park of a pub. The evidence and identification all hung on a white, short-sleeved Fred Perry shirt. No one could properly identify the culprit except to say that he had ginger hair, dark Buddy Holly-style glasses and wore a white Fred Perry shirt, which had blood all over it. Anyway, when the police were called in, they figured it was a chap they knew with ginger hair and glasses who was always getting into trouble on their patch.

'The police jumped into their panda car and steamed around to Ginger's where they found him sitting in front of the television watching horse racing. However, he wasn't wearing a blood-stained Fred Perry shirt. He was wearing a blue floppy sweatshirt. But he had a few grazes around his face, so the police asked him if he owned a white Fred Perry shirt. 'Ginger Holly' confirmed that he did and went to fetch it for the police. He returned from his bedroom several seconds later with a very white and very unstained Fred Perry shirt. The police decided to take him into custody anyway, mainly because of the marks about his head and knuckles but also because he was a habitual troublemaker. They brought the shirt with them as well as evidence. Anyway, when it came to the time of the trial, Ginger's defence team offered up the unstained white Fred Perry shirt as absolute proof that their client couldn't possibly have beaten someone up, bloodied his shirt and had the time to wash it before the police came around to his house to apprehend him. The defence lawyer proudly produced the virgin-white shirt from the police's own exhibits and passed it round the jury.

'When it reached our Sheila Watson, she studied it and asked permission to remove it from the plastic bag. The judge gladly granted her permission and Mrs Watson opened the shirt and examined it further. Mrs Watson says she then asked the judge if it was possible to address the defendant. Permission was granted, and she asked him, through his brief, if he would be so kind as to tell the court if he had any brothers or sisters. The defendant whispered to his brief who in turn advised the court that Ginger had one older sister and two younger brothers, none of whom had ever been in trouble with the police. Mrs Watson then announced to the court that she had a son of similar size to the defendant and she'd washed and ironed his shirts all of his life, and she could positively state that the Fred Perry shirt she held in her hands would never, in a million years, fit the defendant. She further suggested that it was one of his younger brother's shirts and that the original bloodstained shirt had either been washed or destroyed. The defence lawyer did lots of grunting and groaning. Mrs Watson invited the defendant to try on the shirt for the court. The defendant declined and was found guilty as charged, thanks to Mrs Watson's expert opinion.'

Both Kennedy and Irvine were entertained by Wood's digression. For his part, Kennedy was very impressed by Wood's talent for detailed recollection and was happy to follow his flow.

'Mrs Watson made friends very quickly,' Wood continued. 'She and Michelle Roche were always hanging around together. Mrs Watson always carried her black-and-white checked coat neatly folded over her arm, even while sitting – she never hung it up on a hook.

'After her we had Desmond Grant, the only Jamaican on the jury. He was always smiling. He'd lived in the UK for 30 of his 54 years. He had a large family and his children and grandchildren were absolutely his life. He was extremely anxious for the trial to end so that he could fly off to Jamaica for his Christmas vacation. One big point in his favour though, was when we were assessing the evidence in the jury room he'd always go to great pains to slow people down, to make sure he understood the point they were trying to make.

'Next at the table we had our cartoonist, Maurice Stidwood – yes, another Maurice, but this one was always doing cartoons of people. He did a brilliant one of Mai Chada, the defence lawyer. Stidwood was solidly built, but not what I would describe as fat. He always looked like he was going to break into a smile but it never actually rose to the surface. He was concerned about ideals and principles and seemed to have a bee in his bonnet about protecting the underdogs. He formed an unlikely holy trinity with Mrs Watson and Miss Roche.

'How many is that?' Wood asked, opening his eyes for the first time since he started.

'Ten,' Irvine replied immediately.

'Oh, I thought it was only nine,' Wood announced somewhat puzzled.

'Of course I'm counting you in with that total, sir,' Irvine offered.

'Right,' Wood smiled, 'of course, and I make it up to ten, which leaves only Cock and Wilson Murray.

'Leonard – Lenny – Coburn. He'd always say: "Never call me Cock, cock. It's always Co." He was very fat and, with him, fat was an issue or "a tissue" as he would say. He'd more bleeding catch phrases than Bruce Forsyth. "Super-duper" was another one. To his credit, not to mention the advantage of his health, he was a non-smoker. While he was sitting he had this very annoying habit of moving his stomach around this way and that to find a more comfortable position. He'd catch his tummy here and here…' Wood demonstrated by putting a hand on each side of his non-existent stomach and then pretending to move it, first to the right and then to the left, in demonstration.

'And finally, we had, sitting immediately on my right-hand side, Mr Wilson Murray. Very easy for me to remember him because the Beach Boys are one of my favourite groups,' Wood began. 'No doubt you recall that the father of Beach Boys' members Brian and Carl Wilson was called Murray. So Wilson Murray is Murray Wilson reversed, see?'

Irvine and Kennedy saw.

Wood continued: 'Wilson Murray was a lot like you'd imagine Murray Wilson to be, in fact. He dressed very '50s, in old-fashioned glasses, a cardigan, slacks and a shirt. Unlike Murray though, I doubt Wilson ever made the mistake of selling all his son's songs right from under his nose for a few hundred thousand dollars to a company that has since come to be worth in the region of 100 million dollars. But don't get me started on any of that Beach Boys stuff or we'll be here all night.'

Irvine sighed discreetly with relief.

'Anyway,' Wood continued, 'that brings me very neatly back to myself as the final jury member at the table. And I've got to say, I enjoyed it all very much. Even just walking around the courts when I was out of session. You'd pass the different briefs and if you got a chance to eavesdrop – as I often did – you'd hear them talk just like jockeys. You'd hear things like: 'I'm on a winner with the James versus James. I'd have to be a Rumpole to lose it,' or: 'Mine's a total donkey – I'll be well beaten in the first few furlongs.'

'Oh yeah, another thing that I learnt is the reason they wear those heavy wigs in the courts. Turns out they'd die of frostbite if they didn't.

'Sometimes during the Lloyd trial, you know, I felt like I was watching a movie. And you know in a movie when you sympathise with a character, you don't want to see any harm come to them, so you become very protective of them – on the other side of the screen, I mean. In this instance I'm talking about the victim, Miss Eve Adams. Whenever she came on-screen in the dock, I wouldn't want the defence lawyer to catch her out. But I knew it was wrong, so I tried to take my feelings out of it and just listen to the evidence.

'The trouble is that you're hit with so many feelings as a jury member. There was something strange about it. I'm not sure I can explain it properly but there was something about it that made me feel guilty. When people look at you on the jury benches – the way they look at you, that is – it seems to be almost the same way that they look at the people in the dock.

'Then there's the much lighter side, where you see female jury members – girls who, on their first day of jury service, arrive dressed very casually in jeans or whatever and without make-up, who then realise there may be some eligible men also doing jury service, so on the second day they arrive fully made-up and wearing figure-hugging clothes, ready for some action. I mean, on our jury, Sean and Mary seemed to be hitting it off and perhaps if they had met in different circumstances, i.e. they weren't both already dating other people, well then, something might just have happened. For my own part, there was this absolutely gorgeous woman I really fancied from a distance but I never even got to know her name because we were serving on different cases.

'Anyway, enough of that, back to the Lloyd case. We were in the jury room going though the evidence and about halfway through, Michelle Roche announces that she thinks Lloyd is innocent. I mean, I think most of us already suspected that she might be of this opinion. I don't really know why she felt so strongly this way from early on and I might be oversimplifying things by saying that perhaps her bad leg made her sympathise with the underdog. She'd made it so clear during the trial which side she was on. At one point, Lloyd was getting a severe tongue-lashing from the prosecution lawyer, and right in the middle of it Michelle Roche went and asked the judge if she could go to the toilet! I mean, I was completely flabbergasted. I don't know where she learnt that trick from. I never even saw anything like that on television. Obviously Hutchinson lost her momentum. I thought that was a deciding moment in the case.

'So, when Michelle Roche announced, during our evidence assessment, that she thought Lloyd was innocent, it was like she was sabotaging the proceedings again. I was livid, but I decided to just bite my tongue. I tried to understand what I was feeling. Was I feeling livid because I thought Lloyd was guilty and Michelle Roche was spoiling my party? If that was the case, then I was guilty of being as biased and bigoted as I thought she was, and we were both equally intent on achieving our preconceived outcome.

'I told her that we should wait until we'd reviewed all the evidence. She said that there was no need to waste more time. She said that the prosecution had not proved their case that Lloyd had raped Miss Adams beyond all reasonable doubt. I said that's what we were there to discuss. She said no, the fact that we had to discuss it meant that there was a reasonable doubt, and if there hadn't been reasonable doubt then we'd all have walked into the jury room and said, "Right, that's it, he's guilty!" She said that we didn't and the reason we didn't was because there was some doubt about his guilt, and that same doubt was the reasonable doubt the judge had been referring to.

'I said that the judge, in his two-hour summing-up of the case, had also stated: "When someone lies, you have to believe that they lie to hide either the truth or their guilt; for what else is the benefit of lying?"

'At that point in our jury-room discussion, Maurice Stidwood stopped doodling and said: "Hutchinson, the prosecution lawyer, also made a very telling statement in her summing-up. She started to say something like: 'The truth lies', and then she paused for a split second before continuing, 'in the fact that Christopher Lloyd did something to Miss Adams that he should not have done,' or words to that effect. But she paused in the wrong place and what she inadvertently appeared to say was: 'The truth lies.'" Maurice was grinning from ear to ear at this point and he continued: "I think she may have hit upon something important there. I for one thought there were so many lies floating around that none of us were ever going to be able to establish where the real truth lay."'

Wood paused here. He looked like he was either trying to remember something or else was dwelling on the "the truth lies" phrase. He shook his head from side to side and continued.

'And you know, to some degree he was right. We know Lloyd lied. But the prosecution also dealt in lies. At one point, Margaret Hutchinson said to the German, Lloyd's next-door stall owner: "Didn't you also break an appointment to come down to the police station to make a statement?" And he replied: "No, I was never asked to come down." Hutchinson didn't pursue the matter so we had to assume that the German was telling the truth. Now from the jury's point of view, the German seemed to be the only one standing up for Lloyd, but Hutchinson managed to throw doubt on him – just a little, granted – as to why he might break an appointment to come down to the police station. Why would she ask that question? Why would she be allowed, in a court of law, to make an implication that was so obviously groundless? Were we meant to think: "Agh, there's something going on here but she's not allowed to go after it. Why would he not go down to a police station? Possibly he's a criminal. If he's a criminal then surely he's going to stick up for another criminal?" And all this stuff is going around in your head because she threw a curve-ball in her questioning.'

Again Wood stopped talking.

'Are you okay, sir?' Kennedy asked after a second.

'Yes, yes sorry, I was just trying to recall the exact sequence of events,' Wood replied, shifting in his seat and taking a sip from his mineral water. 'Sorry, I'm taking forever on this, aren't I?'

'No, no, not at all, sir,' Kennedy replied immediately. 'This is all invaluable to us – it's the closest we're going to come to finding out exactly what happened at the trial. Please continue, in your own time.'

'Thank you. Let's see. Oh yes, that's it. I tried to get my fellow jurors to continue to review the evidence. We discussed the defence next. Mai Chada was useless, absolutely useless, and then some of her expert witnesses were so keen to back their own side that they were prepared to give expert information outside their area of expertise. The forensic woman, for instance, said that Miss Adams wore her trousers too tight to be provocative. Apparently this was shown by the lines along the front of them, just at the top of the legs. Mrs Hutchinson then proceeded to demonstrate that the majority of those present in the court wearing trousers had similar lines. People simply sitting down and rising again, she explained, formed the lines. She asked the forensic woman whether she found people sitting down and standing up again provocative. That raised a few chuckles around the court.

'I have to say I liked Mrs Margaret Hutchinson, the prosecution lawyer. She was blonde and confident, but not cocky. It was as if she had seen a character similar to herself on television that she liked, and this fact had given her confidence. She was confident in her case. Perhaps she was confident because she had recently been married.'

'How could you tell that?' Irvine asked.

'It was just something about how she looked – all new and fresh-faced,' Wood replied.

The detectives left that particular line of questioning and nodded to Wood to continue.

'Yes. She came across as confident, but not cocky. Mai Chada, on the other hand, was always saying, "Forgive me, Your Honour," or, "I stand corrected, Your Honour." That sort of thing. She always seemed to be out of her depth. She was forever pulling her cloak back up onto her shoulders and asking her brief for advice.

'Eve Adams, although obviously money-motivated, always came across as believable, even though she seemed to have been somewhat coached in advance. She was in a separate room, which we had a video link to – all part of the new approach on rape trials to help the younger victims feel less intimidated, more comfortable. She seemed to have been much happier with her friend and her friend's mum – the Duncans – than she was with her own mum. Her friend, Madonna Duncan – now there's an easy name to remember – came across as very bubbly and honest. Madonna's mother liked to give off an air that she was nobody's fool but when everything was over, I thought that perhaps she was. I got the feeling that, although she might not necessarily have been lying, she wasn't exactly telling all of the truth either.

'Eve's mum – I forget her name just now, possibly because I, and the rest of the court, immediately felt sorry for her...'

'Mrs Angelina Adams,' Irvine offered helpfully.

'Yes, that's it. I'd say that she was definitely a medication casualty. She was fidgeting when it suited her to have a distraction to fidget and she looked in really bad shape. She was possibly even too far gone to be worried or concerned about her daughter's well-being.'

'What about the suspect?' Kennedy asked. 'What was he like?'

'Well,' Paul Wood said quietly, 'he was at least guilty of being involved in some kind of a relationship with a girl who was under-age. His demeanour and language didn't really give much away. His police statement seemed out of sorts with the vibe he was giving off in the courtroom.'

'Did he act like he was guilty?' Irvine asked.

Wood smiled. 'I wouldn't know. To me, I suppose he did look guilty. Mind you, I feel guilty every time I walk through customs in a foreign airport, so I must look guilty, and I'd never even try and get away with a penny chew. I don't know why but I just always feel guilty. So if I were sitting in the dock instead of Chris Lloyd, would I look and feel guilty? I don't know.

'But why did I feel that he was guilty? More because of the evidence than his demeanour, I'd have to say. There were several things that just didn't seem quite right with the case. The defence lawyer claimed that Eve Adams watched porn videos. Eve denied this but Madonna Duncan seemed to confirm that Eve watched them. Chada further claimed that Eve had a friend who had been raped. I think she was implying that that's where Eve got the idea, but Eve denied having any such friend. Once again, Madonna contradicted her friend and in her statement said that Eve did have a friend who was once raped. Why did Eve lie in both these instances? Was her only sin that she thought people would think poorly of her if they knew she watched porn videos? Or was she using these lies to hide something more?

'These were a couple of the points Michelle Roche picked up on and she was like a dog with a bone over them. In a way I'm not sure she understood the subtleties of the points she was trying to make herself. She seemed to know instinctively that there was something amiss but she would argue her case badly, often trying to connect unrelated points. This only seemed to confuse several members of the jury.

'Sean, with his homespun logic, immediately picked up on what the essence of the case was. He thought that Chris was guilty but he, like several of us, was confused by the fact that the police had failed to charge Lloyd with having sex with a minor. Mary thought it might be due to the fact that the police were so confident about their case and their ability to prove it that they wanted to go for the greater sentence carried by the rape charge than the underage sex charge. Underage sex, she said, implied a degree of consent, whereas rape suggested a definite violation. That made sense to most of us.

'At the first count we stood seven to five, guilty to innocent. That was Sean, Mary, Andrew, Susan, Lenny, Maurice Morrison and myself going with guilty; and Michelle Roche, Mrs Watson, Desmond, Maurice the cartoonist and Wilson Murray going with innocent. I was taken aback by that. Totally shocked, in fact.

I'd figured we'd be ten guilty to two innocent, with Michelle and Mrs Watson voting innocent.

'I said I wanted us to go around the table again, and this time I wanted everyone to say what they thought and why they thought it because up to that point, everyone on the jury had been giving off a very friendly feeling. No one, apart from Michelle, had been prepared to speak out against the idea that Christopher Lloyd was guilty. On this round, most people seemed happy to have a platform and to have their say. Although having said that, some people, like Andrew Sainsbury and Susan Golding, were incredibly shy and hardly said anything when their turn came.

'As jury foreman, I spoke last and made again what I thought was the important point, about him changing his evidence. I quoted the part of the arresting caution, you know the bit: "…and if you don't say something that you may try to use later in evidence". You know the one?'

Irvine gave the exact quote.

'Yes, that's it, that's the one. Well, I told the jury that I hadn't originally understood it properly and I still wasn't clear about it when the authorities revised the original caution several years ago. But now it was clear to me that anything that is relevant is relevant right from the start, so why not declare all the facts that will prove your innocence from the word go? It kind of reminded me, in a small way, of that Plato quote: "When people speak ill of you, live your life so that no one will believe them."

'But that clearly wasn't the case with Chris Lloyd,' Wood sighed, 'was it? I tried to show that on three separate occasions the police produced evidence to show his guilt. On each occasion he dramatically changed his story to protest his innocence. In the first instance, when he was accused of the rape, he replied: "Of course I didn't rape her. She probably only said that because I wouldn't give her a job." Then, when the police proved that someone had been physical with her, he claimed it wasn't him. He admitted that they were boyfriend and girlfriend but that they'd only kissed; he claimed that she was making up the story of the rape because he was going to break it off with her. Next, when the police had DNA proof of Lloyd on her undergarments, he claimed that they'd only ever messed around – "only touched each other" – that there had never been penetration, and that she'd claimed rape because he wouldn't take her to Denmark, he wouldn't buy her a mobile phone and he wouldn't give her money.

'I really thought I'd managed to make it clear to Michelle Roche that there was a period of eight weeks between his first and last stories. I tried to get it through to her that he only changed his tune and admitted that they'd messed around when the police managed to produce DNA proof of his semen on her garments.

'She got the point that he'd been in custody for several months by the time the trial came up, only, instead of reading into it that the police must have been pretty convinced of his guilt to remand him, she said how unfair it was for him to have been locked up all this time without anything concrete having been proved against him.

'Then we reviewed the evidence of the prosecution witness, Dr Susanne Reiger, who everyone agreed was confident, likeable and, consequently, believable. The doctor was German and used her hands a lot to make her points. She made her points well. At least I thought so, but Michelle would only concede: "Of course she made her points well; the prosecution are hardly going to use her if she was going to make her points badly."

'Michelle made a very passionate speech about how Lloyd was a victim of circumstance. He was black, he was poor, he had a wife and two kids. He probably wasn't having much fun at home, so he was distracted by Eve Adams's adolescent attentions. Yes, Michelle Roche argued, Chris should have chosen to have nothing to do with Miss Adams; he should have told her to get lost. He shouldn't have messed around with her, but he did and that was as much as he was guilty of. "He's a man, for heaven's sake," were her actual words. "What do you expect? But no one has proven to me that he raped Eve Adams."

'When it came to the next vote, for some reason the guilty side had gained two votes: Wilson and Maurice the cartoonist. Then we went around the houses a few more times until it was back to seven guilty to five innocent again. I was starting to get the feeling that some of the members of the jury didn't want to get involved in a stalemate. They wanted to get away from it all. The trial had been going on for long enough for them. You see at this point, for some of us, it was the second trial and this one had been dragged out for a quite some time. There always seemed to have been some point of law to be argued over in the jury's absence or the judge had to attend to some sentencing issues from his previous trial. Then, one day, we were allowed out so that we could see the Queen opening Parliament. I suppose someone wanted to remind us whose name we were working in. On another occasion we'd have to sit around and wait for two and a half hours because the security van transporting Lloyd from his prison was delayed in traffic.

'Anyway, for whatever the reason, one by one we lost our guilty support until it was down to ten innocent to two guilty, and that was myself and Maurice – not the cartoonist, the other one. Then it was eleven to one and I had to give up. I still registered my guilty vote for the sake of my conscience, and we returned to the courtroom to give our verdict.

'They say that, if the jurors refuse to look whoever's in the dock in the eye when they come back into the courtroom, it's a guilty verdict. If that's the case, then we certainly put the defence lawyer through a few last-minute heart palpitations. As far as I could see, no one except Michelle Roche and Mrs Watson looked at Christopher Lloyd as we returned to the court.

'The judge was totally gobsmacked when I gave the verdict of the jury. Lloyd showed no emotion whatsoever on hearing the verdict. Mai Chada smiled at us all in sheer, unadulterated joy. I got the impression that she had to restrain herself from jumping up and punching the air. Margaret Hutchinson looked at us with such utter contempt in her eyes that I felt about two inches tall.

'Anyway, that was our duty done, verdict delivered, and all of us, except Susan and Lenny, went around the corner for a last-minute drink. A few of us made promises to meet up and keep in touch but that was the last I heard from any of them, and then I read that Christopher Lloyd had been found dead. What happened to him?'

'That's exactly what we're working on at the minute,' Kennedy replied, as Irvine started to pack away their notes. 'Was there anyone on the jury who seemed totally incensed that Lloyd got off the rape charge and walked scott-free?'

'No, we all just kind of fizzled out. We all had our say during recess, and no one seemed to want to join me in another round of discussing the evidence.

'Now the judge, though, he was a different matter altogether. If looks could kill he'd have vaporised the entire jury in the split second after I'd announced the words: "Not guilty."'

Chapter Nineteen

'SO WHAT DID we learn there, sir?' Irvine asked, if only to shorten the journey back to Camden Town.

'Good question, James,' said Kennedy, slouching back into his seat and turning the volume of the radio down. 'What exactly did we learn?'

'Well, we learnt that Mr Lloyd was a very lucky man to walk away from the rape charge.'

'What else?' Kennedy pushed.

'Well, I suppose we had it confirmed, as if we needed it confirming, that justice isn't always carried out in our courts.'

'And what else?'

'Oh, that a single juror can pervert the course of justice,' Irvine replied, visibly starting to struggle.

'And?' Kennedy kept on pushing.

'That maybe Eve Adams did have something to hide?'

'No, no, much simpler than that, James, there's something else. Come on, what else did we learn?'

'Well, we learnt...' Irvine started on another fishing expedition.

Kennedy playfully ran out of patience. 'The only true fact we learnt was that a Formula One car takes one minute and twenty-six seconds to complete one lap – which is approximately three-point-two miles – of the Silverstone Racetrack. That is the one and only fact that we learnt on our trip. Now we have to take that piece of information and put it to use.'

'I don't follow, sir.'

'Well,' Kennedy smiled, 'by learning that it takes a Formula One car one minute and twenty-six seconds to travel around Silverstone Racetrack, we learnt that if we were in such a car now it would take us about 15 minutes to drive back to Camden Town instead of the 90 minutes it's going to take us in this heap of junk.'

Irvine smiled but didn't laugh.

'Seriously though, James, we've learnt that Michelle Roche is a very persuasive woman. Perhaps we should check to see if she had any connection with Lloyd. We're definitely going to need to talk to her.'

'You're not suggesting, sir, that she was planted on the jury to persuade the rest of the jury to find him not guilty?'

'That could be a distinct possibility, James.'

'How on earth would she ever have been able to plant herself on a jury?'

'Well, all you would need to do would be to hijack someone who's turning up for jury service and persuade them to give you their case.'

'It's that easy, sir?'

'Well apparently, the majority of people like to avoid jury service as much as I like to avoid the music of Michael Bolton, so I couldn't imagine they would need too much persuasion. The only problem would be if you approached a conscientious juror who then went and reported you to the authorities. I suppose the other flaw in this theory is that, say you wanted to get on a jury and you were successful in convincing someone to let you stand in for them, there still would be no guarantee that you would be called to serve on the jury of the particular case you have a vested interest in.'

'So, for this theory to work, you'd need to replace several of the people turning up for jury service?' Irvine said sounding very unconvinced.

'Yes indeed, and even if it was technically possible to stage-manage such an event, I'm not sure that Lloyd would have the resources to carry it off. No, I think it would need the clout and money of someone much further up the criminal ladder. Apart from which, this justice system of our has had centuries to get its act together so I'm sure they'll have worked out all the little loopholes by now.'

'Which you knew all along, sir?'

'Yes,' Kennedy grinned, 'but sometimes it's interesting to fly these theories up the flagpole just to get a good look at them.'

They drove on in silence for a few minutes.

Kennedy went to turn the radio on again but just before he did he said: 'I suppose the other thing we've learnt in all of this is that there seems to be some sort of poetic justice on the streets around us, James.'

'Like?'

'Well, like Lloyd managing to get away with his crime in the courts but outside the courtroom, people weren't so forgiving.'

'So you think that's what this is all about, sir, vengeance?'

'It must be a distinct possibility.'

'But not the only possibility you mean, sir?'

'Exactly,' Kennedy replied, then turned on the radio. 'Let's cheer ourselves up and hear just how bad the traffic is going to be around Hanger Lane, shall we?'

Surprisingly, the traffic wasn't as bad as either of them had anticipated and they arrived back in Camden just before 7.30 pm. As they pulled up outside Kennedy's house in Rothwell Street, Irvine said: 'You've got a visitor, sir.'

'Sorry?' Kennedy replied as he undid his seat belt and looked all around him. He spied ann rea's maroon saloon parked directly opposite his house. 'Oh, yes,' the detective continued, with perhaps too noticeable a sigh.

'Do you want me to come in with you, sir?' Irvine offered helpfully.

'No. Thanks all the same, James,' Kennedy replied as he opened his car door. 'I think being seen going into my house with a beautiful young lady is going to do my reputation much more good than going into my house with a bachelor, no matter how eligible he may be!'

Chapter Twenty

'HI!' KENNEDY MOUTHED the word through ann rea's windscreen.

ann rea was looking as stunning as ever, in blue denim jeans with a Beatles-bob haircut acting as an effective hood to her battle-worn black duffel coat.

It seemed to Kennedy that she'd been miles away, daydreaming. She snapped back into reality and offered Kennedy one of her all-encompassing and sincere smiles.

Kennedy thought it was funny the way people smile when they meet you, even though in the majority of cases they didn't really mean it. When you meet someone on the street, both of you will unconsciously offer each other at least some attempt at a smile. Or if you're introduced to someone at a party, the first thing both of you will do is break into some kind of awkward grin. Most times it's not like it's even an attractive face that we pull. Heck, even criminals caught in the act of a crime will involuntarily break into a foolish grin to greet their captors. Shouldn't our smiles, particularly our warmest smiles, be used for when we greet friends or members of our family?

Kennedy felt he qualified for a warmer smile from ann rea. He'd known her for just over five years now and they'd been as close as it was possible for two humans to be, physically and mentally speaking. But maybe that was it, he thought. Maybe that was what had happened to ann rea and himself – and to all other couples who thought they'd made a perfect match and been proven wrong – they discovered that they didn't really have the connection they thought. A couple come together and they grow to be so close that they feel the next step has to be a colossal one. Something as radical as becoming part of one another. Then when they don't, they feel let down and disappointed with each other. We all want so much from our lives, thought Kennedy, we need to feel there's something superhuman in this world. We're surrounded by so much mediocrity that, when love doesn't take us on a fast-track to perfection and bliss, we start to look at our partner and wonder why. We try to find a reason why they, or we, if we're being very truthful, didn't manage to make the leap across the great divide.

Maybe the reality of our lives was similar to a concert given by the Three Tenors, thought Kennedy. Not that he was an expert or anything, but he had watched an entire televised concert to see if he could work out what all the fuss was about. He was unsuccessful in his endeavours. But, during the ninety-minute performance, the artists did reach four mind-blowing highs where the power, blend and versatility of their voices managed to lift the roof off both their concert venue and Kennedy's home. In the hour and a half they were on stage, they managed to create four pieces of sheer, unadulterated magic. Now, Kennedy thought, you might be forgiven for wondering, if they were able to reach these four peaks during each performance (and he had to assume they were), why they didn't do it all the time, for heaven's sake. Would that be too much for a human to take? In fact, was that it? Was it impossible for humans to enjoy too much bliss, so the three generously proportioned men on the platform didn't even bother to try?

Kennedy wondered whether he and ann rea should have taken a lesson from the three sweet-singing, wise men, and not continued to look for an undiscovered paradise across the road. Should they have been happy to settle for the three or four pieces of perfection they had enjoyed in their relationship? He didn't know.

He didn't even know why they had split up in the first, second, not to mention the third place either. Yes, he had his theories. Perhaps ann rea had never really recovered from the disappointment of losing her previous boyfriend. Maybe it was that Kennedy didn't have the experience to deal with the relationship properly. It could have been all or any of a host of equally silly reasons that were to blame. But it shouldn't have mattered. Nothing should have mattered: they'd met and that should have been enough. They'd connected physically, mentally and emotionally. Surely that was enough? But it hadn't been and they had split. And what they were left with was what Kennedy was grappling with the night ann rea parked her car outside his house.

In the weeks during which he tried to come to terms with the death of their relationship, Kennedy had been haunted by thoughts like these. And when he saw her sitting there in her souped-up maroon Ford Popular – she was always saying that the only thing it couldn't pass was a petrol station – they flashed again through his mind. He arrived at the same conclusion as ever: their relationship had died and all that was left for them to do now was to mourn it.

Mind you, ann rea wasn't really helping him in this process. She could have done him a favour and dressed in sackcloth and ashes. That wouldn't have been too much to ask of her, would it? Dream on, he thought, as ann rea finally exited her car. She scrubbed up well, did ann rea.

'Look, I hope you don't mind,' ann rea said as she locked her car door.

She must want to come into the house, Kennedy thought, noting the exaggerated car-locking procedure.

'No, no, not at all,' Kennedy replied sincerely. 'It's great to see you. Let's get out of the cold.'

She stood on his doorstep looking slightly apprehensive as Kennedy opened the blue door to his house, the warmth from inside flushing their cheeks.

'I hate doing this,' she started to say once they were in his kitchen. 'I hate just turning up on your doorstep like this.'

'No, honestly it's fine, it's great to see you again. We didn't really get a chance to speak earlier today,' Kennedy replied.

'If I saw someone else behaving like this, I'd say: "Oh for heaven's sake, get a grip, girl,"' she said, definitely forcing a smile this time.

Kennedy contemplated this further use for a smile, to sell something we thought was feeble. He didn't say anything, but mimed drinking a cup of tea.

'I brought wine,' ann rea said, grateful for the distraction searching around in her bag provided. She produced a bottle of Sancerre.

'It's funny, when you're a couple,' ann rea started as Kennedy helped her off with her duffel coat. 'When we were a couple, we'd just talk, we wouldn't worry about leaving a silence hanging in the air. But now, and earlier today on Parkway, I'm conscious of trying to find things to say to fill the gaps. It's frightening really, how quickly we change – how we're all in such a hurry to change our cloak.'

Kennedy hung her duffel coat on the back of the kitchen door. When he turned around and looked at her she took his breath away. It looked like her blue jeans had been painted on; painted on perfectly over her perfect bum and perfect legs. As ever, ann rea wore the minimum of make-up; just enough to highlight her classic features. Kennedy wondered if it had been the oriental look to her eyelids that had attracted him to her in the first place when he spotted her in the bookstore in Terminal One at Heathrow Airport.

'Gosh, it is warm in here,' ann rea declared as she removed a red, hooded sweatshirt to reveal a skintight white T-shirt that left nothing – least of all her magnificent, full breasts – to the imagination. 'That's one of the things I love about you, Kennedy, you never try and hide your jaw when it hits the floor. You never try to conceal your admiration or your lust.'

'Oh both, believe me, definitely both,' Kennedy replied, averting his telltale gaze to find a corkscrew for the wine. 'Have you eaten yet?'

'No. How's about we order an Indian takeaway and just have a quiet night in with a bottle of wine?'

'Sounds like an idea to me,' Kennedy agreed.

'You see, there's another of your qualities. You're always totally prepared to go with the flow. None of this: "And why are you around here tonight?" or: "We've been through all of this before. Blah, blah, blah."'

'Oh,' Kennedy searched in vain to find words to fend off the compliment.

'Neither are you the kind of man who'll say, or even think: "Oh, here she is, back again."'

'I'd never...' Kennedy protested.

'I know, I know, Christy,' she cut him off immediately. 'It's just that you're so... you're so... I want to say "nice" but even that implies a kind of insult. Oh, blast! Let's just have a glass of wine.'

'Yes, let's,' said Kennedy filling the pause awkwardly.

'Let's!' she agreed.

So they each had their glass of wine. Kennedy ordered some food and put on a CD – The Travelling Wilburys volume 1 – a classic, and the perfect soundtrack for the atmosphere between them.

'You're comfortable now about us being over, aren't you?' she said at the end of 'Handle With Care.'

'Yes, I am actually. I've accepted it totally. I was just thinking earlier that, now I'm mourning the end of our relationship, I guess that means I – I mean we – accept that it's over.'

'Me too. But I still find myself sitting at home and thinking about you – about us.'

Kennedy shot her a 'Where's this going?' look.

'No, no, hear me out, please,' she continued, taking a large gulp of the deliciously crisp, cold wine – her bag had certainly acted as an effective cooler. 'When I saw you yesterday in the graveyard and earlier today on Parkway, I wanted to be your friend. I wanted us to act as friends not as estranged lovers. I don't mean that as a compromise – as in, if we can't be lovers let's at least be friends. I have an overwhelming feeling that I want to be your friend, I want us to be best friends. I want us to be able to meet when we want to as mates and not pussyfoot around wondering if it's too early, if we're over each other. I've never liked anyone the way I like you, Kennedy, and by being your lover I got to see and be with a part of you I don't imagine anyone else has ever seen. It's been so special a thing, you're so special a person, and I need to know you and have you as a friend. I will not let you disappear out of my life.'

'I'll drink to that, ann rea,' Kennedy said, slightly shell-shocked.

'When we met earlier today and we were distant with each other, it nearly broke my heart,' ann rea continued emotionally, her voice very close to cracking. 'It might have had something to do with losing and burying Daniel Elliot. He and Lila, his wife, were just so good to me when I first moved to London. They'd had such a hard life, and then, just when you thought it was time for them to enjoy a respite from all their hardships, it got even worse; Lila died and their daughter, Bella, got caught up in the Fountain Of Sorrow murders. It all seemed so unfair to me. Not what he had planned for the end of his life, when he was scrimping and saving his way through it.'

'There's no logic to it all, ann rea. You can't get bogged down in such thoughts and try to second guess why luck falls all around us just as it does. We make plans and God laughs, isn't that what they say?' Kennedy said, using the phase for the second time in a day.

'I know, I know,' ann rea replied and stopped to listen to the music for a time. 'God, another great song. I really love this album.'

Kennedy's doorbell rang five simple notes, cutting through the music. Their food had arrived. A few minutes later they were sitting down to their feast.

Following their onion bhajis, ann rea proclaimed: 'Goodness, I didn't realise just how much I needed that.'

She let Kennedy serve their next course: chicken tikka masala for her and chicken korma for him, plus Bombay aloo, plain dhal, plain rice and a Peshwari nan to share. Just as he was splitting the nan, she said: 'You know, I'd like us to be comfortable enough to discuss each other's new boyfriends and girlfriends.'

A few bites later, ann rea was the one to speak again.

'You see, you're most definitely over us.'

'Why do you say that?' Kennedy asked soaking up the remainder of the delicious korma sauce with the last piece of the nan.

'Well, the obvious thing for you to have said would have been: "What, does that mean you have a new boyfriend?"'

Kennedy merely smiled; he too knew he was definitely over them but he still couldn't help wondering if she did have a new boyfriend.

'Mmmm,' ann rea appeared to realise that she wasn't going to draw anything out of him. 'Does this mean that you have got a new girlfriend?'

'No!' Kennedy replied, but immediately found a vision of Anne Coles flash through his mind. How strange was that? he thought.

But ann rea was right, they were over and it was time to move on.

After their second bottle of wine – and long after the food was finished – they were listening to their third album of the evening, Nick Lowe's beautiful and perfectly written The Convincer, and she hit him with a statement that was barely audible.

'I think we still have something we need to resolve, Kennedy.'

Kennedy flashed through their recent conversation about the Lloyd case, about Dr Ranjesus, about Bella Forsythe, about Bella Forsythe and James Irvine, about music, about George Harrison and about Esther Bluewood – the second album they played had been Bluewood's Axis, a personal favourite of ann rea's – and he wondered what exactly it was that they still had to resolve.

'The last time we made love,' ann rea began, the slightest hint of coyness creeping into her voice, 'I didn't think it was our last time, if you know what I mean.'

'Sorry?' Kennedy asked, amused and puzzled.

'Well, when we were making love, I didn't think: "This is the last time we'll ever make love." Did you?'

'No, I didn't.'

'When we were making love for the first time, did you think: "This is the first time we've made love," or did you think: "At last!"?'

'I will admit to having had both of those thoughts.'

'Well, I've been thinking, Christy, that in order for us to put our relationship to an end, we have to put it to bed, so to speak, just so that we can accept that it's finally over.'

'The things I have to do for my best friends,' Kennedy said as he drained the remains of his wineglass, took her hand and let her lead him to his bedroom on the top floor for the last time.

The last time for Christy Kennedy and ann rea was like one of those incredible occasions when Pavarotti hits that thunderous soaring note. They both melted back into the sheets, damp with the sweat of their recent energies, and applauded the butterfly's final encore.

Chapter Twenty-One

WHEN KENNEDY AWOKE the following morning, his new best friend had already left. He remained under the piping-hot, furious shower for an extra five minutes to dissolve the last of the alcohol from his bloodstream. As he walked over Primrose Hill he had to admit that he felt great. He didn't know whether that was because the final exorcising of his lover had been successful, or because it was a Saturday morning and the Hill was empty. He didn't really care; perhaps that showed just how successful ann rea had been with their one final piece of business.

He skipped up the steps of North Bridge House and reviewed his notes until Irvine arrived forty-five minutes later, at 08.13.

'I'd like to meet up with the judge today please, James, as soon as possible. Could you fix it up, please?'

DS James Irvine dutifully went off to do just that as Kennedy took out the statement Eve Adams' eldest sister, Janice, had made to WDC Coles and PC Allaway.

Reading between the lines – and there were certainly lots of spaces between them to read – Kennedy decided that Janice must be deeply upset about something or other. He couldn't quite work out if it was with her father and mother not protecting Eve or with Christopher Lloyd for taking advantage of her youngest sister.

One thing you could often glean from a person's statement was their demeanour and the attitude. When Janice Adams ran out of the house on Kennedy and WDC Lowe's first visit, she looked fit to kill. She was throwing all the shapes to show that she had attitude, and more to spare.

Lowe had mentioned to Kennedy that Janice didn't really fit into the Adams household – giving off a bit of a superior air or something.

'I just get so incensed when I go around there again, it makes my blood boil,' Janice Adams had stated to Coles for the record.

The interview had continued:

WDC Coles: You don't live there any more, then?

Janice Adams (JA): Yes I do, but it's my official residence, so to speak. I'm living with my boyfriend just now, but his wife gets suspicious, so he tells her he's crashing at a friend's pad. I mean, of course it's his flat – he does very well, you know – but if his wife even dreamt that he'd bought a flat of his own she'd go absolutely spare. She'd want to get her greedy mitts on it. If she knew I was living with him, oh God, would feathers fly or what! World War Three, I bet you.

WDC: Why do you still get angry when you go home, then?

JA: Well, I suppose it could be a form of release, do you know what I'm saying? There but for the grace of God go I. But it's a disaster at my Mum's house, an accident waiting to happen. I mean, my Mum, she's constantly out of it and Eve's not the brightest spark. I mean, that's unfair, but it's like she's still ten years old, though a very clever ten-year-old. She had some illness when she was young and it left her a bit – she missed a lot of school…so… well, she hasn't been able to develop, intellectually speaking. I hate to admit this to you but I did request that the authorities took her into care and they ignored me. I thought that, with the right treatment and attention, they could help her, help her cope, maybe even help her catch up. I knew something bad was going to happen but I never dreamt it would turn out to be as bad as this. Do you know what? She's scarred for life now; she'll never be able to enjoy a natural relationship with a man again in her life. I mean, I can say that and it might sound flippant, but it's the truth and it's devastating because none of them at my Mum's house realise it. I go around there and my Mum's always out of it, as I say, only this time the police are there and I hear that someone's gone and topped Lloyd and brought even more trouble to the door. I saw the police there and I just couldn't take it. I felt that Lloyd had already stuffed us once in life and now he was doing it again, this time from the grave.'

WDC: Did something happen to your mum?

JA: The '60s happened to my Mum.

WDC: Sorry?

JA: She was a bleeding hippy. She took absolutely everything that there was to take; "from Harpic to heroin," she claimed. When I was born her nervous system was shot to hell, but by the time she gave birth to Eve my Mum was like a complete zombie; a fully paid-up member of the walking dead. Every time my boyfriend tries to get me to do something – you know, I'm talking recreational drugs here of course – or take an extra drink I just force myself to have a quick think of my Mum and believe you me, it's the best deterrent you'll ever find.

WDC: What about your father?

JA: Next question please.

(Pause)

JA: To this day I don't know who my father is. I have suspicions. But I don't know for sure. The same applies to Eve's father. My Mum always had an open house for strays and they were dogs, one and all.

WDC: What about…?

JA: I know what you're thinking. I know you want to say: 'Well, why didn't you stay and look after them?'

WDC: Actually I…

JA: Well I did, and I did it for longer than I should've, until I began to see myself ten years down the line ending up the exact same as my Mum, with a life so miserable that you just take whatever tablets you can to avoid facing reality. And so the circle begins. Do you know what I'm saying? Then I met my boyfriend – he was married at the time. Actually, I was dating his mate, that's how we met – I know this is going to sound crass here and when you listen back to it on the tape, someone will probably think 'What a slapper' – but what I was going to say was that something just clicked between us immediately. He wouldn't do anything about it because he was married. In point of fact, he tried to make another go of it with his wife but their marriage had been falling to pieces before I came along so, needless to say, it didn't work.

They obviously married too young. He said that they should have just lived together and never bothered with marriage. Anyway, he split up with her and then he asked me out. At the same time I was offered a good job in Marks and Sparks – doing research for them on new food dishes – and I just thought, sod it, I owe it to myself to make something of my life. There's only so much energy you can waste trying to swim against the current to save somebody who obviously doesn't even want to be saved. So I just decided I was going to be totally selfish, that it was about time I saved myself, and so I took the lifeline of a new boyfriend and a new job.

WDC: I don't think that was being selfish…

JA: I don't need any compliments or nods of approval from you or your sort. I did what I did. I was telling you the facts, not justifying my actions.

WDC: Can you tell me a bit about your boyfriend? What does he do?

JA: Well, he's not a petrol-pump attendant, if that's what you're thinking.

WDC: Look, I'm not thinking anything here. I'm asking you questions because I hope that your answers will help us with our investigation, that's all I'm trying to do.

(Pause)

JA: He's smart, isn't he? He installs computer systems in big companies. He's a bit of a whiz kid really.

WDC: And his name?

JA: Robbie Stevens.

WDC: Does he know all about Eve and Chr…?

JA: Yes, yes, of course he does. We don't hide things from each other. What sort of relationship would that be? And he's not put off by my family, if that's what you're getting at.

WDC: Finally, could you tell me what you were doing on Monday night?

JA: I can, as it happens. Robbie and I were out at a party. John – that's Robbie's mate, the guy I dated first – was having a birthday bash and we went to it.

WDC: Would you know what time you were there from and to?

JA: Yes, of course. We arrived around eight o'clock and left around two-thirty the following morning. The party was still in full flow when we left. I would have stayed on longer as we were having great fun but Robbie had an important installation to do the next morning – sorry, the same morning in fact.

WDC: Thank you, that's all I need for now.

JA: What, that's me done?

WDC: Yes.

The statement noted that the interview had ended and the tape recorder was then turned off.

Kennedy wondered, as you do, whether the conversation between WDC Coles and Janice Adams had continued after the recorder was switched off and, if so, what had been said. There was an easy way of finding out, but Kennedy wondered why he seemed to be avoiding contact with WDC Anne Coles.

Chapter Twenty-Two

NO SOONER HAD Kennedy finished reading the report than Irvine stuck his head around the corner of the door and said: 'We're in luck, sir. Lord Justice Bailey is still in town and, even though it's the weekend, he says he'll see us right away. He's not too far away, he lives up on Avenue Road.'

'Luck, yes, I can live with a bit of that. I'll meet you in the car park in two minutes,' Kennedy said as he started to tidy up his paperwork and add a few notes to his Guinness is Good For You notice board.

At the top, central as usual, he had written the name of the victim – in this case, Christopher Lloyd. There was a photo of him underneath. Then Kennedy had written the names:

Eve Adams
Janice Adams
Mrs Angelina Adams
Brian Adams
Mrs Christine Duncan
Madonna Duncan
Dionne Duncan
Frankie Hammond
Manfred Hodges
Ivan Hodges
Greg Whitehead
Valerie Lloyd
Mabel Lloyd
Michelle Roche
Paul Wood
Margaret Hutchinson
Mai Chada

Daniel Elliot
Dr. Bella Forsythe
Phostek tablets
Graveyard.
SOCO?

Kennedy, on his office notice board, preferred to read only the large print of the names of the people involved in his case as opposed to the complete description in smaller lettering on each name card. The main theory behind this was that if he read the character details on the cards (for instance: 'Frankie Hammond, common-law husband of Christine Duncan etc. etc.') then he tended to glance over the cards rather than study them (for instance: 'Greg Whitehead, now what do we know about him? Oh yes, he was Lloyd's fair-weather friend'). Sometimes this form of concentration on the characters would produce something. This morning, however, it produced absolutely nothing but wasted brain cells. Now that surely was a question for his new best friend, ann rea.

The judge had omitted to give Irvine the exact address, offering only the following description: 'the large white house on the right-hand side of Avenue Road as you travel towards Swiss Cottage'. As Kennedy and Irvine pulled into the circular drive of the above residence, they were totally in awe. There was no other word to describe their feeling.

The lawns were perfectly kept. It was the middle of a particularly wet summer but there wasn't a blade of grass sloping the wrong way; just pure emerald-green for what seemed like acres. Obviously it wasn't acres but that effect had been created by not having lots of silly little bushes and plants dotted about the place. There was just a thick, high privet hedge around the perimeter of the land and the rest, apart from the driveway, was well-maintained lawn. The house was painted spotlessly white and was a three-story building with the flat front broken by an arc, which reminded Kennedy of the Underground sign.

Bailey's man, a real-life butler, dressed, as you would expect a traditional real-life butler would dress, in black and grey striped waistcoat, grey trousers and black, highly polished shoes, greeted them at their car door.

'Lord Justice Bailey is expecting you,' he announced in a refined accent. 'Would you be so kind as to park the car in the car park on the right-hand side of the house,' he instructed Irvine as he opened Kennedy's car door wider.

The car park was a three-berth affair, which was sheltered by a large oak tree whose branches seemed precariously close to the side of the house. Irvine did as he was bid and joined Kennedy and Bailey's man on the front steps.

As they stepped through the front door of the house it was as though they were leaving present-day London and stepping back in time to the mid 1800s. The entrance hall used the front arc to great effect and was double height, with a majestic oak staircase to their left that led to a balcony. All the interior of the entrance hall was in oak-wood panelling. There was a very large painting on the wall to their right, probably about ten-foot square and spanning two levels. It was a painting of a battle in the background and a scene of domestic bliss in the foreground, with a man about to break the news to his young wife, the mother of his two children, that he must soon be off to do battle.

Kennedy studied the picture as Bailey's man went off to find his master. The detail and the perspective were great and it had probably been painted by some master several hundred years before, but was there really much point? Kennedy supposed it created the desired mood of solemnity in the hallway. Underneath this work was a long, narrow, oak table with tapestry-covered grand chairs at each end. There were a couple of smaller, spot lit paintings directly in front of the front door, under the balcony. No other furniture was visible.

Lord Justice Bailey made a grand entrance on the balcony above them. Kennedy had to blink twice, feeling as though he was staring up at Peter O'Toole. The resemblance was uncanny; they could easily have been brothers. He was even wearing the loud, yellow-based Donegal tweed suit that O'Toole made famous. Paul

Wood, the juror, hadn't mentioned this resemblance; Kennedy could only assume that he didn't know the actor. He had, however, mentioned the constantly twinkling eyes, which smiled now on Kennedy and Irvine from above.

'Good morning, gentlemen,' the fine baritone voice bellowed from on high. 'I shall be with you presently and we'll have coffee and croissants. It's a French custom, I know, and one of their better ones in fact, but I absolutely adore to kick-start my midmorning this way. Just follow Kelloggs through.'

Kelloggs? Kennedy and Irvine looked at each other in amusement.

'One of Lord Justice Bailey's little jokes. My name is Kelogiwisti. If you'd like to follow me.'

A few seconds later they were in a sitting room, which overlooked one of the most beautiful gardens Kennedy had ever seen. Again, lots of grass and very little ornate landscaping excepting the high perimeter hedge, which was itself broken only by a gateway in the bottom right-hand corner.

The room was oak-panelled, but the overall effect was somewhat softened by the matching rose-patterned curtains and sofas, three of which surrounded the grand fireplace. The walls were covered with paintings of varying size and content. The only one Kennedy recognised was a Charles McAuley. It was smaller than McAuley's usual work and was of a blacksmith shoeing a horse. It was a truly wonderful painting and Kennedy was admiring it up close when Lord Justice Bailey entered the room.

'Ah, the McAuley,' Bailey's voice boomed. His brown eyes broke into an even wider smile as he said: 'It always draws people to it. Do you know his work?'

'Well, just a little...' Kennedy began.

'Oh, the accent, of course you would; one of your fellow countrymen.'

'Yes,' Kennedy agreed. In such company he felt safer keeping his words to a minimum.

'From what I can tell, this is the only example of work on such a small canvas and it might just be the best work he has ever done.'

Up close, Lord Justice Bailey looked even more like Peter O'Toole, though the years had been a little kinder to his features. His jaw line was perfectly sculptured in lines an actor would die for. His complexion was unblemished, with a hint of tan, and his face was line-free except for a few laughter lines, which gently broke the contours around his eyes. Kennedy wondered if the judge had a painting hidden in the attic. He had salt-and-pepper hair, which was parted traditionally and bordering on the long side. He wore a mustard-coloured waistcoat under his suit jacket and the ensemble was topped and tailed with a blue bow tie and brown-and-cream brogues. The combination shouldn't have worked but on Bailey, for some strange reason, it gelled perfectly.

As they were all gathered around the McAuley, the door behind them literally creaked open and there stood Bailey's man, Kelogiwisti, with a laden silver tray.

'Good man, Kelloggs,' Bailey said as he invited his guests to take a seat. 'Tell me, did we get a good stash today?'

'I think so, sir,' Kelloggs replied, positioning the tray on the coffee table in front of the fire.

'You see, we have a damned difficult time getting good croissants around here. Most of the ones you pick up are, to all intents and purposes, inedible. But there's a splendid little streetside café in Primrose Hill called Cachao and, when we can get them from there, they're always first class.' Bailey studied the two policemen for a few minutes before continuing. 'These little things, you know, they're important. They make our days and our lives pass much more pleasantly.'

No sooner had Kelloggs closed the door behind him than Bailey said: 'I understand you wanted to talk to me about the Christopher Lloyd trial?'

'Yes,' Kennedy replied.

'Well, I've got my notes here,' Bailey said. He was comfortably spread out over the sofa to the right-hand side of the fireplace and consequently had his back to the window. 'Fire away.'

'Well, we could start with your views on the case,' Kennedy said.

Bailey smiled another large smile. 'Well, let's cut to the chase here, as our colonial friends are fond of saying. You want to know if I thought Lloyd was guilty?'

'Among other things, yes.'

'In a word, yes. I did think he was guilty. I guarantee you, there was no one more shocked in the courtroom that day than Miss Chada, Lloyd's lawyer. She was completely out of her depth and yet she won her case. Probably the only victory she'll ever win in her career. There are very few things that shock me any more. I'll let you into a little secret here. I was so confident of a conviction I had already started to think about his sentence.'

'What happened? What went wrong?' Kennedy asked.

'I'd say that there was a liberal do-gooder on the jury with a very loud voice. The prosecution presented an excellent case. The defence was a disgrace, a complete waste of time, but I've already said that, haven't I? I thought I did a fairly decent job of summing-up. You have to be very careful, you see. We continually walk a fine line between sending someone down or giving them their freedom, not to mention a fair few shillings on appeal.'

'You don't think there was anything untoward going on?' Kennedy asked.

'No,' Bailey replied, dunking the remainder of his croissant in his milky coffee. 'It was, purely and simply, a miscarriage of justice. If it had been a miscarriage of justice the other way – if we'd sent an innocent person down – there would have been documentaries, articles, appeals and committees, not to mention Robin Hood, William Tell and possibly even The Lone Ranger beating their drums to have the person freed. But when a guilty man gets off there's no opportunity for appeal.'

'Well, that's not exactly true, Your Honour,' Kennedy said, and, when the penny had failed to drop, he continued: 'In the final analysis, if he was guilty of a crime, Christopher Lloyd didn't get away with it.'

'Oh, he was guilty, believe you me. I see what you mean though; I suppose in this instance you might be right, although I'm not sure you could successfully argue that the punishment fitted his crime.'

'So you think that he wasn't murdered for what he did to Eve Adams?' Kennedy continued in Irvine's silence.

'Now that's the question we're all looking to you to answer, Detective Inspector. I'm intrigued by this part of the process. I'll admit something to you here, Detective Inspector. I'm envious of you and your work. You see, when a life is taken it's an extraordinary event. It transforms the normal. The final hours, and even days, of Christopher Lloyd were probably pedestrian enough to say the least. But now that we know they were the final hours of his life, all his actions are miraculously transformed into a harvest of spotential clues for you. Where he went, who he talked to, where he walked, where he drove, what he said, and so forth. All the areas and space Lloyd covered in his final hours are now your hunting ground and you know better than I that it all depends on you and your procedure whether penance will be paid for the taking of a life. That's the important thing in all of this. My colleagues and I on the bench can only deal with what you bring to us; we can't go out and find the perpetrators of the crimes continuously going on all around us. We rely on you to apprehend the criminals and present them to us.'

Here Bailey broke into another smile. He looked at Kennedy, then he looked at Irvine and moved around a bit in his sofa before continuing. 'I should say here, Detective Inspector Kennedy, that your reputation does precede you. I have every confidence that, if it is at all possible to catch the person – or persons – who sought to do Lloyd harm for whatever reason, you'll be the one to snare them.'

Irvine seemed to draw more satisfaction from Bailey's compliments than Kennedy did.

'Thanks,' Kennedy said bashfully. He never felt comfortable when praise was being dished out. He felt, as his mother would have put it, that he had a lot to be modest about. He also felt that none of this praise was getting him any further down the road on the Christopher Lloyd investigation.

'Tell me,' Kennedy continued as the dust settled, 'might you have any suspicions about any particular juror?'

'Well, yes,' Bailey began hesitantly. 'I'm not sure my suspicions would be relevant but I think at least five of the jury, possibly even six, were totally convinced that Lloyd was guilty, and of the remaining lot, I'd say the girl with the bad limp was probably the one who argued for Lloyd. She even interrupted the trial, claiming that she needed to go to the toilet. Her trip to the toilet, incidentally, coincided with a few sticky questions to Lloyd from the prosecution.'

'There was nothing you could do about that?'

'First time around, no. If she had tried again and raised my suspicions then I would have taken some kind of action.'

'Like?'

'I could have dismissed her from the jury and continued the trial.'

'With only eleven jurors?' Irvine asked his first question. 'Is that possible, sir, sorry, I mean Your Honour?'

'Yes, of course. Rare, but not unheard of. You see, I would have accepted an eleven-to-one verdict and it would still have been possible to get it. We couldn't afford a mistrial and it's getting harder and harder to get convictions that stick. Listen to me for a minute, I'll tell you something. I sit up on the bench in judgement of these… these delinquents all day long, and the only thing they think they did wrong was getting caught. They think crime is a vocation; it's a career to them, a job just like you and I do. Of course, they have more of an arsenal of manoeuvres to protect them than we have. But we can't become preoccupied with that; we have to use what we're permitted to use to put them away. For heaven's sake, someone's got to protect the homeowners and the old people and the young. All this crime has got to stop; we've got to do something to bring it into check. Anarchy on the streets is closer than we think. How long do you want to keep doing your job if I'm not backing you up?'

'I don't see the two as being connected, Your Honour,' Kennedy replied.

'You don't?' Bailey said arching an eyebrow.

'No. I believe it's my job to catch the criminals and then it's out of my hands.'

'Yes, you're right, of course. Then it becomes my responsibility to make the sentence fit the crime. It's just that there's no respect out there. I remember in my father's day, even the most hardened of criminals would show him respect. "Yes, Your Honour" or "No, Your Honour," they'd say. But now they – the rabble from the streets – treat me like dirt in my own court, can you believe that? We're never going to get that respect back again. I can tell you this, I'm only doing this because my father wished it.'

Bailey paused for a moment and observed the two policemen with a wry grin before continuing. 'I'll let you into a little secret. It was actually a little more than a wish from my father that I sit on the Bench. It was a condition of my inheritance that I could have all of this,' Bailey swung his outstretched arm around the room, 'and a few shillings as well, if I served in the name of Her Majesty. I mean, it was a great idea of his really. I'm proud of the old codger. You see, it wasn't just that he wanted me to put something back into the community; he wanted me to make something of my life. It took a while but I did it, and mostly it's been enjoyable. But it just keeps getting harder to bring criminals to justice.'

'You had four days to observe Christopher Lloyd. How did his demeanour seem to you?' Kennedy asked.

'Strange,' Bailey replied. 'He didn't give much away. He'd rarely return my stare and when he did, it was always with a "what am I doing here?" look. He'd have been a superb poker player. Even when the jury gave the "not guilty" verdict he barely batted an eyelid. He could quite possibly have been shell-shocked by the decision. I'm afraid there's not much help I can give you in that direction. You've got a tricky one here, Inspector Kennedy. You have before you what Winston Churchill called "a riddle wrapped in a mystery". You have a body but no scene of crime. You have, I imagine, several suspects but perhaps they have too obvious a motive. Is anyone under particular suspicion this stage?'

'Much too early in our investigation to say,' Kennedy replied.

He was silently chastising himself for not really entering into a full conversation with Lord Justice Bailey. Did he feel inadequate in the company of a man of such obvious learning? Did he fell inferior? Was that what Bailey and his friends on the Bench wanted, to feel comfortable passing judgement on lesser mortals? Was that why Bailey was getting upset about felons coming into his court and treating him like dirt? Was that where the system was falling down?

'Well, Eve Adams' mother wasn't even capable of crossing the road by herself, so we have to assume we could rule her out,' Bailey continued, obviously wanting to discuss the subtleties of the investigation further.

Kennedy didn't really want to go down this road, discussing all the suspects. Equally he knew that all the main players in the Christopher Lloyd case had been under Bailey's scrutiny not too long ago. He searched for safe ground.

'Well, Your Honour,' Kennedy began shakily, 'it very nearly was the perfect crime, wasn't it?'

'Yes, indeed,' Bailey replied thoughtfully, 'if such a thing exists.'

'If it hadn't been for the heaviest rainfall in years,' Kennedy went on, feeling that he wasn't giving anything away 'Christopher Lloyd would have shared Daniel Elliot's grave for eternity.'

'Yes, yes, you're absolutely correct,' Bailey said sounding positively jubilant.

'That's a very important point,' Irvine said from nowhere, very reflectively. 'If we assume that our murderer was confident that he was going to get away with his handiwork by having the body disappear, then perhaps he didn't go to great pains to tidy up the scene of crime properly.'

'Let me get this right,' Bailey said, rubbing his stubbleless chin. 'You're saying that somewhere out there is a scene of crime waiting for you to discover it and uncover all the clues it has to offer?'

'Perhaps,' Irvine replied.

'Mmmm,' Bailey said and then added: 'What about the rest of Eve Adams' family? Anyone there who might have been so disturbed about the rape that they would be prepared to take the law into their own hands?'

'But murder, sir? – I mean, your Honour?' Irvine exclaimed.

'Oh, I wouldn't be so sure that there aren't a lot of people out there who feel that a death penalty is the only penalty for someone who commits rape,' Bailey offered. 'I've certainly sat on the bench enough times, having to listen to what these animals are doing physically and mentally to their victims, to feel completely impotent when I dish out the maximum sentence I am permitted. Most of them are back out on the streets again within a few years. Some even within a few months.'

'If Christopher Lloyd had been found guilty,' Kennedy said, ' what would his sentence have been?'

'Seven years,' Bailey answered immediately. 'I would have been justified in sentencing him to seven years but if you take into consideration the eight months he'd already served, plus any time off for good behaviour, he'd have been free in about three and a half years.'

'And Eve Adams and members of her family would have had to have lived with it for the rest of their lives,' Irvine said despondently.

Kennedy felt Irvine had again started to associate Eve Adams with Bella Forsythe.

'Yes, I'm afraid so,' Bailey said. 'I'm not personally in favour of locking someone up and throwing away the key. The system is in meltdown already, but we do have to find something that will be effective in sending out the message that you simply cannot be allowed to get away almost scott-free with raping a woman. I don't know exactly what that something is, but when you offend our society, you should not be allowed to take a full place in it and enjoy all the joys and benefits it has to offer. When you oppose society, society must oppose you.'

'Yes,' Irvine agreed. 'I think you're absolutely correct.'

'Well,' Kennedy interrupted the judge and his DS's conversation, which was verging on the maudlin. 'You've been more than generous with your time and hospitality, Lord Bailey.'

'No, no, it's fine. No inconvenience whatsoever.' Bailey began, rising from the sofa and dusting the crumbs from his waistcoat. 'Perhaps you could keep me in touch with the progress on your investigation. Here's my direct line.' He handed Kennedy a white business card containing nothing but an eleven-digit telephone number.

'Thank you, we'll try and do that,' Kennedy replied, accepting the card.

'Oh, and do me a favour,' Bailey began in what sounded like an authoritative conclusion to the proceedings. 'Please pass on my best wishes to Superintendent Thomas Castle.'

As they returned to the car Kennedy realised that he still hadn't managed to check out the York & Albany, the building opposite North Bridge House, for the aforementioned Thomas Castle.

'Now what?' Irvine asked, pulling out of Bailey's subtly-marked exit gate. As they were doing so, a lemon-yellow Smart car was pulling into the entrance.

'Now we head back to North Bridge House and see how we're getting on. We can have a good, honest cup of tea at the same time. Coffee is for the Americans; I can take it or leave it. And quite frankly, I prefer to leave it.'

Chapter Twenty-Three

'THAT WAS A cheap shot you and that WDC took yesterday.'

The speaker was a scrubbed-up Frankie Hammond and he was addressing DI Christy Kennedy and DS James Irvine, who had just pulled onto the forecourt of Tyres R Us. They were just in the nick of time; one minute later, Hammond would have been off on his lunch break.

Kennedy thought it was quite remarkable how some mechanics looked like mechanics 24/7, while others, like Hammond, were meticulous about leaving the grease, grime, oil and dirty overalls behind at the garage. He was dressed in black tracksuit bottoms, a traditional blue shirt, a dark-blue hooded windcheater and a pair of white running shoes. His face was verging on chubby even though the rest of his body appeared quite trim. His white hair was cut back to the skin and he was clean-shaven. His eyebrows were bushy and his eyes were a lifeless blue-grey colour. He looked at you, but if he caught you looking back he would immediately redirect his eyes to the ground about two feet in front of him.

Irvine had already filled Kennedy in on the incident and it was that which had drawn Kennedy's suspicious nature.

'Did they tell you about their little game?' Hammond said, addressing Kennedy.

'Yes, I seem to remember that you were somewhat confused over which night you and Mrs Christine Duncan enjoyed the Indian takeaway,' Kennedy replied.

They were now loitering around the forecourt close to the unmarked police car, an out-of-date and over-the-hill Granada. Hammond seemed unwilling to invite them into the garage.

'You see, I was nervous, wasn't I?' Hammond said as he lit up a

Player. 'You guys have a habit of doing that to innocent people, don't you? You make us feel nervous when you question us. I think it's because you have this way of implying that everyone is a little bit guilty of something, and of course we all are. Hey, I'm sure even both of you have things you wouldn't want strangers to know about.'

Kennedy wondered at this point whether Irvine would consider that his relationship with Forsythe fell into this category. But then he started to examine his own thought processes. Was it strange that he thought about what Irvine would feel guilty about, rather than what he should feel guilty about? What would he, DI Christy Kennedy, feel guilty about? He paid his taxes. He'd never, since school days, cheated on a girlfriend. He'd once dated someone who'd been cheating on her husband. That could probably be filed under: 'Don't do unto others what you wouldn't like done unto yourself.' The only things he could think about that he felt he needed to do, wanted to do, were to ring home more often and live longer. Did all of this mean he was living a sad life?

Neither Kennedy nor Irvine seemed prepared to share any of their guilt.

'So, when you were questioning me last time,' Hammond continued, breaking the temporary gap in the interview, 'I was nervous. Of course I was nervous. But I'm innocent, and I want to make sure that you know I'm innocent, so I'm trying maybe a bit too hard to give all the correct answers to your questions. Of course I know that Monday night was the night Lloyd was murdered, so when you asked me what I was doing on Tuesday night, well, my mind was racing ahead and I was thinking, right, they want to know what I was doing the night Lloyd was murdered and that's why they've asked me that question, so I immediately came out with what I was doing on the night he died rather than the night you asked me about.'

'So what were you doing on the Tuesday night?' Kennedy asked.

'Tuesday night?' Hammond said, stumbling around a bit verbally. 'Tuesday? God, you know, I honestly can't remember.' He gave a very bad stage laugh.

Irvine flashed Hammond a 'dumb' look.

'You see, there you are, you're doing it again,' Hammond said, immediately and confidently. 'You're making me feel nervous and, by extension, making me behave guiltily, I'm sure. I've just forgotten what I was doing on Tuesday night. If you give me a bit of time I could think about it or ring up Christine and check exactly what I was doing. But it's like I need to give you the correct answer and I need to give it to you now.'

'We're not trying to put you under pressure,' Irvine said, maybe feeling guilty for his earlier look, 'we're just looking for the truth.'

'The truth, is it?' Hammond said, sticking his hands in his pockets. 'Well, the truth quite simply, is that I've forgotten what I was doing on that Tuesday night.'

'Okay,' Kennedy said. 'Look, you seem to be on your way somewhere. We've got a few things we need to ask you so do you want to go inside?'

'No, it's okay,' Hammond said. 'I was just going to the pub for a pint and a pie. Do you want to join me?'

'Why not?' Kennedy shrugged, and they headed up to the nearby, strangely-named Bartok pub.

So, had Hammond been en route to see someone only to be waylaid by Kennedy and Irvine? If that was the case he certainly led the way willingly to the pub. But could it all be a continuation of the 'you caught me out on the alibi' act? If he had been on his way to anywhere of significance – significant in terms of the Lloyd case, that was – then would it have been just too much of a coincidence that Kennedy and Irvine would have come by just as he was off on some devious business? And what could his devious business possibly have been about? The problem with being a policeman was that you tended to be overly suspicious of people.

Kennedy got in the drinks – one pint of Guinness, one still mineral water and one orange juice. Hammond, for his part, insisted on paying for three Cornish pasties, which looked like they were homemade and tasted delicious. 'Best Cornish pasties outside of Cor...k' was chalked above the bar. The same joker had written:

'Wanted: Customers', in large letters on the blackboard on the street outside the pub.

'I wanted to talk to you a bit more about Christopher Lloyd,' Kennedy began.

'Now there's a surprise,' Hammond laughed into his Guinness.

'I want to talk about when he was involved in the scam with Tyres R Us. Were you working there at that time?' Kennedy asked, helping himself to another piece of delicious pastie.

'I think you already know I was,' Hammond replied, his Guinness half drunk and his pastie untouched.

'You told DS Irvine here,' Kennedy continued, nodding in the direction of the second policeman, 'that you knew Mr Lloyd was a bad lot because of his earlier dealings with Tyres R Us?'

'Yes, basically someone in the garage, I forget who it was now, was marking up brand-new tyres as seconds – or retreads as they were then called – and selling them to Lloyd who was selling them on as new tyres.'

'Couldn't it have been possible though that the corruption was all on the inside? You know, where Lloyd genuinely thought he was getting a good deal on new tyres?' Irvine asked.

'Oh, come on now. Let's not be naive,' Hammond replied, hiking his shoulders. He had a habit of using his voice, eyes, eyebrows – lots of eyebrows – arms, shoulders, hands, dimples, crow's-feet and even his ears – his entire body, in fact – to communicate. All of his features were in full, uninhibited flow as he continued to address the policemen, particularly DS Irvine. 'Let's say you go into your local newsagents, week in and week out, to buy your pack of 20 Players – okay? Now, one day you're in and the owner isn't around, so the shop assistant says: "Twenty Players as usual… Mr Connery?"'

Here Hammond paused so that at least he could enjoy his joke at the expense of Irvine's distinctive accent. He had a smile in his voice as he continued. 'And you say "Yes." But instead of taking your cigarettes from the shelf behind him, the assistant takes them from a carton that is sticking out of his rucksack under the counter. Instead of the usual £4.81 he only asks you for £2.50. Better still, he says to you that he could sell you a fresh 200 carton of Players for £12.50 instead of the usual £24.00 or £15.00 at the airport duty-free. Now, you mean to tell me that, if you go through with the transaction, you're not aware that you are buying stolen goods?'

A funny thing happened at that point. Just as Hammond was saying the words "buying stolen goods," the rest of the drinkers in the semi-packed pub stopped talking. They might have done so to have a drink or to think about what they or their friends had just said; to eat some food, or to think of their loved ones; to stare at the TV in the corner above the door; to rise and go to the toilet; to tie their shoelaces, to light a ciggy; or to ogle the barmaid. But no matter what their numerous and varied reasons were, the entire occupancy of the pub dropped into an impromptu silence so the words "buying stolen goods," as spoken by Hammond, rang out loud and clear, and everyone turned as one and stared at the three would-be conspirators.

In a microsecond, Kennedy felt a red flush move from the tip of his toes to the crown of his head. Hammond nonchalantly drained the remaining third of his Guinness as if nothing untoward had just happened, and Irvine took the opportunity to visit the bar to order another round. In as much time as it had taken the silence to appear, it disappeared, with a knowing laugh here and a snigger there and an "I wonder what they're shifting" just about every-fecking-where.

'So,' Kennedy, composure regained, began, 'who was this man on the inside, the one who was supplying Lloyd with the illegal tyres?'

'I don't remember, to be honest,' Hammond said, staring into the bottom of his empty glass, turning it this way and that as if some Guinness might be miraculously hiding in some crevice and preparing to spring forth. 'I'd forgotten all about it, to be honest, until the Eve Adams case cropped up.'

Hammond continued staring into his glass, apparently deep in thought. The hustle and bustle of the pub was back up to a full gale force and the noise would have drowned out any conversation between them, but Hammond put his elbow on the table and leaned in very close to Kennedy.

'I'll tell you something, Inspector,' he began, his voice close to a whisper. 'When I heard that someone had topped Lloyd, I have to admit that my first thought was that it might have been Christine. I mean, I now know and accept, having given it careful consideration, that it couldn't have been Christine – she was with me when it happened, wasn't she? I mean we were together at the time of the murder. But for a split second back then I panicked and I thought: "Jeez, she's gone and topped him."'

'Why?' Kennedy asked. 'Why did you think that?'

'Why?' Hammond smiled. 'Why? I'll tell you why. Because she said that she would swing for him when he got away with the rape.'

'But…' Kennedy coaxed as Irvine returned with the drinks.

'But of course she didn't – we all say things like that in the heat of the moment, don't we? You say you could kill someone who offends you, but you don't actually mean that you could literally murder them, do you?'

Kennedy experienced a strange sensation as Hammond was speaking. It was as if the look in Hammond's eyes did not equate with the words he was saying. Although he was mouthing the words "but you don't actually mean that you could literally kill them, do you?", his eyes looked like they were saying, "would that be a possibility, that that could happen?" It was quite freaky, and the moment was gone in a second. Irvine awkwardly negotiated the setting down of the three glasses, simultaneously breaking the exchange between Hammond and Kennedy.

'But you don't think she did it?' Kennedy said as Hammond tore into his second pint of Guinness.

'No, of course not – apart from anything else, I know it would have been impossible – but it's just that she was so incensed about what he did to little Eve that… well, I still think that if she had come into personal contact with him in those few moments, well… let's just say that I for one couldn't have guaranteed his safety.'

'In that time,' Kennedy said, pushing further, 'when you thought that Christine might have killed Lloyd, did you consider how she might have done it? You know, how she might have actually killed him?'

Hammond looked at Kennedy – he had totally blocked out Irvine – and seemed to be choosing his words very carefully.

'Well, the obvious way for a weak woman to murder a strong man would be for her to poison him, wouldn't you say?' Hammond laughed loudly. 'That's why I like to do all the cooking in our house. Yes, I like to know exactly what I'm eating, thank you very much.'

'But then how about physically getting Lloyd to the graveyard?' Kennedy continued as Irvine looked on with great interest.

'Oh, I didn't ever get that far. I didn't need to, did I?' said Hammond, this time breaking off into a hearty laugh. 'I realised that Christine and I had been together at the time of his death.'

'And how did you know the time of Lloyd's death, sir?' Irvine asked.

'Elementary, my dear Watson,' Hammond chuckled. 'I assumed, as one does, that the time you were looking for people to verify their movements was in fact the approximate time of death.'

'Tell me, Mr Hammond,' Kennedy said, hijacking the conversation again, 'how long have you and Christine been together?'

'Let's see, we'll have been together six years this November,' Hammond replied, near-enough immediately.

'That's a long time for a romance,' Irvine chipped in.

'What? Oh, you mean the fact that we've never married?'

'No, I meant the fact that you've stayed together for so long when there wasn't a marriage there to bind you together,' Irvine replied, appearing genuinely awed.

'Oh,' Hammond said blankly.

'You find it preferable not to marry?' Kennedy asked, not really interested but merely throwing down a hook for his next line of questioning.

'Well, I certainly wouldn't want to break the law, gentlemen,'

Hammond replied, mock-sheepishly.

'Oh, you mean you're already married?' Kennedy said.

'Yes indeed,' Hammond admitted, 'and never divorced.'

'A bad ending then?' Irvine asked.

'Her choice, not mine.'

'But why no divorce?' Irvine again.

'It takes two to get married and it also takes two to get divorced. You also need to communicate with each other to end a marriage and I'm sorry to say that she seems to have disappeared off the face of the earth.'

'Any children?' Kennedy asked.

'Yes, we have two beautiful daughters – they'll be 24 and 25 now and probably starting off their own married lives,' Hammond replied. It was obviously still painful for him to go over this matrimonial stuff.

'What went wrong?' Irvine asked, where Kennedy would probably have stopped this line of questioning. There was no point in getting Hammond morose and distracted.

'Oh, I think that's more of an end-of-the-evening kind of conversation. Let's just say that we were childhood sweethearts. God, she was so damned beautiful when she was a teenager, but the sad truth was that we were both too bloody young. She got pregnant and we had to get married. In hindsight, that's rarely a solid basis for a good union.'

Kennedy and Irvine both swigged from their drinks, as though implying: "We'll drink to that!"

'But,' Hammond continued expansively, 'that was then. It had to end and end it did. About three years later I met Christine through her elder daughter, Dionne.'

'Okay,' said Kennedy. They all mentally turned over to a new page. 'So you'd no further dealing with Lloyd since the earlier Tyres R Us incident?'

'Well, why would I? I heard about him when Eve started working on his stall. I warned them all about Lloyd and then I heard about the rape and I couldn't believe it. Then again, I suppose a leopard never changes his spots.'

'What?' Irvine murmured in astonishment. 'You mean Lloyd had a previous for rape?'

'No,' Hammond said, 'not as far as I'm aware. No, what I meant was when you're a bad'un, you'll be up for any kind of dealing that comes your way.'

When Hammond saw that the police weren't reacting positively to this, he continued. 'You don't think so? Well, I certainly believe that after someone steps over the line by breaking the law, from that point onwards it's in for a penny, in for a pound.'

'I'm not sure I agree with that, sir,' Irvine offered politely. 'I mean, I think if you rob a bank you do so from a need... a need for money.'

'Or greed,' Hammond added.

'Perhaps, but then again perhaps not,' Irvine said, choosing his words carefully. 'But what I was going to say was that, even if you're the kind of person who robs a bank to clothe and feed your family, I don't think that you're necessarily the kind of person who would go and molest a young girl.'

'But that's a need as well,' Hammond interrupted again. 'A different kind of need.'

They all pondered that thought for a moment. Kennedy broke the silence.

'What about Manfred's son? Do you think he could be behind this?'

'What would be his motive?' Hammond enquired, seemingly happy that the questioning had now developed into a conversation; the kind of conversation any three mates might have in a public house, and exactly the way Kennedy liked the questioning to go.

'Well,' Kennedy said picking up the thread, 'his girlfriend's sister's friend was raped by Lloyd, Lloyd got away with it and no one seemed to be doing anything about it.'

'Well, I suppose it could be a possibility – I don't really know him. I mean, as a person I don't really know him, but he's young and probably has a fertile imagination, but I can't help you any more than that with him.'

'And the old man?' Kennedy continued, moving further down the road.

'Nagh, not old Manfred,' Hammond laughed, his whole body convulsing this time. 'He's so keen to keep on the right side of the law, he won't even allow his son to throw away his sweetie papers. Nagh, he's so in love with his Corgi collection he would never do anything that would separate him from it.'

'Yes,' Kennedy said, finishing his second glass of mineral water, 'I suppose that's always easier for us, you know, people who are obsessive about their hobbies. Tell me Mr Hammond, do you have any hobbies?'

'Nagh.'

'No? Not even something therapeutic like gardening?' Kennedy pushed.

'By the time I get home from the garage I've neither the energy nor the inclination for anything other than Christine.'

'I suppose that could be taken two ways,' Irvine noted as he too finished his drink.

'I suppose it could,' Hammond replied, not taking the trouble to make it clear what he meant. 'Well, if that's all gentlemen, it's around about that time I got the harness back on again.'

'No, no. Yes, that will be fine,' Kennedy said and added, as Hammond rose from the table, 'for now.'

Chapter Twenty-Four

'WHAT DID WE learn from that, sir?' Irvine asked, as they pulled out of the forecourt of Tyres R Us.

'Oh, we learnt that the Bartok pub makes exceedingly good Cornish pasties.'

'What do you make of him?' Irvine asked. 'Hammond?'

'Mmmm,' Kennedy sighed as he sank back into his seat. 'I don't know, James. There's something about him I'm not entirely sure about. But I'll tell you this; I'd like to know a lot more about him. Let's run a few checks on him and see exactly what has been going on in his life.'

They drove in silence for a time, on their way to East Kilburn, better known as West Hampstead, to the address they had on file for juror Michelle Roche.

The original plan had been to talk to her at her place of work after the weekend but, when Coles tracked her down, Miss Roche quite forcefully stated that she'd prefer to be interviewed at home – she said she didn't want the people at her place of work knowing her business. So, the police were getting to see her two days early.

The houses all flew by unnoticed by Kennedy. He usually liked to look at them – he loved houses – but today the Lloyd case had his mind miles away.

'So, James,' Kennedy said as he sat upright in his seat and snapped himself out of his meditations. 'What's the story with you and Dr Forsythe? Have you made any decisions?'

'I have, as a matter of fact, sir,' Irvine admitted, with a keenness that revealed how he'd been yearning to discuss the subject.

'Oh?'

'Well, I've decided that I would like to get to know her better.'

'Oh?' Kennedy said again.

'Yes, but I've decided that as she's going to be in prison for at least the next ten years, there's no reason for me to do anything rash.'

'Quite,' Kennedy agreed.

'Even if something were to happen between us, I'd still have to find something to occupy myself with for the next ten years and… well, you know, I quite like my career, so when I thought it out I realised that I needn't do anything about it for the next decade or so.'

'Will you write to her?'

'I've thought about that as well,' Irvine said, with a distinct emphasis that suggested: "I'm very glad you've given me this opening too." 'Actually, sir, I was wondering… you know, as we are still technically working on a case that she's indirectly involved with, I was wondering, sir, if…'

'If you could go and visit her in an official capacity?' Kennedy smiled, cutting across Irvine's hesitancy.

'Well, yes, sir.'

'I can't see that there would be anything wrong with that, James,' Kennedy said, happy that Irvine no longer seemed hell-bent on throwing his career down the drain. 'As soon as you possibly can, in fact, might be very helpful.'

'Thanks, sir,' Irvine said as they pulled into Dynham Road. 'I'll see how I feel after the visit. But I know if I write to her it will go on record, so I thought I might, you know, pursue a different approach…'

'I don't want to know, James. I just don't want to know.'

'Of course, sir, sorry.'

Dynham Road inclines steeply from the heights of West End Lane to the bottom of the valley that acts as a border between West Hampstead and Kilburn. It's a road of neat, symmetrical, terraced houses, most of which have been split into flats due to the fact that West Hampstead is the 'Heartland of Flatland.'

Michelle Roche lived in a flat on the top floor of a house midway down the left-hand side. She buzzed the police into the common hallway on their first buzz. She'd probably been watching

out for them from the window, not wanting a couple of policemen to be spotted loitering on her doorstep.

When they were in the hallway, a disjointed voice called out:
'I'm up here, at the top of the stairs.'

The drab, grey-carpeted stairs came to a halt on the second
floor, at a window overlooking the rear of the terraces. The police
saw red brick, grey brick, black brick, grey slate, partially
obscured curtains, dustbins aplenty, occasional swings, bikes
and rocking horses. Their view of the normally hidden sights of
suburban domesticity was interrupted as the door to their immediate left creaked open. A woman who looked like she would
never see her mid-thirties again peered out from a small, security-
chained opening.

'Cards, please,' the voice said flatly.

Kennedy and Irvine produced their warrant cards and introduced themselves in clear, distinct tones.

The door closed again and Kennedy and Irvine heard the metallic
jangling as she undid the chain from its catch. She opened the door to
its widest and, with her eyes, invited the two policemen into her flat.
She was dressed in a dark blue tracksuit. Her long hair looked like it
was unwashed but closer examination revealed that it was, in fact,
the dye streaks she'd added that made it look... well, 'very unattractive' were the words Kennedy settled on. Michelle Roche was frail
and her tracksuit hung awkwardly from she shoulders as though
they were a coat hanger. She had very engaging eyes, however, which
tended to distract you from the rest of her features. She shooed them
up the stairs to her flat without saying a word.

The magic, Kennedy thought, of having a grubby hallway was
that it made the inside of your flat all the more impressive if, that
was, you bothered to spend any money and attention on it.
Michelle Roche had done just that.

The grey hallway carpet gave onto a plush, royal-blue carpet
inside Ms Roche's accommodation. The walls were covered with
Laura Ashley-type patterned wallpaper and, half a flight up, the
trio arrived on a tiny landing that was the hub of a small but ele-
gantly decorated and furnished flat. Straight ahead of the stair-

well was a comfortable kitchen with a dining area that over-looked Dynham Road. To the right of the kitchen at the front of the house was a study-cum-sitting room, with the same blue carpet as the hallway. Next to the study was a partially-opened door. Kennedy assumed that if her enthusiasm to close it was anything to go by, it led to her dishevelled bedroom.

The three of them loitered on the landing for a time, the police waiting to be directed to a suitable interview room and Michelle perhaps waiting for them to state their business. The already small landing space also contained a teak unit, which housed a shelf of ornaments and several books. These were all similar in content, concerning people like Lee Harvey Oswald, the Kennedys, Watergate, Biko, Mandela, the Guildford Four, the Birmingham Three and the Primrose Hill Dead Pets Society. There was one by David Icke, *Them* by Jon Ronson, and one that summed up the entire collection, Jim Driver's classic *Just Because You're Paranoid, It Don't Mean They're Not After You*.

'Let's go upstairs,' Michelle Roche said, in a bemused kind of way. 'There are no phones or distractions there.'

She led them up another flight of stairs, past another bookcase packed to overflowing with conspiracy books. At the top of the stairs was a small but incredibly clean bathroom, and, just immediately before it, the trademark royal-blue carpeted stairs veered around to the left and led them into a windowless, wainscoted room that had been stolen from the roof space.

'This is great,' Irvine said, as they went up into the attic room.

The room had been very sparsely furnished: a smoked-glass covered coffee table surrounded by two large, green sofas, and a matching armchair and leather swivel chair.

'Thanks,' Ms Roche said as she limped across the room and flopped with a sigh into the leather chair, inviting Kennedy and Irvine to sit on the sofa. The offer of refreshments was noticeably absent. 'What can I do for you?' she said.

'We wanted to talk to you about a trial you recently did jury service on,' Irvine began, removing a notebook from inside his jacket.

'I'm not sure I'm allowed to talk about that,' Roche replied, swivelling to face first Kennedy and then Irvine. 'Isn't it sub-judicial something?'

'Ah, no Miss Roche,' Irvine began. 'The trial is over, the verdict has been handed down and so the case is no longer under judicial consideration.'

'Well,' Roche replied, swinging her armchair back in Irvine's direction, 'I'm not a schoolgirl so please don't insult me with the title "Miss." Michelle will do fine but if you find that too informal, try Ms Roche. Secondly, it's all very well for you two to just waltz in here and say you're officials of the justice system – the very same justice system that nearly locked up that poor boy for something he obviously didn't do – but shouldn't I have a solicitor present to ensure that I am not leaving myself open to some kind of future prosecution for discussing the internal workings of a jury?'

'No, Michelle, you're fine here with us,' Kennedy began quietly. 'We're only here to find out what happened to Mr Lloyd. Rest assured, if our investigation leads us into a legal minefield then we'll be calling for your solicitor louder than you will.'

'You won't mind, then, if I record our conversation?' Roche said, taking both the policemen by surprise.

'No, not at all,' Kennedy said. 'By all means.'

'Good,' Roche replied, rising with apparent difficulty from her chair, 'because if you hadn't agreed, I would have stopped this interview immediately.'

She crossed the room to where the half wall intercepted the slope of the roof and appeared to press a section of the varnished wainscoting, which sprang out to her touch. Inside the panel was a compartment housing a mismatch of amplifiers, cassette desks and a record deck. Kennedy glanced around the room, assuming that the spherical, football-size perforated objects at the apex of the roof at each end must, in fact, be the famous Grundig speakers. 'Picture me impressed, he said under his breath.

Roche did not operate any of the aforementioned equipment. Instead, she removed two Sony Professional Walkmans and placed them both on the coffee table between them.

'I'll do a copy for both of us, shall I?' Roche continued as she inserted the microphone leads into the respective recorders. 'I'd hate for you to suggest afterwards that I doctored the tapes.'

Kennedy and Irvine stole a 'What have we got here?' glance at each other.

Michelle Roche's voice seemed somewhat unreal – not quite mechanical but with tones close to alien as she lit the magic eyes on the recorders with a loud 'Testing.'

Now Kennedy realised what it was about her voice that sounded unreal. It was as if her nose was blocked, not from a cold or flu but with something more physical than that, maybe a growth or something in her throat or windpipe that was making it near impossible to speak and breathe simultaneously without her voice sounding like an electronic wheeze.

'Right, I'm ready for your questions, gentlemen.'

'Okay,' Kennedy said, introducing himself to the recorder and giving the date, time and names of those present before continuing. 'Had you ever met Mr Christopher Lloyd before the trial?'

'No!' Roche screeched at such a volume that the equaliser lights on the tape recorders went off the scale.

'Did you meet Mr Lloyd at all after the trial?' Kennedy continued.

'By the time the trial was over, Chris was proven to be not guilty and it is no business of yours who he did or didn't see,' Roche wheezed, in one of her more comfortable tones.

'No, that's not an answer to the question I asked you. Did you…?' Kennedy asked.

'That's the only answer I'm going to give to your question,' Roche interrupted.

'It's a simple question. Did you or did you not see Christopher Lloyd after the trial?' Kennedy asked again.

'It's none of your business. Next question, please.'

'Of course,' Irvine said sympathetically, 'you realise that if you refuse to answer our questions we will have to assume that you did see Mr Lloyd after the trial.'

'Of course I do, but you should also realise that that would be a naïve and childish assumption,' Roche replied, clearly enjoying herself.

'Okay, let's leave that for now,' Kennedy said, trying to avert the looming farce. 'Let's go back to the trial for a minute. Can you tell me why you felt so sure that Mr Lloyd was innocent?'

'Excuse me Inspector, but surely it's irrelevant what I personally thought. The jury found Mr Lloyd not guilty of the charges brought against him.'

'But from the evidence available...' Kennedy began.

'You've got to be kidding!' Roche said, raising her pitch again. 'You trump up your charges; you incarcerate the poor man for several months; you bring him to trial; you lose and, surprise surprise, he wins – he is found not guilty – and then he's murdered and you still won't leave him alone.'

'What I was about to say,' Kennedy continued quietly, once her tirade was complete, 'was that there was a substantial amount of evidence available to suggest that Lloyd was guilty. We know that there were several members of the jury who felt he was guilty, and we know that you felt he was innocent and your powers of persuasion were so successful that you managed to convince the other members of the jury of that too. So my question to you is, simply, why were you so convinced he was innocent?'

Roche stared at Kennedy as if trying to work out whether the detective had just paid her a compliment or had just insulted her.

'The look in Eve Adams' eyes told me everything I needed to know,' she said eventually.

'Sorry?' Irvine said fishing for more.

'I'd seen that look in a young girl before. Where you're after something and you can't get it, and you regret the things you gave up in the hope of achieving your goal.'

'So you're saying that Eve Adams gave Lloyd sex for something and when she didn't get what she thought would be her reward, she regretted having sex with him and cried wolf?' Kennedy asked.

'In a word, yes.' Roche said. 'Oldest game in the world.'

'But isn't that, to some degree, ignoring the evidence?' Kennedy continued.

'Not to mention having sex with an underage girl,' Irvine chipped in.

'What evidence?' she said, looking at Kennedy and then swivelling round to face Irvine. 'And that's not what he was charged with. We, as a jury, could only deal with the charge that was before us.'

'Okay,' Kennedy began, taking up her point. 'He changed his story three times to suit the evidence as the police were uncovering it. DNA proved he'd been intimate with Eve. Then he obviously decided to admit that he did have a relationship with the girl.'

'Again, I have to say that I would accept the fact that sex took place between Lloyd and Adams but, equally, I don't think it was proven that she was raped. You and his lawyer made a thing about the first point you raised. He changed his evidence.' Roche repeated this a second time to get her point across. 'Now you and the prosecution obviously believe that Lloyd changed his evidence to hide the truth. "Why else would he change his evidence?" the prosecution lawyer kept hammering away at us morning, noon and night.'

'Why else other than to squirm your way out of a tight spot by lying!' Irvine said, pushing the facts slightly. Kennedy was happy about this: Roche had too much control over the proceedings for his liking.

'Why else, other than the fact that three white policemen came along to arrest a black man for having sex with an underage white girl?' Roche said, using her hands and tilting her head in a 'Come on, please' pose. 'Okay, now for just one second put yourself in his position. You're panicking, of course you are, and so you say, "Who? Me?" and you say, "Of course not, don't be stupid." And the further they push you the more you lie. Then some time passes and the police produce some more evidence and you move onto another lie to cover your first lie, and on and on it goes. And do you know why?'

Kennedy and Irvine looked at her blankly.

'Do you know why?' she repeated. 'Because you are black and they are white and she is white and there are more of them than there are of you, and you know that given the slightest excuse they will beat the living daylights out of you. You know that is exactly what will happen.'

'Not every policeman goes around beating up suspects,' Kennedy said, a little too depressively.

'And not every black man goes around raping white girls!' Roche wheezed at them, apparently very happy with her point. 'If things were different and the police were cleaner than clean then perhaps he would have put his hands up right from the start and said: "Look, I didn't rape her but I did have sex with her and I'm ready to face the music on that one."'

'But then he was still guilty of having sex with an underage girl,' Irvine said, totally exasperated.

'But that wasn't what he was charged with,' Roche replied, incensed and sounding like a teacher who was fast losing her patience with two less-than-bright students. 'If that had been the charge at the trial then I'm one-hundred percent convinced that we would have found him guilty as charged. I could tell by the look of both Adams and Chris that they'd had sex together, and I'd say not just once but several times.'

'How could you tell?' Kennedy asked.

'Because of the way he looked at me and, I'm sure, the other female members of the jury. Because of the way he answered his lawyers. Because of the ashamed way he acted in front of the judge. Because of the way she answered her questions. Because of the way the camera caught her eyes on the video screen. Because of the way she avoided answering some of her own brief's questions. Because of the admission of her friend, Madonna, that Eve watched pornographic videos. What's a sixteen-year-old girl doing watching videos where women are being treated as sex objects, playthings, and being degraded by men, for heaven's sake? There is a look that people who have been intimate have and it's impossible for them to hide that look.'

'Even though they were separated by a video screen?' Kennedy asked, interested in Roche's assessment.

'Yes. Mentally, they were in each other's company,' Roche wheezed, the blockage in her nose sounding more acute. 'You can tell a virgin a mile away. Even her friend Madonna, she's no longer a virgin either, though she isn't as body-confident as Eve. Virgins at that age tend to have more of a sparkle about them. And Madonna looked pretty jaded to me, Eve even more so.'

Irvine started to say something but it was inaudible because Roche started up her tirade again, completely ignoring him.

'Yes, it's all greed, all greed.' She paused to smile. Her smile looked like it was an extremely painful exercise. 'Do you know why you lost the case?'

Kennedy shook his head in the negative.

'The police, though perhaps not you personally, were just too greedy.' Roche answered her own question in Bette Davis style. 'The police should have been happy with the charge of sex with a minor, but they got greedy and went for the rape charge, which carried a much heftier sentence. Thanks to that simple fact they lost the case, and because they lost their case a poor man lost his life.'

'How do you figure that then?' Irvine asked, appearing genuinely interested.

'Well, if you had gone for the lesser charge, what with all of your DNA evidence and stuff, you would have proved your case against Chris and he would have received a six-year sentence. But, because you wanted the big ten years, he got off with the rape, someone was pissed off, took the law into their own hands, and now he's dead. It's clearly the police's fault.'

Kennedy didn't entirely agree with her logic; it fact, he didn't agree with it at all. But she had more for them.

'The other way of looking at it is that someone wanted him to get off. You know, there are those out there who don't believe criminals should just be sent down at great expense to the country and live a life of luxury for a few years. No, they'd like them wiped from the face of the earth entirely. So, what if this was an alternative justice system and they organised it so that he would get off just so that they could kill him? Eh? What about that? Even down to the way he was to be buried. Think on that. If you dug up all the other graves, I wonder how many cuckoos you would find.'

'Well, we'll never be able to get to the bottom of that one,' Kennedy said, biting his lip, 'but I am interested in going back to the point you made about Mr Lloyd being murdered by someone who was incensed about his acquittal. Do you think it was one of the family members?'

'Well, the problem I'm finding with my investigation is that they're all a bunch of casualties. Also, I think Eve knows more than she's telling.'

'What?' Kennedy asked in disbelief. 'About the murder?'

'No, I mean more during the trial,' Roche said, her voice so hoarse she sounded like she was using a voice box. 'She kept looking like she was going to say something... something else. She kept glancing about when she was on camera, like she was looking for some support for what she was thinking of saying.'

'What is it that you think she might know?' Kennedy asked, surprised by Roche's insight.

'Speculation is the nail in the coffin of all the conspiracy theorists. I'm not going to fall into that trap – people just dismiss you when that happens.'

'Any other information you could share with us?' Kennedy asked, doubting the wisdom of asking that question to someone who had been telling him of an alternative judiciary system a few minutes earlier.

'I'm looking into it. There are a few theories coming up on the internet, but I'm not sure that I subscribe to any of them at this stage,' Roche replied, offering what appeared to be another painful smile.

'So we have to return to our original question: did you see Christopher Lloyd after the trial?' Kennedy asked.

'You can certainly go back to that question, but you should know that I have no intention of answering it.'

'Well, admittedly, we can't make you,' Kennedy answered, desperately fighting to find another way into this area.

'Exactly,' Roche agreed, 'so why don't we just leave it at that?'

'Okay,' Kennedy said, rising from his sofa. 'We'll leave it there for now. I do have one final question though.'

Roche's sigh of irritation was audible.

'What were you doing on Monday last between the hours of six pm and midnight?'

'Oh, I don't know, Detective Inspector. I was probably in the study working on one of my projects.'

'Would you have been logged onto the internet then?' Irvine asked.

'I wasn't, not all night, no. Do you realise how much it costs to surf the net these days?'

'Yes. Fine. Look, Michelle, I need you to think about this. You might even want to talk to your solicitor first but I'm going to need to find out whether or not you saw Mr Lloyd after the trial.'

'It's none of your business; it's none of my solicitor's business. It's nobody's business but Chris's and mine and that's the way it's going to stay.'

And that was the end of that. She couldn't wait to get them out of her flat. She kept pointing to her throat and didn't bid them goodbye, merely closed the door firmly after them.

'That's a bad limp she has, isn't it? Irvine said after they'd returned to the car. 'It's doing her in.'

'I don't think she's ill because she limps, I think that's a side effect of her illness. I think the voice thing is a result of the same ailment.'

'She must have seen Lloyd after the trial, sir,' Irvine offered, as he took a left at the end of Dynham Road. 'Why do you think she'd have wanted to do that? Do you think she was a conspiracy groupie?'

Kennedy remained silent. Irvine continued.

'So, she meets up with him after the trial, she tries to date him, he rejects her. She thinks: "You shit. I just saved your arse." And so she murders him in revenge.'

'Either that,' Kennedy replied, 'or that is exactly what she wants us to suspect.'

'God, it's unbelievable what's going on out there, isn't it, sir?' Irvine said as he turned onto West End Lane and headed south in the direction of central London.

'Or not,' Kennedy sighed, 'or not. Let's find out as much as we can about her. Everything: what she does, boyfriends, girlfriends, everything you can.'

Kennedy Irvine making mental notes. At the same time he made a few of his own.

Chapter Twenty-Five

KENNEDY VISITED THE incident room. Already present were Irvine, Coles, Lowe and Allaway.

They reviewed their evidence again but seemed no further forward. They did, however, have a lot more questions they needed answers to.

Supposedly runners, particularly marathon runners, hit a wall of exhaustion. So too had the investigation. Still, Kennedy reflected, it was much harder for runners. When someone like him hit the wall he could hole up in his office with tea and cookies, and drink and eat his way through it. The runner, on the other hand, literally had to physically fight and sweat their way through. Their secret, allegedly, was to try and go on autopilot and just keep on moving, anyway, anyhow, until they reached their second wind. And when they did hit their second wind they experienced this incredible high, a high that would see them through to the end of the race. But who was to say that they would ever get that second wind?

And who was to say if Kennedy would ever hit his second wind on the Lloyd case? He desperately needed a new burst of energy and he needed it now. He had absolutely nothing to go on, he had no leads to speak of, and he certainly had no leads he wanted to speak about. This was the worst feeling that Kennedy knew. It was not as unpleasant as an illness but it was definitely a similar feeling. He felt an emptiness in the pit of his stomach; he couldn't focus his mind; he was lost, stranded, dejected, and the feeling was worsened by the fact that he was meant to be the leader of the team conducting the investigation.

The main difference between feeling ill and feeling how Kennedy now felt was that he knew, with an illness, he had a doctor, medicine and the natural ability of his own body to heal itself and make him feel better. But in his work as an investigator there was no medicine, no inbuilt process, no doctor and no formula to save him from this feeling of hopelessness. Although, now that Kennedy thought about it, there was a medicine that helped and that medicine was following leads. Anything, it didn't matter how dead-end they were, just as long as you had a direction in which to search. Goodness knows what you were going to discover while on that path. And then, there it was; he experienced his second wind and he was sure that the high he felt at that point was akin to the runner going through their wall.

In the Lloyd case he took little comfort from the fact that all was still relatively fresh because he had no scene of crime, no witnesses, no real suspects and scarcely anyone, apart from Lloyd's mother Mabel, who even cared about the fact that this man had lost his life.

'Let's get stuck into a bit of the legwork, the plodding we're famous for,' Kennedy announced at the end of the session. 'Let's knock on some more doors in the area around the graveyard. It can't do any harm to ask that question again: "Did you see or hear anything suspicious in the early hours of the night before last?"'

Coles duly made notes in her book and nodded agreement.

'Let's also check the nuisance report for that night and the previous ones. You know what we're after; nocturnal disturbances, and any unusual comings and goings anywhere in Camden Town,' Kennedy said.

'I'd say we probably have about ten of those a second in Camden Town,' Irvine chipped in.

'Well,' Kennedy sighed, 'the sooner we get stuck into them, the sooner we might stumble upon something useful.'

And that is exactly what they all did for the remainder of the day. What did they discover? Nothing. Absolutely nothing. There were still a few more areas to continue with the following morning but Kennedy knew they were on a chance less than slim.

As he was about to leave North Bridge House, he received a message from Superintendent Thomas Castle. His senior wanted a quick word with him before he went home. Kennedy hesitated.

He was about to tell Desk Sgt Flynn: 'Blast! I don't feel up to it. I'll do it in the morning,' when who should step into the reception area of North Bridge House but Castle himself. Kennedy was caught in a sandwich between Castle coming into the police station and WDC Anne Coles going out of it. On the spur of the moment, Kennedy said:

'Ah there you are, WDC Coles, I'll be right with you.'

He then turned and faced Castle. 'You wanted to see me, sir?'

'Yes, Kennedy,' Castle replied and, taking Kennedy's arm, he led him over to the quietest part of the reception area. They were right by the open window overlooking Parkway. 'We need to do something about this.'

'About what, sir?'

'About that!' Castle hissed in a hoarse whisper as he pointed across the road to Parkway.

'Sorry?' Kennedy stared across the road and could see nothing but buildings.

'The York and Albany, Christy,' Castle whispered. 'It's a disgrace. If it's left any longer in that condition it will fall down around our ears, just you wait and see.'

Kennedy was bemused by the outburst. Once again he'd forgotten all about Castle's preoccupation with the building's condition. His superior was right, but what could they possibly do about it?

'What can we possibly do about it, sir? No one's been hurt yet. No one I know of, any road.'

'That may well be, but prevention is part of our work as well,' Castle continued, his forehead in a furrow of lines that Euston Station would have been proud of. 'Why don't you get onto the council and see if anything can be done about it.'

'Okay sir, but don't you think the complaint would have much more chance of success if it came from someone in a position of real authority?'

'Who were you thinking of, Kennedy?'

'Well, I was thinking of yourself, sir,' Kennedy replied very quickly, perhaps too quickly.

'Do you really think it would make a difference?'

'Most certainly, sir,' Kennedy said, hoping his grovelling wasn't too obvious. He hoped he was out of earshot of both Flynn and Coles. 'Now sir, if that's all, I need to get on.'

'Any breaks on the Lloyd case?'

'No, not as yet, but it's early days, sir,' Kennedy replied. 'We're just off to review the evidence again.'

'Yes, well, good. Keep me posted, won't you?'

'Yes sir, of course, and good luck.'

'Good luck? Good luck with what?'

'With the York and Albany, sir,' Kennedy said, accompanying Castle back to Flynn's desk and motioning WDC Coles out onto the street.

'Sorry about that,' he began when they were both out on Parkway. 'I just wasn't in the mood...' Kennedy was about to say something negative about his superior, but caught himself just in the nick of time. 'I didn't want to hang around in North Bridge House any longer tonight.'

'No problem, I know the feeling,' Coles replied.

They both stood awkwardly on the pavement.

'You have plans?' Coles asked after a few seconds.

'No, I just didn't want to stay in there,' Kennedy had answered before the penny dropped.

'Do you fancy a drink or a bite? It's my turn, remember,' Coles pushed, assuming, it appeared, that the advantage was hers.

'That would be great,' Kennedy replied graciously, thinking that at least he wouldn't now be guilty of lying to Castle. Technically, at the very least, he'd be justified in claiming that he was going to review some evidence with WDC Coles.

They decided to avoid the Café Delancey since it had apparently forgotten, or lost, the original recipe for its famous rosti potatoes. Café Delancey's loss was the Trattoria Lucia's gain, not to mention the fact that the fine, family-run Italian restaurant was much closer. Saturday night was their busiest night of the week and so Kennedy and Coles were lucky to get a table.

Frank, as ever, was excited because the Arsenal was doing

okay. Kennedy reminded him that as long as they were 'doing okay' they would have no chance catching Manchester United.

Kennedy wasn't really a football fan. Actually, he wasn't a football fan full stop. He'd been to three football matches in the 27 years he'd been in London and on all three occasions he'd witnessed the genius of Manchester United – especially on the first occasion when he saw George Best, Bobby Charlton, Dennis Law and eight of their mates trash Chelsea. Kennedy wasn't sure that the three visits qualified him as either a Manchester United fan or someone who could engage in a proper football conversation with football-mad Frank, but banter they did and it usually filled the time until Kennedy's usual dinner partner, ann rea, could decide what she wanted.

Kennedy always stuck to the same dish – spaghetti with pesto sauce and peas. Coles, in her only outward sign of nervousness, ordered the same and agreed to join Kennedy in a bottle of the fine house red wine. When they discovered there wasn't enough room in the bottle for both of them, they used glasses instead. Kennedy thought this; he didn't say it, although he was tempted, if only to lighten things up a bit between them.

'Do you mind if I ask you a question?' Coles asked, the moment Frank disappeared with the order.

'No, not at all.'

'Well, it's kind of personal.'

'Oh. Well, let's see what it is then first, shall we?' Kennedy replied, trying his hardest to smile a friendly 'I'm not your boss out here' smile.

'Well, this is awkward but I'll just come right out and say it. Are you and the journalist, ann rea, are you still… you know… still dating?'

Kennedy smiled. 'No, we're no longer seeing each other.'

'What happened?'

Kennedy didn't reply immediately so Coles spoke again.

'Are you okay talking about this?'

Kennedy looked at Coles. Was he just flattering himself or was she interested in him in a romantic way? What age was she?

Twenty-eight, twenty-nine tops. That would make her around fifteen years younger than him. ann rea was only ten years younger. Kennedy could never remember going out with a girl or woman who was older than him. When he was a teenager, older girls interested him but he had neither the knowledge nor the courage to do anything about it. Like the rest of the youth of Northern Ireland, he dreamed of being seduced by the older woman; the image that would always flash into his mind was that of Barbara Parkin from Peyton Place. He stepped out with girls on one of Portrush's two strands, and had a few investigative sojourns among the sand dunes, always dreaming he was with someone else, maybe even Barbara. Now he was an older man. He must be an older man, he thought. When you begin to notice that even Gloria Hunniford's daughter is starting to show wrinkles around the eyes you were definitely entering that state of being older. But did that state make him attractive to younger girls?

Hey man, wise up, he said to himself under his breath. She's a colleague and she's concerned about your well-being. She's not compromising herself in the slightest. Coles, without saying a word, was demanding that he treat her as an equal.

'Yes, I'm okay talking about it, Anne,' he said, realising that he'd never called her by her Christian name before. 'In fact, it's probably good to talk about it.'

Just then their wine arrived.

'I'll drink to that,' Coles said, as Frank very generously filled their glasses.

'What are you two drinking to? Putting another criminal away? Or are you drinking to Wenger signing up for another term with the Arsenal?'

'Kind of,' Kennedy replied, winking at Coles. 'We were drinking to another four years on top for United.'

Frank tut-tutted, or the Italian equivalent, his way into the distance.

'I didn't think you were a football kind of person.'

'You were right, I'm not,' Kennedy replied, deadpan.

'So, you were saying that you're okay talking about it. What happened to you and ann rea? I always thought you looked great together.'

'Agh.'

'What?' Coles said, looking hurt.

'That's a hard one, that's a very hard one. When you split up with someone and people say: "Oh, you were great together," or "You were the perfect couple," well, that does hurt.'

'I'm sorry; I meant it as a compliment. Neither of you appeared to be paid-up passengers on the dating roundabout, and so you assume – I assume – that when two people like you two get together there's hope for all of us meeting the right one.'

'You come here not to bury Caesar?'

'Sorry?' Coles replied, visibly confused.

'No, it's okay. I was probably mixing my metaphors. I know you didn't mean to hurt me when you said that. And you know what, you really didn't. The fact that you didn't and that I could joke about it proves in a way that it's really over. The truth is that we've been ending for the last year or so. We got to a point and we just couldn't get beyond that point, and I don't really know why. She's not a bad person but we just couldn't take it to the next level, whatever that level might be.'

'Did you fall out with each other?'

'No, we didn't really. Maybe we were getting frustrated with each other because we didn't know what was happening. I think we'll be fine as friends though. We do get on very well on most levels,' Kennedy said as his mind wandered back to how well he and his friend had been getting on in the early hours of that morning.

The food arrived, a thankful distraction for Kennedy.

'You were right, this is delicious,' Coles said enthusiastically, following a few bites. 'This pesto, pasta and peas combination shouldn't work, and I can imagine some of the telly chefs looking down their noses at it, but it really is scrumptious.' After a thimbleful of wine she continued: 'Have you got used to not being part of a couple yet?'

'Not quite,' Kennedy admitted, although he kept to himself exactly how 'not quite.'

'Yes, that got me. You know, you're so used to doing things as a couple it's never quite the same when you go back to doing them by yourself. How long had you been single before you and ann rea hooked up?' Coles asked tentatively.

She had this habit of asking Kennedy a question and then concentrating intensely on his facial expression to see how it had gone down before deciding whether to make any necessary follow-up qualifications. He must have looked relaxed about the last one, because she let it lie exactly where she'd originally left it.

'Oh, about twelve years,' he replied honestly.

'What!' She nearly spat a mouthful of food out all over him. She managed to retain it just in time in her hand and napkin. 'Sorry. God, I'm sorry about that,' she added apologetically.

Kennedy was in such convulsions of laugher that he found it hard to get a word out. Eventually he managed: 'It's okay, it's fine. You'd be terrible at poker.'

He thought for a moment.

'I mention that only because when Irvine and I went to see Lord Justice Bailey this morning, he said that Christopher Lloyd was so stony-faced in the dock that he would have been a great poker player.'

'Goodness, that was so embarrassing, I'm really sorry. That was unforgivable. But you mean to tell me that you didn't date anyone for twelve years?'

'Yep, that's correct.'

'Were you getting over someone?' Coles ventured.

'No, not really.' Kennedy paused for another swig of wine. 'It wasn't a conscious decision or anything. The time just passed me by. I mean, when I first came to London I very definitely had my heart broken and that was the pits, the real pits, and it took me ages to get over that. And then I started to date again and I went out with a few girls, nothing serious, and then before I knew it, twelve years had passed and I couldn't remember dating a single girl during that time.'

'How about married girls?' Coles asked impishly.

'Very good! I think you might have been hanging out with DS

Irvine a wee bit too much.'

'But that really is incredible: twelve years without a girl. No girls in twelve years. Did you never feel...?'

'Let's not go down that road,' Kennedy said, cutting her off.

'Oops, sorry,' Coles backtracked quickly.

'No, it's fine. I mean, it's not like I've ever been one of those boys, or men, who go out looking for a date every Friday or Saturday night. I've never been very comfortable with that. For me it either happens naturally or not at all. I was just doing my thing, enjoying my work, enjoying my life and, as I say, I woke up one day and realised that it had been twelve years since I'd had a romantic encounter.'

'By romantic encounter do you mean...?' Coles again chanced her arm.

'Use your imagination,' Kennedy interrupted, cutting her off for the second time in as many questions.

'What an incredibly gentlemanly way to describe it,' Coles said, more to her plate than to Kennedy. 'Who ended the twelve-year drought?'

'The very same ann rea.'

'Worth coming out of retirement for, I'd agree,' Coles said, finishing her drink.

Kennedy poured her another. When her wine glass was no more than half full she raised her hand to stop him, but instead of raising it to the brim of the glass she merely touched his wrist with her slender, white-skinned fingers and mouthed the word 'Thanks.' Kennedy remembered that Coles had a habit of mouthing words when in meetings and such, like she would mouth a word discreetly to Allaway or Irvine – anybody except one of her superiors. Maybe it was a sign of shyness or maybe she just didn't want to interrupt the flow of the meeting.

As Coles started to talk again – about having to drive her scooter home and not wanting to get stopped by the police, and about how in reality there was a fat chance of that with the number of officers on the streets of London and other such things – Kennedy studied her. She had a great smile that started at the corner of her mouth and worked its way up by degrees to a full-blown smile, which lit up her entire face. When she was smiling, she was what you could describe as truly beautiful. However, when she wasn't smiling, she acquired a more schoolmarmish face, which just might have been what Coles felt was appropriate for a policewoman.

Kennedy was still getting used to seeing her shoulder-length blonde hair in all its glory. For as long as he could remember, and up until recently, it had spent the majority of its time clipped up under her uniform hat. Kennedy had never seen her outside work before now, so he'd never had any reason to see her with her hair down. Anne Coles was full-figured and claimed that since she'd given up smoking she was forced, for the first time in her life, to watch what she ate very closely, for fear of it going straight to her thighs. Kennedy might be mistaken but she seemed to have become slightly more figure-conscious in recent months and he certainly noticed her new-found ability to turn a few heads, including Superintendent Castle's, along the corridors of North Bridge House. She dressed very soberly while at work and Kennedy had started to wonder how she dressed when off duty. The only make-up she wore during working hours was a vivid crimson nail-varnish. Kennedy wondered whether that gave a hint of how passionate she was. Years ago, when he'd been a teenager in Portrush in Northern Ireland, that was what the boys used to say: you can always tell how passionate a woman was by the colour of her lipstick and her nail varnish. Mind you, they also used to say, make them laugh and they'll fall into bed with you. Or was that if you make them laugh they'll never fall into bed with you? Kennedy could never remember.

Coles was great at accents. She did an incredible imitation of James Irvine; if Bond was ever going to be female she could certainly get the part. Her Thomas Castle was near perfect as well. It was not a side of her Kennedy had ever witnessed before and the more the evening wore on, the more comfortable she seemed to be to drop into them. She did a few movie stars, Bruce Forsyth and her Robbie Williams – 'I'm so bored, I hate everything I do, but as long as I keep smiling cutely all the school girls will buy my CDs in truck loads' had both Kennedy and Frank in stitches. Coles hadn't actually been confident enough to perform for Frank but he'd overhead her as her came to collect their dirty plates.

'I bet she does a great one of you, sir,' Frank claimed as he shuffled away.

Coles blushed. She went bright red, or it just may have appeared that way because of her blonde hair.

He tried to start a conversation about music and her likes and dislikes but it was a short conversation because she was not a music fan. She wasn't scared about admitting it either; it just wasn't something she particularly cared about. Yes, she grew up with her parents playing The Rolling Stones, Pink Floyd, Led Zeppelin and things like that, none of which turned her, or Kennedy, on. When she was going to school, all her mates were into Spandau Ballet, Duran Duran and Adam Ant, none of which turned her, or Kennedy, on. Movies were her passion. She was into movies in a big way and seemed, to Kennedy, to be able to discuss movies under, over, sideways and down. Kennedy wondered if she would get that particular Yard-bird message.

Kennedy considered how people's behaviour changed the more you grew to know them. They didn't mind dropping some of their tricks of the trade or characteristics into the conversation; they'd do a funny routine, have a few catch phrases, favourite accents they'd take off, dunk their finger in their cappuccino, dunk their biscuits, tell you their favourite jokes or stories about friends, etc. etc., but you were only allowed to share this when they felt they really knew you or they felt safe with you. They have the ability, we all have the ability, to shield things from people we only have a working relationship with. Kennedy wasn't sure he wanted to become familiar with anyone, particularly someone he worked with. It was too much: 'Oh, here we go again, it's time to learn someone else's set of tricks.' But you have to accept that it's going to happen. The alternative is that you only enjoy a 'working relationship' with everyone you come into contact with. If you're not careful, perhaps you'll even find you begin to act distantly with your family in that strange way that family members sometimes behave with each other.

The difficulty for Kennedy was that, with ann rea, all these things – quirks, call them what you will – didn't come as optional extras, they all just developed naturally the more he grew to know her. Every week of their relationship, more of these little foibles would come to the surface. In fact, if anything, that was part of the joy of getting to know her, peeling off layer after layer of her reserve and getting to know and enjoy some of what was hidden beneath. The true magic about ann rea was that none of it was ever predictable.

Around nine o'clock Anne Coles paid the bill – she insisted. She touched and then squeezed his arm, saying how much she'd enjoyed herself, and then went off to find her scooter.

Kennedy walked home thinking about how important it was, professionally speaking, not to step over a certain line with your colleagues.

Chapter Twenty-Six

'DON'T WE NEED to know more about Christopher Lloyd?' was Coles' opening line the following morning as she, Kennedy and Irvine met up in Kennedy's office. Kennedy was impressed by how relaxed – and more than Sunday-morning relaxed – she appeared about their previous evening. Absolutely nothing had happened of course, and there was no reason whatsoever for either of them to feel any embarrassment. Nonetheless, he had been wondering how she would handle it. Two colleagues had enjoyed an innocent dinner together. Yes, one female, beautiful and single, and the other male and recently unattached, but what did that mean? Hadn't Coles, by her presence in the reception area of North Bridge House, saved Kennedy from a potentially interminable delay as Castle bent his ear about something or other? Yes? Yes. So what was there to handle?

She handled it – or perhaps more to the point she didn't handle what wasn't there to handle in the first place – by waltzing into Kennedy's office and disturbing his and Irvine's early morning tea with: 'Don't we need to know more about Christopher Lloyd?'

'Good point,' Kennedy replied, 'indeed we do. Indeed we do.'

'Okay, so what were you thinking of?' Irvine asked, visibly taken aback by Coles' forthright manner.

'Well, I was thinking of his wife actually. She seemed quite communicative.'

'Right, that's a plan,' Kennedy said, jumping up. 'James will continue to monitor the progress on the disturbance calls here at the station and we'll go and visit…' Kennedy nodded towards Coles and then checked his notice board, 'Valerie Lloyd.'

Coles drove and talked; Kennedy sat and listened. She talked her way through the case and through the suspects. She wasn't babbling, though. Kennedy noticed she was doing what he'd often encouraged members of his team to do; to go over and over the details of the case so that they were familiar with all its finer points. After doing so, hopefully you wouldn't overlook some of the subtler evidence as and when it came to light.

When they reached Edis Street, Coles found a gift of a parking space right behind a lemon-yellow Smart car.

'Let's leave this until later. I need to get back to North Bridge House,' Kennedy said before Coles even had a chance to turn off the engine.

Without batting an eyelid, Coles engaged the car into gear and carefully pulled out into the street again.

When they parked the car at the back of the police station, Kennedy said: 'Could you find out the name of the owner of the car with the registration number W 745 VHJ, please.'

Kennedy returned to his office to find two messages, both marked 'Urgent'. One was from Irvine and the other one, ominously enough, was from Castle. Obviously he was back on his good neighbour hobbyhorse via the York & Albany.

On reflection, Kennedy wasn't entirely sure about the next sequence of events because they happened pretty much simultaneously. Irvine and Coles reached his office just as Kennedy was dialling Castle.

'The car belongs to Valerie Lloyd,' Coles said.

'I think we might have something from the disturbance reports, sir.' Irvine started.

'Kennedy? Good. Do you realise what's being going on in the York and Albany?' Castle said at the other end of the telephone, cutting across Irvine.

'It seems that there was something suspicious going on at the York and Albany, sir, the night before last,' Irvine continued, in Castle's telephonic space, not even aware that there was one.

Chapter Twenty-Seven

CASTLE HAD GOT so fed up that no one, not even Detective Inspector Christy Kennedy, had done anything about the eyesore across the road from North Bridge House that he had taken it upon himself to inspect the York and Albany first thing in the morning. He had stumbled upon the hitherto missing scene of a crime, after a fashion. He had the good sense to cancel his inspection immediately in order to protect the evidence.

'I found a chair with a rope still around it and traces of food and drink. It looks like someone was imprisoned there. I've ordered the building to be sealed off immediately and you should get your boys in there. Warn them that the building is in pretty bad condition. If they aren't careful, it'll collapse around them.'

'With your permission, sir, I'd like to cancel that order,' Kennedy said, as Irvine and Coles listened in to one side of the conversation.

'What? Are you crazy?' Castle shouted, so loudly that he gave Irvine and Coles ample opportunity to overhear both sides of the conversation.

'Well, you see sir, Christopher Lloyd disappeared for a time before he turned up dead in Daniel Elliot's grave. Now, my guess is that whoever murdered him needed somewhere to keep him for a while. Our murderer was convinced that he had a foolproof plan for the disposal of the body, so I imagine there's a chance, a slim chance, that they might have been less than careful in covering their tracks. So, assuming whoever it was might want to come back at some point, to cover up their tracks as it were, it might just be an idea not to call in the cavalry just yet.'

'Okay, I take your point. But it all sounds a bit Sherlock Holmes to me. You know, sitting in the cupboard waiting for the murderer to walk right in and reveal their guilt.' Castle moderated his tone. 'So, do you intend to do a stakeout, leaving things just as they are?'

'No, sir,' Kennedy replied immediately. 'I think we're safe to assume that we won't have any visitors during daylight hours, so as long as we're discreet and don't display any obvious presence, we can get on with assessing what, if anything, is in there.'

Kennedy set the phone down and Irvine continued: 'As I was starting to say, last Monday night at 3:43am a call came in from a Miss Christina Czarnik, a successful actress who lives in the big Hollywood-style house on the corner of Park Village West and Parkway, directly opposite the York and Albany. She was just returning from a night of clubbing and she was nearly scared out of her wits when she was passing the back gateway of the York and Albany because she heard grunting and groaning behind the gate. She ran into her house and quickly phoned us. The duty desk sergeant asked if she saw any vehicles. She went and looked out of her window, which overlooks the York and Albany, and she saw a vehicle pulling off the pavement and speeding the wrong way up Park Village East, straight across the red lights and up King Albert Road. Miss Czarnik said she didn't have time to get her glasses on to see the make or number of the vehicle, but that it looked dirty and she hadn't remembered seeing it when she was walking past earlier.'

'Okay. Let's pick a small crew and have a look around the York and Albany for ourselves. It must be the most popular closed-down pub in London.'

It would appear that since the year 1827 – the Duke of York and Albany died – there has been an ale house, a public house, a theatre, a livery stable, a tea room and the Regent's Park Riding School on the site of the currently dilapidated York and Albany pub. But it was never what one might call a beautiful building, or even a regal building. No, it was more of a wannabe-elegant Nash building.

Inside, it was an absolute mess. The walls were mostly stripped right back to the original wooden battens and where they weren't, plasterboard hung on in various asymmetric shapes, giving the impression of weird and wonderful undiscovered countries on an atlas. Most of the floorboards had been either taken up or pillaged, but there was an elaborate system of walkways which seemed to take you to the various doorways. Every now and then an extendable hoist would prop up overhead beams, planks or bits of ceiling. Kennedy prayed that the hoists would remain successful in their endeavours so as to enable his small but efficient team to go about their work. It was hard to figure out how the rooms fitted together because they were all a mess.

They moved to the first-floor landing and immediately left behind some of the stench and all of the rubbish – newspapers, beer cans, cardboard boxes, broken chairs, a pram and bottles. Clearly, those seeking shelter knew better than to venture upstairs. The stairwell didn't creak; it did visibly move two or three inches under their weight though. Kennedy cautioned them to use the stairs one at a time. At the top, there was one large room on either side of the landing. The room to their right was in bad shape, with only about a third of the partition wall remaining. The room on the left though seemed to be in the best condition; the wall was complete and the door was still intact. Inside was the evidence Castle had discovered.

The room was lit by a bizarre criss-cross pattern of beamed white light created by the police torches and small tears in the bin liners covering the four large windows, two front and two rear. In the middle of the room, equidistant from the windows, was a wooden-lattice foldaway chair. The chair faced the front of the building and seemed to be precariously placed on a couple of rotten floorboards. The SOCO boys were down on their hands and knees trying carefully not to destroy any potential evidence, while at the same time trying not to fall through the floorboards. One of them, dressed head to toe in a white boiler suit, had a mobile UV light and was using it to help him pick up this and that with his tweezers. Anything of interest was carefully placed in sealed plastic bags. He seemed to be making progress, but the truth wouldn't be known fully until the lab analysed the specimens. One of his other white-suited colleagues was trying to place a large, empty, plastic Ballygowan Mineral Water bottle into a bag as evidence. The bottle was obviously empty because as well as the top being undone there was a one-inch hole roughly cut in the bottom. There was a long piece of twine partially wrapped around the bottle with the remainder snaking its way, haphazardly, around the floor. He eventually succeeded in bagging the bottle and twine but he seemed to be experiencing difficultly picking up the bottle top, which was lying face up nearby.

'Don't try and force it,' Irvine warned.

'It seems to be attached to the floor,' the SOCO officer replied, repositioning his torch to afford him a better view. He turned round to Irvine, keeping his fingers on the dark blue top, his arched eyebrows caught in the beam from Irvine's torch. 'It's actually nailed to the floor, sir.'

'Really?' Irvine said, as he carefully negotiated the floorboard to take a closer look. 'Well, I'll be...'

'What is it?' Kennedy asked, from a position in the doorway, which afforded him an overview on the proceedings.

Irvine explained what they had found.

'See if that floorboard will come away easily,' Kennedy ordered no one in particular.

Irvine worked gloved fingers in the one and a half inch gap either side of the board. It offered a little resistance.

'Let's take the whole thing with us for closer examination,' Kennedy said, remaining in his original position for fear that his intrusion might bring the entire place collapsing down like a deck of cards.

'And what do we have here then?' Irvine said, once the floorboard had been removed.

The SOCO officer who had found the bottle and top shone his torch into the hole created by the missing plank. There, ten inches below and resting on the floor surface, which created the ceiling for the floor below, was a saucer.

'A rat trap?' the SOCO officer offered.

Kennedy felt his skin crawl and noticed that, like him, everyone else in the room stole a quick 360-degree glance around.

'Nagh,' Irvine replied, 'up here it would be like trying to catch an elephant with a piece of thread. No, if it was rat poison there'd be lot more saucers, or tin lids, and they'd all be on the floor surface itself.'

'Bag it,' Kennedy ordered and let them get on with it.

Could this be where Christopher Lloyd had met his end? What a sorry place for even a rat to die.

Chapter Twenty-Eight

KENNEDY OPTED FOR a walk around Regents Park rather than going directly back to North Bridge House. He had a few things he needed to figure out before returning to the bustle of the station. He thought about the empty mineral water bottle on the string. Had it played some part in Lloyd's death? Or was it merely the abandoned toy of some stray child or crazy person, an imaginary pet, perhaps, or a makeshift telephone? Why was the lid nailed to the plank? Surely it must play more than a casual part in all of this, but what?

The conclusion from the post-mortem was that Lloyd had been poisoned. Taylor had found traces of aluminium phosphite and had reported, that due to the absence of marks on Lloyd's body, it was likely that the deadly poison had been inhaled.

Kennedy snapped his fingers and pointed to the ground. The bottle made sense. Taylor had explained to Kennedy that you merely added water to the Phostek tablets and poisonous fumes would immediately rise. So, the victim is restrained in the chair. A floorboard nearby is lifted and the required dose of Phostek tablets is placed on a saucer on the surface below, and the floorboard repositioned. The bottle top is nailed, face-up, to the floor nearby. The bottle is then screwed into the affixed bottle top. Next, water is poured into the bottle via the hole cut in the bottom. The twine is wrapped around the bottle a few times and the murderer takes hold of the end and goes back down the stairs, gently tugging the twine, so that by the time he reaches the bottom of the stairs the bottle unscrews and eventually frees itself from the fixed top. The water inside flows down over the Phostek tablets, which unleash their poisonous gas all around Lloyd. Obviously the murderer is far enough away from the fumes to be safe.

Now that he thought he understood the method of murder, he made his way back to North Bridge House to see what good, if any, his new information would be to him.

Kennedy stopped by Sgt Flynn's desk and asked him to buzz through to WDC Anne Coles, instructing her – via Flynn – to meet him in the car park in a few minutes. Coles was down in two and smiled at Kennedy and Flynn as she said: 'Where are we off to, sir? Valerie Lloyd?'

'The very same, the very same.'

Two minutes later they were back in Edis Street for the second time that day. The lemon-yellow Smart car was noticeable by its absence.

Kennedy had Coles scoot straight round to Lord Justice Bailey's house on Avenue Road. No lemon-yellow Smart car there either.

'Let's go back to Edis Street and wait,' Kennedy said and Coles drove back down Avenue Road via the cumbersome, one-way traffic system at Swiss Cottage.

By the time they returned to Edis Street the Smart car was parked up between two other cars as neatly as the manufacturers had advertised.

Valerie Lloyd greeted them at the front door with a large, friendly smile.

'Didn't I see you up at Judge Bailey's earlier? You were in a car with that Scottish Detective I met, weren't you?' Valerie asked, proving again the age-old theory that the best form of defence is attack.

'Ah,' Kennedy replied, not missing a beat, 'I thought I recognised your car from somewhere.'

Valerie beckoned them up to the living room with a very flamboyant wave of her hand, closing the door with the other.

'So, how long have you known the judge then?' Kennedy asked as he and Coles sat down on the sofa.

'Not long,' Lloyd replied, taking a seat by the cream-tiled fireplace.

'How long?' Kennedy pushed.

'A time,' Valerie Lloyd answered. She looked like she wished he would stop that particular line of questioning. Kennedy gestured with his hands and raised his eyebrows, indicating that he wanted to know exactly.

'I get it,' Lloyd eventually replied. 'You want to know if I knew the judge before the trial. I'm sorry to disappoint you but I didn't meet him until afterwards.'

'How did you meet?' Coles asked, changing the tack.

'Would you like a cup of tea?' Lloyd asked, the smile evaporating from her face for the first time since she greeted Kennedy and Coles.

Nine times out of ten Kennedy would, of course, have answered yes and this was one of those nine times. He decided to ease back a bit with Valerie, thinking that they'd get further with her if she were more comfortable.

Coles stared at Kennedy in disbelief as Lloyd disappeared from the room. As they sat in silence they could hear the sound of running water, a switch being flicked, cups clinking together, doors being opened, packets rustling. Then, after a couple of minutes, she returned with a tray laden down with various bits and pieces.

'I'll be mother then,' she said, taking orders first from Coles, then Kennedy.

Coles kept shtoom; Kennedy assumed that she was following his lead of not questioning Valerie any further on the case when she seemed under pressure.

Kennedy talked to Valerie about nothing but trivial things; the new Harry Potter movie and how important the Potter books were to her kids, how amazing she found it to discover that her children, particularly her eldest daughter Whitney, expressing, for the first time, opinions and tastes of their own. Valerie was impressed at how, apparently from nowhere, her daughter had dissed S Club 7 in favour of Ryan Adams. Coles had no idea where it could come from either but Kennedy suggested that the traditional playground peer pressure was obviously still alive and well.

'Okay,' Valerie announced, drawing a line under their small-talk, 'you want to know how I met Judge Bailey?'

Kennedy nodded.

Valerie rose from her chair and went over to her grand Ambassador radio, which she turned on and tuned in to Radio Two's gentle sounds. She returned to her seat and said in a voice not much louder than a whisper: 'I met him through an escort agency.'

Kennedy thought he hadn't heard her properly and said, 'Excuse me?'

'Yes,' Valerie laughed, 'you heard right. I met him through the escort agency.'

'You're trying to tell us that you met Lord Justice Bailey through a dating agency?' Coles asked, her eyebrows tickling her fringe.

'No,' Valerie replied smoothing down her red dress across her knees. 'I'm trying to tell you that I met him through an escort agency – Fine Friends.'

Fine Friends indeed! Kennedy thought

'I'm a single mother. I don't have a lot of friends, I don't have a lot of money and I don't have a lot of free time to go out clubbing and trying to find men friends. So I found a way of solving all these problems: I found work with a high-class escort agency for which I get paid, and I also get to go out with some nice men.'

'But...' Coles started in blatant disbelief.

'Does that make me a hooker?' Lloyd finished Coles' question for her and smiled graciously. 'No it doesn't. For the record, I've been out with about thirty men this year and I've only had... erm... sleep-overs with two of them.'

Kennedy slumped back in the sofa. The single word that kept repeating itself in his mind was 'unbelievable', modulating rapidly into 'un-fecking-believable'. Not 'un-fecking-believable' that Valerie Lloyd was enjoying her 'sleep-overs,' but that she was actually doing the wild thing with the judge who had delivered the not guilty verdict on her husband on a charge of which – even from the most liberal viewpoint – he could never have been considered precisely innocent. What a mess. A mess that perhaps explained why Christopher Lloyd had escaped sure punishment, with a little help from the judge who was sleeping with his wife. A mess that also helped explain why the same Christopher Lloyd ended up dying in very mysterious circumstances. Irvine had told Kennedy that, according to Valerie, Christopher Lloyd had boasted to Manfred Hodges that he was close to something. Could that something have been a rich, fat-cat judge who'd been tied up – probably physically as well as figuratively – with his wife? The perfect scam, really. But the timing was vital. Who did what to whom was not as important as when who did what and to whom.

'Okay, let's backtrack a wee bit for a minute,' Kennedy began, composing his thoughts. 'Let's just go back to the beginning of all of this. How did you find out about Fine Friends?'

Valerie Lloyd seemed totally unperturbed by the proceedings. She didn't look like she was taking Prozac, Kennedy thought, but whatever it was she was on, it was working. She smoothed her skirt down again and said:

'Well now, let me see. It was one of Whitney's school friend's mothers.'

It just gets worse, Kennedy thought. He couldn't help but smile at the image of Valerie Lloyd taking her daughter, Whitney, to school and then standing around the school playground, striking up a conversation with one of her friends' mothers. He could visualise the conversation. 'Oh, Mrs So-and-So, that's a really nice outfit you've wearing. Gosh, isn't that the new, top-of-the-range Mercedes? Oh my goodness, Mrs So-and-So, are they traces of nose candy I see around your nostrils or was it perhaps just a tad too much talcum powder after your shower?'

And then Mrs So-and-So would take Valerie off for a cappuccino and Mrs So-and-So would spill the beans on her new-found riches. Kennedy's musings were hijacked by Valerie saying:

'It's incredible how easily you slip into it. She said it was really an escort service for wealthy businessmen who don't have the time or energy to go out looking for women but sometimes they either need some female company or they are invited "as a couple" to a function. Fine Friends has a great reputation and before either the client or the girls can go on their list, they do a check on you that is as thorough as the Inland Revenue. In the interviews with the girls they tell them that they are not after call girls. They want only to provide an escort for their discerning clients. They charge £200 for an evening, and the girls receive 60% of that. By today's standards that's high but Fine Friends state that they want to pay their girls well so that we don't decide to turn tricks to supplement our income. On top of which, they charge their clients quite a high annual membership fee; we don't see any of that, of course. But then, equally, if the client chooses to give us a tip or gift, Fine Friends doesn't see it either. The fee is taxed and the agency looks after all of that. The gifts obviously aren't taxed.'

'Now I'm sure you'll agree...' Lloyd paused and stared at Coles for a few seconds. She smiled at the policewoman as she continued: 'You don't sleep with every man you go out with on a date but equally neither do we abstain from sex on every single date. Just exactly like you, Miss, it depends on the man, doesn't it?'

Coles looked like she didn't know where to put herself. Kennedy was sure he saw the beginnings of a blush. Lloyd continued: 'It depends on the man. It depends on how well you know him and how long you know him. Of course there is also a chance that he may not find you attractive in that way. He may not be interested; he may only want to have some female company or he may only want to be seen in public in the company of a woman. So from my point of view, I was having someone professionally screen all my dates; I didn't have to rely on my intuition. I enjoy going out, I enjoy the money and no one is being hurt. Where's the harm in it?' Lloyd said, smiling directly at Coles.

'How many times have you been out with Lord Justice Bailey?' Coles replied, holding and returning Lloyd's stare.

'Must be about a dozen times,' said Lloyd, adding as an afterthought: 'Sorry, did you mean to ask how many times have we been to bed together?'

'No, I didn't actually,' Coles replied, matter of fact. 'What I would like to know is when you had your first date with him.'

'I don't remember exactly, but I could find out for you from Fine Friends if you like.'

'That would be helpful,' Coles replied.

Kennedy broke in cautiously. 'Did you discuss your husband's case?'

'The funny thing was that I didn't recognise him at first, without his wig and gowns and that. But he recognised me immediately. Shows how observant he was, doesn't it? Here he is, conducting this trial, and he's still sharp enough to observe everyone in his court. I found it incredible that he could do that. On the first date we went to his club, Home House, off Baker Street. It was pretty funky for a judge, I thought, and one of the first things he said to me was that we'd been in each other's company before. That was a pretty strange way to say it. I mean, I thought what he meant was that we knew each other or we'd met or something like that but he said we'd "been in each other's company." I racked my brain but I just couldn't think when that might have been. I mean, he looked so dignified with his two-tone hair and booming voice and all that.'

'Did you eventually remember where it was you saw him?' Kennedy asked. He still had the timing of the meeting uppermost in his mind and was trying to find a way back to that point.

'No,' Lloyd replied simply.

'So how did you find out?' Coles asked.

'We were getting on well. He was a perfect gentleman and treated me with the greatest of respect. Towards the end of the evening I asked him what he did. He told me he was a judge and we talked about that for a time. He's great at sending himself up, you know; he's got all these great courtroom jokes. Like he said he once had this regular criminal in his court and at the beginning of the proceedings the criminal stood up and said: "I don't recognise this court." And the judge said he replied: "Why on earth not? We haven't redecorated it recently."'

Coles and Kennedy had a bit of a laugh at that.

'And then there was another one,' Lloyd continued before the laughter subdued, 'a true one. What was it now? Oh yes, this old criminal was up before the judge again for the umpteenth time. The judge sentenced him to something like nine or ten years and the criminal says: "Oh goodness, Your Honour, I couldn't do as much as that." The judge said he couldn't help but smile and when he'd regained his composure he said to the criminal: "Well, do as much as you can."'

This one didn't exactly get the police detective and his WDC laughing but it did raise a smile.

'So he told you he'd been involved in your husband's trial?' Kennedy asked.

'Yes. He said I'd been in his court. He said that was when we'd been in each other's company before. And I still didn't get it. At first I thought he was referring to me and I became quite indignant. I said I'd never been up before a judge. He said not directly. He asked me when I'd been in court recently and I said I'd never been in court, and then he said had I not recently been in the public gallery of a court. And then the penny dropped, I realised he meant Christopher's trial. I still didn't equate him with Christopher's judge. I asked him what he was doing at Chris's trial and he said that he was presiding over it.'

'Did you discuss your husband's case further?' Kennedy said, quickening up the pace a little.

'He said right from the start that he felt Christopher was guilty and that he'd been very lucky to get off. He didn't really want to discuss it more than that, to be honest. He felt it would be improper jurisprudence or something like that. I was quite happy not to be discussing Christopher, actually. That's all anyone ever seemed to want to discuss.'

'What about when Christopher was found dead?'

'Well, we'd been on a few dates by then. I'd been to his magnificent house a few times, we'd exchanged personal telephone numbers and were contacting each other outside of the escort service; I wasn't seeing anyone else through them since my first date with the judge, in fact. When I heard about Christopher I admit he was the first person I went to talk to about it.'

'How did he react?' Coles asked, taking her turn at a question.

'Well, he seemed nervous. He said the police would be around to see me and that we really shouldn't be discussing it any further. He said it was kind of okay after the trial because his business with Christopher was done, but now, because of the murder, the trial would surely be revisited.'

'Did he want to stop seeing you?' Kennedy said.

'No. In fact he invited me up to his house, which is when I saw you. That's the first time I'd been up there in daylight. He wanted to make sure that I was okay but he still said that we shouldn't really talk about Christopher. I told him that I was okay about that. I told him that I'd lost Christopher a long time ago and that was probably why I wasn't as upset by the death as everyone thought I should be.'

'Did he suggest that you shouldn't see each other for a while?' Kennedy said, trying hard to keep a little pace to the questions.

'No. Actually, we arranged a date for tomorrow night. We're going back to his club, in fact,' Lloyd replied.

'Surely you must see how this looks, Mrs Lloyd?' Kennedy started. 'First off, you're dating your husband's judge. Then, your husband gets off on a pretty watertight case...'

'But I didn't know Judge Bailey at the time,' Lloyd said quickly, interrupting.

'You're sure of that?' said Kennedy.

'But I just told you, the first time I met him was after the trial and I didn't even realise he was Christopher's judge.'

'And you're absolutely sure?' he said again.

'On my children's lives,' Lloyd offered, then as an after-thought added: 'But you can check the dates with the escort service. They'll have it all documented.'

'Okay,' Kennedy replied, implying that they would do just that. 'Tell me, your other dates with the escort agency...'

'The escort service. Fine Friends like to be known as an escort service; they think an agency implies prostitutes,' Lloyd said, by way of correction.

'Sorry,' Kennedy said, 'service, I'll accept that. I was about to ask you if any of your other dates with the escort service knew Lord Justice Bailey?'

For the first time Valerie Lloyd looked a little flustered. Just a little, but enough for both Kennedy and Coles to notice.

'I couldn't possibly say,' Lloyd admitted after a pause. 'I mean, it would be extremely unprofessional of me to discuss one client with another, wouldn't it?'

'Quite,' Kennedy replied, his disbelief very evident. 'Tell me, Mrs Lloyd, would you by any chance know a Ms Michelle Roche?'

'Who?' Valerie replied, very matter of fact.

'A Ms Michelle Roche?' Kennedy repeated his question.

'Was she one of Christopher's girlfriends?' Valerie Lloyd in turn asked, and when neither Kennedy nor Coles replied she continued: 'No, can't say I've every heard that name mentioned before.'

'Thank you, Mrs Lloyd,' Kennedy said as he and Coles rose to their feet. 'You've been very helpful. We'll probably need to see you again. We can let ourselves out.'

'Can you believe that?' Coles said, as she closed her car door and secured her safety belt.

'It gets worse,' Kennedy replied, deadpan, flexing the fingers of his right hand energetically.

'Sorry?' Coles said, turning the car radio down. It too was tuned to Radio Two and Robbie and Nicole's mistreatment of the Sinatras' classic was playing. Kennedy thought that at low volume they sounded like two mice whispering; he just hoped they weren't distressing the mice half as much as they were distressing the humans.

'Well, DS Irvine advised me that Valerie's alibi for the night her husband was murdered was a "sleep-over" on a date.'

'A sleep-over with Lord Justice Bailey?'

'Right first time,' Kennedy replied, turning up the radio again. Now Johnny Walker, Radio Two's coolest DJ, was playing Tell Ol' Bill, a very fine track by Eric Bibb. 'Which would make them each other's alibi.'

'So Bailey must be our man?' Coles asked in a whisper.

Kennedy just blew air through his lips, partly in exasperation and partly anxiety.

'I can't believe she admitted that she'd been up to Bailey's,' Coles continued. Like Kennedy, she was trying hard to take it all in.

'That was probably Bailey. He probably told her to admit the whole thing before we got to it,' Kennedy replied, trying out his theory. 'He's probably going to say that they have nothing to hide. They are a man and a woman…'

'One of each…' Coles said, looking like she couldn't resist and then like she wished she had.

'Well, don't expect me to draw you pictures,' Kennedy offered in the spirit of the moment. 'They're both free and he's implying – via her – that they've nothing to hide.'

'But he found her very guilty husband not guilty.'

'No,' Kennedy disagreed, 'the jury did that.'

'But at the least it's all very suspicious,' Coles, pausing for thought for a moment. 'But if Bailey did help her husband get away with rape, why would he murder him? If he wanted to get him out of the picture, all he had to do was steer the jury towards a guilty verdict and then have Christopher Lloyd locked up for ten years. That way he could have kept his hands squeaky clean.'

'No, I doubt that he had anything to do with Lloyd getting off,' said Kennedy. 'I think all of that was a strange coincidence. Nagh, Bailey had no need to remove Lloyd from the picture. Valerie Lloyd also admitted to Irvine that Christopher had been out of her and the children's life for the past three years. I think we need to forget Bailey's involvement in the trial; that's a red herring. I think he met up with Valerie, Christopher found out about it and went to him looking for money. You know the sort of thing: high-powered judge, call girl and wife of a petty criminal, a criminal the judge had already set free – the press would have had a field day with it. So, Bailey sets up this elaborate, foolproof way of murdering Lloyd and, if it hadn't been for the extraordinary weather he would have gotten away with it.'

'Shit!' Coles said, and added shortly thereafter: 'Sorry.'

'And you know?' Kennedy added. 'From what Bailey was saying earlier today, he may have taken some satisfaction in bringing someone to justice who he felt had cheated the system, and in his own court too.'

'So do you think Valerie was involved with him in the murder?'

Kennedy thought about this until the end of the Eric Bibb cut.

'Well, it makes some sense that whoever carried out this murder had an accomplice,' he began expansively. 'But I doubt that Valerie Lloyd would be involved in taking her children's father's life.'

He went quiet again.

'So we need to see Bailey next?' Coles said, taking her eyes off the road and looking straight at Kennedy

'No, not quite. We're not ready for that. I think we'll leave it until tomorrow. That is, of course, unless we run into him somewhere in the middle of the night, if you see what I mean.'

They travelled in silence for a few minutes. About five minutes from North Bridge House, Coles spoke again.

'Look… I wanted to say something, to ask something really.' She frowned with concentration. 'If I'm out of line, can you promise me we'll forget the conversation ever took place?'

'Okay,' Kennedy replied, intrigued.

'No, I need you to promise,' Coles pushed.

'Ah,' said Kennedy with a smile and a sigh, 'if only we could undo what we said by pretending we never said it. It's an interesting concept. Go on, I'll buy it.'

'No, I need you to say that you promise.'

'Okay, I promise,' Kennedy replied, turning to look at Coles. Concern really brought out the classic features of her profile, particularly around her eyes.

'Well, I wondered if it would be okay if I asked you out to dinner…'

Kennedy was about to say something when Coles added:

'Like on a date, you know, an official kind of date-type thing.'

Kennedy was still looking at Coles. She had scrunched up her face and hiked up her shoulders the way you do when you were expecting the schoolteacher, while passing behind you, to clip you around the ear.

'I think I'd enjoy that,' said Kennedy. And he meant it.

Chapter Twenty-Nine

CHRISTY KENNEDY RANG ann rea, to clear his head. He wondered how she'd react to the news that he'd been invited out on an 'official date-type thing': the first time in his life a girl, or a woman, had ever invited him out on a date. He decided not to – tell ann rea, that was. Afterwards he wondered why he hadn't. He hadn't done anything wrong, had he? Hadn't ann rea herself said that she wanted to become good enough friends that they could discuss their respective dates. But he wasn't sure she had meant the very next night.

She seemed genuinely pleased to hear from him. She too invited him out to dinner and, unlike Coles, she actually pinned him down to a time – the following evening, in fact. Hey, he thought, things are looking up. Here he was, planning to socialise with two beautiful women over the next two days. Wasn't life great after all?

Five hours later, Kennedy was beginning to think that perhaps Castle's assessment that his plan was more Sherlock Holmes than Z Cars was right after all. Maybe it was a wee bit far fetched. On the other hand, in the previous twelve hours Kennedy had homed in on three suspects. And not just three suspects: one of them was a prime candidate, in the shape of Lord Justice Bailey.

Yes, he had three suspects. But on the other hand – if he could find a third hand – he didn't have a lot of proof. In fact, he had none.

The SOCO team had uncovered a load of evidence but, as yet, there wasn't one positive lead.

So, what exactly did he have to lose by going ahead with his harebrained scheme? Nothing!

But now his main problem was going to be one of endurance. Owing to the set-up at the York and Albany, it wasn't going to be possible to change shifts. Those on the inside would have to stay there, possibly all night. The back-up team though, in the beat-up old van Kennedy had positioned across the road from the road in Park Village East, would be able to discreetly change shifts every three hours.

As it was Kennedy's idea, he decided to take the all-nighter inside. He chose Allaway to accompany him because he needed Irvine to run things on the outside, and because he didn't feel it appropriate to spend the time with Coles. Was the possibility of a romantic relationship with one of his colleagues compromising him? he wondered. The thought disappeared from his head as quickly as it had entered. He had chosen Allaway for professional reasons and their long night would be starting soon.

They walked up and down Park Village East several times to ensure that no one was watching the York and Albany. There was nobody around, so, observed only by Irvine in the van, they slipped quietly through the gate at the rear of the disused pub.

Using red-filtered torches, which wouldn't betray them with telltale flashes through the holes in the window covering, they carefully picked their way through the rubble and gingerly climbed up to the first floor – the floor on which Kennedy was sure Christopher Lloyd had spent the final hours of his life.

He advised Allaway to immediately find a comfortable posi-tion to avoid any possibility of cramp, and the two of them settled in. Allaway positioned himself behind an old armchair that had been lying against the rear wall just by the window, and Kennedy moved into the corner of the same room, again just under a window. He was dressed in black chinos and a black hooded wind-cheater, figuring that, with his hood up, he'd blend in with the darkness.

At ten o'clock he was still confident about the stakeout. By eleven he thought it was stupid and was seconds away from calling over to Allaway and abandoning the project altogether. The flaw in his theory, he thought, was that no one would be stupid enough to murder their victim right across the road from a police station and then leave all the evidence for the police to find. Had he been so desperate for a break on this case that he had broken his own golden rule and made the evidence fit his theory?

He evaded these doubts by tuning in to the groans and creaks of the building to see if they followed any set pattern. It was amazing the way an old building had a life of its own. It seemed to breathe in response to the wind and the rain, the heat and the cold and the water pipes, which Kennedy was surprised to hear seemed to be fully operational. Why would that be?

By midnight he thought he was going to be the laughing stock of North Bridge House, but at 12.25 precisely he heard a dull thud from over in Allaway's corner. It didn't appear to be one of the characteristic sounds of the house but he couldn't be one-hundred percent sure. He also thought he heard the wind rustling on the outside of the building. He couldn't quite determine what it was. As his brain was running through the list of possibilities, he suddenly realised that it had been a still, clear night when they entered the York and Albany and so there wasn't any wind. Even if there had been a wind at that time of the year, there wouldn't have been any leaves to rustle.

'Allaway?' he whispered across the room.

No reply.

'Allaway?' he said, a bit louder this time.

Still no reply.

'Allaway?' he called hoarsely.

No reply.

'Allaway, are you okay?' Kennedy shouted, this time standing up and flashing his torch in the direction of Allaway's corner.

Still nothing.

He can't have fallen asleep on a stakeout, can he? Kennedy wondered, smiling to himself.

Kennedy carefully made his way across the room to the position he imagined Allaway should be in. The floorboards creaked in competition beneath him, betraying his progress. He thought he heard a creak or two that didn't fit in with his journey, then he remembered the floorboard they'd removed as evidence. He thought he knew approximately how far the missing board was from the back wall and Allaway's position. Just the same, he gave the area a wide berth – a berth wide enough to come upon Allaway from a different angle to reach behind the tatty chair Allaway had used as a hiding place.

Then he saw him. He looked like he had literally taken Kennedy at his word in his endeavours to find a comfortable position. He was sprawled out on his side between the chair and the wall – he looked like he'd fallen asleep.

Surely he couldn't be asleep?

Kennedy stopped in his tracks and then, in a flash, what had appeared to be a darker part of the back wall moved towards him. Before he had a chance to rally his senses, he noticed that the red beam from his torch caught the reflection of some shiny, reflective object.

He felt the gentle breeze of displaced air as the black form moved swiftly and deftly past him to his right. Kennedy couldn't be sure but either part of the form, or the mirror-like surface, must have made a connection with him because he was momentarily winded. His nostrils twitched at the memory of a smell but he didn't quite register it.

Whish!

He felt only the slightest pain as the object pierced his clothes and the skin of his stomach. He actually heard the hiss of the air from his deflating lungs as the object was withdrawn from his body as quickly as it had entered.

He turned and tried to catch the form before it got away, but as he did so, his legs buckled under him. He attempted to shout but all he heard was the gurgle of an irregular supply of air in his throat.

He sank to the floor. His right knee fell onto a piece of glass and the surprising thing was that the pain he felt when the skin was punctured was much more intense that the pain from the wound in his stomach.

By now he had lost complete control of his body movements

and no matter how hard he tried to steady himself on his knees, he could feel himself continue to topple over.

For some strange reason – something to do, he felt, with physics, body mass and body velocity – he fell onto his right side. He grabbed the pit of his stomach with both hands. He'd kept hold of the torch throughout and the beam now flowed across the room like a river of blood.

As he wondered what had happened to Allaway, he felt moisture gushing through his fingers and experienced a throb of panic.

Blood!

Blood was flowing freely from his body. His entire body produced a thick film of sweat. At least he hoped it was sweat and not even more blood. Blood. He was shocked by the amount of liquid seeping away from him onto the floor. How much blood was in a body? How much could we afford to lose? Why was the heart continuously pumping the blood through the veins? He supposed it was a wee bit like the way people and traffic are always moving around the streets. Now surely it would make a lot more sense for the blood, and the people and the traffic for that matter, if they just all stayed continuously in the one place? In the case of people and traffic it would certainly lead to a lot less stress, not to mention conserving humanity's natural and dwindling energy supplies. Perhaps it would mean Kennedy couldn't now be bleeding to death. How could he save himself? He needed to understand exactly what had happened to him. Someone had punctured his body and his lung with a sharp implement. Some of his blood was flowing out of his body through his clothes and some must be simultaneously flowing into his lungs. When his lungs were full he would drown. So how could he, in this semiconscious state, solve the problem? If he were a car it would be easy; he'd just turn off the engine and remove or repair the damaged parts. But if he turned off his heart he'd surely die. He couldn't do anything, he couldn't move. Why couldn't he move if he was just bleeding? He wondered if Allaway was dead, killed by the knife of the same assassin.

If he'd been fatally stabbed how come he wasn't feeling more pain? He had to admit that what he was now feeling was more discomfort than actual pain. He remembered experiencing worse times in his dentist's chair, far worse in fact. He felt like he was dying but if he was dying, how come his brain was still working and working as well, or as badly, as ever?

He rummaged through his brain to see if now, in this state, he could get a different perspective on the Lloyd case. He searched through his memory to see if there was anything whatsoever he could possibly have missed. It was like trying to find a bit of food that was stuck in his teeth. He knew it was there, somewhere, and he knew he was going to feel brilliant when his tongue eventually discovered and dislodged it, but he just had to keep hoaking around in the dark recesses for a while. Sometimes you think you've discovered it but then it will totally disappear a few times before you eventually successfully locate it. Could that be the real meaning of the saying: 'On the tip of my tongue'? What was on the tip of his tongue as far as this case was concerned, he wondered?

He'd wanted so desperately to solve this case – what would now apparently turn out to be his last case – and here he was, having just been stabbed by the perpetrator, and he still didn't know who it was. Kennedy couldn't even remember if he had smelt his attacker's breath. Now, how unobservant was that?

He could see his life flash past: his early days up in Portrush; his first feeble attempts at romance in the sand dunes beneath Barry's Amusement Arcade; college and college romance. He fast-forwarded his memory through this section: the vibey, out-of-sorts, early days in London; his first murder case at the back of The Hammersmith Odeon; him being sick on seeing the corpse; his move to Camden; meeting ann rea. He played all of this section in slow motion: the views from the top of Primrose Hill at two hundred and twelve feet and eight inches above sea level. He could see everything vividly and he was aware of the scenes from his life flashing past him but did that mean that he wasn't dying because he was aware of them flashing past him? Now that he'd been able to stop the replay of his life, what did that mean?

He enjoyed his life, he loved his life, and he didn't want to lose it. Was his vanity the reason he was losing the thing he loved and cherished the most? Had he done a great wrong to deserve this or had he just been in the wrong place at the wrong time?

What was dying like? Would it be like falling asleep? When would the exact point of death come? You know, that time you actually crossed over the line?

The last thing DI Christy Kennedy saw before he lost consciousness was Allaway's ghost-white face washed in the red beam of light from his torch.

Chapter Thirty

THE MOST AMAZING thing about dying, thought Kennedy – for he was convinced that he had died – was that he could still think.

Incredible!

Sure, wasn't that just the greatest discovery of mankind? The only drag was that you had to wait until you were dead before you realised and understood it.

Your thought process doesn't end when you die, Kennedy thought, to prove his point like a lion tamer sticking his head in a lion's mouth. For the lion tamer didn't seek to tempt fate but only to prove that he could do it. When the novelty wore off, he wondered, did the dead only continue with their thought process for as long as their bodies were still warm or intact, as it were? Would he be aware of his body as it decomposed and crumbled away? He had a vision of an entombed Mozart composing as he was decomposing. Could Kennedy experience the process of being at his own funeral and then lying around until his body wasted away?

If so, would he be able to see and hear people talking about him at his funeral? He imagined God chastising him. 'Come on now, just because I'm letting you carry on thinking after you've died doesn't mean I'm also going to give you X-ray vision.'

Had it been within God's power to save him? If so, why hadn't God saved him? What sin or sins had Kennedy committed that had warranted God forsaking him? Why did God forsake innocent children while saving others who had obviously turned their backs on Him? How did He make that choice? Was He more interested in sinners? Did saving sinners just make for better entertainment? Or was it an impossible choice even for God to make: who to save and who not to save? Had He got so bogged down in the decision-making process – you know, reviewing the whys and wherefores of each case – that He found, to His cost, that there were just too many casualties? Did He find that it was easier to do what He could when He could and never consider why He did it? That would make a lot of sense and even suggest that there just may be a few human flaws in God's personality.

Kennedy's thoughts returned to the graveyard scene. He wondered what it would be like to see and hear how ann rea acted with others, unaware that he was observing her. Kennedy was convinced that people had different personas in different company. He couldn't wait to eavesdrop on her life.

Great. Here he was, dead for only a few minutes, and he was thinking about ann rea already. 'For heaven's sake, man, get a grip!' he scolded himself. If he had been a smoker he'd have found the perfect way to give up now. But ann rea wasn't so simple. He wondered if, in his new state, he'd be able to eavesdrop on her entire life? That might be too painful, even for a dead man to take. At least he'd never now die of a broken heart. Good to see his cynicism wasn't killed off by death either, he thought. He hoped this novelty would wear off shortly as he was beginning to become irritated by all his little sidetracks.

He returned to the eavesdropping scene and thought it would eventually prove to be impossible anyway. Imagine being alive and aware of all the dead people looking over your shoulder, all the people you knew plus a few people who were just downright nosey.

What would people say about him now that he was dead? And would he be aware of it? Would he be able to accept in death the compliments he'd never been able to stomach in life?

Kennedy imagined and hoped that, in life as in death, you were aware only of the people in your immediate vicinity. Did that mean that when he was in his grave he would be aware of all the people in the graveyard but no one else?

His detective mind clicked into gear again and he realized that if he were to be buried in the same graveyard as Christopher Lloyd, he could find out one, who murdered him and two, if he had raped Eve Adams. That could be very handy, very handy indeed. But then again, what could he do with the information?

Nothing.

He wondered why he hadn't been properly focused on the Lloyd case? Had he been too preoccupied with ann rea or Anne Coles?

He wondered who would replace him. Someone dying or being killed on a case wasn't going to get in the way of the giant, outstretched, hand of British justice. Heck, even in Taggart, two different stars of the show had died only to be replaced seamlessly in the next series. So if they could do it on the telly, they could certainly do it in real life. Who'd replace him? James Nesbitt? James Nesbitt, how the hell did he slip into the thought process? He meant James Irvine of course. Detective Sgt James Irvine, he was well capable of taking over. But had Castle noticed this? Maybe the Super was so into the politics of policing that he cared only about his current heads of department.

But wasn't all of this thinking a waste of energy, now he was dead? Nothing he would learn in the graveyard was going to be any good to him now. Of all the millions of people who'd lived and died, not one of them had ever been able to transfer their new-found information back to the living. Some, even those as great as Houdini and Arthur Conan Doyle, had made vain attempts to do so when they were on this side – no, sorry, that should surely be the other side. He was now on the other side, the dead side, and they'd tried when they'd been on the side with the living. Either way, they'd made no connections.

Then Kennedy had another panic attack. He remembered that when he'd been on the other side – the living side – and he would turn off the amplifier of his quad stereo system, the on/off red light never went out immediately. The power-indicator on/off light burned as bright as ever for several seconds and then gradually, ever so gradually, it started to fade. The same thing happened with a computer terminal, and the very same thing with the old television sets, where the picture would be reduced to a white spot in the centre of the screen and would seemingly take forever to disappear.

Could the process of his life ending be similar? Someone had just turned off his power supply and it was taking a while for his brain to shut down completely? It certainly made sense. Was he now, in the words of Jackson Browne, 'Running On Empty'? When empty was done, was that it? Would he go to where all the people before him had gone, and turn to dust?

Who'd turned out his light? Was it Bailey? Kennedy hadn't recognised anything or anybody in the final few minutes. He'd been aware of a dark form standing against the wall, a darker shade of pale as it were, but even in his memory vision it was still; still as a column of bricks, in fact. He'd dismissed it as exactly that, a column of bricks, a brick pier supporting something in the ceiling but now, when he re-ran the scenes from his memory bank, he realized that there had never been any such columns or piers on the back wall.

This realization confirmed that his death had been his own fault. He'd clocked someone standing motionless against the wall and he'd interpreted them as an inanimate object – a column of bricks. If only he'd taken the time and patience to assess the information correctly he could, and would, have taken another course of action – an action that just might have saved his life.

There it was, his mistake. It was just like the computer games. You make a mistake and you lose a life. Kennedy had made a mistake and lost his only life. Unlike Game Boy, though, he couldn't just push another button to bring the next life up.

He'd always credited himself as a thinker, a fairly decent thinker in fact, and mostly he'd been able to use his brain to keep himself out of trouble. Of course, he'd been involved in a few scraps during his years on the force, but he couldn't remember ever suffering anything other than bruises to both his body and his ego.

Talking about being gentle and a thinker made him realize that neither had really gotten him any further forward in life after all. But did he really think that being gentle and a thinker should have got him further forward in his life? And in any case, he couldn't really have been as nice and gentle as he thought he was because he had still frequently lost his temper with people. But his temper had never gotten him into scraps. Being a policeman he'd have thought he would have been involved in more serious fights.

Obviously, there must have been a certain amount of luck involved in it over the years. Someone could just as easily have pulled a gun on him and put a bullet through his forehead. He wondered if that had happened, would he still have been able to think during this time after his death?

The main problem with the ABBA (Annulled Body, Brain Active) Club that he'd just joined was not being able to communicate with any of the other members, so he didn't really know what the rules were or how long life membership would actually mean. He was half expecting his power supply to beep out at any second so he was forcing himself to enjoy his thoughts right up to the last moment, whenever that might be.

So who was the person who'd materialized from the dark brick pier? Bailey? Surely the dark form was too agile for a man of Bailey's advanced years? Michelle Roche had a bad limp and was, Kennedy imagined, physically inept; surely it couldn't have been her. Frankie Hammond? Now he was solid, fit and looked to be in extremely good shape. Did that move him to top of the list? Or was Kennedy way off base and someone else entirely had been responsible for Christopher Lloyd's and his own death?

He wondered what killers felt when they killed. Yes, possibly that should have been a frequent thought for him in his line of work but he had always felt, while on a case, that that thought process could be too much of a distraction. Now, when it was closer to home, he wondered what his killer had been thinking. Had Kennedy just been something that needed to be disposed of and he'd just been disposed of? What was the killer doing now? Was he preoccupied with Kennedy's demise? This was a line of questioning Irvine could follow up with Dr Forsythe.

So, who could it possibly have been? Perhaps it was one of the people on the outskirts of the case. Kennedy started to think of scenarios for everyone involved so far and tried to imagine the circumstances under which each and every suspect might have murdered Lloyd.

A wee voice in his head distracted him with a question. 'If you'd lived, how long would you have continued your work as a policeman?' Kennedy wondered where it had come from. Kennedy had always been more preoccupied by what he would do after he finished being a policeman. He'd thought about that a lot. He certainly didn't want to live out his life to retirement in the police force. So what were his other ambitions? Well, he didn't really have any passionate ones. He felt it would become clear to him at the right time. And when would that have been? When he'd met a partner? Was that when he'd have started the next part of his life? He thought ann rea had been that person but he'd never considered giving up his work to be with her. What would they have done together? Moved to LA and started a small-time detective agency? Yeah, and gotten eaten alive in the process, he laughed. Would his ambitions only have become more apparent to him when he met his real life partner? Would that have been when everything would fall into place? Did that mean if he didn't meet her – whoever she was – he'd never discover what he should be doing with his life? Did he really want to be alone? Was that why he'd kept on being a policeman? Was that why he would have kept on being a policeman if he'd not been stabbed?

He started to get the shivers. The shivers? Did that mean that he hadn't gone to hell? Surely he couldn't have gone to heaven; he didn't believe in heaven. Is hell only hell because the devil keeps the home fires burning all the time? Sure, hadn't his mother always done the same? No, but seriously though, he felt so cold he could feel his teeth chattering. This wasn't pleasant, he thought.

Was this... could this finally be the end; you know, the point where the white dot on his television screen disappeared altogether? He certainly could hear a bit of a commotion start up all around him. He started to panic again. Why would he panic if he were already dead? He heard screeching, he heard crying, he heard wood breaking, he saw flashing lights.

YES! Fire and brimstone, this was more like the death he'd been expecting, a lot more. Here was a scene from a Ken Russell movie. Reds, lots of reds; lights, lots of flashing lights; lots of weeping and gnashing of teeth; yes, this could be it, Kennedy thought. Rather than lying around thinking great thoughts as your body wastes away, you're going out in a final blaze of glory. Houdini and Conan Doyle had both arrived at the same conclusion, Kennedy thought. Surely that was why they'd never bothered to communicate from beyond the grave. Why the feck bother? What would they say? 'Hello? Yes, I'm dead and you're alive but I still love you, still love you as you spend my hard-earned cash and forget me and take up with someone else.'

No point, no point whatsoever, Kennedy conceded. If only he could get rid of the shivers he'd be fine. Fine with his final exit. He started to think of all the things he would miss. He wasn't going to see what was going to happen on ER and Coronation Street. He wasn't going to hear the new music his favourite artists made. And the saddest thing to Kennedy was that he didn't care anymore, didn't care at all. All he cared about was how cold he was. He was still sweating but he felt cold.

So cold.

If he'd only tuned in to how cold he was he would have realized that he was, in fact, still alive.

Medically speaking, that was – and only just.

Chapter Thirty-One

AT MIDNIGHT THE same night, ann rea suddenly felt an over-whelming compulsion to visit Primrose Hill. Later she would describe it as a nostalgia surge. She wanted to go where they had gone, where they had spent some of their good times. She'd parked her car outside Kennedy's house. She didn't bother to check inside; she knew somehow that Kennedy wasn't in. Seeing him wasn't what this visit was all about. She'd been feeling such a strong connection towards Kennedy during the day. It was sadness and emptiness over the end of their relationship, the end that they'd recently celebrated. The method of celebration brought a flush and a smile to her cheeks as she wrapped her duffel coat tightly around her and wandered up the steep incline of the hill.

She was frustrated by her inability to deal simultaneously with her professional and romantic lives. She'd come to the conclusion that this was the source of her problem. She hadn't wanted to become Kennedy's 'other half', but, at the same time, she didn't feel his equal. She'd never have admitted this to him; she knew 'annoy-ance' would not have adequately described his feelings. She tried to examine what unfulfilled ambitions she harboured. She enjoyed writing and having her work published in a newspaper. But, at the same time, there was something about the title 'journalist' that felt alien to her. When she'd been growing up, when journalism was a more honourable profession, she would have been happier work-ing under the title. Somehow though, she had always felt out of sorts with something. Kennedy was great in that he'd always grounded her, made her feel better about herself. He was very together, and she wasn't. That, she felt, was the simple reason why it hadn't worked. He had his life in order. He knew what he wanted. At one point she would have been happy just to follow his lead, on the grounds that he knew where he was going. How wrong could that have been? Probably not at all, but she felt that if she'd followed along blindly and woken up several days, weeks, years or lifetimes later to discover it wasn't what she wanted to do or where she wanted to be, then she'd have made a drastic mistake and wasted her time – or life. Kennedy probably wouldn't have forgiven her for that mistake, no matter how hurt he was at their break-up.

Recently though, since her last night with Kennedy, she'd been thinking that maybe she'd gotten her priorities wrong. Her dad had always told her never to put her work before her life. 'You work as a means to an end during your life; you don't live this life to work.' In the remainder of his lengthy 'Consider the Lilies of the Valley' lecture, he told her that everyone he knew, including himself, did exactly the opposite and ended up wasting their lives, which was bad enough, but even sadder when you got around to admitting it.

It was a beautifully still night. The sky was clear and ann rea could see for miles. At exactly twelve-thirty, at a height of two hundred and twelve feet and eight inches above sea level, ann rea had a sudden sensation of her heart jumping out of her chest.

The sensation was as physical and as violent as that. At first she thought it was a heart attack of some kind but, apart from the initial thud, the sensation had transferred from a physical to a mental one. The next flash she had was that Kennedy was in trouble of some kind. She didn't know why she felt it, but she was completely convinced that he was. She started running down the hill. Instead of going to his door and banging on it or ringing on the door bell, she got into her car and drove straight to North Bridge House, illegally parking her car on the footpath by the main, but always locked, gate.

Sgt Flynn was on duty. ann rea breathed a sigh of relief when she spied the reliable and steadfast desk sergeant. Had it been anyone other than Flynn she knew she would have been thrown back onto the street again.

'Christy's in trouble. Where is he?'

'He's okay, Miss rea, he's out on duty,' Flynn replied, careful not to be flippant about her remarks.

'I know he's in trouble, bad trouble. Where is he?' ann rea persisted.

'He's on a stakeout and we'd have heard if anything had gone wrong,' Sgt Flynn replied, politely but firmly.

'Look, I don't know what kind of trouble he's in, I'm just telling you that I've never felt as convinced about anything in my life before. Please tell me where he is.'

'I can't do that, Miss,' Flynn said apologetically, 'but what I can do is check up with them.'

ann rea nodded positively.

Flynn raised a walkie-talkie to his mouth and, through the crackle, asked someone for a status report. No reply.

Again, Flynn tried to raise some life at the end of the line. Again, no success.

'We're wasting time, Sgt,' ann rea said, this time pleading. 'Please tell me where he is. I need to be with him. It might be too late.'

A few seconds later WDC Anne Coles rushed into the reception of North Bridge House. 'Have you been trying to raise us?' she shouted at Flynn. 'For goodness' sake, Kennedy ordered radio silence on this.'

'ann rea here feels Kennedy's in some sort of trouble.'

Coles looked at ann rea who was trying to use every bit of her soul to communicate to the other woman how serious this really was. Coles seemed to accept the urgency without hesitation and she turned and ran out of the station, followed closely by ann rea.

Both women ran straight across the top of Parkway, nearly getting knocked down in the process by a white stretch limo. Coles still hadn't said a word to ann rea.

Coles, dressed all in black, ran straight to the stakeout van and banged on the side with her fists. The back doors burst open and out jumped Irvine who took a quick look at both women. 'What on earth…?'

'ann rea feels that Kennedy's in trouble,' Coles said.

For the first time, ann rea felt she'd come up against a stumbling block. She accepted that Flynn, who'd just joined them on the street, could have turned her away. She accepted that Anne

Coles could have turned her away with a less than charitable reply – and perhaps if it hadn't been for selfish reasons, that's exactly what would have happened – but Irvine looked like he was having none of it, none of whatever it was ann rea was feeling. He was resisting her. However, Coles was now running across the street in the direction of the back entrance to the York and Albany. ann rea turned and went after her. After a beat, Irvine and Flynn followed on their heels. They say that panic is infectious; it can travel through a large crowd in a matter of moments without one person saying a word to another. The animal in us remembers the non-vocal language our ancestors used to transmit warnings about impending danger. This was the opposite though, ann rea thought as she blindly followed Coles and the pathway picked out by her industrial-strength torch; here they were all running madly and aggressively towards danger.

ann rea thought that the inside of the York and Albany looked like the set from a Hammer House of Horror movie. Coles was the first to reach the top of the stairs, the first to stop – to stop so suddenly that ann rea ran into the back of her – and the first to scream. As ann rea regained her senses she saw what had drawn the scream from Coles.

Kennedy was lying, shivering, on the floor in a large pool of blood.

Coles seemed incapable of going to his aid. She just stood there, stunned, and screamed for about twenty seconds. ann rea didn't scream, she sank to the floor beside Kennedy. She raised his head onto her knees. She struggled to hold onto his head with one hand and take off her duffel coat with the other as she heard Irvine on his mobile, summoning all kinds of help. He might even have thrown in a fire engine for good measure.

ann rea covered Kennedy with her duffel coat as best she could. She found herself absentmindedly trying to push some of Kennedy's blood back into his body. She looked at Irvine and her eyes pleaded with him to do something and do it quickly.

'They're on their way,' he said, through Coles' continuing screams.

ann rea couldn't be sure but she thought Irvine might have slapped Coles on the face to stop her screaming. The WDC had obviously lost it completely. Sgt Flynn had one of the back-up WDCs take Coles away.

Irvine moved over to Allaway who was now starting to groan in the corner. One of the other back-up constables moved towards them. He wasn't aware of the condition of the floor and was totally gobsmacked when his foot went straight through it and into the ceiling of the room below. He was badly, but not fatally, cut. Irvine and another WDC helped him up again and she then attended to the cuts on his leg as best she could while Irvine went back to Allaway.

Pretty soon, ann rea heard the sirens of the emergency vehicles coming through the park. She held Kennedy as close as she could, trying to give him some of her warmth, some of her life, maybe even some of her soul. Her blue cardigan had fallen open and Kennedy's blood was fast turning her white T-shirt crimson. She took it as a positive sign of life. The paramedics came rushing upstairs, followed by two firemen. ann rea had been right, Irvine had summoned them as well. The floor, he told them, was in such a bad state that he wanted to make sure the paramedics could get Kennedy and Allaway out of the building without further danger.

ann rea rode to the hospital in the back of the ambulance with Kennedy, who was taken straight to theatre, leaving ann rea and Irvine on a coffee binge until about four am when they were joined by Superintendent Thomas Castle.

At five-twenty Dr Leonard Taylor came out to see them. He told them that Kennedy was going to be fine.

For the first time since standing atop Primrose Hill five and a half hours earlier, ann rea broke down and cried. It wasn't Irvine's shoulder she cried on, it was Dr Taylor's. He told them that, if the doctors had gotten to Kennedy as little as ten minutes later, they would have been too late. He also told them that when the hospital staff realised exactly who they were operating on and how serious his condition was, they'd rung him at home.

Allaway, on the other hand, had suffered nothing more than a severe bang on the head and was kept in overnight for observation purposes only. As Dr Taylor took the two seniors through to see their junior, he advised Castle and Irvine that Allaway should be well enough to be back on duty within hours. Kennedy was in intensive care but Taylor returned for ann rea and made sure she was allowed to stay with Kennedy for as long as she wanted.

As he was leaving, he turned to her and said: 'I can't think of a better dose of medicine for him when he wakes up than to see you.'

'How long do you think before he'll be out?' she asked, watching the coloured lights blink on and off across banks of monitors.

'Physically, he should be fine with just a weekend off; that is, if he's prepared to take it easy and let the rest of them do the running around for him when he goes back,' Taylor replied. 'But mentally, it's difficult to say. Hopefully that won't get in the way of the healing process.'

Chapter Thirty-Two

AT THE EIGHT-THIRTY briefing later that morning, Superintendent Thomas Castle took charge of the Lloyd case. Truth be told, technically, as Kennedy's superior, he'd always been in charge of this and every case being worked on in North Bridge House.

Irvine was anything but disappointed. He felt Castle's action would retain the stability of the team. Sure, hadn't Kennedy himself always worked on the principle of the power of the team to great advantage? So, if Castle had promoted Irvine to take charge, or even worse, brought in another Detective Inspector, it could have very easily upset the workings of the team.

Castle seemed a little distracted as he was filled in on exactly how far the case had got. He was able to shed a little bit of light on one of the suspects himself. Around the time Kennedy was being stabbed by the dark form – who was now automatically promoted to chief suspect in the Lloyd case – Castle had been at a police function in the Swiss Cottage Marriott Hotel. The guest speaker had been none other than Lord Justice Bailey, and Castle assured Irvine and Coles that Bailey had not left until 1.40 am. How could he be so sure? Castle had left at the same time and Bailey had bummed a lift from him. Castle delivered Bailey directly to the front door of his white house at exactly 1.45 am.

Irvine didn't think losing one of their four suspects immediately was a great start to the new Kennedy-less phase of the case. In a way, there had only been three suspects as one of them was a double act: Lord Justice Bailey and Valerie Lloyd, the wife of the original victim.

So the team broke up, each to go about doing what they did best – amassing information. They had agreed to focus on getting more information on Bailey and Lloyd, Frankie Hammond and Michelle Roche, and they also wanted to question Eve Adams again. Kennedy had indicated to Irvine that he thought Michelle Roche might have had something when she suggested that there was more to be learnt from the victim, Eve Adams.

Kennedy's approach had always been to gather as much information as possible. Then and only then could you start to piece your puzzle together. Each and every member of the team had a part to play. Some used the modern, hi-tech approach; others, in particular Desk Sgt Tim Flynn, used the old bush-telegraph approach. Kennedy had set him about trying to locate details of Frankie Hammond's first wife.

He was on the phone as DS Irvine and WDC Coles were leaving North Bridge House a few minutes after the briefing. Flynn held his hand high and nodded at Irvine as he continued to chat to someone on the phone. Coles looked slightly embarrassed hanging around the reception area so she suggested that she would go and get the car.

'Great, Smithy,' Flynn was saying into the phone. 'I knew you wouldn't let me down. I owe you one.' Flynn paused and smiled as the crackle in the phone translated into some well-known phrase or saying. 'Okay, the Edinburgh Castle it is. See you there.'

'Good news?' Irvine asked before Flynn had even a chance to return the handset to the cradle. He hoped the desperation wasn't showing in his voice.

'Might be,' Flynn said, scratching his forehead with a pencil. 'DI Kennedy asked me to check with my contacts to see if I could find out about Frankie Hammond's first wife. Well, as it happens, Smithy – a mate of mine up in Finsbury Park – knew her dad, worked with him for quite a few years. Anyway...'

Irvine turned his hand around in increasing faster circles, indicating that he wanted the short version of the story and the telephone number.

'God, I really lost it this morning, James, didn't I?' Coles said before Irvine even had a chance to do up his seat belt. She was speeding down Parkway at nearly twice the legal limit. Luckily for them the Saturday morning traffic was a lot lighter than it was during the rest of the week.

'I don't know what happened, I just lost it,' she said again.

'I mean,' Irvine said, motioning 'Come on, please' with his hands, 'it's not as if there was no reason.'

'Yeah,' Coles sighed, 'but I'm a police officer.'

'And you're human and you saw a colleague in pretty bad shape,' Irvine said. There was something about the way his Sean Connery accent polished these vowels that made the words sound comforting.

'Yes, and I'd just asked Kennedy out on a date earlier in the day.'

'What?' Irvine gushed. He was convinced that if he'd been driving at that point he would have crashed.

'I know, I know,' Coles said sheepishly.

'No, no, no, Anne,' Irvine replied in a half whistle. 'We haven't got to that stage yet.'

'What stage?'

'The third stage,' Irvine laughed. 'The first stage is where you tell me you've invited Kennedy out. The next, rather protracted, stage is where I quiz you in great detail about it, and the third and final stage is where we're winding down and I start to sympathise with you.'

'Well, you knew how I've been feeling.'

'I did?'

'You did,' Coles asserted. 'And you know what it's like when you are attracted to someone and you know they're single, and you kind of want to make sure that you don't leave it too long in case they meet someone else.'

'And you don't want to be in too much of a hurry in case you catch him on the rebound,' Irvine claimed.

'Correct,' Coles agreed, ' but don't you think it's better to be in early rather than late?'

'Sorry?'

'Well, for instance, say I left it so late that when I asked him out he said, "Sorry I'm already seeing someone," it would be too late. You know, he'd already have made arrangements.'

'Arrangements?'

'Don't keep pulling me up on my words, James.'

'Sorry,' Irvine replied, enjoying himself.

'However,' Coles continued as she pulled out on the Euston Road, 'suppose I asked him too early, well, all he could say would be: "Sorry, I'm not over ann rea yet." That would be fine because after he'd gotten over her then he'd remember I'd been interested in him and maybe he'd give me a call.'

'Okay, that makes sense,' Irvine reluctantly agreed. 'But I have to admit that I'd never have pegged you as a lady who would make the first move.'

'Well, it's a sign of the times, I'm afraid,' Coles said. 'He's too much of a gentleman and too much of a professional to ask me out.'

'What did he say?'

'He said, and I quote: "I think I'd enjoy that." That's what he said to me.'

'Goodness!' Irvine said. 'Colour me impressed. So when were you to go out on the date?'

'Well, that's as far as we got,' Coles said reflectively. 'But do you know when I realised that I *had* been too late?'

Irvine didn't know but he didn't feel the need to say so; he knew Coles would continue when she felt comfortable.

'Remember when you sent me over to see why Sgt Flynn was breaking Kennedy's order on radio silence?' Coles started up a few seconds later. Irvine nodded that he did remember and Coles continued. 'When I entered the reception area at North Bridge House and I saw ann rea standing there, I knew she was on the verge of breaking down but she had enough resolve, or class, or call it what you will, to keep it together. She was keeping it together because she knew that's what she needed to do to be of any use to Kennedy. She said she felt he was in trouble. I could tell immediately that it was her instinct; she had no proof and she was prepared to hold herself up to be ridiculed if she was wrong. She was prepared to look like a fool for her man. How many women would do that? No matter what she felt up to that point about herself and Kennedy and whether they should be together or not, she knew then – and I knew then – that there was something bigger than the sum total of the two of them.'

'What happened when you saw Kennedy?' Irvine asked.

'Well, believe it or not, I don't think I lost it because of the state he was in, it was more because I could see Kennedy and ann rea had been so tight that she knew when he was in mortal danger. I think that that freaked me out the most, to be honest, and then when I started to get over that I began freaking out at the amount of blood he'd lost. I felt he was either dead or going to die, and I found the whole thing – about people knowing when their loved ones are in danger – all just a bit too freaky for me. I was just overwhelmed and I lost it totally.'

'Well, it was lucky for Kennedy that they were so tight, even though neither of them seemed to accept it. Dr Taylor reckons that if Kennedy had been left even another ten minutes, he may not have survived,' Irvine said quietly.

Coles blew air through her teeth. 'How is he this morning?' she asked, as they took the upper fork outside of Kings Cross in the direction of Islington.

Irvine looked at the mess caused by the road works around King's Cross Station. People were expected to just put up with traffic nightmares on the promise that eventually the system would get better. No sooner was one part of the system better than they'd start to dig up the roads half a mile away and then the nightmare would start all over again. Irvine was amazed at people's resilience to just get on with it; no matter what you threw at them they would just get on with it. Kennedy was a lot like that. Irvine felt that of all the people he knew, Kennedy was the best prepared to accept his lot.

'Apparently, he's remarkably fit,' Irvine answered. 'Dr Taylor said they were going to let him go home this afternoon.'

'Is that wise?' Coles asked incredulously. 'I mean, only last night he nearly died and now they want to send him home alone.'

'I don't believe that he's going to be alone,' Irvine said, carefully choosing his words.'

'Oh, is the Police Federation going to have a nurse look after him?'

'Not exactly,' Irvine replied.

'Oh,' Coles said, the penny finally dropping. 'ann rea is going to look after him?'

'I believe so,' Irvine said, not wishing to labour the point. 'We're nearly there. It's up on the right, but we can't turn here. We have to go around the block so take the next right and then back into Amwell Street.'

Irvine looked at the memo page Flynn had given him containing the following address:

Rachel Harris
77c Church Street
Stoke Newington
London
N16.

Chapter Thirty-Three

RACHEL HARRIS WAS a survivor. That was the overwhelming feeling Irvine had about her when she answered the door. She looked like she was in her mid to late forties but was trying desperately to appear ten years younger. Her hair was long and straight – too long and too straight. From a distance she probably did look younger, but all that served to do was to make you think, 'God, you're a lot older than I thought' when you came up close. She wore skintight black trousers, creating the impression that she was all hair and trousers. She wore her make-up subtly and she made maximum use of her full lips, which were certainly her best feature. She refused to let Coles and Irvine into her house, so they stated their business on the doorstep.

'I understand you were once married to Frankie Hammond?' said Coles.

'So this is about Frank?' Harris began. 'Hang on here a minute while I get my coat and we'll go for a little walk.'

For two and a half minutes Coles and Irvine kicked their heels on the doorstep. Irvine hoped that every time Coles caught him looking at her, his 'so you've made a move on Kennedy' expression wasn't too obvious. He still couldn't believe that she had done that. He thought it would probably have been a bit of a turnoff for him on the grounds that the less interested the woman was, the more interested he always seemed to be. The way Coles dropped her head but then turned her eyes back up to his face meant that she knew he was thinking about her and Kennedy but she didn't say a word about it. Eventually Rachel Harris returned in a dark-blue donkey jacket. Irvine was bemused by the fact that she was wearing her waist-length hair inside her coat, not outside; surely that must limit her head movement somewhat, he thought.

'Let's head across the road to the park. We'll have a bit of privacy there,' she advised, leading them away from her house.

Irvine felt that she must have been entertaining a friend at home and that she didn't want to be involved in a conversation about her ex-husband in front of them.

'The girls, my two daughters that is,' she began, immediately blowing Irvine's theory out of the water. 'Well, let's just say that neither of them would be paid-up members of Frank's fan club, so I thought we'd be able to talk more freely out here. I hope you're okay with that.'

'That's perfectly fine, Rachel,' Coles smiled.

The footpath was only really wide enough for two so Irvine hung back and let Coles and Harris lead the way. Because of this, there was no further conversation until they reached the square, just lots of path staring.

'I think it's incredible in here,' Harris said, leading them over to a bench. 'I often come in here just to hear myself think. Don't you think it's incredible that you can be in the centre of London and still have this little oasis?'

'Quite,' Irvine agreed, taking a seat on the left-hand side of the bench and leaving Harris in the middle. 'Am... how long were you married to Frankie?'

Rachel Harris seemed to consider this question for longer than one would have thought necessary. Either she'd genuinely forgotten or she'd pushed the memories so far back into the recesses of her mind that she was having trouble digging them out again. Eventually she spoke.

'Sixteen years, seven months, one week and five days, if you need to know the exact time.'

'A long time to stay together,' Irvine said, not really knowing where this might go.

'You mean a long time to stay with someone and then get divorced from them?' Harris said, turning to look Irvine straight in the eyes.

'No,' Irvine began confidently. 'I meant it's a long time for two people to have been together.'

'Yes, I suppose it is,' Harris continued, somewhat relieved.

'What was he like when you first married?' Coles asked, changing tack.

'He was... he was...' Harris again seemed to be searching for something from deep within. To Irvine and Coles, the beginnings of a gentle smile seemed to play on her lips but apart from that, she looked to Irvine like she was absent. Yes, Irvine thought, absent was the word that best described Rachel Harris. Now she became distracted by a couple who walked into the square with a baby in a pram and a boy who looked about four and who couldn't wait to run around the square and experiment with every bit of apparatus and bench and tree, and even dog-do.

'That's when it's perfect,' Harris said, ending her block. 'You meet someone, you get to know them, you fall in love with them, you marry, you have a child, then you have another child, then you are so preoccupied with your children that you neglect your own relationship. Years pass, then you realize that you never really knew the father, you knew only the part of him that he wanted you to know. You keep saying to yourself that you couldn't have been so wrong about someone, so you deny your thoughts. That's what we do, you know, we deny our thoughts and our instincts.'

'So Frank wasn't the man you thought he was?' Coles asked quietly while looking straight ahead.

'What do you mean?' Harris said, turning to her left.

'Well, was he cheating?' Coles asked.

'What, cheating with other women?'

'Yes,' Coles said.'

'Oh, I wish.'

'Was he into crime?' Irvine asked, thinking that he hadn't really considered Hammond smooth enough to be a womaniser.

'You know what, if it wouldn't mean hurting people, I'd have wished he was a criminal.'

In the space of a couple of minutes Harris had grown visibly upset. She looked like she was barely keeping it together and her composure seemed about to disintegrate all around her long, straight, brown hair.

Coles and Irvine both backed off at that point and just sat in silence with Harris, both trying carefully not to put the slightest hint of pressure on her that might cause her to break down.

'Frank's trouble was that he liked teenage girls,' Harris eventually said.

'Oh,' Coles said.

'Agh no,' Irvine said simultaneously.

'But that wasn't the worst thing...' Harris continued after a few seconds.

'Wh..' Irvine was about to say something but stuttered to a stop mid-word.

'It was our daughters he liked.'

Harris let out an abrupt sob, and then, just as suddenly, she seemed to regain her resolve and composure.

'I'm sorry,' she began.

'No, don't be, for goodness' sake,' Irvine replied.

'No. It's just that I haven't even considered this for so long. It's been buried so deep. My doctor says I should be dealing with all of this stuff or it will destroy me. Ha, what's left to destroy!'

Coles lifted her arm and put it around Harris' shoulders.

'Has he been up to his old tricks again?' Harris asked, turning away from Coles and looking at Irvine.

'No, no, not at all,' Coles said quickly. 'We're investigating a case that he's indirectly involved with and we're just trying to get some background information on him.'

'We've checked him on our computer and he's never been in trouble before,' Irvine said.

'That's my fault. I just couldn't bring the charges. I couldn't put the girls through it again,' Harris continued, apparently happier to discuss the subject. 'I made all the classic mistakes. When Gina, my eldest, started complaining about her father, I thought she was suffering from an overactive imagination. I mean, he couldn't be doing that to our daughter, could he? Eventually Gina stopped complaining, and I thought it had all been a storm in a teacup. Then Frances, who'd always been very outgoing, started to get withdrawn and moody. I thought it was just, you know, the pressures of being a teenager. Then Gina confronted me and said that he was at it again, only this time, if I didn't do something about it, she was going to go to the police.'

Coles kept her arm around Harris' shoulders and Irvine was bent over, elbows on his knees, looking up into Harris' face. Neither of the police officers said a word, feeling that she'd continue when she was ready, which was exactly what she did a minute or so later.

'I was beside myself. I didn't know what to do. I mean, I watched him but he still seemed to me to be a normal man. We hadn't had a sexual relationship for quite a few years by that stage but I put that down to the fact that we'd been together for ages and had grown too used to each other. I thought that was normal. All my friends were always laughing about their old men not paying them attention anymore. I must admit, though, I did start to watch him like a hawk. I stopped taking my sleeping pills and then one night, sure enough, he got out of bed in the middle of the night. I waited a few minutes and, when I thought I heard Frances cry ever so softly, I went into her room.

Frank always kept a piece of wood under our bed, you know, in case any thieves would try to do our house while we slept. So I took that bit of wood with me. I didn't even realize I had it until I went into Frances' room. I don't know what came over me but I just said in a very calm, natural voice: "Frank, could I see you for a minute." By this time our Gina was behind me and when Frank came out into the hallway I pushed Gina into her sister's room and closed the door. Then I went absolutely berserk. I battered him about the head. It was like I was possessed. I didn't worry whether or not I killed him, and I know one wrong blow to his head could have done exactly that. When he put his hands up to protect himself, I battered them with the wood and then I chased him down the stairs and out into the street. I locked the door after him. And that's when my legs just went from under me. I collapsed in the hallway on the inside of the door and I felt that my heart was going to burst it was pumping so hard. Then Gina and Frances came down the stairs and instead of being scared – I'll never forget this – they were smiling. They looked so happy.

'The three of us ran around the house like mad things, collecting all his things and stuffing them into bin liners. We threw everything out the window after him and told him if he ever came within a mile of the house again we'd bring the police in. He sent lots of letters asking for forgiveness, but I told him that I wanted a divorce or I would go to the police. We got the house because it was rightfully ours but I've never taken another penny from him. We looked after ourselves and that was it until you arrived at my door asking me if I was once married to Frankie Hammond. I had a panic attack because I thought he'd been up to his old tricks again and it had been all my fault because I hadn't gone to the police instead of throwing him out of our house.'

Coles and Irvine walked Rachel Harris back to her house and as they were saying their goodbyes, Irvine asked one final question. 'Tell me, can you remember if Frankie was ever a keen gardener?'

Harris laughed for the first time since they met her. 'Keen gardener? Frank's idea of gardening was to lay all the front of the house in concrete and use it to park his cars on.'

When Coles and Irvine were driving back to North Bridge House they received a message that Kennedy would like to see them at his house as soon as possible.

'What's that all about?' Coles began tentatively.

'I imagine, knowing Kennedy, that his mind is in gear no matter how poor his body is, and he's still thinking about the case.'

'Maybe I should just drop you off there?' Coles offered.

Irvine sighed. 'Not sure that's such a good idea.'

'I can always see him later,' Coles offered in hope.

'Nagh,' Irvine said. 'Let's get it over with. If you put it off now it will make it twice as hard next time.'

'But ann rea is going to be there.'

'I would imagine ann rea is going to be around from now on,'

Irvine said, slapping his knees in time to the music on the radio. He didn't know what it was and he didn't care. He just wanted to give Coles the impression that what they were talking about was no big deal.

By the time they'd reached Regents Park Road and Coles had taken a right into Chalcot Crescent and then another left into Rothwell Street, the song, and Irvine's drumming, had finished. They parked opposite Kennedy's house and as they were walking across the road, Coles broke the ice by saying: 'James, did I ever tell you what a crap sense of rhythm you have.'

Irvine smiled and rang the doorbell. They heard voices inside and a few seconds later ann rea, looking stunning in a tight black T-shirt and pants (more like thick tights, Irvine assessed) and a pair of black flip-flops, opened the door and greeted them with a huge smile.

Kennedy was sitting in the kitchen. He was looking remarkably healthy and fit for someone who'd nearly died the day before. Just shows you how fine the line is between life and death, Irvine thought, as he and Coles each pulled up a chair at the large oak table.

Chapter Thirty-Four

KENNEDY WAS MORE interested in talking about the case than talking about his health. He did say that he felt incredibly weak but was surprised at how mentally alert he felt.

'ann rea tells me that if it hadn't been for you, Anne, I might not have been feeling anything at this stage,' he said.

Coles made to protest but ann rea continued with Kennedy's line. 'No. If you had questioned me, doubted me, or even stopped outside the York and Albany, we could have been too late.'

'I think you're being very gracious,' Coles hesitated. 'I think I could have, erm, behaved more appropriately...erm, when we found you, sir.'

'I've got you all to thank,' Kennedy said, offering an air of finality to that part of the conversation. 'Now, how are we progressing on the Christopher Lloyd case?'

'Well,' Coles said, jumping in before Irvine had a chance, 'Superintendent Castle was at a function with Lord Justice Bailey at the time of your attack, sir, so that rules him out, I suppose.'

'Unless he had an accomplice?' Irvine added.

'Well,' Kennedy said, accepting ann rea's offer of a cup of tea as Irvine rose to help her, 'the most obvious person would be Valerie Lloyd and I'm sure whoever attacked me was more lithe and agile than her.'

Coles then recalled for Kennedy the interview she and Irvine had just conducted with Rachel Harris.

'So, Sgt Flynn turns up trumps for us again,' was Kennedy's only response.

They chit-chatted away generally for the following fifteen minutes as they drank their tea. Kennedy seemed to have less of a passion for his favourite brew than usual.

'What I'd like is for you to have Flynn pick up Frankie Hammond,' Kennedy ordered, taking control of the case again, 'and bring him into the station for questioning. But in the meantime, could youse two go and interview Eve Adams again. I've got a hunch that Michelle Roche's view that Eve knew more and, more importantly, wanted to tell more may be quite accurate.'

'Okay,' Irvine said, indicating he was happy to accept the reinstated chain of command. 'Should we question Hammond when we get him back to the station?'

'No,' Kennedy replied, sounding winded. 'I'd like to leave him to stew overnight and I'll talk with him in the morning.'

Coles, Irvine and ann rea all stopped in their tracks. Kennedy felt they were all thinking 'You're a fool!' But no one, except ann rea, had the courage to say it. Her exact words were: 'You're a fecking eejit!'

'Ah,' Kennedy smiled, 'glad to see you've picked up some Ulsterspeak during our time together.'

'Well, in this case, it's the perfect word to describe you,' ann rea replied, visibly upset but still in control.

'Let's see how I feel in the morning,' Kennedy said, in an act of compromise. He didn't want to waste the little energy he did have on arguing, particularly with the woman who'd saved his life.

ann rea let Coles and Irvine out and Kennedy could hear them giving it lots of whispering and concern out in the hallway.

'What I'd like to do now is to go to bed and try and get a good night's sleep,' Kennedy said when ann rea returned.

He liked having her around all the time and he liked the way she didn't pussyfoot around him. The other thing he liked was that they hadn't discussed 'them' since the incident. She was there as a friend and he couldn't think of another friend he wanted around him more.

She helped him up the stairs via the bathroom and helped him into bed.

'I'm not going to lecture you, Christy. You and you alone know what you're capable of. I know that Dr Taylor thinks you shouldn't lie around the house for ever, but I'm not sure that even he means you should be back at work as quickly as you want. I'll ask you to be careful though. You've been through a lot, okay?'

'Is that the end of the lecture you weren't going to give me?'

'You know what I'm saying, Christy, that's all,' ann rea said as she picked up her book, *First of The True Believers* by Theodore Hennessy. By the time she sat in the chair close to Kennedy and found her page, Kennedy was asleep. It was three-thirty in the afternoon, probably the earliest in the day he'd been asleep since he was a child.

Chapter Thirty-Five

FIFTEEN MINUTES AFTER leaving Kennedy's house, Irvine and Coles were ringing on another doorbell, this time that of the Adams' household up on Talacre Road, around the corner from Primrose Hill in Chalk Farm.

Eve Adams wasn't at home. Her mother thought she would be down at the café in the Stables Market, not too far away.

And not too far away from Lloyd's stall, Irvine thought. Ten minutes later they were looking for Eve around the Stables. Twenty minutes later they found her in the archway between the Stables and Camden Lock, trying on an afghan coat of the sort that was very popular in the '60s, and which seemed to be making a bit of a comeback if the number on display in Camden Market was anything to go by.

'Buy us a cup of tea, will ya?' was Eve Adams' reply when Coles said they'd like a few words with her.

It was Saturday afternoon and the market was in full flow with every sex, race and creed imaginable. Cash was changing hands at an amazing rate, and the hustle and bustle drew pickpockets like iron filings to a magnet. Eve, in her own words, was 'pretty hip to all the shit what was goin' down.' She also seemed well known by the locals. She nipped into the back of one of the stalls unchallenged, with a fiver she'd blagged from Irvine, and came out a couple of minutes later with two cups of steaming hot tea, a can of Coca-Cola and no change.

She took them to an unused stall up in the Stables, far from the madding crowd. Coles started the proceedings.

'We wanted to talk to you some more about the Lloyd case.'

Eve downed the majority of her can in two minutes and took a large intake of breath. 'Yeah, Madonna's mum told me somefink this morning. She said the police was going to be around soon looking under stones because someone had topped the cop who was looking after the case. I hope it wasn't the Ulster geezer who interviewed me last time. He was nice. He listened to me properly. He got what I was saying, you know, not treating me like an alien or somefink.'

Word gets around fast, Irvine thought. How do people find out these things so quickly? It was Saturday and there'd been no radio or newspaper reports about Kennedy getting stabbed. Yet, around Camden Town, already people were talking about it. How exactly does that happen?

In this instance, the bush-telegraph trail was easy to follow. ann rea had organised to meet a non-journalist friend of hers from the Camden News Journal for lunch on Saturday. Being ann rea and being conscientious, she had rung early that morning to cancel. She hadn't said what was wrong with Kennedy, other than that he'd been involved in a bit of an incident and she was going to look after him for a few days. This friend rang up another journalist friend who worked on the paper to try and fill the gap in her lunchtime schedule. The second friend already had a lunch date in Café Delancey with a show business contact of hers: Christina Czarnik – the very same Christina who lived opposite the York and Albany. When the journalist rang to see if she was happy for another friend to come along too, Miss Czarnik told her that she'd been up half the night with police and ambulance sirens going on about one o'clock in the morning. She said she'd taken a look out of the window to see what it was all about and seen ann rea – she was sure it was ann rea – and someone she was convinced looked like Christy Kennedy being taken out of York and Albany on a stretcher and placed in an ambulance that went speeding down the street.

From there the journalist put two and two together and was on the phone to see what else she could find out to scoop ann rea on her own story. She rang a contact of hers who sold newspapers in Camden Market. The stall owner didn't have any new information but he was repeating word for word what the journalist was telling him – in apparent disbelief. It just so happened that Mrs Heather

Walker was buying her daily copy of The Sun at the same time. Mrs Heather Walker was next-door neighbour to Mrs Christine Duncan, the mother of Madonna. Mrs Walker and Mrs. Duncan were good friends; in fact, they enjoyed elevenses together on Monday, Wednesday and Friday, alternating houses for the midmorning, sweet-tooth treat. Mrs Walker thought her news too good to keep until Monday so she knocked on Christine's door and over tea told her what she had heard at the newspaper stall in the market. Christine told her daughter, who immediately rang her best mate, Eve, who was just about to go down to the market and, an hour later, Eve gave her somewhat embellished version of the story to Coles and Irvine.

'So is he dead, then?' Eve asked, breaking into Irvine's thoughts.

'No, he's not dead,' Coles said, a tad too quickly.

'No,' Irvine added somewhat calmer. 'In fact, we've just been to see him. It was he who sent us down here to have another chat with you. He told us to tell you he was sorry he couldn't come himself – he enjoyed your chat about connecting eyes to a computer.'

'Oh, I bet he had a good old laugh at that one,' Eve said through gnashing of chewing gum and teeth.

'On the contrary,' Irvine said, breaking into a smile as he recalled the actual conversation he and Kennedy had had. 'He thought that, like all revolutionary ideas, it sounds a wee bit far-fetched when you first hear it but he felt that, in a few years, it could be the norm.'

'Exactly!' Adams shouted, not caring to hide her enthusiasm. 'I'm always telling Madonna that the geezer who first invented the television was probably laughed at. I mean, can you imagine going to someone – in those days – and saying that you're going to make a radio but it will be one that will show you pictures at the same time? There were probably a few people who wanted to throw him in the loony bin.'

Adams was grinning from ear to ear as she continued. 'Did he, the Ulster geezer, really say that it was a revolutionary idea?'

'Yes, he did,' Irvine replied truthfully. 'His name is Christy Kennedy, Detective Inspector Christy Kennedy.'

'Is he the boss or somefink then?'

'Well, he's certainly our boss,' Coles replied.

'And is he really okay?' Adams said. She was sitting awkwardly on a crate. She wore loose-fitting, shiny blue tracksuit bottoms with Camper trainers and a red, glittery top under an open, hooded, grey zip-up sweatshirt. Her mousy brown hair was pulled tightly across her head, away from her face and into a ponytail. This made her look, not exactly plump, but certainly more full. She was at that vital stage where she was going to either lose the puppy fat by disciplining her eating habits, or watch it meander out of control.

'Yes, he's going to be fine,' Irvine confirmed, touched by her genuine concern.

Irvine's gaze followed the line down to her feet. She was squelching something under her foot. All of a sudden the penny dropped and Irvine clocked the number of reefer remains lying around the floor. She was obviously feeling guilty because she had brought the police to this spot and had apparently only just remembered what she and her mates did in the stall.

'Don't worry about that,' he said with a smile he hoped would diffuse the situation. 'Probably a bunch of hippies were here last night.'

'Probably. It is Camden Market, after all,' was all that Eve managed to offer in explanation but Irvine noted that she did visibly relax a little.

'Detective Inspector Kennedy wanted us to ask you a few more question about the trial,' Irvine continued.

'Oh,' Adams replied, still staring down at her feet. She seemed reluctant to engage in direct eye contact with them.

'Yes,' Irvine said, deciding to keep on playing the Kennedy card. 'He thinks that we may have missed something.'

'Really?'

'Yes. He thinks we're missing something important and that you might be able to help us some more.'

'He actually said that he was missing somefink important?' Adams said, keeping her head down but flashing her eyes up in Irvine's direction.

'Yes. I think he felt you have some more information that might help us with all of this,' Irvine continued, trying not to push too hard and scare her away. He also felt that if Coles were not with him, Eve Adams would probably be much more forthcoming.

'You know, when someone was trying to top him, Inspector Kennedy that is, was that anyfing to do with this case?' Adams asked, her words speeding up.

'We believe so, yes.' Irvine said, happy that Coles had tuned into what was happening and was trying to sink into the background.

Adams looked Irvine in the eyes for the first time; she looked like she was trying to make a difficult decision.

'Okay, look, could you tell the detective from me, and this is very important, very important: Christopher Lloyd did rape me. That's vital. Have you got that?'

'Yes,' Irvine replied, barely audible above the racket going on outside.

'Have you got that?' This time Adams was addressing Coles.

'Yes,' Coles replied, a little louder than Irvine.

'That's not the reason I went to the police, though.'

'Sorry?' Irvine said.

'No,' Adams said, looking back to the ground again. 'You're meant to ask me why I went to the police.'

'Yes,' Irvine replied in a stutter, 'of course. Why did you go to the police?'

'Well, you know that all these child psychologists claim that when someone shouts rape, they are often just looking for attention. I mean, I've had them up to here, probing away to try and see what makes me tick and all that tosh,' Adams said, resorting to a grin that suggested, 'and I came out of it alive.'

'Well, I have to tell you somfink. They're right; at least in my case. I was shouting rape to get some attention. As I've said, I want you to tell Kennedy I was raped. I told Chris no but he went ahead anyway and that is rape. I'm not sorry about going to the police and the trial. I mean, obviously I'm sorry that he died, but that was nothing to do with me and I can't feel bad about everyone who dies, can I?'

'But if he raped you, then you couldn't possibly be calling rape to get attention, could you?'

'You still don't get it, do you?' Adams replied, her frustration very evident. 'Duh!' she continued, aping the Flintstones.

'Right, so you were drawing attention to something else?' Irvine said, having to correct himself from her 'somfink' inflection.

'Okay,' Adams grinned, 'or maybe someone else?'

'Christopher Lloyd raped someone else?' Irvine said in disbelief.

'No, no, no,' Adams replied.

Irvine was worried she was growing impatient with them for not picking up what she was offering. If they didn't make the proper connection soon she might close down altogether.

'Someone else raped someone else?' Irvine replied.

'Good,' Adams said, the relief written all over her face, 'you're getting warm. Not exactly rape, though.'

Still Irvine was drawing a blank.

'Okay, let's go back to the night in question, the night Chris raped me and I went to the police.'

'Yes, okay,' Irvine said, thinking that Kennedy would probably have put it all together by now.

'So what happened?' Adams prompted.

Why was she not spelling it out? Irvine wondered. Was that a clue?

'You went home?' Irvine suggested.

'Yes?' Adams kept on pushing him. Why? Maybe she wanted to be able to say to someone: 'I didn't tell the police, they worked it out for themselves.' Yes, Irvine thought, that's a distinct possibility.

'You went to the police?'

'Not directly.'

'You went to Madonna's?'

'CORRECT!'

Irvine felt like he should have registered something significant from Eve's big revelation, but he still didn't get what she was on about.

'Madonna was being molested by Frankie Hammond,' Coles said sadly, very sadly, 'and you felt that by reporting Christopher Lloyd you might force Madonna to report Hammond.'

'YES!' Adams shouted. 'Not just a pretty face.'

A blush rose to her face as she realized what she had just said, and as the information sank in with Coles and Irvine.

Adams drained the remainder of her Coke and then spat her chewing gum into the empty can. She was unwrapping another piece of gum as she stood up. 'Well, if that's all, I need to be on my way. People to see and all that stuff.'

'Tell me,' Coles said standing up as well, 'just one final question. Is there any chance that you may have mentioned to Christopher Lloyd what was going on between Frankie and Madonna?'

'Bingo!' Adams said with a contented smile. 'Full house. You've got it all now, haven't you?'

Adams sauntered off leaving the two detectives following her every step. As she was about to fall in with the Camden crowd she turned to face the two detectives and shouted: 'Give my regards to Christy, won't you?'

Chapter Thirty-Six

KENNEDY SLEPT FOR the rest of the day and through the night. He woke as fresh as a daisy. He sprang out of bed in search of the shower but a violent stitch in his back arrested all further movement and he stood frozen in agony like Edvard Munch's Scream.

ann rea found him a few seconds later. If Kennedy hadn't already been worried by his situation, he was when he saw the look of shock in ann rea's eyes. It reminded him of something Staff Nurse Rose Butler – an old flame of Irvine's – had once told him. She said that one of the most dangerous moments for a patient if they wake up or to come round when they're being worked on. The look of alarm on the nurses' and doctors' faces is one of the biggest causes of a heart attack.

She helped him back to the bed.

'I've got to take it easy,' Kennedy said when his wind returned.

'Really?' ann rea said. 'I was hoping we could have run around Primrose Hill.'

'I think a run around the bedroom is as much as I'm capable of.'

'Wishful thinking, Christy,' ann rea said, and then after feeling his head for his temperature, added 'dream on.'

'Okay,' Kennedy began. 'I don't want to argue with you about this, ann rea, but I do need to go to North Bridge House.'

'You're an adult,' ann rea said. 'You're going to get no argument from me.'

'No, I know, but I want you to know why I need to do this. I feel that I have to confront the person who did this. I know it's stupid but I feel so passionately that if I don't do it now I'll never properly recover from this. I also think if we don't get him in the next day or so, he just might get away with it.'

'Kennedy, you don't have to explain anything to me,' ann rea said, putting her arm around his shoulder.

He felt so helpless. He hated, more than anything else in this world, feeling helpless.

ann rea sensed this.

'Don't worry Christy, we'll get over this,' she said. 'After all the shit we've been through, we're not going to let something like this get in the way.'

That said it all for Kennedy. That was one of the reasons he loved ann rea. She wasn't one for advising caution or taking the soft route. At that moment he felt, with ann rea at his side, he could take on anything or anybody. It wasn't that he felt he could take them on and surely win. But it was worth the risk, because if he failed, with ann rea there, his disappointment would not be a disappointment after all.

ann rea drove Kennedy to North Bridge House and helped him into the police station. She had a way of helping him that didn't make him feel like a total invalid. He insisted that he be set up first in the interview room. He stayed in his seat for about ten minutes to get his breath back. The journey from his house to the station – a journey he usually took for granted twice a day, most days of his life – nearly wiped him out. It's funny, he thought, as he sat in the interview room with no company except the ticking of the second hand of the large clock on the wall and the buzzing of the harsh neon light about him, how when you've almost lost your life, you treasure it the most.

Well, that wasn't exactly true. Kennedy loved Primrose Hill with a passion and he enjoyed nothing more than strolling over it every morning, with only a flock of magpies for company. Kennedy was convinced there were more magpies per head of population in Primrose Hill than anywhere else in England. He couldn't wait to get back out there for a walk. He didn't care if it was a quiet morning, the busy noon or the slightly dangerous night-time. He wondered if he was putting his health and enjoyment of Primrose Hill in jeopardy now by preparing to subject himself to he knew not what.

The sad thing was that if a doctor had told him that going into the office that morning could do his health irreparable damage, he knew he would still have had to do it. How irresponsible was that?

The noise of the door to the interview room being opened by Irvine chased all these thoughts from Kennedy's head. As pre-arranged, Irvine stood with his back to Kennedy, shielding him from Frankie Hammond. Kennedy wanted to see the look in Hammond's eyes when he realized who was about to question him.

As Hammond crossed the room and walked to the opposite side of the table, Kennedy received a strong whiff of cigarettes and he remembered immediately when he'd last been exposed to that smell.

Two nights ago in the York and Albany, as the dark form against the wall had glided past Kennedy, stabbing him in the process, Kennedy's nostrils had registered the rush of the breeze of displaced air and the smell of stale cigarette smoke – the same smell Kennedy was now receiving from the opposite side of the table. Kennedy also had an admittedly unproven theory that the more pressure people were under, the worse their breath smelt. He took some comfort therefore from the foul aromas wafting their way across the interview room.

Kennedy's little stunt of setting Hammond up so that he wouldn't see him worked perfectly. It was as if the mechanic had seen a ghost. But his shock turned to a smirk as he turned to his solicitor.

Round one to Camden Town CID, but now what? Kennedy didn't feel he could start off the proceeding with: 'I smelt you the other night.' It would hardly stand up in a kangaroo court, let alone the court of someone like the honourable Lord Justice Bailey.

Soon they were all seated around the table: Kennedy and Irvine on the near side and Hammond, who chose to sit diagonally opposite to Kennedy, and his brief – introduced for the record as Daniel MacAllister – on the far side. MacAllister worked out of Kentish Town and was in his late twenties, which was possibly why neither Kennedy nor Irvine had come across him before.

Irvine turned on the recorder and stated the names of all present, the exact time and the location. Kennedy had asked Irvine to bring several files with him into the interview room. He had asked Irvine to mark them up in large letters, using a black felt-tip pen. The names visible for all to see were: 'Christopher Lloyd', 'Madonna Duncan', 'Gina Harris' and 'Frances Harris'. Kennedy spread these four files in front of him as if they were a large deck of playing cards.

Frankie Hammond hardly flinched as the names were displayed in front of him. He stared only at the one marked 'Christopher Lloyd'.

Neither Kennedy nor Irvine said anything. The solicitor, MacAllister, did some grandstanding of his own by removing a clean note pad from his briefcase. He very elaborately removed a Parker fountain pen from the breast pocket of his pinstripe suit, unscrewed the top, and poised the nib over the virgin page.

'It's remarkable how, when you're young, you sometimes have a tighter bond with your friends, your school mates, than you do with members of your own family,' Kennedy began, hoping his voice wasn't betraying how weak he felt.

None of the other three felt sufficiently compelled by Kennedy's statement to reply.

'Yes,' he continued, 'I suppose what I'm trying to say is how incredible it is, the secrets that the young will share with their mates. Secrets they will never ever divulge to members of their immediate family.'

Kennedy now seemed to have Hammond's attention, at least to some degree, but the floor remained open to Kennedy.

'In a way, I suppose, you can't really blame them for keeping certain information from their family. There's just some dirty laundry that's better left buried at the bottom of the basket.'

Irvine looked as if he was trying to appear impressed and intrigued by the proceedings but he wasn't really carrying it off.

MacAllister seemed bored without having to stage the look in the slightest.

'Is there a point to all of this?' he asked, seemingly irritated. 'We're all busy people and you've already held my client overnight without the slightest justification.'

'Well, Mr MacAllister,' Kennedy began, 'we're got four charges to bring against your client, and possibly a fifth, but I have to consult my doctor further to see how serious the last one is.'

'May I suggest that we get on with it then,' MacAllister continued in his trademark irritated manner.

'Fine,' Kennedy said, continuing to draw the file marked 'Gina Harris' towards him but not opening it. 'Do you know a Miss Gina Harris, Frankie?'

'Of course I know her, you dickhead. She's my daughter, isn't she?' Hammond snapped back and then whipped out a packet of Players from his Michelin jacket pocket.

Irvine pointed to the 'No Smoking Please' sign pinned to the back of the painted door.

Hammond prepared to light his cigarette. Irvine pointed once more to the sign.

'What are you going to do? Summons me for smoking in a public place? Your man here has got five charges on me; I don't think anyone is going to take any notice of a sixth.'

'Actually, I'd prefer it if you didn't smoke,' said MacAllister as Hammond struck the match.

He lit the cigarette. He was about to take his first puff when Irvine stood up, leaned across the table and snapped the fag out of Hammond's mouth. 'The sign says 'No Smoking Please',' he said as he stubbed the ciggy out. 'We only say 'Please' the first time, then it's 'No Smoking' full stop!'

Hammond looked at his brief for support but found none, just a man waiting patiently to write on his clean page the way children, fresh back to school, are eager to start on the first page of their exercise book.

'Okay,' Kennedy continued. 'We have reason to believe that

over the course of several years you sexually abused your daughter, Gina Harris.'

Hammond just shook his head. 'No way.'

'Your wife and Gina say different,' Kennedy said. 'We have reason to believe that over the course of several months you also sexually abused your other daughter, Frances Harris.'

Hammond looked at his solicitor who was writing down the charges as quickly as he could.

'It takes a lot of courage,' Kennedy continued, 'for a child to make such accusations, but with the support of a mother – well...'

Kennedy waited until MacAllister stopped writing before he continued.

'We have reason to believe that you also took advantage of another minor, Miss Madonna Duncan.'

'You've no proof of...'

'Oh, but we have,' Kennedy replied smugly, or at least hoping he came across as smug as he patted the first three files in front of him.

'Is that all?' said MacAllister, staring at the file marked 'Christopher Lloyd'.

'Well no, not really,' Kennedy said, appearing puzzled. 'I mean, there is more but I'm sure that'll be enough for now. We've enough here to convict your client and, you know what, these days he'll probably get as big a sentence for these three charges as he will for the Lloyd murder. I'm not one-hundred percent sure about that, but I can assure you that whatever the length of the sentence, it will be a lot more unpleasant than if he goes down for the murder of Christopher Lloyd. Child molesters, for some reason or other, always seem to have a very unpleasant time in prison. There'll be no book contracts, television interviews or movie deals for a start. There'll certainly be no hardman respect on your wing, wherever it may turn out to be. What I'm saying, Mr MacAllister, is that I'm not sure whether justice would be better served by just leaving it at that.'

Kennedy started to pile the files on top of one another again, ensuring the one marked 'Christopher Lloyd' was on the top.

Hammond fidgeted. 'I'd like to talk to my brief in private.'

This was going to be awkward, Kennedy thought. He nodded to Irvine to kill the tape, and as Irvine recited the time and the break in the proceedings, Kennedy stood up, hoping that Hammond and MacAllister wouldn't take too much notice of him as he turned and walked as confidently as he could out of the room. He collapsed against the wall in the corridor just outside the interview room. Irvine was there in a flash to steady him and prevent him from falling.

'I couldn't believe it was so simple,' Irvine whispered to Kennedy.

'It wasn't. We're not there yet,' Kennedy hissed rather than whispered. 'Hopefully he's asking his brief to make a deal with us but if he doesn't, we don't have anything really, just our suspicions. Even if the three girls were willing to come forward and press charges, I'm not sure I'd want to put them through it all again. Maybe if we didn't have anything else we'd have to, but...'

Just then the door opened and MacAllister's head appeared from within. 'We're ready to continue.'

As they were following MacAllister back, Kennedy whispered to Irvine to fall over the table as he turned on the tape.

Irvine's hamming-it-up performance was enough to let Kennedy sit down without either MacAllister or Hammond being aware how much pain the detective was actually in.

'My client is willing to confess to the Lloyd murder if you'll drop the other charges,' MacAllister said once the tape was rolling again.

He didn't admit that his client had wanted to go for a manslaughter charge but that he had stated that, in his honest opinion, Kennedy would never accept it. He had also reminded Hammond that, as a father himself, he felt that Kennedy had been right in his assumption that Hammond would have an easier time in prison while serving a murder sentence. Not strictly the best legal advice that a brief has ever given a client, but when it comes to crimes against children there are few who are prepared to help the guilty escape their punishment.

Kennedy hoped that his mental sigh of relief wasn't outwardly visible.

'Why?' Kennedy said, his dangerously low energy level interpreted as exasperation. 'Why murder him?'

At first Hammond seemed reluctant to talk. He looked at MacAllister, who merely shrugged his shoulders, and then started to talk. 'The dickhead left me no option. He tried to blackmail me over Madonna. I didn't have a penny to my name.'

Hammond started to laugh. Kennedy couldn't see the joke, and supposed he was releasing pent-up tension.

'He was always getting his crimes wrong, was our Christopher. I mean, he was either selling our stolen reject tires, as new, on our doorstep, or he didn't genuinely believe they were stolen. And the coats! I think he even sold one of them to you guys. The boys in blue receiving stolen goods! Then he hit on me. I mean the golden rule in blackmail is to make sure that the person you are blackmailing has at least got some bleeding money. Basic stuff, but he was always getting it wrong.'

'Why poison?' Kennedy asked.

'I didn't have the stomach to do it any other way. Besides, he was bigger than me. I thought it through. How do you kill someone without having to do it with your bare hands? And how do you ensure that the corpse is never found? I was watching one of those programmes on television about murderers and it said one of the methods favoured by women is to poison their victims, usually over a long period of time.

'So, I got a book on poison and the aluminium phosphite caught my eye. It's actually for killing vermin. And I'd read how incredibly strong and effective the Phostek tablets were. I worked out a system where I didn't even have to be in the same room as him.'

'How did you know about the York and Albany?' Kennedy asked.

'Christopher used to use it himself as a hideaway. He said we had to go there because it was important no one ever saw us together. Another of his grand plans was to get enough money to

lease the building from The Crown Estate and open a private club
and restaurant there – a gentleman's club, if you like. See, that
was Lloyd again, he never thought things through. It was going to
cost millions to restore the place. How much was he going to turn
over each year with a gentleman's club in Camden Town? He kept
saying that it wasn't Camden Town, it was Regents Park and he
was going to call the club The Regents. See, that was Christopher.
He was more interested in the club's name and the artwork and
what uniform the doorman would wear than he was in thinking
about how to start the whole project up. The window-dressing is
the last thing you think of. Anyway, he came to see me and said
that Eve Adams had told him what Madonna had told her. He
said he hated to do it but now that he had a rape charge over his
head he was going to need an easy way to get funds.

'I stalled him. I mean, at first I told him not to be a fool. I didn't
have a penny. Christine takes all the money I earn the minute I
walk through the door. That's her deal; if she's going to be my
housekeeper she's going to be the money-keeper as well. That's
the golden rule, that's the only way she can make it work. When it
became clear that Lloyd didn't believe any of this, I told him I
needed time to get some funds together. He kept phoning and I
kept thinking. Eventually, I came up with a plan. I watch a lot of
true-crime stuff on the telly and I came to the conclusion that the
chances of a murderer getting caught diminish significantly if
there's no body. So I worked out how to get rid of it. Simple, I bury
it. But then I wondered how I could bury it so that a freshly dug
grave wouldn't be discovered. I was driving past the graveyard
near King's Cross and I suddenly thought, why not bury it in a
graveyard? I was all set on that idea for a time and then I worried
about them finding an unauthorized grave in the graveyard. Then
I had this amazing idea: why not bury the body in someone else's
grave. It's perfect, you see? They're never going to dig up a grave
where someone was publicly buried and everyone knows, or
thinks they know, exactly who's in there.

'I checked the local papers for death and funeral notices and
found one. I rang Lloyd and told him I'd meet him later that night

with the money. I made noises about needing some kind of guarantee to ensure he wasn't going to come back and hit on me again in the future. First, I went to the graveyard and dug an extra foot or so in the grave. That was a lot harder than I thought. Manual labour – who'd do it these days? I still managed to arrive at the York and Albany early, with a few bits and pieces. I put the Phostek tablets in a dish under the floorboards. I rigged my plastic mineral-water bottle and nailed the top to the wood. It was a variation on something we do in the garage. We have lots of these jars for various sized nuts, bolts, screws and washers, and we nail the lid to the underside of the shelf. Then we simply screw the jars into the 'in' position and it keeps it all neat and tidy. I just worked on the reverse of that. One of my initial problems with the system was how to get the water into the bottle when the top was already nailed to the floorboard. I went around the houses on that a few times, I can tell you. But in the end the solution was so simple. I nailed the top to the floor, screwed the bottle into its top so that it was standing upside down on the floor, and then I carefully cut a hole in the bottom of the bottle – which was now the top, of course – and simply poured the water into it. I was scared shitless in case I spilled the water, so I took the tablets out from under the floorboards while I was doing that part.

'The rest was easy. I wound the twine around the bottle. I experimented with it a bit to get it in the correct position and to make sure that it didn't topple over when I pulled the string. I found that I needed to prop something against it to keep it in position, so I used an old crate that was lying around; it also helped to hide the bottle from Lloyd. I replaced the tablets on their plate under the floorboards and then I waited for him to arrive.

'He came on time. He had a worse case of the jitters than me. I don't think he really had the stomach for crime, you know. After a few minutes sitting in his spot in his makeshift chair on the first floor where I'd set everything up, I told him I was sure that nothing was wrong and that I would go down to the van and get his money for him. As I went down the stairs I pulled the string I'd laid out. I made a bit of a noise as I pulled it, just in case the bottle made any noise turning. I went as far as opening the door and closing it again, then I went back to the bottom of the stairs and whispered up to Lloyd to be very still and very quiet because I'd just seen a police panda car parked outside the door.

'I hung around for about twenty minutes or so, whispering up to Lloyd that they were still there. Once he said he wished they'd hurry up and move on because the pong up there was unbearable. It always smelt something rotten up there so he wouldn't have been suspicious. Maybe it wouldn't even have mattered. He was so desperate for his cash that he'd have put up with any smell. Then I heard the crash of him tumbling over and waited for another ten minutes before going up. He twitched around for about half an hour or so, nothing violent, and then he stopped moving altogether. I felt for a pulse but he was dead. I couldn't believe how easy it had been. But now came the really hard bit – getting him out of the York and Albany and into my van. It was about two in the morning and it was belting down so luckily there weren't many people around.

'I drove over to the graveyard and had the same trouble getting him out of the car. But this time at least I'd a wheelbarrow, which I'd discovered in the graveyard. And that was it. I really thought that I'd found a foolproof way of getting rid of the body.'

'But you hadn't counted on the rain?' Kennedy said, happy now that it was all down on tape.

'No, I hadn't considered the rain and I hadn't bothered to clear up the stuff at the York and Albany. There was no reason to, was there? There was no body there, therefore no crime.' Hammond looked at Kennedy. 'But the truth is, if I hadn't come back to tidy up the stuff I'd have been okay. You'd never have proven a thing. I was stupid, I should have made sure you were dead.'

This remark sent Kennedy reeling. He couldn't believe that Hammond could be so hardhearted. For him, Kennedy was just someone who stood in the way of his freedom and had to be dealt with. Admittedly, he went about it in a clumsier way than he had done getting rid of Lloyd, but he was under pressure, and the net effect was exactly the same. Kennedy and Lloyd were two obstacles that needed to be removed so that Hammond could live his life untroubled.

When you accept that most murderers have this outlook on life, it can't help but hurt you emotionally, but as a detective it certainly gives you a better understanding of your work.

As Hammond was charged and taken away to the cells, Kennedy remained in his seat. He was thinking about murderers in general, and Dr Ranjesus in particular. Dr Ranjesus was the only person who Kennedy was convinced was a murderer but who was still enjoying his freedom.

Chapter Thirty-Seven

KENNEDY WENT HOME, mentally and physically drained. WDC Anne Coles drove him and helped him to his door. ann rea answered and both women helped Kennedy into the kitchen.

Kennedy sat down. He was exhausted. He needed to rest but he was scared, always scared, of falling off the horse. He'd always assumed it was hard to get back up again. Usually, as one case ended, he avoided the trauma of it by getting straight into the next one. There always was a next one.

Now though, he was forced to take a break, and this time, instead of getting the jitters about it, he found himself looking forward to it. He heard Coles and ann rea talking in the hallway but he blanked out what they were saying. He was thinking about what he would do with his time off. Apart from having time to recuperate, he was looking forward to doing nothing, just listening to music and reading. ann rea had been raving about the book she was reading, *First Of The True Believers* by Theodore Hennessy, which was a novel about the Beatles. He couldn't wait to read that one. He was looking forward to listening to the radio – Radio Four – and not just having it on in the background while on the go. He thought it would be great to make himself a cup of tea, get a few pieces of shortbread and settle down in his favourite leather chair to listen to a good, solid couple of hours of radio. He was looking forward to getting his strength back again and going for walks in Regents Park and on Primrose Hill. He was looking forward to slipping into little routines, like going to buy the papers every morning and then having a tea and a toasted poppy-seed bagel in the Cachao café on the way home.

Maybe in the afternoons he'd get a video from the store around the corner and catch up on the ever-growing list of movies he kept promising himself he'd watch. It would also be nice to be able to go to the cinema in the afternoon and not feel guilty about it. The theatre was a different thing altogether for Kennedy. ann rea had dragged him along quite a few times over their years together but whereas he found it very easy to get lost in a movie, he had great difficultly achieving the same blissful state in the theatre. On the way back from the cinema, he'd stop off in Parkway at his favourite bookstore, The Regents Bookshop, for a bit of a browse.

Goodness, this is going to be great fun, he thought. In the evenings he'd make himself a bite to eat à la Marks and Sparks and settle down to some quality television, to the radio, a book – or even a combination of all three. Then he'd retire to bed early so he could rise fresh the following morning and enjoy the best part of the day.

Then another thought hit him. In all his plans for his time off, he hadn't once thought of or considered ann rea's involvement in his day. Nor did he want to think any further of it.

Coles stuck her head back in from the hallway and said goodbye with a strained smile.

ann rea led her to the front door.

Coles seemed to be searching desperately to find something to say. Both women stood on the doorstep in silence for a few moments.

Eventually Coles said: 'He's a good man, you know. Please take care of him.'

ann rea lifted her hand and patted the policewoman's back a few times but didn't say a word. Then Coles turned, left ann rea standing on the steps, and in a few moments pulled out of Rothwell Street and then left onto Regents Park Road.

Paul Charles

was born and raised in the countryside of Northern Ireland. He now lives with his wife in Camden Town, where he divides his time between writing and working in the music industry. He is currently writing the eighth Christy Kennedy mystery, *Sweetwater*.

The Do-Not Press
Fiercely Independent Publishing

www.thedonotpress.com

All our books are available in good bookshops or – in
the event of difficulty – direct from us:
The Do-Not Press Ltd, Dept JF,
16 The Woodlands
London
SE13 6TY
(UK)

If you do not have Internet access you can write to us
at the above address in order to join our mailing list
and receive fairly regular news on new books and
offers. Please mark your card 'No Internet' or 'Luddite'.